THE KEEP OF AGES

THE KEEP OF AGES

CARAGH M. O'BRIEN

BOOK 3: THE VAULT OF DREAMERS TRILOGY

ROARING BROOK PRESS
NEW YORK

Library of Congress Control Number: 2016953573

ISBN 978-1-59643-942-9

First edition, 2017
Book design by Elizabeth H. Clark
Printed in the United States of America

1 3 5 7 9 10 8 6 4 2

For my aunt,
Nancy J. Walsh

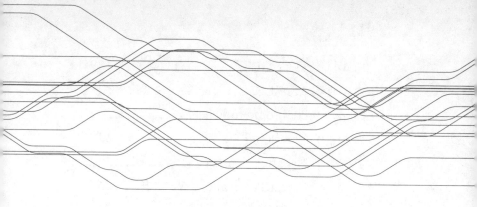

CONTENTS

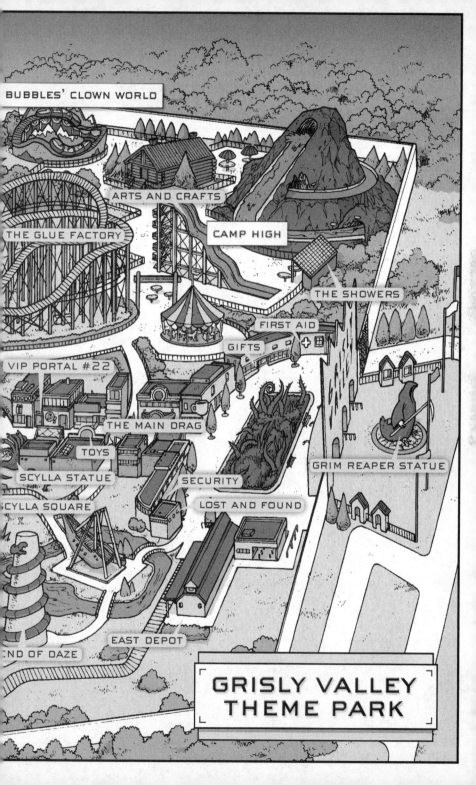

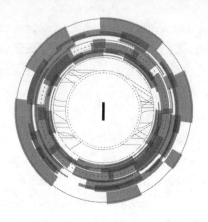

THE BOXCARS OF HOME

APART FROM A LONE cicada's keening, the desert evening is quiet. I lean my shoulder against a boulder and aim my binoculars toward the boxcars, where the empty laundry line cuts through the heat of our backyard like a white slash. Rolling my focus knob, I shift my circle view up the back steps to the screen door and then to each window, one by one. Nothing moves. I watch until the colors go drab, until the stillness corrodes my hope.

No one's home. After all I've survived to come back, my family isn't here to greet me. I'd laugh if I didn't ache so much, and if I weren't sick with worry. Ma and Larry haven't answered the phone since I started trying to reach them yesterday, but they normally never leave Doli. They have no other place to go. Their absence makes no sense.

Training my binoculars on the desert surrounding the box-cars, I pick carefully over each clump of creosote to see if Berg has anyone staked out to watch my home and wait for me. From this side of the old train, out of sight of the tourists, nobody bothers with fresh paint, and each boxcar home has faded to a rusty brown that's barely distinguishable from the desert.

A neighbor steps out the back of her boxcar and descends to a row of chicken-wire crates that huddle in the shade of a stunted oak. First she pours a measure of feed pellets in the top, and then she takes a rabbit out by the ears. It kicks its legs, indignant, but she holds it to a stump and dispatches it quickly with an ax.

The thunk reaches me a moment after the flash of the blade.

If I were smart, I'd go to the McLellens' place at the far end of the train and ask what they know about my family, but I can't yet. Hope and fear keep me here, peering at my home, waiting in case someone comes. Dubbs should be back from school. Larry should be drinking a beer on the couch. Ma should be frying onions. Those windows should be open like mercy to let in the air.

As the shadows turn and grow longer, I get too anxious to wait anymore. I have to see what's left, even if my family's bodies are baking inside that shimmering box of heat, bloating into a feast for flies.

No, I tell myself. *They're gone. They have to be gone, not dead. They can't be murdered.*

But my fear is real. I know how sick Berg can be. I lower the binoculars so they hang from my neck, brace a hand on the boulder, and rise. Hitching up my jeans and crouching low, I pick my way between brush and rock, until I cross the dusty slope of the valley. I duck under our laundry line and when I open the screen door, it gives a dry squeak. We never lock our back door, but since it sticks, I give it a kick at the bottom, and for the first time in half a year, I'm home.

"Ma?" I ask into the hot, hollow stillness.

Late sunlight sifts through the skylights, intensifying the gloom in the corners. I take a cautious breath and step inside. The stifling heat has the familiar, egg-sandwich smell of home. Dipping my head out of the strap, I lift off the weight of my binoculars and set them on the shelf. The ceiling is lower than I remember, the room more cramped. Books and dishes are left in a typical mess, but nothing looks ransacked. In the kitchen nook, a paperback props open the door of the fridge, a sign it's unplugged, and now I know: this was a planned departure. The nearest lamp is unplugged, too. I can picture how Larry examined the electric meter while Ma went around disconnecting everything—hot water heater, toaster, clock—so not even the smallest appliance could draw any current and cost them while they're gone.

But where to?

And when did they go? Sweating, I shove up the kitchen window for a cross breeze, and then I look around hopefully for a note. My gaze scans over my little sister's school photo and a box of ammo on the coffee table. The pencil bucket stands spiky on the desk. No note. I try to tell myself that they didn't expect me, which is not the same as being forgotten, but still, it stings. As I trail my hand along the orange plaid couch, part of me clams over a lost pearl of grief. Where'd they go?

They wouldn't just leave for no reason. This is our home. They'd have to be driven or drawn away by something huge. Even then, they should have left me some message.

Despite my stepfather Larry's paranoia about surveillance in electronics, I'm sure my parents have a computer now. They've been coordinating the search for me and accepting donations online. Yet I can't find a computer or tablet anywhere. They could have taken it with them, but they haven't answered any emails lately, either. Things don't fit.

I try to think where my little sister, Dubbs, might have left me a message. Turning to the red curtain that gives some privacy to our bunk beds, I drag it aside along the wire, and I'm suddenly, keenly homesick, right here at home. Dust motes float in a beam of sunlight that lands on an upturned sandal. A gleam reflects off the little framed photo of my dad and me, him in his uniform and me in his hat, still on the wall where he hammered in the nail and hung it for me over a decade ago. My sister's bed, on top, is neatly made with her yellow patchwork quilt. Below, my red quilt has collected several drawings, a bird's nest, and a handmade, ceramic soap dish. I turn over the drawings, which have her name and age on the back, but no clues for me. Then I remember Dubbs's journal.

I drop to the floor, roll to my back, and push under my bed. Ignoring the dust bunnies, I inspect the pattern of metal wires for the little homemade booklet that she used to hide under the mattress. The booklet is gone, but in the same place, I find a folded piece of paper. *Yes*, I think. I pull the paper between the wires and stand to hold it in the sunlight. It's a lined sheet of notebook paper with the ripped parts still fringing one side, and it feels faintly brittle, like it was wet once and then dried. It says

To Rosie. From Dubbs.
See you

I turn the note over, looking for more, but though the paper is large enough for more writing, those are the only words. Frustrated, I check under the bed again. That's all she left. Was she interrupted? That seems unlikely, considering she had time to fold up her message and hide it under the bed. Absently, I brush the dust from my hair and shirt.

The phone rings. I jump and bolt past the curtain to the living room. My gaze flies to the doors. The front one is still closed. The back one is still empty. When the phone rings again, I grab it to my ear.

"Hello?"

A faint click is the only reply.

"Hello? Who is this?" I ask.

I spin around the room, searching for a camera lens on the lamp or the wall or the skylight. One could be anywhere. I instinctively back into the kitchen, taking the phone cradle with me on its long cord, and I peek through the window toward the road out front.

Still no voice comes from the phone, though I hold it hard to my ear. It doesn't disconnect, either, so someone's listening.

A Jeep is newly parked beside the tamarack tree, its windows rolled down, a gun rack clearly visible on the back window. A young man with a wispy mustache is smoking behind the wheel, and my lungs tighten with fear. Ian. My former captor from the Onar Clinic. He wasn't there when I entered the boxcar, but now he's watching it.

My heart thuds. "Is that you, Berg?" I ask into the phone.

The faint clicking comes again.

I slam the phone down in its cradle. Horror flashes along my skin. Out front, Ian opens his car door and flicks away his cigarette butt. He's lanky in a black tee shirt, gray pants, and army boots. Beneath his pale hair, his expression is unsmiling, but I can tell he's jazzed. He loves tracking me down.

Before he can get any closer, I move swiftly toward the back door. Quickly, quietly, I step out and shut it. I wince into the setting sun, and then I sprint around the ragged fences and rabbit coops and grills behind the boxcars, heading for the McLellens'. A surprised voice calls out to me, but I don't answer. A crashing noise makes me look back as I run. Ian vaults over a pile of cement pavers. He's coming fast and aiming a gun.

A popping shot fires out behind me, and a spat knocks a water jug spinning by my right ear. I dodge left and run even faster.

"Peggy!" I scream.

My heart's pounding and my lungs are bursting from fear. I'm running so fast that everything's a blur except when I leap over a shovel or launch off a garden post or flip a folding chair behind me. My ears are primed for another gunshot. My scalp anticipates pain. I don't dare to look back again.

I scream for Peggy again, and now the McLellens' boxcar

is in sight. It's ten yards ahead. Five. I'm almost there when I hear a much louder shot and jolt instinctively sideways before I realize the blast came from in front of me.

Peggy McLellen is standing on her back stoop, with her rifle raised. Her sundress rides up to show her sturdy knees and rugged boots.

"Get behind me," she says tersely.

I fly up the steps and stop in her shadow, panting. I look over her shoulder toward Ian, who has stopped back in the abutting yard. He hugs a bleeding hand to his chest, and his gun has fallen in the dirt.

"Explain yourself," Peggy says. "This next bullet's aimed somewhere more permanent."

"I've just come to collect Rosie," Ian says, panting. "I wasn't going to hurt her."

"She doesn't want to come," Peggy says. "That's what running away means."

"She doesn't know her own mind," Ian says. "She's sick in the head."

"*I'm* the sick one?" I say. "*You're* the one who works for Berg."

"Who sent you?" Peggy says.

"Her guardian, Sandy Berg," Ian says. "If you aid her, you're kidnapping, and that's a felony." He leans to reach toward his gun with his good hand.

"Leave it," Peggy says.

"I need my gun," Ian says.

"You need to get out of here or you'll get yourself mistaken for a gutless coyote and shot," Peggy says.

"It's just tranquilizers," Ian says. He lifts his voice. "I wasn't going to hurt you, Rosie. You know you're supposed to come."

"Where's Berg now?" I ask. The one good thing about him still being alive is that I can't get prosecuted for killing him.

Ian tilts his head and gives his bangs a little flip. "At Forge, like normal," he says. "But he'll come now that I've got you. It won't take him more than a few hours to get here. You can stay awake and talk with me in the motel 'til he arrives. Or sleep, if you'd rather. But it seems to me we've got things to discuss. You shouldn't have ditched me back in Montana."

"Where's my family?" I ask him.

"Looks like they ran, like cowards," Ian says.

Peggy takes another blasting shot toward Ian, who screams and ducks to the ground.

"Mind your manners," Peggy warns him.

Ian swears in a squeaky voice. "You don't have to shoot me! I haven't done anything!"

Peggy frowns. "Your folks are looking for you," she says to me, her voice low. "They got a tip. They left yesterday. Come on in and I'll tell you about it."

"What about him?" I ask.

Ian is crouched way down, with his hands over his ears. The right one's bloody. It also looks like he's peed himself.

Peggy gestures with her gun. "Stand up, idiot. Quit your crying. I'll only shoot you if you run."

He stands slowly, keeping his hands high, and he looks taller and more awkward than ever. Peggy walks behind him, picks up his tranquilizer gun, gives it a quick inspection, and tucks it in the belt of her dress. She gives him a nudge with the muzzle of her rifle.

"In you go," she says to him. She nods back up at me. "Rosie, take the hash browns off the stove and see if you can't find some duct tape."

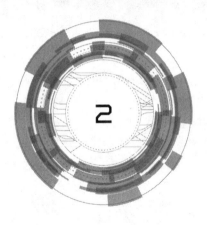

2

A GOOD DAUGHTER

I SHIFT THE HASH BROWNS off the hot burner and locate the duct tape like I'm told.

Peggy has me hold the rifle while she ties Ian's wrists behind him. When he resists, she clouts him on the head. "You watch it. I'm running out of patience," she says. She directs him into the closet off the living room and tells him to sit before she secures his ankles with more duct tape. She wraps a wad of medical gauze around his bleeding hand, gags him with an old scarf, and locks him in the closet.

I won't lie. I find this deeply satisfying. Ian kept me captive for months when I was helpless in a sleep shell, and I relish that he's the victim for a change. Once in a while, Ian kicks, and the muffled noise gives me another little thrill.

Peggy parks Ian's tranquilizer gun on the bookshelf next to her Bible. Without another word, she dishes up two heaping plates of omelets and hash browns, and passes me the Tabasco. It's the best food I've ever had in my whole life. I have to moan with pleasure.

"Glad you like it. There's plenty more," Peggy says, smiling. "I cooked like everybody was home."

I glance around. The ceiling fan is on, silently alleviating the press of heat, and the windows are open. I can't hear any noise from upstairs.

"Where are Rusty and the kids?" I ask.

"Visiting Rusty's mother in Phoenix," she says. "No offense, but you look real bad. You could use another ten pounds, easy. Eat up," she says, and she empties the rest of both skillets onto my plate.

The McLellens' boxcar has the same footprint as ours—a long, narrow rectangle—but it feels completely different because they jacked up the ceiling to fit in a loft and added a ton more windows. Money'll do that. I babysat and ran errands for the McLellens for half my life, so I know my way around. Their place is freshly painted and up-to-date, with a huge flat-screen TV and an open laptop on the kitchen counter. My gaze goes instinctively to the camera lenses, which are uncovered, and prickles rise on the back of my neck.

"Do you mind?" I ask. I step over to her laptop and close it. Then I take a dish towel and fold it over the top ridge of the TV to cover the lens there. I check the bookshelves, the lamps, and the corners where the paneling meets until I'm sure no other lenses are aimed at us.

Peggy, chewing thoughtfully, watches me and makes no comment. She's a tall, big-boned woman with short hair, dark skin, and a penchant for wearing red. Her sleeveless dress today is no exception, and I can see the soft, swirly mark of an old scar on her upper arm.

I get back to my fork. "What do you know about my family?"

"You just missed them. They took off yesterday afternoon," Peggy tells me. "They got a credible tip on your whereabouts. Someone had a photo of you sleeping, and your parents decided to go in person and check it out. They wouldn't say where."

"Sleeping how?"

"It was just your face on a pillow. In profile. Very little color, but some. It was pretty artsy, actually," she says.

Inside, I go still. "It was just a picture? Not a video clip?"

"Just a picture. I take it you know the one I mean," she says.

I do. It's from a video taken when I was lying in bed with Linus. It sickens me to remember how we were spied upon. Was that really only a few nights ago? So much has happened since then. "How'd my parents get the picture?" I ask. "Who sent it?"

"I couldn't say. Your ma showed me the picture, but otherwise, she was tight-lipped about the whole thing," Peggy says. "She was trying to protect me, or so she said."

As far as I know, the only person who could have sent that image is Berg, and if he's luring my parents to him, they're in real danger.

"Were they driving?" I ask.

"Yes. I sold them a car a while back," she says. "They got a little money from people who donated to help search for you.

12

You wouldn't believe how stressed your parents have been. When that picture came yesterday, your ma was beside herself."

In a sick, painful way, I'm almost glad to hear she was upset. "Really?"

"Of course!" Peggy says. "And Larry, too. What's wrong with you?"

Guilt shuts me up. A good daughter's not supposed to have ugly feelings toward her parents, but I have layers of them. Resentment and anxiety are uppermost at the moment. It's so easy to blame Ma for letting Berg take control of me. She's responsible for bringing Larry into our lives, too, and what a prize he's been. The one thing I'm clear on is that I miss my sister, Dubbs, and I'd do anything to keep her safe.

"Once I find them, I've got to convince them to leave the country with me," I say. "We have to go somewhere else and start over with new identities. It's our only chance to have a normal life now. Berg'll never stop looking for me."

Peggy wipes her fingers daintily with a napkin. "If you ask me, that sounds like fear talking."

"It is," I say. "I'm not ashamed of it. Fear's healthy when you want to stay alive."

She looks doubtful. "I don't buy that. Rusty and I have been here, what, thirty years? Plenty of times I've been scared. Plenty of times we've had trouble at the business, but you don't let someone run you out of your home. Now, if you're tired of that boxcar and have better prospects, that I'd understand. But our kind, we don't run. I don't see Larry as the running type, nor your ma, either. And certainly not you."

I throw up my hand. "I'm not talking about local trouble. Berg has allies all over the world."

"So?"

I can't explain this to her. She isn't going to get it.

"Don't you make that disgruntled face at me, Rosie," Peggy says, pointing her finger at me. "You just lay it out properly. Start back at the beginning. Don't leave anything out. I saw you on that fancy show of yours. We all did. But I never understood why you got out of your bed and broke the rules. Did you *want* to get expelled?"

So I try. I tell her I wanted to expose what Berg was doing with the dreamers, but I got caught. Berg took me from the school and stuck me in a vault with more dreamers at the Onar Clinic in Colorado. For months, I was kept asleep there and mined for my dreams. Once I finally escaped, I made my way to Burnham in Atlanta, and then I went back to Forge, where I met up with Linus again.

I pause, remembering the morning in Linus's bedroom when we were joined by Thea and Tom.

"Go on. I'm listening," Peggy says.

I try to explain that this girl Thea has my mind in her body. Unsurprisingly, Peggy looks skeptical. I skip the part about nearly killing Berg in the dean's tower, but when I get to how Berg kept Thea captive in the basement even though she was in labor with her baby, Peggy looks more thoughtful. Meanwhile, I go through my second helpings. Peggy opens a jar with a pop and pours me a sloppy serving of applesauce for dessert. The sweet, wet taste is heaven.

She leans back and fixes a bobby pin over her ear. "That is

14

some wild story," she says at last. "If even half of what you say is true, Berg's a psychopath. How can anyone be that evil?"

"I don't know," I say. "He doesn't think he's evil. He's trying to save himself and his kids. He's mining dreams for medical research."

"How's that now? He's the dean of a boarding school," Peggy says.

I nod toward her laptop. "Look up the Chimera Centre and Dr. Huma Fallon. Berg's connected to that research. He sells dreams from Forge students and other dreamers to doctors who try to heal or rejuvenate brains, like for coma patients. That's how Thea got my memories into her. Berg has a personal stake in it, too. He wants to find a cure for his Huntington's disease before it gets worse, and he wants to be sure his kids don't get it." He also spoke about wanting to be immortal, but I spare Peggy that outlandish detail.

She leans back in her chair and crosses her arms. "Suppose what you say is true. I'm not saying I'm convinced, but just suppose. It still doesn't explain why Berg is pursuing you, specifically," she says. "What is it that makes you so special?"

"Not me. My dreams," I say, and I rise to do the dishes. I squirt plenty of blue dish soap on a yellow scrub sponge. "Berg told me my dreams are unusually vivid and versatile, especially when I'm scared. He said he's trying to figure out why. There's a lot of money involved, I guess." I nod toward the closet. "This is just the beginning. Berg's never going to give up looking for me. He needs me too much."

"I'd like to give him a piece of my mind," Peggy says. "Not literally, of course."

15

I laugh. "I don't suppose my parents took a phone with them."

"No. You know how Larry is about cell phones."

I do. My stepfather believes cell phones are a government scam so they can eavesdrop on us all. I don't agree with him, but I am convinced Berg has ways to tap into my calls, given half a chance. It's happened too many times before. I have a few recyclable phones that I consider safe, but I know the best way not to be traced is to never call anybody. I turn on the hot water to rinse a cup and set it on the rack.

"Speaking of phones, I had a call for you yesterday," Peggy says. "A young man named Linus Pitts left a message in case you contacted me."

Hearing his name aloud gives me a start. I turn from the sink. "What did he say?"

She reaches toward a yellow sticky note. "He was quite insistent that you call him. Fancy that. Handsome young man, if you ask me. I like his accent."

Peggy passes over the sticky note, and I take it with wet fingers. A small flutter attacks my lungs and won't stop. I told him I'd call him when I could, but what is there to say? It's painful to speculate that he has a camera in his eye, and that Berg has always been a silent spectator in our relationship. Berg may have even seen yesterday's kiss.

"I do believe that is a blush I see at last," Peggy says, her voice amused. "What did I tell you before? Smart boys like smart girls. It was only a matter of time."

"It's not that simple," I say. "I just realized yesterday that he must have a camera in his eye. He said he didn't know about it, and I want to believe him, but it freaks me out." I stare at the note, and now the blue ink is bleeding where it's wet. "We've always, *always* had someone else with us, spying along with everything we've done." I can't explain how this makes me feel, like our relationship has been defiled.

"So talk to him about it," Peggy says.

I shake my head. Linus is inextricably linked to Berg. Too many feelings to face. "I tried," I say. "It's no use. I just can't right now." I shove the sticky note in my back pocket.

"That's too bad," Peggy says. She folds her napkin. "Your sister Dubbs likes him."

"What?"

"She near idolizes him, from what I can tell," Peggy says. "She watches that show of yours more than what's healthy. There's some fan site that has all your old footage on it, and she watches your episodes with Linus over and over. Gorge on Forge. That's what it is. A born romantic, that kid."

"I guess," I say. I let out the drain so the dishwater can gurgle down. "How am I supposed to find her and my parents?"

"Larry said they'd call me from a phone booth when they could to check in, in case I heard anything about you." Peggy taps absently at her collarbone. "You could stay here with me. That's probably the smartest move, at this point. When I tell them you're here, they'll come home and you'll be reunited."

"Ian's in the closet," I say, pointing out the obvious and all it implies. A tick of fear reminds me I shouldn't linger. "He must have told Berg when I showed up. It isn't safe for me here."

"Your parents were working with a lawyer to try to stop Berg's guardianship of you," she says. "We could contact him."

It's all I can do not to roll my eyes. "You don't get it. A lawyer can't keep me safe," I say. "This isn't a fight that will wait for the courts. Berg is utterly ruthless. He wants to mine my dreams, and nothing's going to stop him until he's dead or I'm dead. Even then, I wouldn't put it past him to keep mining me somehow. He's just like that."

"I see," she says slowly.

Her gaze shifts toward the afghan on the couch, so she's not looking at me directly anymore, and I'm instantly uneasy.

I've known Peggy McLellen for as long as I can remember, and I can read when she's figuring out how to say something I won't like. She's probably the closest thing I have to a second mother. Ma taught me my letters and how to read, but it's Peggy who took me to the library and braced her dark fingers on the paper form while I signed up for my first library card. More than once growing up, I wished Peggy and Rusty would adopt me, and not just because Peggy made better grilled cheese sandwiches. Effortlessly, casually, they made me feel safe and welcome, and I never want to lose that.

"There is one other possibility here," Peggy says. "Now don't get mad at me. We could try calling a doctor."

"For what?"

"You might need a little help," Peggy says. "There's no shame in it."

I look at her in disbelief. Even with Ian in the closet, she thinks I'm making up my problems. "You think I'm crazy."

Peggy opens both her hands like stranger things have happened. "I'm just saying. Your ma and I talked this over. A lot.

She has a mess of regrets about how she handled you when your dad left."

I stare at her. "What's Dad have to do with anything?"

"You don't remember," Peggy says in a tone somewhere between sorrow and resignation. Her eyes go serious. "You and your dad had a special connection. He was a dreamer, just like you. Big imagination. No goal was too far-fetched. And he loved this country. He believed in it. When he went MIA, you got real quiet. You barely talked. Your ma didn't know what to do."

"She never told me this," I say.

"Why would she?" Peggy says. "She tried everything with you back then, but you were a mouse. You had this dreamy, faraway look. Rusty said you were downright spooky. When we asked you where you were, you said, 'Talking to Dad.'"

A tingle lifts along my skin. "I don't remember any of this," I say.

"I don't blame you," she says. "Memory's a strange thing. When we heard the news that your dad was presumed dead, your ma was afraid to tell you, but you heard about it somehow. You stopped eating for three days. You wouldn't talk at all. Not for weeks."

I keep waiting for a resonating prickle of recognition. I was four when my dad went missing and eight by the time he was presumed dead. That's old enough for memories, but I don't recall going silent or talking to him in my head. I just remember missing him.

"And you think that old stuff is connected to now?" I ask. "You think that excuses why she signed me over to Berg?"

"I'm just saying, she was afraid you'd need some help once you came home," Peggy says. "It can't hurt to talk to a doctor. She wishes she'd brought you to see somebody when you were little."

Her wishes come too late.

"We can't blame everything on the past. My mother is weak," I say, coldly. I brace my hands on the edge of the metal sink and think of what she's let Larry do to me over the years. "You know her. She's always been weak."

"Don't you think you're being a bit uncharitable?"

Stung, I frown at her. "Would you ever sign a contract to give up control of one of your kids?" I ask.

She bites her lip, and then shakes her head slightly. "No."

"Because you're a normal, decent mother," I say. "Ma *wanted* to give me up. It wasn't the money. It was *easier* for her that way."

"Rosie, no. You're not being fair," Peggy says.

The ugly, old anger I feel toward Ma makes me twist the dishrag extra hard.

"I've always been too complicated for her," I say. "She's never understood me. She let Doli High put me on the pre-prison track! She married *Larry*, for heaven's sake!"

"We all make mistakes," Peggy says. "And Larry's not all bad."

I let out a pained laugh.

"Would you quit defending her?" I say, but it comes out as a squeak.

Peggy rises slowly from her chair and comes over to give me a hug. I stand stiffly in her arms, wishing this would all just go away. I thought going to Forge was going to fix everything. Give me real skills and a place to belong, away from my family. Now I'm right back where I started, only my life's a thousand times worse.

"My parents were supposed to be home, waiting for me," I say, my voice tight.

"I know, baby," she says.

What am I doing wrong? How can I be so angry at my parents and miss them this much, too?

A banging noise from the closet makes me jump. Peggy loosens her arms.

"Keep it down in there!" I yell to Ian.

He shouts something back, muffled but angry.

Peggy releases me completely and turns toward the closet. "We're going to have to check on him. Tell me what you know about this boy."

I wipe my sleeve across my eyes and focus on the simpler, immediate problem of our hostage. Our disgusting hostage.

"His name's Ian. Ian John Cowles," I say. Of course I know his middle name. It's so annoying, what I had to listen to from him. "He's nineteen. He used to take care of dreamers like me at Onar. He liked to put makeup on the girls. He brought me little gifts, like lip balm and fresh mint leaves." He liked me helpless. A shiver of revulsion ripples through me. "He had a crush on me, and I tricked him into thinking I liked him back so he'd lighten up on my sleep meds. That's how I finally got away. He normally lives with his granny in Colorado. He likes to hunt, but he also rescues hurt animals when he finds them on the road. I thought he quit working for Berg, but obviously, he didn't."

"And you hate his guts," Peggy says.

"Can you tell?" I say dryly. "Oh, and he had a cat named Peanut. She died. He still keeps her cage in his car."

Peggy rubs her hands together. "Let's see what Mr. Cowles has to say for himself."

She steps over to the closet and opens the door.

Ian's narrow features are normally pale, but now he's red-faced and snotty. His teeth bite into the scarf gag, which has darkened with saliva. Still tied securely, he has shifted into an awkward sitting position among a jumble of hiking boots and a broom. His shirt is twisted, and with his wrists bound behind him, his skinny arms look unexpectedly strong. He flips his head, trying to get the sweaty, wispy blond hair out of his eyes. Angry, guttural noises explode around his gag.

"It won't do you any good to yell," I say. "No one can hear you. Okay?"

He says one more loud, indecipherable thing, and then goes quiet, looking at me through vicious eyes. He's never looked more dangerous to me, and I think, *This is the true Ian. This is who he is underneath.*

"Myself, I'd give him more time to stew," Peggy says.

He garbles into the gag again and looks furiously toward me. His demand is obvious.

"Hold still," I say, and I lean in to get the scarf out of his mouth.

"Untie me," he says, spitting. "This is ridiculous! I'm on your side."

I wipe my fingers on my jeans. "What do you know about my family?"

22

"I told you. They're gone. That's all I know," Ian says. "Berg sent me to get you, not them. Why don't you call him if you want answers? Use my phone. Go on. It's right in my pocket."

I glance at Peggy, who shrugs. Then I reach into his pants pocket to find a phone and a small, clear box with a bunch of colored pills inside, red and yellow. I give it a shake, and Ian's gaze glues to it.

"What's this?" I ask.

"Nothing. They're for my heart. For when I'm stressed."

I toss the box to Peggy and stand. "Do you realize what Berg wants to do to me?"

"It's no secret," Ian says. "He's going to mine you again. He's going to take out your worst dreams and leave the rest to help you heal, like before. You're overdue. We need to get you back to treatment before you hurt yourself."

He is so completely wrong that I'm actually impressed.

"Interesting," Peggy says.

"Berg's so-called treatment nearly killed me!" I say. "He ruined me!"

"You're not ruined," Ian says. "You're overexcited. Unpredictable, maybe, but that's not incurable. You just need the right care." He tries unsuccessfully again to flip his sweaty hair off his forehead. "Untie me, Rosie. Let me help you."

No possible way. "Why would you want to help me? Aren't you mad that I ditched you?" I ask, genuinely curious.

"I was, at first. Any guy would be. I offered you everything," he says. "But then I remembered how sick you are. I was worried for you." He tilts his head to get a better look at me. "I've

23

only ever wanted what was best for you. You know that. I'm not giving up on us when you need me most."

Loathing renders me speechless.

Peggy clears her throat. "Touching devotion."

Ian's gaze never leaves my face. "I'm ready to forgive you, Rosie. You only have to ask."

"Here's what I have to ask," I say. "I want to know the scope of Berg's operation. A few days ago, I saw a picture of a vault of dreamers much bigger than the one at Onar. Is that the one in California that you once talked about? Where your dad works?"

He tries to sit up a little straighter, and the broom knocks out of the closet.

"It could be," he says cautiously. "The big vault's in Miehana."

"Are there other vaults in the U.S.?" I ask.

"I don't know. I haven't heard of any."

"Where is the one in Miehana, exactly?" I ask. "Do you have an address?"

He blinks at me, frowning. "No, he never told me."

"But you've talked to him," I insist. "You must have some idea where your dad is."

"We email," he says. "His phone doesn't work underground."

"Can you email him now?" Peggy asks.

"I will if you want. He doesn't always answer." He arches back and sniffs like he's had a sudden jolt of pain. "Call Berg. Just talk to him. If he knows where your parents are, he'll tell you."

Peggy shakes a couple of Ian's colored pills out onto her palm. "You're looking a little stressed. Want one of these?"

Ian looks from Peggy to me and back. "No. I'm fine."

"What are they? Roofies?" Peggy asks.

"No. Like I said, they're for my heart," he repeats.

"You're a total liar. Are they for me?" I ask. "Were you going to drop one in my drink?"

His cheeks turn a livid red. "No," he says. "They're just nothing!"

He can rot in the closet for all I care. I yank the broom out of the way and slam the door.

"Rosie! Don't do this!" he yells from inside the closet. "Call Berg! I didn't mean anything with the pills!"

I turn and chuck Ian's phone on the couch. I can't believe how pissed I am. Ian's a scuzzbag, but the real monster behind everything is Berg. If he has my family, I'll kill him. This time I really will.

A rattle of a drawer makes me turn. Peggy pulls out a magnifying glass and holds one of Ian's pills to the light, a red one. "Echo eight. I know a chemist who could take a look at these."

"Be my guest. Keep the whole box," I say.

She takes up a yellow pill next. "The idiot is rather compelling," she says.

"So you believe me now?" I ask.

She lowers the magnifying glass enough so that I can see her eyes over the lens.

"You're not safe here. That's clear. I suggest you call up one of your rich friends, Linus or whoever," she says. "Go hide somewhere far from here, and once I hear from your ma and Larry, I'll send out a signal."

I can't just hide, though, not when my family is in danger. I run through my options. Calling Linus is out. I could reach Burnham if I could get on a computer, but he's all the way in Atlanta. Thea's the one I'd most like to connect with, but she just had a baby two nights ago. I'm not even sure where she is. The medic said she'd be okay, but what if she isn't? Supposing her parents have brought her back to Texas, I can't exactly show up there. Her parents are looking to buy more Sinclair 15, so going to their ranch would be like saying *here, mine me*.

A phone buzzes. Make that Ian's phone. It's on the couch, visibly vibrating, but the caller name is simply OTHER. I pick it up and swipe the answer button.

"Hello?" I say.

A click and a cool silence reach me before a voice comes on.

"I see Ian found you," Berg says.

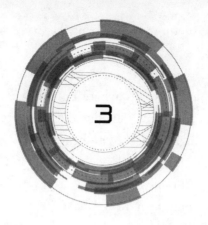

3

A TRADE OF DREAMS

BERG'S VOICE SHOOTS through me like icy poison. I glance quickly at Peggy and then sink down on the couch, pressing the phone to my ear.

"What did you do to my family?" I ask.

"Nothing. They're perfectly fine. They're in Las Vegas."

"Vegas?" I say, surprised. "How do you know?"

"I had a tracking device put on their car," he says. "I was hoping they'd lead me to a certain elusive prodigy of mine, but I was wrong. Is Ian with you?"

I am not Berg's prodigy. "Yes."

"Put him on."

I glance toward the closed closet door. "Not possible," I say.

"Rethink possible," he says. "I need you to put him on, and I need you to stay put where you are. I can be at the McLellens' in three hours. If you run, it will only be worse when I catch up with you."

Fear ripples through me, and I cast my worried gaze toward Peggy. Berg knows exactly where I am. Peggy comes and sits next to me on the couch. She puts her arm around me, and I tilt the phone slightly so she can hear, too.

"You need to leave me alone," I say to Berg. "I'd kill myself before I'd let you mine me again."

"No, you wouldn't. Not if I have your family. Wait there nicely now, Rosie," he says. "It won't be that bad. We'll work out an exchange that's fair to all of us, I promise."

I let out a tight laugh. "Are you serious? You've ruined my life."

"Actually, you made the choices that messed up our system at Forge," he says. "Time and again you've thwarted me, but we have lives depending on your dreams now, Rosie. Countless lives, today and in the future. I'm not going to jeopardize other innocent people just because you're being self-centered."

I can't believe the way he's reframing everything.

"You stole my dreams," I say. "Why don't you admit you did it for yourself, for your Huntington's disease? I know about you and your kids. Your daughter hates you, and I don't blame her."

He audibly sucks in a breath. I can imagine his ruddy face going bright with color.

"You've managed to surprise me, I must say," he says. "Let me guess who you have spying on me. Linus? Has to be." He hums a short note. "It hardly matters. I'll grant your point. I am personally invested in finding a cure for my illness. But you also must see that our research goes far beyond my own needs. If we can truly regrow brain tissue, we're at a turning point for all humankind, and you're pivotal to our progress."

"I don't care," I say. I shift the phone to my other hand and stand, turning away from Peggy to focus all my vehemence on Berg. "Just keep away from me and my family, or I swear, I'll turn this around and come after you myself. I should have killed you when I had the chance."

Berg makes a faint tapping noise on his end. "Why didn't you?" he asks.

I balk. In a flash, I'm back at the decision point, when I plunged the syringes into him and he watched me, glassy-eyed, while I tried to decide how much more of the sleep meds to give him. I hated him, but I couldn't kill him. It couldn't go over that line. He had a telltale bulge in the skin over his heart that matched mine.

"You had a port," I say.

"I see," he says. His voice grows slow and thoughtful. "We're more alike than you realize, Rosie. Both of us suffer. Both of us are dreamers. How would you like to know there's some of you in me already? If you killed me, you'd be killing a part of yourself."

This can't be true.

"A conscious part?" I ask, horrified. The phone feels suddenly heavy in my hand. It's excruciating to imagine part of me trying to exist in Berg. "Do you hear my voice in your mind?"

"No, but that would be a welcome side effect, I'm sure," he says. "Does Thea hear such a voice? It's a tantalizing prospect. Clearly, we have more studying to do."

"But I don't want to be studied. Don't you get it?" I say. "I don't want anything to do with you, ever, period."

"And yet I know where your family is, and you don't," he says.

I restrain an impulse to smash everything in reach. "Don't you dare hurt them," I say.

"Stay where you are. I'll collect your family and bring them back to you. We can make a trade."

I turn toward Peggy to see if she's following this. Her eyes are wide with astonishment.

"You mean, trade my dreams for my family?" I say.

"Since you put it so crudely, yes," Berg answers.

I can't bear to listen any longer. I jab the red button on the phone to disconnect, and then I throw the phone back on the couch. I tighten my hands into fists and squeeze with all my might to stop from screaming.

"Heavens almighty. You weren't kidding about him," Peggy says.

"I have to go," I say. Everything is suddenly very clear. I have to warn my family before Berg kidnaps them, but I'm also near panic because how can I possibly find them? He's always one step ahead of me. I can't stand it. "I don't have a minute to spare."

"I mean, really. The man's a raving monster," Peggy says.

"He says my family's in Vegas." I look at Peggy. "What are they doing there?"

"Take a deep breath," Peggy says. "Let's think this through." She heads into the kitchen area, takes a couple grocery satchels from a hook, and starts loading one with bagels.

But I can't wait. I pat my pocket for my keys. I can't stop for anything.

"I have to leave now," I say. And then I have a terrible realization. "Oh, Peggy. I'm so sorry! He knows where I am. He'll come directly here, or he'll send somebody. You aren't safe!"

"Don't worry about me," Peggy says. "I can look after myself."

"But Rusty and the kids," I say.

She shakes her head. "Not a problem. I'll tell them to stay with his mother until we sort things out here." She nods her chin toward the pot bar in the next boxcar. "I've got three vets working next door. They're as good as an army. They'll handle anything Berg can throw at us, and they'll welcome the chance."

She's packing more food and gear into the satchels for me: cans of soup, dried fruit, water, a camp stove, matches.

"What about him?" I ask, pointing toward the closet. I feel a pinch of guilt. "He's been awfully quiet. What if he really has a heart condition?"

"I got him," she says. "Don't worry."

My eyebrows shoot up. "Shouldn't I at least look in on him?"

"I wouldn't if I were you," she says. She adds a box of Band-Aids to the bag. Then she sticks her hand in the cookie jar and pulls out a wad of twenties in a rubber band. She stuffs that in the bag, too. "Either he's okay or he isn't."

I step near and press my ear to the door. It's dead quiet in there. I set my hand on the doorknob, and then reconsider. She's right. I can imagine Ian in there, snot-faced and twisted. Either he'll bluster and complain, or he'll be silent and passed

31

out, or worse. It's bizarre to feel responsible for him after all he's done to me. I let go of the knob and back up.

Deliberately, I scoop up Ian's phone again. I check the settings to turn off the GPS, and then I power it down. If I could take out the battery, I would. I put it in my pocket.

Peggy passes me a set of keys.

"Take the Toyota," she says. "It has a lot of miles, but it will get you where you need to go. Just call me when you're somewhere safe," she says. "Hopefully I'll hear from your parents soon so I can warn them."

"But what if Berg taps your phone by then?" I ask. "It won't be safe for me to call you. It won't be safe for them, either."

She frowns a moment. Then she reaches on top of the fridge to where she keeps things she's confiscated from her kids when they misbehave. "Here. Take Freddy's tablet. I'll put a post on Facebook if I hear from your parents. We'll figure it out from there. Where's the charger?" She puts her son's tablet and a plug in the lighter bag, instantly giving me access to the world.

Her generosity floors me. "I don't know what to say. This is too much."

She waves off my thanks. "You might as well take some of these, too," she says, reaching for Ian's pills. "When I find out what they are, I'll let you know." She takes a few of the pills, puts the rest back in the box, and snaps the lid closed. Then she tucks the box into my bag.

I throw my arms around her in a hungry hug. She feels so solid, so real. I wish I didn't have to leave her. "I'm so sorry," I say. "I didn't mean to bring you so much trouble."

"It's nothing I can't handle. Who do you think I am?" She

smiles, letting me go. She plucks her red dress back in place. "Go on, now," she says. "And drive carefully. When did you get your driver's license, by the way?"

"I never did."

Peggy lets out a booming laugh and shakes her head.

I pick up the heavy bags and clatter down her front steps to her old green Toyota. The night has come. I drive back in the desert hills and stop at my old car, the one Burnham lent me, long enough to grab my supplies. I still have two syringes of narcotics I took from Ian, all that's left after I injected two into Berg. I have a bag of clothes, including a few new essentials I bought the night before, when I also picked up a sleeping bag. I have way too many phones: the crappy disposable one I used for a few calls with Linus and Burnham, Ian's phone, and Berg's phone, which has gone dead. I have no charger for it, either. I also have two more recyclable phones that Burnham gave me. What is that, five? I dump them all in my backpack. I've left my binoculars back at home, but there's no getting them now. For a moment, I peer back toward the boxcars in mournful regret. This isn't the way I expected things to go when I came home.

A minute later, I'm driving west, toward Las Vegas.

I make twenty miles before I realize I'm heading exactly where Berg wants me to go.

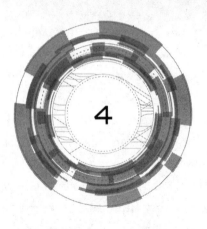

WAFFLES67

FOR A SECOND, I can feel Berg crowding in on my mind, playing me again. Then I step grimly on the accelerator and get back up to speed. I am not going to be paranoid. I'm five hours from Vegas. He doesn't know what car I'm in, and it would be nearly impossible for him to send someone to intercept me. Still, I have to be smart.

He definitely has the upper hand. All he has to do is send some lowlifes to pick up my family and stash them someplace. It infuriates me to think of Ma, Dubbs, and Larry in his control. Berg could drug them and mine them, just like he did me. Or he might keep them hostage until he can persuade me to do whatever he wants. My skin screams off my bones.

Think, Rosie. What's my next move?

A truck roars past on my left and sends a mini tornado around my car.

I wish my dad were with me. Hearing Peggy's perspective on him was unsettling. I should have taken the photo of me and him from the wall of my bedroom. Better yet, I should have taken the nail.

But I didn't, and my dad's dead. The truth is, I need help. It stings to admit it, but I do. I can't outwit Berg on my own. I have to run over my options again.

I have a distant cousin in Calgary. It's almost comical how unhelpful that is.

Linus.

Whenever I allow myself to think of him, even his name, an anxious, melty sensation curls in my gut. I can't call him, even though his number is in my back pocket. Berg would trace the call for sure.

Burnham.

I chew on the inside of my cheek and allow myself to fully consider my friend in Atlanta. The last time Burnham and I spoke, it was by phone, and I was in the dean's tower at Forge. Burnham's computer was getting fried by a virus from Berg's computer. That was Friday night, or technically early Saturday, and Burnham has probably replaced his computer by now, Sunday night. I can't imagine him existing long without one. He's far away in Atlanta, but he could help safely from a distance. On the downside, his parents own Fister Pharmaceuticals, the company that makes the sleep meds for Forge and half the country. He's loyal to his family and hypervigilant about anything that could tarnish the Fister reputation.

I squirm uncomfortably in my seat and adjust the vent to get a stream of air on my neck. Okay. So there's an added hitch to me and Burnham that I haven't much wanted to admit to myself.

A week ago, that first night when I was visiting Burnham in Atlanta, I had a vicious nightmare and woke in a panic. Burnham got up to make me cocoa in his kitchen, and shirtless Burnham is quite the sight. The whole memory makes me uneasy, and not just because I feel guilty about hanging with Burnham while my relationship with Linus was murky. Now that I have a little space from the cocoa episode, I feel like Burnham shouldn't have kissed me. I know that I came to the kitchen dressed in, well, not much, and I didn't resist the kiss as it was happening. And yet, if Burnham was really as noble as I always thought he was, he should have known I was vulnerable.

I check my gas. I'm at half a tank. I put on my blinker to pass a slow car and then ease back into the right-hand lane.

The worst thing is, I apologized to Burnham the next day, like the whole thing was my fault, like something was wrong with me for not being into him more. I kept trying to be honest, but I didn't really owe him anything.

Then the other night, when Burnham and I discovered that clip of me in Linus's bed, Burnham was not pleased. I could tell. I wish none of this bothered me, but I feel this ick about Burnham and it isn't going away.

I turn my thoughts to my last real option: Thea. She changed me. I wanted to stay angry and not care for anybody ever again, but when she was suffering and having her baby in that dark, filthy tunnel, I wanted so badly to help her. I felt like I was seeing myself struggle in pain, and in the end, she broke me open. She's me. That's why. She's truly me no matter how much we change. And if I can feel so fiercely protective of Thea, I must have the ability to care for other people, too.

Fine, I think, *but this isn't helping me come up with a plan.*

I'd love to talk to Thea and find out if she's all right, but I don't have a secure way to reach her. Anything I plan now needs to be kept from Berg if I'm going to have any chance of beating him, which brings me back to Burnham.

He set up a dark web Tor site so I could reach him securely if I needed to, and that's exactly the situation I'm in now. When I consider how devoted Burnham has always been to discovering what Berg's up to, it reassures me somewhat. Despite our turbid chemistry, I can count on Burnham. I'm probably making too big a deal out of the kiss, anyway. Could be he doesn't even remember it.

At the next chance of a turn, I ease off the main highway onto a narrow, unpaved road and head north. My headlights bounce over the gravel, and phantom bushes fly past my windows, but I hold the jittery wheel steady until I find a decent place to pull over. I turn off the ignition, and in the quiet, the gravel road gleams a ghostly, pale line through the dark desert brush.

I dig into a satchel for Freddy's tablet, doubtful I'll even get a connection here, but after a moment of a searching signal, I get a Google window.

Yes.

I check Facebook and look up Peggy's profile. Her latest post says, *The idiot is gone.* Nothing about my parents. It's disheartening, and I shiver, thinking of Ian on the loose again.

I pull up the Tor site Burnham created when I was with him in Atlanta and type in our passcode, *Waffles67*. A string of messages pops up, and I feel a jolt of surprise. They're from Burnham, and the first is time-stamped from last night.

From: BurnFist51
To: LKRose
Sent: Sat 3/26/67 8:59 PM
Subject: Hey
I'm finally back up. Berg's virus totally fried my computer. I had to buy a new one. Call me. 404-484-1223. The line's secure.

From: BurnFist51
To: LKRose
Sent: Sat 3/26/67 9:14 PM
Subject: FW: Hey
Are you there?

From: BurnFist51
To: LKRose
Sent: Sat 3/26/67 9:23 PM
Subject: FW: Hey
Reply if this reaches you.

From: BurnFist51
To: LKRose
Sent: Sat 3/26/67 9:32 PM

Subject: FW: Hey

I get it. You're not online yet. It'll prolly take you a while to get to a computer. I'm not going to panic. Call me as soon as you can. Waffles says hi.

From: BurnFist51
To: LKRose
Sent: Sun 3/27/67 6:06 AM
Subject: FW: Hey

I just saw Berg on the Forge Show like nothing's wrong. Where are you? Don't be dead. That would be uncool.

From: BurnFist51
To: LKRose
Sent: Sun 3/27/67 10:34 AM
Subject: FW: Hey

The now is miserable.

Burnham once professed that he didn't worry because it made the now miserable, but clearly I've pushed him over the edge. I scramble for one of my new, recyclable phones and pull off the wrapper. *Please have a signal*, I think. I punch in Burnham's number and listen to the rings. What time is it in Atlanta? Before I can calculate time zones, the connection comes on.

"Hello?" he asks.

I bolt up in my seat, smiling. "So you do worry after all."

"I'll be," he says in his Southern drawl. "You're not dead."

I shake my head, clutching the phone hard. Hearing his

voice twists me up because he sounds so close. A thrum of wind surrounds the car, and the desert outside my windows is impossibly vast and dark. "Nope," I say.

"Don't do that again," he says. There's a fumbling noise like he's arranging something, maybe reaching for his glasses or shifting his brace. "Where are you?" he asks.

"About an hour west of Doli. I'm in my car, by the side of the road," I say. I glance out the window. "In the desert."

"Alone?"

"Yeah."

"And you're really okay? Berg didn't hurt you at all? It sounded bad when I got cut off."

"I'm okay," I say. "I was able to jab a couple syringes into him and dose him with sleep meds. That was fun." I explain how I escaped, and how my friend Thea had her baby down in the tunnel. "Berg kept her prisoner down there."

"That guy is seriously twisted," Burnham says. "But now, who's Thea?"

I'm startled to realize I've never told him about her. I didn't really know who she was myself when I visited him in Atlanta. It's tempting now to tell him the whole story, but I have a sneaking suspicion he'll want to tell his parents, which would not be good. Besides, I should check with Thea before I divulge what's basically her health history. Come to think of it, I really should have checked with Thea before I told Peggy about her, too.

"Thea's a friend of mine from way back," I improvise. "We're really close, actually, and she showed up at Linus's house looking for me. She's normally in Texas with her family, and I really need to talk to her and find out how she is, but I don't have a safe way to call her. In fact, I haven't been in touch with anybody 'til now."

"No problem," he says. "I can send her a recyclable phone and give you the number. Do you still have one yourself?"

"I have one left," I say.

"Then what else? What else do you need?"

He is truly such a nice guy, and it feels so good to have his support.

"I have to find my parents and my sister," I say. "Berg said they're in Las Vegas, and he pretty much promised to kidnap them if I didn't let him mine me."

"You can't let him do that."

"I know, but I have no way to warn my parents," I say, frustrated. "They don't have a phone. I'm scared, Burnham. He could take them anywhere. Anywhere in the world, actually, even Iceland. The Chimera Centre's there."

"He can't take them personally, though," Burnham says. "He still has to show up regularly on *The Forge Show*. He could hire people to kidnap them, but I doubt he'd take them out of the country unless he had you, too." A tapping comes from his end. "This isn't good. I could get a PI, but that would take time. Do you have any other ideas? Why are your parents in Las Vegas?"

"I'm not sure," I say. "I'm not even sure Berg was telling the truth about them being there. My neighbor Peggy said my parents had a lead on where I might be and that's why they left. Vegas might have been their destination, or they could have been heading somewhere west of there and just stopped on the way." I frown out my window as a shimmer of dust passes through my headlights. "There's supposed to be another vault of dreamers in Miehana, California. A big one. I can't help thinking it's important."

"You mentioned that once before," he says. "Miehana," he adds slowly. "Isn't that near the Olbaid Nuclear Power Plant? The one that blew up?"

The name tickles a memory of a story from science class. "Possibly," I say. "Let me take a look."

On Freddy's tablet, I do a quick search for the Olbaid Nuclear Power Plant, which is right on the Pacific coast, about halfway between L.A. and San Francisco. It had a major meltdown in 2048, about twenty years back. The town of Miehana is thirty miles inland, just outside the Olbaid Exclusion Zone. Images of the OEZ show the rusty ruin of a roller coaster and decaying, overgrown summer cottages.

"You're right," I say, impressed.

"Okay," he says. "We'll see what we can find out about that vault in Miehana. And here's another idea. I can search the Fister database to see if there are any significant sleep med orders in that part of California."

"You think that vault of dreamers uses sleep meds?" I say. "The dreamers are already asleep."

"They used sleep meds for you when you were at Onar, didn't they?" Burnham says.

He's right. They did. "But I was an exception," I say. "Berg buys bodies from a pre-morgue. They're legally dead. He's just found a way to boot up their bodily functions. He can reignite their brain stems."

"Who told you this?"

"Berg did," I say, remembering Gracie, a little dreamer girl from the vault under Forge. "From what he said, the dreamers are sort of half back from the dead, just enough for their old dreams to stir. Berg uses their brains almost like potting soil. He could implant dreams from Forge students into them and they'd take root. That's what he said, at least."

"Holy crap," Burnham says. "Why didn't you ever tell me this?"

"I don't know. It didn't come up."

"That is one creepy dude," he says.

No kidding.

"Hold on. I've got another thing," I say. I locate the pill box I took from Ian and fish out a few of the little pills. I turn on the overhead light so I can inspect a red one. "See if you can find out anything about a red pill marked 'Echo eight,' and a yellow one. I think this is a double theta marked on it."

"Send me a picture."

It takes me a couple seconds, but I do. "This phone camera's not the best."

"That's okay. Where'd you get the pills?" Burnham says.

"I found them on a guy who works for Berg. Remember Ian? He came looking for me in Doli."

Burnham wants to hear all about that, too, and I tell him how Peggy and I stuck Ian in the closet.

"You're really not safe anywhere, are you?" Burnham says.

I focus out my window again. The place where I've pulled off is still dark and quiet. If I turn off my headlights, I'll practically disappear, but I'm too anxious to stay here doing nothing.

I switch the phone to speaker and prop it on my knee. Then I start the car again and turn back toward the freeway.

"I'm going to keep driving toward Las Vegas," I say. "I'm going to hope Peggy warns my parents about Berg in time and they start driving back toward me."

"Sounds good," Burnham says. "But maybe get some sleep in there."

I laugh. Like I could sleep. "And you'll do your research and send a phone to Thea," I say.

"What's her address?" Burnham asks.

"I don't have it on me. You'll have to look it up. Her name's Althea Flores. She lives in Holdum, Texas, and her family owns a ranch. They're super wealthy." I realize he'll learn a ton about her online, but that's for another conversation. "How long will it take to get her a phone?"

"I can have it delivered first thing tomorrow."

"Thanks, Burnham," I say. "This is so nice of you. I mean it."

"Don't mention it," he says. "I'm glad to be back doing something. I was worried about you."

A louder shifting noise comes from his end. I think he's about to say goodbye, but instead, he clears his throat.

"Listen. Do you have another minute?" he asks.

I've just reached the highway again and I turn on my blinker, which clicks in loud rhythm. I look to my left for on-coming headlights and wait while a pair of headlights gets bigger.

"Sure. I'm just driving," I say.

After the car passes, I pull out onto the road and pick up speed.

"I was talking to my sister, Sammi, yesterday," Burnham says. "I kind of told her about when you were staying with me here in Atlanta. That night. After you had your nightmare."

I know exactly what he means. A cold furball lodges in my lungs. I can't believe he told her about us.

"I remember," I say, trying to sound nonchalant. "What about it?"

"Sammi says I owe you an apology," Burnham says quietly. "She got me thinking I came on too, well, strong, and then I wasn't exactly cool the next morning."

I feel a snap of relief, like a cord breaking. I grip the steering wheel harder and aim straight ahead as an overpass whooshes above. "Wow," I say.

"So she's right?"

She's brilliant is what she is.

"Yeah," I say.

"I'm sorry, then. I really am," he says. "The trouble is, I can never tell if the vibe between us is good or bad, or if I'm just imagining it, you know?"

I do know, unfortunately. It's not like I have everything figured out. "Let's just agree never to kiss each other again," I say.

"Not ever?"

I throw up a hand. "Burnham!"

"I'm apologizing," he says. "I'm trying to be straight-up honest with you."

"And you're making me really uncomfortable," I say. "Just stop."

"Okay. All right," he says. And then, "Just tell me one thing. One last thing."

"What?"

"That picture of you in Linus's bed. Does that mean what I think it does?"

I frown at the road ahead and watch the white lines flicking by. I don't owe Burnham an answer. I know that. I'm certainly not going to tell him that Linus and I didn't have sex. But I have to say something.

"Linus doesn't pressure me," I say.

The car hums over the smooth road.

"Touché," Burnham says softly.

I shake my head. He asked; he got his answer.

"If you don't want to help me anymore, that's fine," I say.

"Wait a second," he says. "I'm not helping you just because I like you. We're a team, Rosie."

"We are?"

"Berg messed up my life, and think of all those other students at Forge. We trusted that place, and he stole our dreams. I don't mean mine, literally, but it's effectively the same thing."

A prickling of hope gathers in me. "You're right," I say. Burnham has always had an innate sense of justice. I knew that.

"We're going to bring him down, Rosie. You can be sure of that."

Wow, I think, and my hope is buoyed into something more certain. "Thanks," I say.

"Of course," he says. "Now, I've got stuff to do. Don't drive too late. And be sure to eat something. Cheetos, at least."

I smile. "All right," I say. "Thanks again."

46

He hangs up, and I'm left alone, still driving. It's funny. With all the dips and turns our friendship has gone through, I feel closer to him now than I did when I was standing in his kitchen. I wonder if he feels the same.

My smile fades. If only I knew where Linus was.

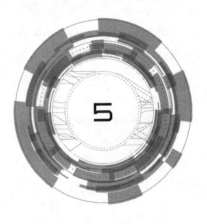

5

LEMON SMOKE

INKY DARKNESS PRESSES against the windshield. It spreads, clinging, an ultra-blackness that blots out the stars, the road, and the headlights. And yet the Toyota's speeding along. I can feel the momentum and hear the wind whipping past. In Fagan gloves like Ian's, Linus has taken my place behind the wheel. Elation lifts my heart, but then I remember his eye and misery follows. With the dashboard casting a faint glow over his features, I can just make out his profile, but he won't look at me. When I ask him where he's taking me, he doesn't reply, and then comes the creeping feeling that he won't look my way because something's wrong with his face. I know this, but I can't see it yet because he hasn't turned, and suddenly I don't want him to. What if his other eye and his cheek are melting? My voice box locks onto itself. I can't speak. A prickle scatters through my body, and at the same time, a leaden heaviness consumes my muscles. My heart beats harder, but it also feels thick. It feels wet.

I look down at my chest to find that black ooze is seeping through my shirt, from my heart. *Linus!* I whisper, terrified. *Help me!* I press against the wound of my heart, trying to keep the ooze in, and finally Linus turns to me. Where his face belongs, a boil of black sludge slowly churns around a single, clean, protruding eyeball. The eyeball slices open mechanically to reveal a tiny figure inside, a man at a control center with levers and cogs. It's Berg. He smiles at me knowingly, and the black ooze gushes from my heart.

I jolt awake, gasping.

The car is filled with murky light. A film of moisture beads the windows. I'm in the backseat, parked on a deserted side road where I stopped when exhaustion caught up with me. My heart's beating wildly, my skin's slick with sweat, and I'm clutching my bulky sleeping bag to my chest.

"I'm okay," I whisper desperately.

It was a nightmare. Just a nightmare. A horrific blend of fears. Linus betraying me, Berg in charge, me helpless—these are all terrors I can't bear to face.

I pull on my shoes, shove open the car door, and step out onto the dirt. Depthless violet touches everything, near and far. Dawn has come, the stars are fading, and I can't see another car or a house in any direction. The only truth is red sand, mesquite, and saltbush sloping toward the distant horizon. I take a deep breath of the cool, tangy air and push my thick hair back from my face.

"I'm all right," I say again, more certainly.

But my heart still aches. It's been two full days now since I've seen Linus, and it feels like so much longer. I pull out the sticky note Peggy gave me and look at his number. It's possible, I suppose, that it's a secure way to reach him, but I don't know if it's worth the chance. He could be waking up in St. Louis, in an apartment I've never seen, sitting alone at the side of his bed, checking his messages to see if I've tried to contact him. Or he could be on location somewhere, drinking a cup of coffee in his stylish clothes, prepping to shoot another episode of *Found Missing*.

Finally, self-indulgently, I choose to imagine him asleep in his rumpled bed where we lay together. Early light is sifting in the dormer window, crossing his knuckles at a slant. He's half in shadow, with his face relaxed and his dark hair a mess. He smells of cotton and salt, and his chest barely moves with his slow, even breath.

"No," I mumble, sliding the note back in my pocket.

It's no good thinking of him this way, reducing the real Linus to nostalgia. He isn't mine. I can't be with him now. My dream made that clear. No matter how little Linus is to blame for the camera in his eye, Berg rides along inside Linus like a tiny, perpetual spy, seeing everything he does, invading every aspect of his life.

A buzz in the car makes me turn, and I instinctively think it's Linus calling. Instead, I find a message from Burnham that says he's had a recyclable phone delivered to Thea already. It occurs to me then that Linus might have tried my old disposable phone, so I dig it out of my backpack. Sure enough, I've missed two calls from him. An odd little thrill goes through me, part relief and part power. I compare the callback number to the one Peggy gave me, and they're different, which makes me all the more skeptical that either is secure.

What am I thinking? I *just decided* not to contact him. I'm not going to change my mind.

I do a quick check of Peggy's Facebook page, but she hasn't added anything new.

Unwrapping my last fresh recyclable phone, I dial up Thea. As it rings, I grab a bagel from my supplies and step out of the stuffy car again.

A girl's quiet, uncertain voice comes on. "Hello?"

"Thea? It's Rosie," I say. "Did I wake you?"

Thea gives a soft laugh. "No, but this phone showed up only ten minutes ago. Imagine my surprise. How are you? Where are you?"

I am so, so relieved to hear her sounding normal. I barely allowed myself to think that she could be dead or back in a coma. Grinning, I meander into the desert, where dew has darkened the dust and the tops of pebbles.

"I'm in Arizona," I say. "And I'm good. How are you? How's the baby?"

"I'm exhausted," she says. "You wouldn't believe how tired. But my baby's unbelievable. She's absolutely incredible."

"Really? I'm so glad. What's she like? Tell me."

"She's the sweetest thing," Thea says, her voice warm and dreamy. "She has these stern little eyebrows that'll melt your heart. And she never cries. She's sleeping now in a little bassinet right next to me. I just want to watch her, every second. Tom's in love with her, of course. He's a big fat marshmallow."

"What did you name her?" I take a bite of bagel as I listen.

"Valeria, after my grandmother," Thea says. "She was a pistol, apparently."

Valeria was not our grandmother's name. We had a Kelly and an Alvina, but I let it pass.

"Thanks for helping me with her," she adds. "That was bad in the tunnel."

"I know. I'm just glad you made it okay. I've been worried," I say.

"Tom was fit to be tied when he found out."

"I bet," I say, smiling. It's easy to picture the big, protective guy in a state over Thea.

A bird chirps from nearby. I turn my gaze in the right direction and search the bushes for movement.

"Want to hear something kind of different?" she asks.

"Sure."

A shifting noise comes over the phone before she goes on.

"When I was in labor, I had the strangest vision right before the baby came," Thea says. "I could see Althea's grandfather on the porch here at the ranch, and Althea's old dog Gizmo, only Gizmo was still a puppy. A little collie. And I was a girl with little-kid hands. The thing is, it felt like a real memory, like my own. What do you think that means?"

"I don't know. Has that sort of thing happened before?"

"No. I've had some of Althea's feelings before, around Tom especially, but that's the first time I've ever had anything like a real memory."

"What feelings for Tom?" I ask.

"Just feelings. That's not the point. It just made me wonder if part of her is still alive in me."

I pause a moment to idly push a dry stick with the toe of my sneaker.

"You said something," I say. "That night, you asked me to give a message to Althea's parents and her grandfather. You told me to thank them and tell them they did right by you."

"I did?" Thea asks.

"Yes." At the time, her voice even sounded a little different. I was terrified, actually. I thought she was dying. I chomp down on my bagel again and work through a thick, stale bite. She's quiet for so long, I start to wonder if we've lost the connection. "Thea?"

"I'm just thinking," she says. "It's scary. It was a nice memory, but I don't want Althea to come back. I couldn't handle sharing my brain with her, and I wouldn't want her taking over, squeezing me out. Is that selfish of me?"

I hadn't thought of Althea taking over.

"No," I say. "Or yes, it is, but you deserve to feel selfish about your own mind."

"Even if it was hers first?"

"Thea! You're not giving up, are you?"

"Of course not."

"Are you having headaches or déjà vus? Any dizziness?" I ask.

She exhales a big breath, and then speaks very quietly. "Actually, the headaches are pretty bad."

"Have you told your parents?" I ask, alarmed.

"They know," she says. "Did you say you're home? How's Dubbs?"

"You're changing the subject," I say.

"I want to hear about you," she says firmly. "And our family."

I squash down my anxiety for her, but I'm not forgetting it. "You're not going to like this," I say. Then I tell her about my visit to the boxcar and how our family was gone. I add in my run to Peggy's and the mess with Ian. "Berg's after me," I say. "He wants to mine me again, and I'm worried he's kidnapping Ma and Larry and Dubbs to force me to cooperate with him."

"And you think they're in Vegas?"

"That's what Berg said."

"I'm trying not to freak out here," Thea says. "It's weird that they didn't leave any note for you. Did you look everywhere?"

I'd completely forgotten Dubbs's note. Now I chuck away the rest of my bagel and pull the scrap of paper out of my pocket. "There was something from Dubbs, actually, but it didn't say much. She hid it under the bed, where she usually kept her journal." I smooth the paper and read the message into the phone. "It says, *To Rosie*, period. *From Dubbs*, period. *See you*, no period." I hadn't noticed the periods before. Dubbs is eight. She's not big on punctuation. Then again, maybe she is. I'll take any clue.

"There's no drawing?" Thea asks.

"No."

"Does it smell?" she asks.

I lift Dubbs's note to my nose and breathe in the dry scent

of lemon. An odd possibility occurs to me, and I inhale the scent again. *No*, I think, awed. Then I smile.

"The little sneaky genius," I say. "It smells of lemon."

"You know what that means," Thea says, excited.

"Yes. Just a minute. Let me find a match."

"We're like twice as smart now," she says. "This is so exciting. Check quick. Valeria's waking up again."

"Hold on. I have to go back to the car."

Dubbs and I once had a trick for secret messages that we wrote with lemon juice. I read about it in a magazine from the library, and we spent a string of summer afternoons squeezing lemons, writing messages to each other with the juice, and letting them dry so the writing disappeared. Sometimes we'd write a decoy message on the paper with regular ink, so no one would ever guess a hidden message was layered beneath.

Now, with the phone tucked under my ear, I light up a wooden match and hold it beneath the paper, close enough to feel the heat, but not near enough to catch fire. At first, nothing happens, and then the heat makes brown letters appear where the dry juice is hidden in the paper and completes the message.

> To Rosie. From Dubbs.
> See you at 240 Mallorca Way
> in Miehana, CA.
> Don't tell. I miss you.

The last line encircles my heart and squeezes. I hold the match an instant longer to see if any other writing will appear, and then I wave it out.

My brilliant, *brilliant* sister left me an address. And she hid it, too, like she knew someone might come looking through our house, like she knew she was in danger. Not good. The address is in Miehana, the same place as the big vault of dreamers. It can't be a coincidence.

"What did you find?" Thea asks.

"It's an address in Miehana, California: Two forty Mallorca Way," I say, trying to remember if I've ever said anything to Thea about the vault in Miehana. I don't think so. "It has to be where my family was going. She says not to tell anybody."

"Dubbs is a genius," Thea says. "You're going there, right? I wish I could go with you!"

"You just had a baby. Your head's a mess." Already I'm walking around the car to get in the driver's seat. I toss the matches on the dashboard and take another sniff of Dubbs's note. Now it smells like smoke as well as lemon, and it's almost as good as having her in the car with me.

"At least tell me what can I do to help," Thea says. "I have money now. What do you need?"

"You sound like Burnham."

"Burnham! Exactly. We have to tell him. He'll be a huge help."

I look again at Dubbs's note where it says *Don't tell*.

"I'm not sure I want to tell him," I say.

"Why not? How much does he know about you and me?" Thea asks.

"I wasn't sure you'd want me to tell him about us."

"What is wrong with you? That's ridiculous," Thea says. "Call him back. He already knows I was in a coma. You should at least explain to him how we're connected. Then he and I can put our heads together. He'll be a brilliant ally. He knows all about computers. You know, I bet he could even break into the Forge computers if he tried."

I switch the phone to speaker and rest it on my knee. Then I start up the car and shift into gear.

"He did try," I say.

"What?!" she exclaims.

"He tried and failed, just a couple days ago while you were locked in the vault at Forge. In fact, the whole thing back-fired," I say. I turn the car around and head back toward the highway. "The point is, for the very first time, I might actually have an edge over Berg. This address could be the key to the vault of dreamers in Miehana, and he doesn't know I have it. I have to be careful who I tell and what I do next."

"*We* have to be careful," she says. "Don't you dare try to do this on your own. Imagine how I feel. I care about Ma and Dubbs as much as you do."

I notice she doesn't mention Larry.

"And Larry," she adds. "Besides, we don't know anything about that address. It could be a trap. Why don't you come to Holdum instead? We can work together and figure out a plan."

"I think we're both safer apart," I say.

She lets out a laugh. "What are you talking about?"

I hesitate, not certain how she's going to take this. "Berg told me your parents want to buy more of my dreams for you."

I aim around a pothole.

"They probably think you're dead," Thea says, her voice

low. "They wouldn't want to mine you if they knew you were alive."

"No? Have you told them about me?"

"I have, obviously, but it didn't do much good," she says. "They won't believe I'm you inside. They know Rosie Sinclair was a star on *The Forge Show*, but they think I'm just obsessed with you. They don't realize Sinclair Fifteen comes from you."

"What are they? Stupid?" I say.

"You know what?" she says calmly. "Sometimes you sound just like you used to when you were a little voice in my head and you said the sort of thing I knew not to say out loud."

"And sometimes you sound like a superior butthead."

"I'm trying to be rational here," she says. "Madeline and Diego are very shrewd people, but they're not cruel. They must think the original source of my dream seed is dead. Or a volunteer. A dream donor or whatever."

Thea's deluding herself, but I keep my opinion to myself this time.

"Did they tell you to invite me there?" I ask.

"They suggested it," she says. "When I told them how you helped me deliver my baby, they said you would always be welcome here."

"I see," I say, coming to a stop before the highway. I crack my window to let in a little air. "I hate to point out the obvious, but having me nearby would be awfully convenient if they ever needed to mine me."

"Rosie, they wouldn't. I promise you. That would never even be a possibility."

"No? What if you fall into a coma again? What if your headaches get worse?" I say. "Why not tap old Rosie? She's got dreams to spare."

From her end of the phone, a muffled shuffling happens.

"I'd give you my dreams in a heartbeat," she says.

I laugh. "Oh, great. Now I'm a selfish jerk."

"I didn't say that."

"No?" I say. "I guess I'm not as generous as you. I wouldn't sacrifice my dreams for you. I already did that when it wasn't my choice, and I'm not doing it again."

I'm surprised at how vicious I sound. But they mined me and mined me until I was a pathetic shred of myself. I barely survived. I've never been the same.

"Rosie," she says sadly. "You know I had to leave you."

"Don't."

I already feel ugly and bad enough as it is. I don't need her bringing up her justifications again for why she abandoned me, and sure as I live, I don't need to think any more about what it was like in the dream hell of Onar. The simple, bitter truth is, I'm never letting anyone mine me again, ever.

"You said you're sorry. We're done," I say.

A little squawking noise comes over the line, and then a guy's murmur. It's disconcerting to think Tom might have been overhearing her end of the conversation.

"Valeria's awake," Thea says. Another shuffling noise follows. "She needs to nurse. Listen, will you call me later? We'll figure out what to do about Berg, okay?"

"I'll try," I say.

"Don't be mad at me."

"I'm not mad," I say. I am, obviously, fuming mad.

"Then will you please tell Burnham about me, really? Please?" Thea says. "He'd never believe me if I tried to tell him myself."

"I will."

"Call me after you talk to him."

She's off.

I ease onto the highway and get up to speed. She thinks we belong together, like we're still halves of the same whole. She's wrong, though. We aren't the same. We have completely different lives now. What's more, we don't even really think alike. We never did, actually, even when we were part of the same mind. That's why we could disagree with each other before. You have to be separate to disagree.

And yet. We still have fifteen years of shared memories, and she helped me find the lemon juice clue. I hold the note above the steering wheel and take a moment to memorize the address. For the first time, I wonder how Dubbs got it.

Then I touch Dubbs's note to my nose again and breathe in the lemony, smoky fragrance. It's a small, churlish comfort to think that Dubbs will recognize me rather than Thea if we ever all meet together.

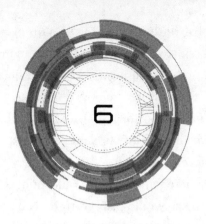

6

LINUS: HALF BLIND

HE HATED DOCTORS and doctors' offices and hospitals. He couldn't stand being asked to undress, or feeling a paper gown against his skin, or knowing he'd be touched with impersonal, efficient hands. His mum had died in hospital. His dad, too, an ocean later. The slimy guy who'd photographed him at age thirteen, Floyd, had divined this revulsion somehow. He'd worn a stethoscope around his neck while he took the shots of Linus, posed half-naked on the brown, carpeted podium. The hidden tension was what gave the photos their power, Floyd had said.

Sweating in his suit, Linus sat in the waiting room of the top eye surgeon in the country and tried not to think about the past. To look at his eye, they weren't going to make him undress, that was for sure. He could keep it together. He wasn't a kid anymore. He wasn't subject to Floyd's sick power.

He couldn't live with a camera lens in his eye anymore. He couldn't have Berg spying on every tiny, intimate detail of his life. His gut tensed with hunger. He hadn't been able to eat since he'd found out his eye belonged to Berg, and no matter how much he faked his normal confidence, he was shaking and fizzing inside like a faulty firecracker that spun around on the street and never fizzled out.

If Rosie were here with him, he could calm down, but that wasn't realistic. If she would just return his calls, he would quit wanting to rip her apart. How many times could she break his heart?

A teenage girl and her father looked his way and whispered to each other. They recognized him, no doubt, but he hoped they'd stop at the friendly, knowing smiles and not approach to talk to him. He wore shades, and he had a patch over his left eye. If that wasn't a big enough hint that he didn't want to interact with the public, he didn't know what was. Twenty other patients were waiting as well. The TV beside the receptionist's window was tuned to *The Forge Show*, low volume, and even though he didn't watch it, he could feel the light of it washing over him personally like a punishing, scalding X-ray.

The inner door opened, and the famous doctor herself leaned out. Dr. Keane's long nose and silver hair matched the photos he'd seen. Her dangling blue earrings were a surprise.

"Mr. Pitts?" she asked, glancing up from the clipboard she held. Her eyebrows lifted as her gaze settled on him. "Won't you come in?"

As Linus rose, the girl whispered audibly to her father, "See? I told you."

Linus expected to face an examination room, but instead, the doctor led him to a small office with wall-to-wall diplomas and awards. A snow globe rested on the corner of a shiny mahogany desk, and he relaxed slightly at the whimsical object. Inside, a pair of tiny skaters were poised on a glassy pond. When she gestured him toward a leather armchair, he was too restless to sit.

The doctor crossed her arms in her crisp white coat. She was nearly as tall as he was, meeting his gaze straight on and patiently, as if she didn't have a crammed schedule.

"This is a pleasure," she said. "I've enjoyed following your career, but I never expected to meet you in person."

"Thanks for seeing me on such short notice," Linus said.

"Not at all. What can I do for you?"

"It's of a confidential nature."

"Of course."

"I have a camera lens in my left eye," he said, pointing to his patch. "It was put in while I worked at Forge, and I didn't know about it until Saturday. I called you as soon as I could."

Her eyes widened in surprise. "You didn't consent to the camera?"

"I was never even asked about it. The cook at Forge hit me in the eye, and I couldn't see, so I went to the infirmary," he said. "The doctor there told me I had a hyphema. She said she had a procedure to make it clear, and she worked on me for maybe half an hour. Not long. She put me out while she did it. Then I wore a patch afterward for twenty-four hours, but that was it. When I took the patch off, I could see again. Things were a little bright, but the doctor had told me to expect that, so I didn't think anything about it."

"You want me to testify? Is that it? What you've described is a serious breach of ethics," the doctor said.

"I want you to get it out," Linus said.

She took a penlight out of her pocket and gestured toward his eye. "May I?"

He stiffened. "What? Right here?"

"We can move to an examination room if you prefer," she said.

"No," he said. "Here's fine."

She tilted her face, smiling oddly, as if she were reading exactly how nervous he was.

"It'll only take a minute," she said. "I'll need you to take off your glasses and your patch. Here. Hold this for me."

She passed him the snow globe, which was cool and heavy in his hand. The glass was so smooth it was almost oily, but it felt good, too. Calming. He gave it a tilt, and the snow drifted around the skaters. When the doctor smiled, he set aside his sunglasses and his patch. Then he held the snow globe in both hands and offered her his face. Lightly, she pressed her cool thumb and forefinger around his left eye, stretching wide his eyelid.

"Look up?" she said. "Now down. To the left? Now the right."

Her light beamed into him, creating a blind, silent hollow. He concentrated on the cool sphere of glass in his hands until she lowered the light away, leaving a ghost glare behind. She examined his right eye, too, and then dropped her pen back in her breast pocket.

"All done," she said. "You were right. You have a camera in your eye."

Linus felt an ugly twist of vindication, and then a new shot of anger. He couldn't help wondering if Berg was watching this very scene.

"Have you seen these before?" he asked.

"Yes. Quite a few times. I've installed a couple dozen, usually for the military, but in a few civilians, too," she said. "It can be very stressful for people psychologically, like an invasion. This is the first time I've heard of anyone having a camera inserted against his will, however. Normally, you'd carry a receiver on your person to relay the signal, but I don't suppose you had that?"

"No."

"It could have been bugged into your phone easily enough," she said. "Or while you were at Forge, you could have had any number of receivers in your environment. Do you understand how the camera works?"

"Not exactly."

She held out her hand for the snow globe. Linus turned it over to loosen the snow once more before he gave it back. She set it on the desk and pulled over a pad of paper. She drew a little diagram with an eyeball and a couple of boxes and arrows.

"The camera in your eye has a lens that was inserted between your cornea and your iris," she said. "It collects your visual data. It also has a tiny, built-in, wireless transmitter, which sends a signal to a nearby receiver, usually carried on your body. That receiver, in turn, powers up the signal and passes it along to whoever's watching."

"Is the camera always on?" he asked.

"The camera is, but that doesn't mean you're always

transmitting data," she said. "If you're out of range of a receiver, the camera can stockpile data until you're back in range and send it then, in a batch."

At best, then, some of his visions were delayed, but Berg still saw everything eventually. Even if Berg hadn't bugged Linus's cell phone, he had certainly planted a receiver somewhere in Otis's house, where Linus went back often to visit. Possibly a receiver was in Linus's bedroom. He searched his room often enough for camera lenses, but he'd never thought to look for a small box that could be out of sight.

That scene in his bed with Rosie, the one that Berg had a clip of, could have been watched live. Linus seethed. No wonder Rosie didn't want to be with him. All of their most private moments together had had a voyeur along. He could practically feel Berg smirking. Sick old bastard.

"How long have you had this? Dr. Keane asked kindly.

Linus glanced up. "Months," he said. "Since last September."

She made a quick grimace. "Are you sure you don't want to sue? You'd have quite a case."

"I just want it out," he said.

She leaned back against her desk and crossed her arms again. "The good news is, I can take it out for you. The bad news is, removing it is far more complicated than putting it in, and I'm booked solid for the next six months. I could refer you to a colleague who might be able to help you sooner, but probably not by much."

His heart sank. He couldn't face Rosie again with the camera still in.

When he didn't reply, the doctor moved around to the back of her desk and skimmed a finger over her computer pad. "I can fit you in on September fourteenth, eight a.m. That's a Wednesday. Does that work for you?"

He couldn't wait half a year.

"Isn't there anything sooner? Please?" he said. "I can pay double. Triple."

She shook her head. "I'm sorry. That's my first available date."

He refused to accept this. There had to be a way.

"You don't understand," he said. "I'd be better off half blind. Can't you fry the sucker with a laser or something?"

The doctor considered him for a long moment. "There is one other option. I don't recommend it."

"Let's hear it."

"I could affix a black membrane over your pupil, for now. It would meld to the surface of your eye and block your vision. You'd be completely blind in that eye."

Linus felt the first bit of hope he'd had in days.

"Would it show much?" he asked.

"It would to anyone looking carefully," she said. "Your pupil would appear to be always the same size, not changing with brightness. But it's reversible. When you come back six months from now, I can give you a cornea transplant and a new lens. You'll be back to normal."

That was what he'd been longing to hear. "When can you do this?"

She looked back at her calendar and shook her head. "I can

try to squeeze you in Friday. That'll give you a little time to think it over."

"I don't need any time," he said.

"Nevertheless," she said, coming back around her desk and reaching past him for the door. "Think it over."

7

TABBY IN THE WINDOW

AROUND ELEVEN THAT MORNING, I pull into a gas station to fuel up. In the distance, Vegas is a sun-bleached bar graph rising out of the desert floor, with a swatch of blue, faded mountains in the background. The sight of where my parents last were brings my fears forward again, and I reflexively check Peggy's Facebook profile again. There's still no update. So frustrating. Her daughter has posted twice, though, so at least the McLellens are okay.

I suppose it's possible my parents evaded their kidnappers and they're continuing to 240 Mallorca Way. If so, I'll find them there when I arrive. It's a hope, no matter now slim.

I put on my hat and pull the visor low over my face before I go in to pay for my gas. I pick out a package of donuts, too, and I'm waiting in line, staring at a box of car lighter phone jacks, when, with a start, I recall that I have Ian's phone.

Of course. It won't do Berg any good to kidnap my family if he can't call me and tell me so. He must be trying to reach me.

I hurry back to my car and pull over to a spot of shade next to a pawn shop. Then I dig through my bag for Ian's phone. With an anxious rip of wrappers, I stick a Band-Aid over the camera lenses, and then I turn it on. It's low on power but it's getting decent bars. The phone icon shows two voicemails: one from an unknown number at 11:58 p.m., and one from OTHER, at 12:04 a.m. Eleven hours ago! My heart beats harder.

Which first? I take a steadying breath and try the unknown number.

To my shock, my sister's voice comes on.

"Hi, Rosie?" Dubbs says. Her voice is too high, like she's excited or scared. "This is Dubbs. I'm okay. This guy says—" There's a muffling noise, and then, faintly, I hear Dubbs say, "What do you want me to say again?" A man's indistinguishable voice answers her, and then Dubbs comes on clearly once more. "Okay. This is Dubbs. If you get this? I'm okay, and Ma and Dad are okay, too. They're sleeping here. We're in a truck. You're supposed to call Dean Berg. And don't call the police." The man's voice rumbles in the background again. "I said it!"

A swift bumbling cuts off the connection, and the message ends.

Fear robs me of breath. Berg has my family! I knew it was likely to happen, but now it's real.

I listen to the message again. She's afraid. I know she is, but she's also trying to be calm, like that's the mature thing to do

70

in a crisis. She's only eight years old! My heart tears around my chest. I listen to the message a third time, hoping for clues. They're in a truck, but where?

I want to crush something.

I switch to the next voicemail, the one from OTHER, also known as Berg, and I give it a jab.

"You should have a voicemail from your sister," Berg says. "Call me. The sooner the better."

I'll kill him. For a fierce instant, that's all I can think. I really will. I suck in a painful gasp of air. I'll track him down and slash him into bloody pieces.

Then my gaze lands on Dubbs's lemony note, and my heart crumples in aching pain. He can't hurt her. How could anybody hurt sweet old Dubbs?

I have to think.

If I call him and he finds me, he'll no longer need to keep my family hostage, which means he'll dispose of them, one way or another. It's just the sort of ruthless thing he'd do. So I can't let him find me. I can't call him back.

But then, what do I do?

Berg doesn't know where I am, so far. That's an advantage for me. I turn off Ian's phone again and drop it on the passenger seat. The GPS wasn't on, but if Berg has a way to track calls on Ian's phone, he might know I turned it on for a minute. He might know I've heard his messages. Still, what can he do? Nothing. He has to wait for me to contact him.

I take a shaky breath. And Berg doesn't know I have that address in Miehana, the one Dubbs left me. I notice she didn't say anything about that in her voicemail. Maybe my family hasn't told their captors where they were headed. That destination could still be safe.

Dubbs was smart enough to leave me a secret message. She was brave enough to stay calm when talking on the phone for her kidnappers, too. My little sister! I have to be brave, too. And smart. I'll find her. I will.

I wish I could believe myself.

I curl my fingers around the steering wheel and grip hard enough that I feel all the rest of me is shaking. *Is this what you wanted, Berg?* I think. He has me sick with fear.

>>>>>>>>

I head west, driving long hours, until my initial horror and panic spiral down into a noxious feeling in my gut. I can't eat. Not even the donuts. I can't bring myself to call anyone. Not Linus, not Burnham, not Thea. I'm certainly not calling Berg. All I can do is drive. I'll get to 240 Mallorca Way, and I'll figure out what to do next after that. It's not the greatest plan, but it's the only one that makes any sense. Fear and anger keep me burning, mile after mile, well into the afternoon.

Where Nevada meets California, the long road rises through treeless hills. White wind turbines, with their three reaching propellers, dominate the hills like an army of giants. It takes me a while to realize half of them are rusted and don't spin. Miles later, near L.A., I pass a storage lot filled with trailer classrooms, empty now. Cheery electronic billboards advertise theme parks and tourist attractions, but below them, rows of run-down motels and the ruin of an old mall dispel the illusion of prosperity. I knew California was hurting, but after all the movies I've watched, I still thought it would look better than this.

Late in the afternoon, I reach Miehana and wind through the summery, quiet streets, aiming for 240 Mallorca Way with help from Freddy's tablet. Spiky green foliage and tall fences give way to a narrow, shop-lined street, and I slow with the traffic, curious. Pedestrians in athleisurewear walk their dogs. Four different coffee shops are open on one block. A Walgreens, an old-time movie theater, a computer store, an Indian restaurant, and a bakery occupy another. A woman locks up her bike, and a mailman steers by with his big-wheeled cart.

I can't parallel park, but I finally find a space I can drive straight into. It's warm when I grab my backpack and step out of the car, and the California air has a different, easy brightness to it, as if the sun prefers not to cast real shadows here. Taking a deep breath, I try to let the beauty calm me down a little, and I stride along the sidewalk until I find the right address on a small, vacant stationery shop. Dead flies cluster in the window well. I step back to look up the building, and above, four narrow windows reflect the sky. One of the top windows is open, and a gauze curtain hangs straight in the opening.

I try the bell.

No one comes.

Come on, I think. I know my family was coming here, and they had to have a reason. Once again, I wonder how Dubbs got this address. The place doesn't look very promising.

I try again, several times. I knock. Still no one comes. I take a step backward and crane my neck to look up the building again. Now a tabby cat is perched in the top window, looking down at me like it understands the purpose of a doorbell and would admit me if it could.

Checking around the corner, I find a narrow, littered gap between buildings where the shady air is cooler. I head down the passage, past a sour stink of urine, and at the far end, I peer over a tall wooden fence into a ratty, enclosed area with a few garbage cans. A fire escape zigzags across the back of 240 Mallorca, and a short clothesline runs across from the second landing to a pole. One pale item has been hung out to dry.

A meow draws my gaze upward. The tabby cat steps daintily out to the fire escape and watches me expectantly. That's enough of an invitation for me.

I push open the gate and enter the fenced area, which has an earthy smell. When I try the back door, it's locked, too, unsurprisingly, so I take a closer look at the fire escape. The ladder part hangs above me, just out of reach, and it needs to go up several inches before it will release from a hook and come down. I have to haul over one of the garbage cans and brace it against the back wall, but once I climb it, releasing the ladder is easy.

It crashes down with a clatter and barely misses my head.

"Yikes!" I mutter, my heart pounding.

I look up, expecting a zillion people in the nearby apartments to lean out their windows and yell at me, but nobody appears.

Okay, then. Up I go.

The iron rungs are warm from the sunlight's heat. As I grip the metal, my heart kicks with apprehension. I tell myself that this is different from the ladder on the observatory at Forge, the ladder I fell from when I nearly killed Burnham. I remind myself that since then I've made it up other ladders without fainting. One ladder, anyway.

I can do it now. Carefully, being sure to move only one hand or foot at a time so that I'm always connecting with the ladder at three points, I climb eight rungs. When I reach the first landing, I expel a huge breath of relief, and then I hurry up the fire escape steps to the top level, to the open window.

"Hey, kitty," I say to the cat, and laugh at the way my hand is trembling when I pet its head. The cat slips inside, and I give the window a little tap. "Hello? Anybody home?"

I push the window up higher, enough to lean in.

The room is a small, stuffy space with a large bed and a baby's crib. An empty birdcage stands in a corner near an upright piano. The piano's lid is closed neatly over the keys, and pale, wispy feathers rest lightly on the dark rug as if a bird shed them only moments ago. Awkwardly, I climb inside, fully a burglar now, and my eye catches on a dark painting of a seashore with cliffs and big waves.

"Hello?" I call.

"Is that you, Marnie?" a reedy female voice answers.

Startled, I freeze. Then I take a step forward, and the floor beneath the rug squeaks.

"My name's Rosie Sinclair," I call. "I'm just here for a visit. I think you know my sister?"

A clunk comes from farther in the house.

I move softly out to the hallway. A door at the far end stands ajar, and light drops on the polished wooden floor. I push the door slowly open to find a small bedroom overlooking the street. It's even warmer than the first room, as if the open windows do nothing but trap the heat, and it's laced with a weary scent of lavender. Books and framed photos line a tall bookshelf, and pill bottles fill a woven basket next to a landline phone.

"Hello?" I say, and step in farther.

A thin old woman in a lacy bathrobe is poised on the far side of a four-poster bed, aiming a can of Mace my way. Her gray hair winds in a long, thin braid like extra lacework at her collar, and her pale blue eyes are magnified by enormously thick, round glasses. She reminds me a bit of a black-and-white film star, the delicate, elegant type that goes mad and murderous by the end of the show.

"Well, I'll be," she says in a genteel drawl. She lowers the Mace. "It really is you. Now, here's a surprise."

"You know me?" I ask.

"Heavens, yes. Who doesn't? How'd you get in?"

"I tried knocking but no one answered, so I came up the fire escape."

Her eyebrows lift. "Naturally," she says, and comes around to sit on the edge of the bed facing me. She cradles the Mace in her hands. "How'd you find me?"

"My sister gave me this address," I say. "Dubbs Sinclair. Do you know her?"

"I'm aware that you have a sister, but I'm not acquainted with her personally."

I'm confused. "But then how did Dubbs get your address? Why would she send me here?"

"I haven't the foggiest," the old woman says. "It seems like a rather cheeky thing to do."

Now I'm even more puzzled. The woman is regarding me with a certain amused welcome, like an old friend, and as I study her back, a vague recognition stirs. Her square jaw and broad forehead are familiar, but the connection eludes me.

"Do I know you?" I ask.

"I'm Lavinia Jacobs," she says. "I once taught at the Forge School of the Arts. I believe you've seen my portrait in the dean's office."

Yes. I did see that portrait, only Lavinia didn't wear glasses in it, and she was a good twenty years younger. Lavinia Jacobs was the film teacher who first arranged to have her students filmed around the clock. Her experiments laid the foundation for the current Forge School and *The Forge Show*. The full magnitude of who she is hits me. She's an icon. I try to recall when she started the show. In the early 2040s, I think. She wasn't young then. She must be over eighty now.

But she's here, alive, and my sister sent me to this address.

"I don't get this," I say.

"You thought I was dead, no doubt," Lavinia says. "You wouldn't be the first."

"No," I say. "I'm just surprised. What do you have to do with my family?"

"Nothing, as far as I know."

"But then why did my sister give me your address?"

"That is what we need to divine. I'm not exactly in the phone book, so to speak." She glances toward a clock on her nightstand and shakes her head. "Four-thirty already? Gracious. What is this world coming to? Get Tiny some food, will you? Down in the kitchen? One scoop's fine." She straightens again, sets the Mace on her dresser, and slides open the top drawer. "And start some water for tea. I'll be down in a minute. On your way!" She dismisses me with a wave of her silvery fingers.

I'm more puzzled than ever. This makes no sense, but I do what she says and head downstairs, alert for any clues to explain why Dubbs connected me with Lavinia. A grandfather clock ticks on the lower landing, and a living room is separated from a kitchen in the back by a wide, arching doorway. Old, dark furniture and a worn carpet give the place a hushed stillness, and I don't see a TV or computer screen anywhere. She must watch *The Forge Show* somehow, though, since she knows me.

A distant flushing noise comes from above.

In the kitchen, the cat sits expectantly by a couple of tin bowls. I slide my backpack to the floor. Then I fill one bowl with water and, feeling a bit intrusive, I open cabinets and heavy wooden drawers until I find a smelly bag of dry cat food. I scoop some into the dish, and Tiny digs in with a light tinking noise.

I check for camera lenses and find none. It's a Spartan kitchen, with one blue plate, one soup bowl, and one set of silverware. A pot. A pan. Just enough for a solitary old soul. Plastic measuring cups nest inside a mixing bowl. I fill the metal teakettle, turn on the gas flame with a whoosh, and set the water to boil.

No toaster. No coffee machine. No microwave. Everything's clean and tidy, including a pile of letters under a glass paperweight on the windowsill. It's not at all what I would expect from a woman who was such an innovator in her day. An oval rag rug rests before the sink. The ceiling is the shiny blue of a battleship. Another landline phone with a long, coiling cord is attached to the wall. It could be that she's just into simplicity, Thoreau-like, but it feels more like she's living in another time.

I glance at the pile of letters and notice they're all the size of greeting cards. Since I've been nosy already, I sort through the pile. The faded envelopes are all addressed in the same small handwriting to Lavinia, all from the same S. Schur in Downers Grove, Illinois, all unopened. The postmarks date back over ten years. I set them back carefully under the paperweight, puzzled.

It isn't just that the apartment has the feel of another time, I realize. It's more like I've entered an apartment that's under a spell, where everything's dormant, including the aging princess I now hear coming down the stairs. Yet there has to be a good reason why Dubbs left me this address. Out the window, a breeze stirs the item on the clothesline, and I realize it's a child's faded smock, the plastic kind often worn while finger painting.

Lavinia moves gracefully into the kitchen and heads for a dish of lemon drops. She's dressed in gray slacks, black ballet flats, and a tailored beige shirt that fits neatly on her spare figure. Her braid is coiled at the back of her head, and she's put on coral earrings and a dash of lipstick. She pops a lemon drop in her mouth, pursing her lips while she clicks it around her teeth.

"Now," she says as she eases herself into a chair. She gestures me toward the chair opposite hers. "It's time to decipher this enigma. Where is your sister now?"

A dose of caution makes me modify the truth. "I don't know. She and my parents are missing."

"Missing," Lavinia repeats flatly. She lifts an eyebrow. "Well, that's a start. Does Berg know you're here?" she asks.

"I hope not."

"The man's a fiend. An absolute fiend," she says. "Smart as can be and rotten to the core."

I agree with her there.

"Who else knows you're here?" she asks.

"No one," I say. Thea doesn't really count. "Do you still watch *The Forge Show*?" I ask.

She grimaces briefly. She reaches for a teacup and a short glass, and then fishes tea bags out of a tin. "It pains me. It's a travesty of what I first imagined," she says. "You students never get to see the night and the stars. That alone is downright treachery of the high seas. Still, if you take any school and give it the top talent in the country, it'll be a success. It's the students who make the school, not the other way around."

"So you do still watch it," I say.

She shrugs. "Strictly speaking, I don't watch it. I'm still tapped directly into the cameras at Forge. I can watch the students directly, without the obnoxious interference of idiots like Bones. You recall Bones."

"My techie," I say, startled.

"Yes. I can watch through all the cameras of the show, all the time," she says. She reaches down to stroke Tiny's ears. "Like a techie, but I don't have to log out at night and go home. As you can imagine, it gives me a different perspective."

Amazed, I stare at her. "But you don't even have a TV," I say.

"My dear Rosie. Don't be obtuse. Clearly, I do," she says. "I suppose you're asking for proof. Let's see. You climbed out on the roof in the rain the night before fifty cuts. You got soaked, but you looked happy for once. That's the first time I paid any attention to you."

"Berg showed that same clip to the trustees," I say. "You could have intercepted it then."

"Quite right," she says, straightening. The cat pads away into the living room. "Okay, the night you went down the pit of the clock tower, you waited until the moment that Berg and Otis and Linus were all focused on Parker, Otis's partner, before you ran across the quad. That's how you made it to the rose garden and the clock tower without being seen. Am I right?"

"You saw that," I say, awed.

"There's a camera in the clock tower aimed down the pit. I saw your little penlight as you descended to the bottom. You had me on edge, I must say. I'd have been in a terrible spot if you'd fallen. Fortunately, you didn't."

She could see, she *still* can see anything that happens at Forge. It blows my mind. She can watch any camera at any time, even at night. That's what she's telling me. This means she knows everything, every time I snuck out of my sleep shell.

"Could you see the cameras down in the vault of dreamers under the dean's tower?" I ask.

"Now we come to it," she says, and behind her thick lenses,

81

her eyes go bright and sharp. "There was no vault of dreamers under the school, not that I ever could see. It wasn't there when I worked at the school, and it never showed up on any camera."

"But I was in it myself," I say. "And I know Berg had cameras down there. I saw them. He had my friend Thea on his phone when she was down in the operating room just this past Friday night. He showed her to me."

"Then those cameras must have been on an isolated system," she says. "Think about it. If he did have dreamers hidden at the school, he couldn't have a hundred techies knowing about them."

"Wait. Are you saying you believe me?" I ask, hopeful and uncertain.

"I'm saying that cameras only go so far. The truth is still the truth."

The teakettle whistles, and steam gushes from its spout. Lavinia points to it, and I fetch it over to pour. Fragrant steam rises from the tea, and I automatically inhale, savoring the scent. Lavinia takes the clear glass and politely nudges the teacup toward me.

"Have a lemon drop while your tea steeps," she says.

Obeying, I taste the dissolving coat of powdered sugar before the lemon kicks in, and my whole mouth salivates around the sweet sourness.

Lavinia's gaze slides past my shoulder, out the window, to some distance I can't see. "It just so happens, I'm inclined to believe you about the dreamers," she says. "Now tell me what's really happened to your family. People don't just go missing."

I trust her now with the truth. "Berg kidnapped my family yesterday," I say. "I think they were in Las Vegas at the time. I have a voicemail from my sister from last night, but that's the last I've heard from any of them. She said they were in a truck, but I have no idea where. She warned me not to tell anyone."

"You think Berg's responsible, of course."

"I know he is," I say. A pinch of anxiety tightens my gut. "He left me a message, too. He wanted me to call him back, but I didn't. I came here instead because my sister told me my family was coming here."

"And we still don't know why. Most curious."

It's more than curious. Lavinia has to be an ally I can use somehow. "Do you know anything about a vault of dreamers here in Miehana?" I ask.

Her gaze returns to me. "I have my suspicions," she says. "What have you heard?"

"Not much," I say. "I've seen a picture of a big vault full of sleep shells, and I know a guy who said his father worked at a big vault of dreamers here in Miehana. I don't know where it is. It doesn't come up on any searches."

"I see. Are you thinking Berg has your parents there?" Lavinia says.

I hitch my chair closer to the table. "It is possible, isn't it?" I ask. "I mean, he can't be with them himself. He's showing up on *The Forge Show* like usual, but he could have told his people to hide my family there."

She frowns and dips her tea bag experimentally. "I might have a way to see if a delivery was made this morning."

My heart lifts with hope. She must know where the vault is.

"You have to help me," I say. "You have to tell me what you know. I'll do all the rest, I promise."

She smiles at me, amused. "I see. You'll sneak in and carry your family all out in your pocket, I suppose. Assuming they're there."

"I'll figure out something," I say. "Berg doesn't know I'm here. If I act fast, I might be able to catch him off guard." I push my hands into my hair and squeeze my head. "You have to understand. He's always been the one in control. Ever since I went to Forge, he's just been playing one long, twisted game with me. Even when I'm living out in the world, it's part of his game. He told me once that real life is better for me, like this very moment could be adding value to my dreams."

Lavinia lightly touches her glasses. "That does sound like him. He was very much into control when I knew him at Forge," she says.

"But me being here with you, this is out of his control," I say. "I need to make the most of it."

Lavinia nods thoughtfully. "Supposing you do get into the vault of dreamers out here. You'd be delivering yourself right into Berg's clutches again, regardless of whether your parents are there or not. That hardly seems wise."

"That's why I need your help," I say. "You must know a way I can get in there without being seen."

She laughs. "I don't."

"But you know something that can help me. You at least know where it is."

Lavinia regards me inscrutably for a long moment. "Go on. Try your tea."

When I take a sip of the tea, my taste buds go wild with the lemony tanginess, and I have to smile.

Lavinia nods at me. "What did I tell you?"

"It's good," I say.

She sips, too. "It's the small things that count," she says.

Inside, I'm all impatience. It feels like I'm being tested, like Lavinia can play a game or two herself. I force myself to relax for a moment and try to picture things from my hostess's perspective. If only I had something to trade with her that she wanted.

In the quiet, Lavinia props her chin in her palm, and her gaze goes inward and distant again. I turn to see what has her attention outside and notice the faded smock again. It's a bit odd, considering the apartment is devoid of toys or games. I wonder if Lavinia is a mother or grandmother, and I try calculating years. Supposing Lavinia is eighty or so, a daughter of hers might be in her fifties, which would put a granddaughter in her twenties or thirties. Lavinia might even be a great-grandmother. I study the translucent plastic, noticing how sun-bleached the fabric edges are, as if the smock has been hanging out a whole summer or longer. Much longer.

"Do you have a family?" I ask.

Lavinia sighs, and her sad, magnified eyes shift toward the pile of envelopes on the windowsill. "Not anymore," she says.

I wait, wondering if she'll go on, but she doesn't, and I can't bear to pry. I need her help so badly it hurts. She must know that.

Lavinia nudges her teacup away, takes another lemon drop, and comes to her feet. "All right. I'll help you," she says. "It could be dangerous, mind you."

Hope lifts my heart. "I don't care," I say.

She steps into the hallway, opens the door to a closet, and pulls a chain to turn on a light bulb inside. She gestures with her hand. "After you."

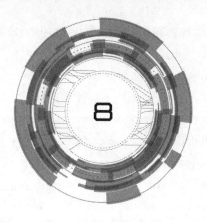

THE PARK IN THE CLOSET

THE CLOSET SMELLS of mothballs, but it has no clothes, only a couple of cardboard boxes on the floor. I sit on a narrow bench along the back wall and keep my feet out of the way as Lavinia comes in and pulls the little, ratchety chain on an overhead light bulb. She rummages in a box until she comes up with a small black puck. After she sticks a cord into it, plugs it into a socket, and pushes a button, a light shoots up and expands outward in a cone, just like I saw once before in Berg's office. Lavinia smiles grimly, sets the puck on a box, closes the door, and pulls the chain to turn off the overhead light.

"Move over," she says, and sits beside me on the bench.

A keyboard of light shines onto Lavinia's lap, and she types in a command. A colorful, 3-D map of an amusement park appears in the puck's projection cone, and I can easily read the sign over the main entrance: Grisly Valley. It's about the last thing I expected.

"Why do you have this?" I ask.

"I designed the original layout for the cameras at Forge when I was there. When I came west in forty-seven, I was head of the team that designed the camera security for Grisly Valley," she says. "Heard of it?"

"No. Should I have?"

Her voice is close in the closet. "It was a famous horror theme park back in the forties. The challenge for my cameras was much like what I had at Forge, just with a bigger stage and thousands more players."

"It wasn't broadcast as a show, was it?"

"No," she says. "The cameras were all internal, for security. But it was the same idea."

"What's this have to do with the vault of dreamers?" I ask.

"I'm getting to that. You're not the most patient person, are you?"

"Sorry."

In the 3-D map, intricate buildings, bridges, and waterways are portrayed with striking detail, filling out the lands of the theme park. Five different horror lands lie inside its borders, clockwise from the entrance: Vampyre Graveyard, Zombieville, Backwoods Forest, Bubbles' Clown World, and Camp High. At the center is a massive stone tower with spired roofs and a moat.

"What's this?" I ask, pointing to the tower. A dark green dragon is poised on one spire with its wings folded back.

"The Keep of Ages," she says. "It was the centerpiece for

all the parades and spectacles, like the dark twin of Sleeping Beauty's castle at Disney. Or was that Cinderella's? I forget. See the dragon? It was a wonderfully lifelike combination of puppetry and projections. The special effects at the park were legendary. The effects team was given carte blanche, and I remember when they'd simulate earthquakes and fires all over the park. Floods, too. People were scared witless, which was just what they wanted, of course."

My gaze is drawn to the signature rides that rise above the treetops, especially the Glue Factory roller coaster, the Fodder Mill wheel, and the End of Daze spiral. "I would have loved this place," I say.

"You and millions of others. It's a ruin now," Lavinia says. "It lasted only nine months. The state condemned it when the meltdown happened at Olbaid. Every acre of Grisly is in the OEZ, the Olbaid Exclusion Zone."

I'm stunned to think of all that work and creativity gone to waste after only nine months.

"When was that meltdown?" I ask.

She shakes her head. "In forty-eight. Nineteen years ago. Not exactly Chernobyl, but bad enough. The Olbaid Nuclear Power Plant was damaged in an earthquake and leaked high-level radiation for two weeks. Everyone was banned from the area for twenty miles around. Thousands of us had to be moved. Even now, the place is dangerous because it was too costly to clean it up properly."

"You had to move, yourself?" I ask, turning to see her profile. Her glasses reflect the lights of the projection.

She nods, her gaze still toward the map. "That's when I came here to this apartment. Me and my daughter's family."

She skims her hands over the keyboard on her lap, and the top surface of the map lifts up and hangs in midair. Beneath, the underground routes and service rooms are exposed to view, including a parking lot and a large assembly area. Smaller cells might have been offices or changing rooms. The cafeteria, the main office, the archives, and the tech rooms are all clearly marked. It looks like an entire underground city.

"What was this space for?" I ask, pointing to the biggest room.

"That's where the parades assembled. It was big enough for full-sized floats. We called this level Negative One." She points to another area. "This was the costume department. Here, the cafeteria. Special VIP routes for celebrities who visited the park are marked with the green dotted lines, so they could move easily between rides without getting gawked at on the surface. These big half circles here in blue? They're the moat around the Keep of Ages. These red lines mark the doors up to the ground level. Stage level, we called it. Everything hidden from the public was backstage."

"Like at Forge," I say.

"Yes," she says. "Same concept."

The green lines for the VIPs go everywhere, like their own web, and I can easily see how the red lines of the stage level match up with the hidden ramps and stairways in the level below.

"And these—" Lavinia touches her keyboard and a galaxy of tiny blue lights comes on through the stage level of the park. "These are the cameras."

"Wow," I say. Each one is a tiny fan shape, showing the angle of its viewing direction, and they cover every inch of Grisly Valley, in some places, many times over.

Lavinia sets the 3-D image spinning slowly, and I stare, fascinated by the complexity of the system, the little buildings and rides. It looks so alive, so vibrant, that it's hard to imagine the place dead and deserted.

"It looks so fun. Did you ever go?" I ask Lavinia.

"Many times before it opened. Once afterward," she says. "It was truly delightful in a dark, twisted way, if you like bat wings and glow powder. The Grisly brothers who came up with it were very creative, obviously, but they also had a sense of humor."

"Who were they? What happened to them?"

"Gone, all three," she says. "Their assets were tied up in lawsuits for over a decade. One of them shot himself. The second died of cancer. The third went bankrupt and moved away to the Philippines. No one's heard from him in years."

"Who owns Grisly Valley now, then?" I ask, curious.

"The state," Lavinia says. "It bought up most of the property in the contaminated zone. They even stored contaminated cadavers there for a while."

As it occurs to me now why she's showing me this, I stare at her dim profile. "You think the vault of dreamers is at Grisly Valley," I say.

She nods. "It may be outlandish, but that's what I think."

"What makes you think so?"

She taps her keyboard so the upper layer settles back down on top of the lower one, and her glasses flicker again with colored reflections.

"The park is supposed to be shut down like all the rest of the OEZ," she says. "Technically, nobody's allowed in, but people are curious. They sneak in sometimes. I know because I used to see them. I left a few cameras behind, off the grid. Simple, solar-powered cameras to satisfy my curiosity. I used to see kids trespassing now and then. A few old hippies, too. Harmless picnickers, really. Then, one day, maybe seven or eight years ago, I noticed a truck pull in."

She taps her keyboard again. The 3-D map recedes, and the projection of a flat screen comes forward into the same space. It shows a grainy, black-and-white film of a truck driving slowly around the potholes of an old road. It passes near the camera and Lavinia freezes the frame. "Forge Ice Cream" it says on the side of the truck in clear letters.

But that's not possible, I think, dumbstruck.

"Seems a little odd that someone at an abandoned theme park is ordering ice cream, don't you think?" she says.

My mind's racing. "Linus and I had a theory," I say. "We never knew for sure. But we thought human bodies were being delivered to Forge in the freezer compartments of those ice cream trucks."

She doesn't bat an eye. "Shortly after I saw that, all of my cameras went dead except for one," she says. "This one here, out by the road. It's practically useless."

She shows me a view of a deserted, overgrown road. It could be anywhere.

"Did you tell anybody about the ice cream truck?" I ask.

"What would I say? That I kept illegal surveillance cameras going on Grisly Valley? That I was concerned about unorthodox deliveries?" She straightens back and folds her arms across her chest. "Since then, there've been rumors the park is haunted. People say the lights and the rides go on sometimes when nobody's there."

"Do you believe them?"

She shrugs. "I'd like to get some new cameras back on the property. That's what you can do for me." She runs her fingers over her computer, and some grainy footage of the road starts playing.

"If the vault of dreamers is at the park, down in one of those big rooms, someone has to be living there, taking care of them," I say.

"That's possible, as long as they're doing it in secret," she says. "It's the perfect place, really. It's officially off-limits, so anything could happen there."

As it starts to sinks in, I get a prickle of anxious foreboding. This could be it. The vault of dreamers could be right there, a few miles away, at Grisly.

"You never went to look and be sure?" I ask.

"No. I didn't want to," she says. She pauses her footage on the view of the lonely road, then backs it up and starts it forward again, slow motion. "But now look at this. This was from this morning, just before dawn."

A pair of headlights comes slowly into view. Details are hard to make out, but the vehicle has the shape of a delivery truck. Lavinia freezes on it.

A sick feeling turns in my gut. "My family could be in there," I say.

Without replying, she fast-forwards through the footage, and half an hour later, the truck comes back out again and passes under the camera.

"That's all I've got," she says, her expression solemn.

The timing would work. It's all adding up. If the vault of dreamers truly exists at Grisly Valley, my family could be hostage there. In fact, a huge number of dreamers could be waiting there, like in the picture I saw. It's starting to feel real. Dangerous.

Lavinia opens the door of the closet so that air and light from outside can shift in. I blink as my eyes adjust. I expect her to lead me out of the closet, but she stays seated beside me, rubbing her thumb into her palm, as if her hand aches. A faint trace of lemon dust clings to her sleeve.

"I wish I knew why you were here," Lavinia says quietly.

"What do you mean? Dubbs sent me."

She shakes her head deliberately. "No. It feels like a giant hand has reached down to shuffle up the tidy furniture of my dollhouse life." She turns the wedding band on her finger. "My daughter and my granddaughter both died of radiation poisoning after the incident at Olbaid."

"I'm so sorry."

Lavinia goes on as if she's barely heard me. "The cemetery wouldn't take them. They had a new policy based on ignorance. In any case, I should have buried them myself, back at our old place, but my son-in-law wouldn't agree, so we sent

94

their bodies to Grisly." Her smile is both bitter and sad. "Ironic, isn't it? The horror theme park became a burial ground."

"I don't understand."

"I don't care to go into the logistics with you," she says. "I'll just ask you, once you're there, to please have respect for the dead."

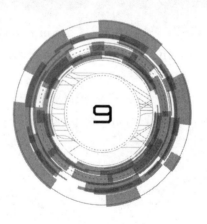

9

THE DRAGON OF
GRISLY VALLEY

OVER THE NIGHT, I study the 3-D map of Grisly Valley
until I can see every turn and angle in my mind's eye. Accord-
ing to Lavinia, cell phone coverage in the OEZ is spotty at
best, so using a GPS map is out. It's best to have my directions
memorized, with the understanding that it may look different
in person, aside from major landmarks. Once I think I know
the map, Lavinia gives me a set of fancy goggles, tabs me up
with a few sensors, and drops me into an expanded version of
the map so I can practice exploring it in full-scale virtual reality. This involves bumping into the walls of the closet until I
get the knack of stroking my steps along the floor to propel
myself through the virtual set. The virtual streets and buildings, the concession stands and rides, even the garbage cans
and streetlamps all shimmer with articulated, artificial brightness. It's pretty cool, actually.

After I learn my way around the street level of Grisly Valley, Lavinia advises me to sleep for a while to cement what I've learned. That reminds me of Forge. She offers me the bed in the spare bedroom, and I crawl under the covers beneath the painting of the seashore. My dreams are full of Grisly Valley, and I wake late the next morning to the sound of Tiny purring in the crook of my bent knees.

"Hey, girl," I say, and curl my fingers around her flinching ears. My mouth feels dry and my muscles stiff, but for once I didn't wake from a nightmare, and I feel well rested for the first time in ages.

The first thing I do is check for news from Peggy on the wild chance she's heard something, but there's no change on her Facebook profile. On the floor beside me is a paper I drew the night before, when I was testing my memory of the map. I'm lifting the paper to puzzle over it when one of my phones buzzes. I have to sort through the bunch of them in my backpack until I find the right one, and it's Burnham. With a pinch of remorse, I realize I should have called him sooner, when 240 Mallorca turned out to be a good lead. Also, Thea wanted me to talk to him about her, and I never did.

"Hey," I say, picking up. "How are you doing?"

"Good," he says. "Where are you now?"

"In California." I let my gaze travel to the window and out to the sunny sky.

I fill him in about my messages from Dubbs and Berg, and coming to Lavinia's, and my plan to look for my family at Grisly. I warn him about ten times that I don't want the police involved. In return, Burnham tells me about Ian's pill, the red

Echo 8, which is a sleep aid. The yellow double theta is a stimulant. Fister produces a slightly different version that's used for depression. He also discovered that Fister does sell pharmaceuticals in the Miehana area, but nothing stands out as unusual.

"Did you connect all right with your friend Thea?" Burnham asks.

"Yes. Thanks. And I have something I need to tell you." Shifting on the bed, I cross my bare legs pretzel style and rake my hair back from my forehead. "The only thing is, you have to promise not to tell anybody," I say. "Not Sammi or your brother or your parents. Especially not your parents."

"I won't," he says. "I promise."

"You're going to have trouble believing it."

"Just spit it out."

I launch into the complicated story of how my consciousness split in two, and half of me ended up in another body, Thea's body. I leave out how suspicious and mean I was to her at first, until she convinced me who she was. "She was pregnant, too," I say. "We have all the same memories up to the point when we were put in the Onar Clinic, but I swear she came out nicer than I am. I ended up helping her have her baby that same night I went to the dean's tower at Forge, and we're friends now. She's back in Texas with her family," I add. "She's having a lot of headaches, and that's a bad sign."

Burnham makes a skeptical humming noise. "And you're positive about all this," he says.

I nod. "Absolutely. I warned you. You can ask her if you don't believe me. She can tell you anything about our time at

Forge before you left. You can ask her about the note you gave me. The one with the P.S. about the lady knight."

I can hear him clicking around on his computer in the background.

"She was at the Chimera Centre, you say? Look at this stuff!" he says. "If this is all true, do you realize what it could mean for medical science?"

"You're making me nervous," I say. "Don't get excited."

"This makes so much more sense now," he says. "No wonder Berg was taking such chances. Rosie, this is huge. If what you're saying is true, you and Thea are huge!"

"We are not huge," I say. "You are not telling anybody about this."

"Are you kidding?" he says. "You *have* to let me tell my parents!"

My heart goes still.

"Burnham Fister," I say. "On the soul of your grandfather *who you helped kill*, you are not going to say a word to your parents! You promised me!"

The clicking stops. I can practically hear his shock in the stillness.

"We're done," he says.

I wait for the sound of him hanging up, but it doesn't come. Is he expecting me to apologize? I pull my knees up to my chest and squeeze myself together.

"I'm sorry," I say stiffly. "I take that back. But you have to understand. You can't tell *anybody*. If you do, I'll deny every word, and I'll never speak to you again."

From down below in the kitchen comes the growing whistle of the teakettle, and then it fades.

"I'm coming out there," Burnham says. "What's your address?"

"No."

"Rosie, I'm coming. We have to talk in person."

"Are you keeping your promise?"

"I will. But we need to talk," he says. "I'm not sure you realize. My parents are the good guys. They use their research to help people, Rosie, and what's happened to you could change the world."

I shake my head. "You're sounding like Berg," I say. "I realize exactly what's at stake, but I'm not going to sacrifice myself for any cure. I just want to save my parents."

"I get it, believe me. You've suffered," Burnham says. "So have I. Can I just ask you one thing, though? Are you glad Thea's alive?"

His words catch at my heart. I tilt my head back to look at the ceiling. Of course I'm glad Thea's alive, but that doesn't mean I want a thousand more versions of me running around like her. Not that she's actually me anymore. But still. He's oversimplifying.

"Why do you always mix me up?" I ask.

"I don't. Just don't do anything until we talk, okay? I can be there in a few hours."

I shake my head. I am not going to let him slow me down. "No. Thanks, but no."

"Rosie!"

"I've got to go."

"Wait!" he says.

But I hang up.

Burnham seriously disturbs me. I just knew he'd want to tell his parents, but if he does, and they start an investigation, then what Chimera did to Thea with my dreams will be all over the news. Every brain researcher on the planet will want a sample of my dreams to experiment with. I'll never be safe again.

I pull on my jeans, take up my map, and head downstairs to the kitchen, where Lavinia's reading a crisp newspaper. She's wearing a silvery-gray outfit today with a fancy brooch, and I wonder if she's dressed up for my sake or if she's always like this. NPR plays low from an old radio. Sunlight reflects on the faucet and sink, and a basket of scones and a pot of apricot jam are laid out on the table.

"Did you bake these?" I ask. "I didn't even hear you."

"Help yourself."

I slide my drawing onto the table and take a scone. Cutting it in half, I try it with a dab of butter, which melts into the warm, white tastiness. I can hardly believe how good it is.

"Oh, my gosh," I say, in raptures.

With a rustle, she sets her newspaper aside. "Glad you like it. Have another."

I will, for sure.

"My grandmother used to read the newspaper," I say.

"Is that right?"

I haven't thought about my grandma in a long time. She let me sit on her lap and showed me the funnies. She would read each bubble of words aloud as I pointed to it. Sometimes I would go backward, and she'd read the words in backward order. I loved that. It was like my finger magically controlled her voice.

"Would this be your mother's mother or your father's?" Lavinia asks.

"My father's," I say. "She died when I was little. I never knew my other grandparents. They all died before I was born." I look thoughtfully across at her. "Do you have other family besides your daughter and your granddaughter?" I ask.

Her gaze goes toward the windowsill, where the paperweight rests on the pile of cards. "No blood relatives. I have a son-in-law. He's remarried. We haven't spoken in years," she says. "When you're old like me, you know more dead people than alive ones." She nods at my map. "So. Have you settled on your route?"

I swallow another bite of buttery scone. "I'll wait until tonight, when it's dark, and leave my car outside the fence that surrounds the OEZ," I say. "It'll take me a little while to hike down to the park, but as long as I avoid any lights, I shouldn't get picked up by any surveillance cameras." I lean over the table and turn my map in her direction, so she can see where I'm pointing. "I'm thinking I'll go in here, by the main entrance, if I can."

"There are probably lights there," she says. "Ideally, I'd like you to put one of my cameras here, overlooking the turnstiles and this little road for emergency vehicles. The second one should go here, facing the Keep of Ages."

"I'll try."

"Then what?" she says.

"I need a way down to the Negative One level. I know the dreamers are in a big room, and it seems most likely that would be underground," I say. "I was thinking of going down this first ramp."

She shakes her head. "That's too open. No place for cover." She taps a finger on my map farther along, up the Main Drag. "There's a VIP portal here, by a gift shop. That'll take you directly down to the greenroom on Negative One."

I don't have it marked on my map. "Where?"

"I can show you in the closet." She shifts her finger. "Or here, by the Bottomless Pit. There's another VIP portal here. That might be even better. It leads down to the grand assembly area." She sits back. "Supposing you do find the vault, what then?"

I don't want to tell her how nervous I am about this whole thing. There are so many unknowns. I'll have to trust to my wits once I'm there.

"I'll look for my family until I find them," I say. "I'll break them out if I have to, and then we'll get back to the car and drive away. That's the best that I've got."

"You'll come back here afterward," she says, frowning. "Do you have any weapons?"

Not really. The only thing I have is a couple vials of sleep meds left over from my time in the dean's tower with Berg, and the pills from Ian.

"For Pete's sake," Lavinia says at my hesitation. She reaches behind her, opens a drawer, and slams a sheathed dagger on the table.

Startled, I slide it out to find a sharp, ragged blade, as long as my hand.

"I don't know how to use this," I say, turning it in the light.

"When you're scared enough, you'll figure it out," Lavinia says.

I take a surreptitious look at her thin arms in her sleeves, wondering how strong she'd be in a fight. Hard to know.

"Thanks," I say. "Does this knife have a name?"

"Please. This isn't an elf kingdom."

I laugh, and she smiles archly back at me. I slip the knife back in its sheath.

After breakfast, she sets me up in the closet again. I practice moving around the lower level of Grisly Valley, in and out of the dressing rooms, the cafeteria, the tech station, and the parking lot. Lavinia has me practice taking the VIP portals and routes, first by following the green lines, and then without them. I make special note of the portals by the Main Drag gift shop and the Bottomless Pit.

When I finally take off the goggles and step out of the closet, the world swims around me for a sec until I get my land legs again. The grandfather clock ticks loudly. Outside, evening has come again and the shadows are long. Lavinia's hunched at the table in the kitchen, tinkering with a small solar panel and a camera.

"When do you want to go?" she asks.

"Soon," I say. "Now."

>>>>>>>>>

An hour later, I park near the outermost fence of the OEZ and get my first look at the evacuated area. As I step out of my car, a dragonfly whizzes past me with a sudden whir. The air smells of dust and a musky, not unpleasant rot of vegetation.

I half expected the OEZ to be blackened and twisted, like a bomb went off, but instead, the landscape is lush with ashy-green coastal trees and scrub. Under the last light of a streaky sunset, the lines of decaying roads and buildings are softened by the encroaching shadows of the forest. Where the roof of a distant church has collapsed, its pink walls stand hollow to the sky.

The Grisly Valley Theme Park lies in a shallow valley, half a mile inside the OEZ. A dusky wasteland of parking lots, dotted with bushes, expands for acres around the main gates. Inside another layer of fences, the theme park itself is a village of shops, restaurants, and rides. It has far more trees than I expected from Lavinia's map. A scattering of security lights cast thin, half-hearted pools of illumination against the twilight, as if they're only on by habit. The swelling roller coaster of Bubbles' Clown World stands rickety but intact against the fading light of the sky, and the Keep of Ages looms with eerie majesty. It gives me a kick of nervous excitement.

I pocket my keys, sling my backpack over one shoulder, and check my knife, which honestly feels more awkward on my belt than reassuring. My phone has one bar. In my jeans and a brown shirt, I hope I'm blending in. I start hiking along the fence where a faint trail dips in the grass, until I find a place where trespassers have wedged an opening between two tilting poles. Sucking in my gut, I squeeze through and pull my backpack after me. Then I descend an uneven, washed-out path toward the parking lots. The evening sky darkens with surprising speed, and a salting of stars appears over my shoulder. I have to crawl through a gap in another fence, and then I start across the cracked tarmac of the parking lots, winding my way past the bushes, old beer cans, and fallen, rusted streetlamps.

My sneakers make a flat, unnatural sound that's eerily absorbed into the distance, and I instinctively try to tread softly. Once, I look back the way I came so I'll be able to find my way out, and that's when I fully realize how dark it has become. Already, the nearest fence is barely visible. I note an upside-down exit sign for a landmark, and then I keep walking until I reach the main entrance, where "Grisly Valley" arches over the gated turnstiles. Four flagless poles stretch upward, standing sentinel, and a floodlight glares across the plaza to illuminate the dearth of visitors. The only movement is a plastic bag flapping in the fence.

I don't like it. The place is too quiet. As if in defiance of the cameras that are posted on poles and corners, the old ticket booth is tagged with graffiti. To the right, the narrow road for emergency vehicles is blocked by a heavy gate. This is where Lavinia wants one of her cameras.

Stopping in a shadow beside a statue of the Grim Reaper, I take off my backpack and pull out her first camera. I climb up the pedestal of the statue, and I affix Lavinia's camera and solar panel to a flat place near the hem of the reaper's robe. I aim it toward the turnstiles and the road, as she requested, and turn it on.

Then I leave the floodlit area, heading around the tall iron fence, looking for a way into the park. In the darkness, I almost miss the place where a bar has been pried out, but then I manage to wriggle through the narrow gap, and I'm in the park proper. Another thrill runs up my nerves.

I've reached a narrow, curving lane with bathrooms to my right. As I tiptoe forward and peer around the first corner, I enter Camp High, the horror land based on summer camp and high school. The maze called The Showers is right in front of me. Based on the maps I studied, the giant Arts & Crafts slide should be ahead to my right, and the Main Drag should be to my left, only I can't see either. Ruin and time have shifted things.

To avoid the lights, I have to take an indirect path, and I get badly lost once before I find the Main Drag. A few widely spaced, pragmatic security lights buzz faintly overhead and cast shadows from the quaint, original streetlamps that aren't on. Across from me, a white statue of a unicorn has a plastic six-pack ring on its horn. The cobblestoned pavement is uneven underfoot, with missing and cockeyed stones. And yet, when I look up the length of the Main Drag toward the Keep of Ages, I can feel a certain aura of excitement, even now.

Grisly isn't just a ruin. It's has the feel of a legendary ghost town, an ironic tragedy. It's a horror park that was closed by real catastrophe, almost as if it tempted fate, and I'm here all alone. I keep alert, walking slowly and staying to the shadows.

Since I promised to set up Lavinia's second camera near the Keep of Ages before I go underground to search for the vault, I head west up the Main Drag, toward the center of the park. I pass a café, a souvenir shop, and a tattoo parlor, all empty. The faded storefronts seem too small for a real main street, skewing my sense of proportion. An armadillo squats in an empty flower tub, and a hubcap lies in the gutter. A kiosk has been burned to a blackened shell.

From somewhere to my right, a tinny snatch of carnival music drifts through the night. My pulse takes off. I step back into a doorway and slip my knife out of its sheath, but though I watch and wait, no one comes. A minute later, the music goes off, and all I can hear is my heart thudding.

Someone's watching me. I can feel it.

I take a deep breath and start cautiously forward again. Three mannequins are draped in American flags and posed on a balcony as if waving to a passing parade. At the next corner, a dim alley is piled with baby strollers. I can tell some of the trespassers before me have been more interested in pranks than vandalism, but that only adds to the bizarreness of the place.

A light comes on in the store beside me, and I jump back. Gilt lettering on the window announces TOYS. I peek in. The toys are long gone. Only a rack remains, and an old price gun. I watch for movement, but no one's there, and a minute later, the light goes off again.

"This is weird," I whisper.

First the music and now the toy store lights make me think someone is following my progress through the park, but who? Why don't they come out and talk to me? They can't be ghosts.

I peer around and spot more camera lenses everywhere, large ones on poles and button cameras on doorframes and trim, exactly like at Forge. Just because Lavinia doesn't have access to the feeds anymore doesn't mean all the cameras are dead. Some of them could still be serving a security system.

But still no one comes. The Main Drag is as dim and motionless as before.

I don't understand this place, but I'm not going to let a little spookiness stop me from looking for my parents. I still have to put up Lavinia's other camera before I head underground. I note the VIP portal she mentioned, the one between a cookie shop and a gift shop, as I pass. Then, at the end of the Main Drag, I reach Scylla Square, the center hub of the park, where the Keep of Ages rises out of its base of thorny shadows.

The keep towers above me, twice as large as I expected, and blacker than the sky. Instinctively, I shiver. A dark, empty moat surrounds the massive foundation, and double bridges with rising stairs cross over the void to a big, arched door. One caged light bulb glows above the arched doorway like a modern afterthought, but otherwise, with a shimmer of moonlight on its pointed roof, the keep looks like it was born straight out of a nightmare.

Clinging to one of the topmost spires, a large black dragon peers over its shoulder with vivid red eyes. It's no longer sleek and green as it was in Lavinia's 3-D map. Instead, this dragon has weathered into a dark, motley beast with ragged scales and bony claws. I'm trying to understand how its eyes can glow so brightly, if they're lit or coated with reflective red paint, when the dragon shifts its head.

My heart stops. I must be wrong. I peer upward, disbelieving. Slowly, with a creak, the dragon turns its heavy head as if to survey the park below, and then it blinks. Nothing more. It doesn't hiss fire or open its wings, but it has the slight, hovering alertness of a beast that breathes, and it seems all the more lifelike and ominous because of its patience.

I've never seen special effects like this—if Lavinia hadn't mentioned how remarkable the technology controlling the dragon originally was, I might have worried that I was hallucinating. As it is, I'm completely captivated.

Cautiously, keeping near to the buildings at my back, I circle Scylla Square and get closer to the moat and the bridge on the left. A small statue of a snaky, six-headed monster presides over a set of defunct water fountains, and I choose the monster's platform for Lavinia's second camera. I fit my knife back in its sheath, and then it takes me a second to secure the camera. I aim it across Scylla Square, toward the stairs of the keep, as she requested. When I try to call Lavinia to tell her it's ready, I can't get a signal, and now I know I'm on my own.

When I look back up at the dragon, its head has turned in my direction. It blinks again. I press back into a shadow, but its gaze never wavers. *This is crazy*, I think. *It's not real.* But I can't shake the feeling that the dragon's eyes are staring right at me. On the double bridge of stairs that leads across the moat, dim blue lights turn on below the banisters. They shine out at knee height and catch in specks of white in the stone steps, giving them an eerie, black-light sort of glow. They almost seem like an invitation.

Above, a purple spotlight flicks on, beaming onto the keep's roof, and the dragon lifts its shoulders in a great double-hunch, as if it's stretching, or preparing for flight.

I could swear a bizarre show has started, just for me. I hear an amplified cricket noise. Then another. The chirping continues with a layer of static from a recording. Next, a gurgling, rusty sound comes from the bottom of the moat, and then fog drifts up, filling the moat below the bridges.

Then, from above, a loud, drawn-out creaking noise heralds the opening of a trapdoor that extends outward from the center roof of the keep. It lowers on two chains until it juts forward like a diving platform or the plank of a pirate ship.

Now the dragon fully awakens. It rolls its shoulders so its wings partially unfurl. It coils an arm more securely around the spire and leans its head forward toward the plank, moving more naturally than any mechanical puppet ever could.

Half a dozen purple and white spotlights are now trained on the plank, and a drumroll signals an event. As the figure of a small girl glides out on the plank, my heart catches in my throat. She's pale and motionless, standing with her eyes closed and her arms at her sides. Her gray gown flutters slightly in the breeze, and her blond hair shifts lightly around her shoulders. Otherwise she doesn't move. She shines with ethereality, and the staging would be beautiful except for one ghastly truth: she's my sister.

She's Dubbs. Up there.

Ready to fall.

And all of a sudden, I can't think of effects anymore. My sister is far too real.

"No!" I whisper, staggering forward. I'm afraid to call out, afraid any noise will disturb her balance.

She's forty or fifty feet up, and a fall into the foggy moat would kill her. The dragon uncoils slightly to inspect Dubbs. It cocks its head and slowly extends its neck forward. If she turns to look at it, she'll be only a couple of yards away from its big head. But she doesn't turn her head. She doesn't seem to move at all, as if she's suspended in a trance.

Go back, Dubbs! I think. *Get down on your hands and knees and crawl back inside.*

Another breeze shifts her gown, and she sways with it. I can't stand it.

"Dubbs!" I shout. I bolt toward the nearest bridge of blue stairs. "Dubbs! Hang on! I'm coming!"

The girl above turns her head slightly in my direction and her eyes fly open. They're wide and frantic, and she lets out a scream. She crouches down to the plank and grips it with both hands. The dragon backs up slightly and flares its wings wide. Dubbs now turns toward the dragon and screams again with wild terror.

I'm frozen on the stairs, watching in agony. Much as I want to run inside the keep and up to the roof to save her, she could slip any second, and I can't go farther up without losing sight of her. If only I could distract the dragon.

"Hold on! Just hold on!" I yell to Dubbs. Then I wave my arms. "Dragon! Over here!" I yell. *"Dragon!"*

But the dragon doesn't see me or doesn't care. It rises up on its back legs and flaps its heavy wings. Dubbs hugs the plank with all her might. Her gown ripples again, and she looks impossibly small and helpless. The dragon opens its mouth and lets out an earsplitting cry, and Dubbs catches her breath and screams once more.

"Dragon!" I yell furiously. "I'm over here!"

It leans its head back and lets out another roar toward the sky. A blast of fire comes out of its mouth, scorching the air above the keep. Wind swirls savagely around Dubbs, who struggles to keep her grip, and then, with a final scream, she's blown off her perch. She topples into the dark night air and pinwheels down toward the moat.

In shock and horror, I run against the banister, and then, just as Dubbs is about to hit the ground, the dragon swoops down and catches her in its claws, soaring with her back up into the sky.

I can't breathe. For another moment, Dubbs and the dragon are visible in the night sky above the keep. The dragon makes an awkward, dipping circle, as if adjusting to the weight in its claws. Then it flies out of the spotlights, disappearing into the night. The spotlights go off. The lights on the steps, too. The entire area around the keep is plunged into darkness. Even the sole, caged light bulb that hangs above the heavy wooden door is out.

They're gone.

They were real. They couldn't be real. My mind's racing with confusion.

"Dubbs!" I cry.

Where is she? My helplessness tortures me. I search the night sky but I can't see anything in the wan moonlight. Then, silently, a single, finely focused spotlight turns on and shines down into the moat, exactly at the spot where Dubbs would have landed when she fell. I lean over the railing, peering closely as the fog shifts. A hole has opened in the bottom of the moat. An opening. A drain, possibly.

Gripping the railing, I swing myself over and wade through the fog to the middle of the moat. A gurgling comes from a dark circle below the spotlit fog. I touch forward with my toe and feel the edge of a void.

What on earth is happening? A dragon that I believed was a special effect tormented my sister and flew away with her. Could Dubbs have been a special effect, too? She looked so real! And now a trapdoor has opened in an empty moat. My mind is still racing, surging with adrenaline and horror, and I can barely make sense out of anything.

But here's what I do know: ever since I stepped into Grisly, I've had the feeling that someone's been watching me. If this stunt with the dragon was a spectacle just for me, then whoever concocted it might just relish traumatizing me, but also they might be trying to tell me where to go. Whoever it is must know something about Dubbs.

Grimly, I realize what I have to do. I take a deep breath and step forward.

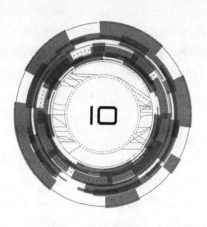

THE WHISTLER

I TOPPLE INTO THE HOLE SIDEWAYS, smashing my arm on some unyielding barrier. Then I'm falling down a wide, slanting pipe. I hit a bend, but there's nothing for me to grab on to, and as I keep sliding down, faster and faster, I duck my head in my arms and let out a scream. It's too dark to see anything. For half a second, my backpack snags me up on something. Then I rip free and I'm falling again. The chute follows a swift, mind-spinning spiral down until I'm disgorged onto a large metal grate. I skid across the bars and bang to a stop.

"Ouch!" I say.

I blink hard in the darkness and struggle to catch my breath. My elbow is sore. My knee, too.

A trickling noise matches a scent of moist stone. Cautiously, I crawl forward toward the trickle, and a faint green luminosity guides me to the edge of an underground gully with a shallow, fragrant stream. Above, gray stone arches unevenly in organic curves. The light comes from the water, where bits of green flicker at the edges of rounded stones. Bioluminescence, I think. Microbes live in the stream. Burnham talked about them once, back when we were at Forge, but I didn't know I'd ever see the shimmering effect myself.

My phone gets no signal, unsurprisingly. I shift to my feet and brush off my limbs, blinking as my eyes keep adjusting to the dim light. My backpack is gone. Behind me, the opening of the chute that dropped me here is a black hole. It has to be part of the drainage system for the moat, and climbing back up it would be impossible.

Fortunately, to my left, a narrow bridge spans the stream. I cross over to a short wooden dock where an old length of rope hangs from a cleat and trails silently in the flow. Beyond, a tunnel is hewn out of the rock. It's dark, but it's the only way to go, so I use my phone for a light, and I edge slowly forward. The air grows musty and close, and then I find a gaping, heavy door. With a creak of hinges, I push past and find the next tunnel extends in two directions. To my left, the dark is impenetrable, but to my right, far off, a faint, cool light touches the walls. I turn off my phone light. With increasing hope, I head toward the light, and as I round the next corner, I can see an archway at the end of the tunnel.

Quietly, cautiously, I creep to the archway, and when I stop in the shadows to look through, I'm rendered breathless.

A large, round cavern sprawls before me, and dreamers fill the space. They lie in sleep shells, in circular rows, and their lids are all glowing with soft blue light. My heart turns sick. Body after body rests in a motionless trance, but I can feel the pulse of them breathing. An attentive presence fills the room, like the hush as a conductor first raises a baton. Far above, faintly visible by the blue light, an uneven dome of rock arches over the room. Half a dozen round holes are cut into the slanting sides like for an overlooking gallery, and above them, a larger oculus at the top is a purply shade of black, like a starless patch of a clear night sky. The color is so deep, I half think my eyes are deceiving me.

This room wasn't on the map Lavinia showed me. It feels older and deeper, like it belongs to another world. It's both wonderful and terrible.

"How can this be?" I whisper.

What am I possibly supposed to do about it?

A lone butterfly drifts silently over the sleep shells, its wings as colorless as limpid glass. I watch it flit from one side of the cavern to the other before flying up into the oculus and vanishing into the deep purple.

I'm still peeking from my archway when a red light comes on over the sleep shell that's nearest to me. All the sleep shells, I notice now, have poles with lights and IV tubes attached, but the other lights are all off. Standing on tiptoe to look into the nearest shell, I see a pale young man with a straight nose and dark hair. Beige patches line his temples, and clear gel covers his closed eyes. Aside from his breathing, he isn't moving, and I can't fathom why his light is on.

Then, far across the room, a middle-aged man steps through

a distant arch and comes down a few steps. I quickly crouch down and press myself against the wall of the tunnel, angling my head just enough so that I can still see.

The approaching man is a thin white guy in green scrubs, with black eyebrows, receding dark hair, and a worn, yellow handkerchief around his neck. He moves with a measured stride and winds his way through the sleep shells until he arrives at the one with the red light, mere paces from where I'm hiding. With his back to me, he opens the lid, flicks his wrists, and checks the dreamer's intake IV line.

"What's troubling you, hmm?" the man mutters.

He gives the IV line a little tap. Then he flips some switch so the blue light inside the sleep shell goes off and on again, like a reboot. The red light above goes off. The worker gives a satisfied grunt and closes the lid. At that instant, the red light goes on again, and so does a red light above another sleep shell, two dreamers down. Then a third nearby light goes on.

The man taps his ear. "Kiri? Something's going on down here," he says. And then, "I don't know. They're restless." As he looks up and partly turns, I catch a glimpse of his long nose and pale complexion. "No. The butterfly's gone. I don't think it's that. Did you check upstairs? Are the cameras back on?"

Me. I have the distinct, uncanny impression that the dreamers have sensed a stranger in the vault. A new jolt of adrenaline courses in my veins. Two more red lights go on.

"Hold on," the worker says.

Then he turns slowly in my direction.

Instantly, I shrink back out of sight. My heart pounds while I hold very still, listening. I'm dreading that he will come up the steps, look into the tunnel, and find me. For a long moment, I hear nothing, but then I catch the sound of him talking into his earpiece again, and his voice is dimmer, farther away. My relief is short-lived. I have to get evidence of the man before he disappears. I pull out my phone, tap the camera icon, and make sure the flash is off. Then I lean around the corner of the arch again to aim it toward the receding man, and I take a picture.

My phone makes a camera clicking noise, and in the cavernous silence, it's as loud as a gunshot. The man spins around. A dozen more sleep shell lights go red.

Crap, I think.

"Who's there?" the man calls.

I turn and bolt back down the dark passage. Blind and afraid, I skim my hand down the left wall, bouncing my fingertips along the rough surface so I won't miss the doorway to the stream. Behind me, running footsteps come from the vault.

Finding the door, I scramble to go through it, but as soon as I smell the water ahead, I stop, remembering. The stream is a dead end. I can't get back up the chute. I'll be trapped.

The footsteps are coming nearer.

On instinct, I reverse back out of the door and turn into the darkness of the unknown passage. I keep my left hand trailing the wall and my right hand stretched out before me. As fast as I can, I lunge through pure darkness, sucking in stale air, until it hits me I could blindly run off an edge and fall to my death. I halt where I am and drop to the floor, huddling as small as possible, and I turn to look back over my shoulder.

The outline of the passage is dimly visible by the light from the far end, and the tall man is silhouetted as a black figure. He reaches the door to the stream, but he doesn't go in. Instead, he faces me. He flashes a beam of light in my direction and takes one more step, but then he stops. I can hear him breathing heavily.

"I know you're listening," he says. His voice carries easily through the silent tunnel. "I just want to talk to you. What's your name? I'm Jules. We won't hurt you."

Like I'd believe that. I try to still my own ragged breathing, but my heart wants to explode.

"You're going to need help to get out," Jules says. "Those tunnels are a maze back there. Don't be stupid and get lost. Hear me? *¿Habla español?*"

I still don't answer him. I pull my knife out of its sheath and grip it tight.

The man takes one more step and lifts his flashlight high. I wince, but I don't think he can see me.

"Okay. Whoever you are, you're going to have to come to us eventually," Jules says. "Just don't disturb the dreamers when you do. Come quietly. We're through the nine o'clock arch. This tunnel leads to the vault through the three o'clock, so we're directly opposite. And don't try to get back out again via the stream. If a storm comes, it gets flooded fast. I've seen it kill people before, and it isn't pretty."

I hold still, barely breathing. I'm not leaving until I have answers, but I don't trust him for a fat second. I wait, watching, until his figure finally recedes. Only then do I really realize why he's content to leave me here. I'm trapped. This entire underground complex could go on for miles. The guy's right.

In an endless labyrinth, it would take one wrong turn and I'd be lost for good. If I don't return to the vault of dreamers, I'm dead.

>>>>>>>>

After he's gone, I keep listening, half expecting him to return with reinforcements, but nobody comes. My suspicion is confirmed: they don't need to bother. Slowly, quietly, I retrace my steps to the main vault and peek through the archway again. The red lights over the sleep shells have gone off again, and the lids glow with their calm, steady blue. The hush is deep, like a forgotten spell.

What do I do? Much as I want to search inside each sleep shell for Dubbs and my parents, I can't risk disturbing them again or Jules will definitely come back. I have to come up with another plan.

By the glow from the sleep shells, I take a closer look at how the ancient, natural walls form the big room. The stone bulges and recedes irregularly, and in places, it's streaked with dark patches as if water has dripped through. The floor is fairly level, and the general shape of the space is semispherical. Only the circular holes in the ceiling and the four carved arches testify to human ingenuity, but they make me wonder what this room was used for in ages past.

Each archway has a few steps and a wooden ramp that lead down to the main floor. I look straight across the vault, to where Jules first appeared. He said his was the nine o'clock archway, and flat fluorescent light glows there. The arches for noon and six, on the other hand, are black and lightless like mine. I glance up again at the dome and the gallery of glassless windows. If I could get up there and look down on the dreamers, I might be able to see some faces.

Quietly, barely daring to breathe, I take a step down into the vault. No red lights go on. I take a step to my right and press back against the wall. I hold still, waiting, and then I take another sideways step to my right. The nearest sleep shell's light flickers red once, but then stays off.

Okay, I think. *Stay calm*. It's almost like they're a sentient beast that can smell fear, and they won't react to me as long as I stay calm.

So many. How did they all get here? And when?

I take another soft step to my right, and when the lights all stay off, I keep going, slowly, step by step. I study the dreamers' faces as I pass, watching in vain for a twitch of a reaction. They're teens and children, all asleep. They remind me of the ones I saw in Berg's control, with their systemic functions rebooted, kept suspended on the edge of death, breathing just enough for him to mine and seed their brains.

Why are they here? Who are they? Are they just being preserved, or does someone mine them regularly?

There's so much I don't understand. The logistics alone are mind-boggling. Somebody had to set this up. Somebody has to tend all the dreamers. And worse, beyond the scale of it, the pathos presses upon me to my core. Seeing each face compounds the tragedy. It's like finding a children's cemetery full of lives cut short and stoppered up at the exact moment they were lost.

It tugs at my soul. How on earth am I going to find my family down here?

Staying with my back to the wall of the vault, I skirt slowly around to my right, counterclockwise, until I'm one-quarter of the way around the room without disturbing the dreamers. At the twelve o'clock arch, I ease up the steps, and a faint breeze touches my face as I look into the next tunnel. No lights or signs of activity beckon ahead, but I have to see if I can find a way up to the gallery.

The floor of this tunnel has two smooth, worn tracks, and I slide my feet forward one at a time, counting my steps. By twenty paces in, the black is a complete, inky emptiness. A plink comes from the darkness ahead of me. I pause to listen, waiting, and then another plink comes, like water dripping into a puddle.

At the next step, my shoe hits sand, wet sand, and I don't dare to go any farther. I turn on my phone light and cast the beam forward. The tunnel has a puddle of black water six feet across, and on the other side, the floor rises at a steady slope. Someone has dropped a pair of boards across the puddle, and I cross over one. On the other side, the tunnel is rough-hewn and narrow, with a turn ahead. I take a few more steps, doubtful, and at the turn, the tunnel branches in three directions. The one to my left has a staircase leading up, and my hope rises. I start up, counting my steps.

At the sixteenth step, I reach a landing with a circular opening, and smile. I've found the gallery in the dome that overlooks the dreamers. I turn off my phone light, set my fingers on the stone ledge, and peer down into the vault. The circular pattern of the sleep shells is even more pronounced from this angle, and the dreamers seem to go on forever. I can't help wondering if this is the vantage place where the photo I saw was taken from, though as I check now, I don't see any cameras.

I breathe deeply. Seeing the dreamers' faces works well from here because I'm not that high up, and the angle is good. Quickly I realize I need a system, or I'll lose track of which sleep shells I've searched. So I start at the outside edge, at the three o'clock archway, and I work my way around and in, row by row, moving carefully around the windows of the gallery.

Even with a bit of distance, even with my determination to search efficiently, it's painful to see all the still, eerie faces. Almost all of the dreamers are kids, from as young as maybe four years old to twenty, but once in a while I find an older person with a gray beard or silvery hair, and it's almost a relief. At least that rare person had a longer life. Then the next one will be a preschooler, and I'm wrenched all over again.

I can't do this. But I have to. Without access to any records, there's no other way, so I force myself to keep searching. Though each dreamer has unique features, their placid expressions give them an overriding sameness and anonymity, and as time passes, I find a numbness cocooning my heart. I don't want to be uncaring, but I need to find my family. I can't think of a better way.

Minutes turn to hours as I peer into hundreds of sleep shells. My elbows grow sore from leaning on the windowsills. Occasionally, a red light goes on above one of the sleep shells, but a few moments later, it goes off again by itself, like this is normal. Nothing else changes. No one comes to look for me.

Despair wears me down. Hunger, too. Without my backpack, I don't even have my water bottle.

I resume my search in the next row, and that's when I find my sister.

My heart plummets and zags. I know it's her. I shift, leaning farther into the dome to see her better.

Dubbs's blond hair is smoothed back from her forehead, and translucent gel covers her closed eyes. She's pale, but not deathly. In fact, compared to the children that surround her, she's practically rosy. I'm wound so tight now, I can barely breathe. An IV line snakes under the neckline of her gown, and I instinctively touch my chest where my port is lodged beneath my skin. She must have one, too.

"Oh, Dubbs," I whisper. She's really here. It's my worst fear.

How am I going to get her out?

I straighten up again and count off the rows to pinpoint where she is, so I can't lose her again. She's in the five o'clock direction, twelve rows in from the outside wall, seven rows out from the middle. I check the other sleep shells near her, but my parents aren't there. Do I keep looking for them, sorting through all the dreamers in view? Or do I try to rescue Dubbs?

I instinctively check for cameras again but still can't find any. The dreamers must be monitored somehow, though, because Jules came when a dreamer's light stayed on before, and I'd be sure to disturb more dreamers if I walked to where Dubbs is. It's going to be impossible to get her out without being noticed. I can carry her. I know that much. But I'll need to move quickly once I get her, and before that, I need to know a way out.

125

I'm scared. I admit it. The only way I know to get out of here is through the chute, but I can't imagine how I'd crawl back up that, especially carrying Dubbs. There has to be another way. Jules warned me not go back out via the stream, which means he thought I entered that way. It must lead out, somehow, but that seems extreme.

A better way out must exist. Logically, Jules and whoever else works here have to use a standard route. They can't live down here always. I just have to find that other way back to the surface.

A faint rattling comes from below, followed by a soft, tuneless whistling. One of the red lights comes on over a sleep shell, and then several more. A man, not Jules, enters from the nine o'clock arch, pushing a wheeled stretcher. He's wearing shabby gray coveralls like an old-time janitor, and he has a bright, round headlamp on his helmet that bobbles a bit with each of his steps. A gray drape over the stretcher covers the contours of a body, which jolts slightly as the man wheels it over a bump. Three or four more of the dreamers' lights go on.

"It's all right, everybody," the man says amiably. "Nothing to see here. Go back to sleep."

The dreamers' lights stay on. Another goes on, as well.

Whistling again, the man pushes his cart through the rows of dreamers while red lights come on around him. Not all, but a few. After he passes, they stay on for a bit, then blink out. When he reaches the center of the room, Dubbs's red light goes on, an outlier, and it stays on when he takes a left and turns in my direction. More lights come on and go off near him as he continues. Then the man pushes his cart up a ramp almost directly beneath me, through the twelve o'clock arch, and disappears. His whistling floats back behind him.

My sister's red light is still on after all the others have gone off, calling to me like a beacon. Then it, too, goes off.

What do I do?

Quietly, swiftly, I hurry back down the stairs and peek into the tunnel just as the man with the stretcher vanishes at the other end. For a last instant, a bit of his light reflects along the two smooth tracks on the floor, and then the tunnel is dark.

I hesitate only an instant before I follow. I run lightly to the next turn of the tunnel in time to see his light at the other end of the passage before he turns again. I follow after him, running in the dark as quietly as I can. We pass several intersections with other tunnels, all just as dark, but I'm careful not to fall behind. I can't afford to get lost.

The whistler finally slows to a stop before a big wooden door. He pushes it open, leaves it ajar, and jockeys the cart through. Peering after him, I see a wide, low-ceilinged room with two square metal doors at waist height. Black scorch lines smudge the walls above the doors, and the place smells ashy, like a kiln. I creep closer, hugging the wall, careful to stay out of sight. The man opens one of the metal doors, and lines up the stretcher in front of one of it. Then he grips one end of the covering and tips up the end of the stretcher so the body slides down, through the open doorway, into the oven.

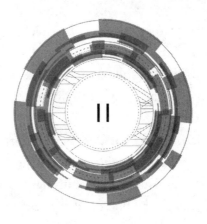

THE STAR OF DREAMERS

THE MAN LOWERS THE STRETCHER again and rolls his shoulders. Then he shifts the stretcher clear of the oven door, closes it, and latches it. Then he pushes a button. A hissing noise of a furnace comes on. The man slides open a peephole on the door and peeks through for a moment while bright orange light escapes. Then he closes the peephole and reaches for the fabric cover on the stretcher to fold it.

I'm stunned. For an instant, I'm pressed back against the wall, bug-eyed and paralyzed. Then I turn and run as fast as the darkness will allow me. I have to get away!

I stub my toe and bang into a wall, where I stop. Idiot. I can't get lost back here. I need the whistling man. He's my guide back to the main vault. How far have I come? I pull out my phone, but I don't turn on my light because I don't want him to see me. I stand perfectly still, listening. The silence is so profound that I can hear my eyes blinking, and the darkness is like thick, black poison in my lungs, stealing my breath and feeding my panic. Softly, slowly, I turn back the way I came, desperate for any sound or a glimpse of headlamp to signal that the whistler is still nearby. I reach a widening in the tunnel and feel around, discovering the three open gaps of an intersection. I have absolutely no idea which way to go. I listen intently another moment and hear, very faintly, a cadence of whistling melody, but I can't be sure which tunnel it comes from.

"*Please*," I whisper desperately.

But the whistling recedes, and I'm alone in the dark. *Think*, I tell myself, fighting back panic. *Stay calm*.

With shaking fingers, I turn on my phone light again. I lift it high, casting a pale shimmer of light along one tunnel and then the next. They look identical. The third one inclines slightly upward. I don't recall going up or down while I followed the whistler with his stretcher, so that's no clue. The floor lacks the double tracks from before, so I have definitely wandered off the original route, but I can't have come very far. It isn't possible. If I can just find the tunnel with the two tracks in it, I can follow that back to the vault.

That's my logic. I have to be methodical. I can't give in to panic, even though the battery life on my phone is now down to fourteen percent. I take off one of my socks, marking one tunnel as number one, and then I walk along it, counting my paces until I reach fifty. It has no intersections. No smell of fire or moving air. I go back to my sock and repeat my search in the second tunnel, with similar discouraging results. But in the third tunnel, the slanting one, at my thirty-fifth step, I find an intersection with the two smooth, worn tracks along the floor. Relief pours through me. I count backward again to where I left my sock and retrieve it, and then I return to the tunnel with the tracks.

This has to be it. In one direction or another, I have to believe I'll find the main vault again. I put down my sock again to mark my place, and I peer to the right. My phone's battery is now down to eleven percent. I can barely stand to turn off the light, but I might need it even more later, so I do. Then I start forward, keeping my shoes on the smooth track and counting my steps.

At twenty-three steps, the tunnel veers left. At fifty steps, I round another corner, and far ahead, I see the faint light of the vault again, reflecting on the puddle. My heart nearly bursts with relief. Forget my sock. I'm not going back. I put my phone back in my pocket and walk quietly to the end of the tunnel to peek into the vault again.

In the five o'clock direction and near the center of the room, a couple dozen red lights are on above the dreamers. The whistling man with the headlamp is wheeling his cart out of the vault, through the nine o'clock archway, and he has a dreamer on top of it. Alarm rocks through me. I stretch up on my tiptoes and scan automatically for my sister. I can't see exactly from this angle, but my gut already knows. Her sleep shell is empty. They've taken her.

"No!" I whisper.

And then my fear turns to raw anger. I have to stop them. I've had enough of being worried. And scared. I have to save her!

I kick a stone by accident and it rattles down the steps into the vault. A red light goes on above the nearest dreamer, and I ball my hands into fists. *Don't do this*, I think. I take a steady breath to cool my temper and frown at the light, willing it to go off. A moment later it does, and then, stealthily, I slide around the perimeter wall of the vault as I did before, circumventing the dreamers.

At the nine o'clock arch, I pause to peer up the tunnel. This one is more cleanly hewn, like a hallway, with small lights set in the walls at ankle height. It smells different, too, with a trace of cleanser or disinfectant in the air. I slip inside and hurry along until the sound of voices makes me slow. Around the corner, ahead of me, light comes out of a larger doorway, and I stop, listening.

Voices talk calmly back and forth. More than two. I can't make out what they're saying. A shifting noise is followed by some clicking. I back against the tunnel wall, flattening myself as much as possible, and then I peek in the doorway.

Medical equipment gleams under bright lights, and five occupied operating tables are arranged in a star, with the dreamers' heads toward the center and their feet out at the points. I can't tell if one of them is Dubbs, but all the dreamers are child-sized. Two women in green scrubs and a man, Jules, stand around one, aiming their attention toward a nearby computer that swivels out by an arm from a central pole. It's odd to see high-tech medical equipment in a room that's rough-hewn from the rock. The black-topped counters near the back of the room remind me of the science labs in my old high school.

I shift back out of sight and glance farther along the hall to a second door that would let me into the back of the room by the counters, but it's closed.

"Tilt that closer, would you, Anna?" Jules says.

A series of quiet clicks follows, and then several squeaks and the shuffle of shifting feet.

"She's younger than she looks," says a woman. "Look at this."

"That's distress," Jules says. "Isn't it time to call Sandy? He'll want to see this."

I need to see, too. Carefully, silently, I edge past the doorway. For an instant I'm exposed to their full view, but they don't look up, and then I'm across.

A telephone ringing sound, amplified through a speakerphone, comes from the operating room. I know the rhythm of the ring. I set my hand on the knob of the second door, and when the phone rings loudly again, I pull the door open and crawl inside. Then I pull the door nearly closed again. When the phone rings a third time, I shut the door all the way, with the softest click covered by the ringing. Then I creep behind the nearest counter. A familiar trace of vinegar laces the air and triggers my fear. I wait, motionless, to see if I've been noticed, but the phone keeps ringing and the doctors or whoever they are remain absorbed by their work.

A generic voice from the speakerphone announces that the voicemail box is full.

"Sandy Berg is the most exasperating person," a woman says. "Can't he tell time?"

"He'll know we called," Jules says. "He'll call back."

"When he's good and ready, you mean," she says. "What do you say? Do we park her again?"

"Let's just take a proper look," Jules says. "No harm in that."

They go quiet. I'm bursting with curiosity and fear. Silently, I shift along on my hands and knees until I can see around the far corner of the counter. I hold my breath. From my angle, I can see the legs and undersides of three of the operating tables, including the one where the doctors are busy. They hover around in their green scrubs. A vast array of equipment extends down from the ceiling on metal arms and coils, and a complex network of IV lines and wires runs between the patients and the computers.

A rustling comes from the doorway, and I shift to see the man from the oven, the whistler, enter with a large plastic bin. If I had stayed in the hall much longer, he would have found me.

"Any word on our visitor?" asks the woman.

She's the same one who spoke before, the one Jules called Anna, and she has a low, cultured voice even when she's exasperated. She stands with her back to me, so I can't see her face, but she has a thick braid of gray-and-black hair tied off with a red band. Tall and slender, with a dark complexion, she rests one gloved hand on the patient's arm.

"Not yet," the whistler says, setting the bin on a counter. He takes off his helmet, revealing a thatch of brown hair.

"Might as well get the dogs," Jules says.

I shudder to think of being chased by dogs in those dark tunnels.

"You know what'll happen to the dreamers with that

133

racket," the whistler says. "Give her another day and she'll come out on her own. They always do."

"Not always," says the second woman. It's the first time she's spoken, and her voice is lighter and softer. I shift to get a better look at her profile. She's petite and delicate-looking, with smooth dark hair, fine eyebrows, and brown skin. She seems younger than the others, and she's wearing green sneakers with her scrubs.

"Kiri's right," Jules says. "If she breaks her leg and dies back there, it'll be a waste. I say we bring in the dogs. Give her a little scare, too."

"I hate the dogs," Kiri, the petite woman, says.

"Why didn't our cameras pick her up when she was aboveground?" Anna asks.

"It was one of those shorts I've been telling you about," the whistler says. "All the cameras crashed last night for an hour and then came on again spontaneously."

"You have to track that down," Anna says. "Didn't I say it could be dangerous if the cameras malfunctioned while someone was in the park? And now it's happened."

The whistler sighs and sorts through a pile of white food containers. "I've looked. I'll look again. Do you really believe Sandy will bring Rosie to us?"

"He has to find her first," Anna says.

"Does anyone know if Linus is in touch with her?" Jules says.

"Sandy could ask him," Kiri says softly.

"Linus won't take Sandy's calls," Anna says. "Berg told me

so, but he's tracing Linus's other calls, obviously. He's talked with his producer, a pizza place, and the ophthalmologist, but not Rosie."

"I think they broke up," the whistler says. "That's what makes the most sense. Otherwise, why isn't Linus with her?"

Anna lets out a laugh. "Since when are you so interested in the romantic details?" she says.

"If they break up, it could be good for Ian," Jules says. "Right, Whistler? Your boy has the hots for her still, doesn't he?"

I listen, agog. This man, the whistler, is Ian's father? I need to get a better look to see if there's a resemblance.

"My son knows what he's doing. He has good taste," Whistler says.

The others laugh.

"That's why you want Rosie down here," Jules says. "You want to get Ian's girlfriend back for him. He likes them dreaming, doesn't he?"

"Are you finding anything over there or just wasting time?" Whistler says.

Jules's next laugh is rather snide.

"Really, Jules," Anna says. "We're not finding much, Whistler," she adds politely. "She's in a pre-REM mode. A bit restless but stable. I'm curious to see what her dreams are like."

A phone rings.

"There he is, finally," Anna says. "I'm putting him on speaker." There's a clicking. "Hi, Sandy. Anna here."

"Sorry I'm late. Did you start without me?" Berg says.

His voice always gives me the creeps, and I can feel myself shrinking inside my skin. It sounds like they coordinated a time for this call.

"We have Dubbs on the table. We're just ready to go," Jules says.

My heart sinks. They *are* working on Dubbs, just as I feared.

"Remember, no mining for her," Berg says. "We're just taking a look. Is she in REM?"

"Not yet. We could boost her," Jules says.

"No. Leave her be," Berg says.

Kiri reaches up to adjust Dubbs's IV, and I hear a few taps on a keyboard.

"What's the status on Rosie?" Anna asks.

"Nothing new. I'm looking for her," Berg says. "I'm sorry it's taking so long. I know how important this is. She's very good at disappearing, but she always surfaces, one way or the other. She knows I have her family."

"Have you tried getting any dreams from Thea?" Jules says.

"No luck so far," Berg says. "The parents have invited Orson over and he's there now, but the girl's resisting medical intervention. It's a delicate situation."

"These are all delicate situations, Sandy," Jules says. "We've been getting some strange ripples here in the dreamers."

"What kind of ripples?" Berg asks.

I half expect Jules to mention that a visitor is in the tunnels.

"We've noticed a turn in the organic code," Jules says.

"A hacker, maybe? A virus?" Berg asks. "Is it spreading? Is Whistler with you?"

Jules looks toward the whistler and nods his chin.

"Not a hacker," Whistler says. "It's internal. A spontaneous mutation, possibly."

"Track it down," Berg says.

Whistler laughs. "Sure thing. No problem."

Jules makes a face at him. "In other words, Whistler's working on it," he says. "The truth is, we only have so many hands down here. Rory Fallon's gone back to Iceland to spend some time with his wife and daughter, and we don't expect him back anytime soon."

"How are you doing with my hybrid?" Berg asks.

"It's coming along," Anna says.

"Be more precise, please," Berg says. "When will it be ready?"

"We've tweaked the CRISPR for your mHtt and crossed that with the Sinclair Fifteen, which appears to cut out the Huntington's," Anna says. "We're running trials with the seeds in a dozen dreamers now, but we won't know how it works in a live host until we try. Is your coma patient standing by? Has his family signed on?"

"No," Berg says. "I've hit a snag there. Chimera's a dead end."

The doctors look at each other with varying degrees of surprise.

"Then what's the point, Sandy?" Jules asks. "I thought you wanted the Berg-Sinclair hybrid for a live host."

"I do. I'll get you a host. Don't worry about it," Berg says.

"You'll *get us one*?" Jules says. "We don't do live hosts down here. You know that, Sandy. Dreamers only."

"So you say," Berg says.

Jules shakes his head. Kiri lifts both of her hands in a *what now?* gesture.

"Are you going to tell us who you have in mind as a host? Have you found a volunteer? Your son, maybe?" Kiri asks.

Berg's laugh comes over the phone. "Not my son. Someone else. I'm just working out the logistics."

Anna frowns. "You're not going to ask us to put the hybrid dream seeds right back into you, are you? That won't work, Sandy. You're already too far along."

"I'm well aware, thank you," Berg says. "I'm already taking the maximum dosage of tetrabenazine, and my chorea's noticeably worse. No. I've got someone else. I need to make the leap, like Orson did. Like Rosie's transfer into Thea."

The team exchanges glances again. Jules ducks back his chin and frowns. I'm getting a bad feeling about who Berg might want for his host.

"Haven't you learned anything from Orson, Sandy?" Anna says.

"Many things. What's your point?" Berg says.

"Orson's not the happiest of men," Anna says. "What makes you think you'd be any better off than him?"

Berg laughs again. "Let me worry about that. For now, keep your trials going and take care of Dubbs. No mining for her. Absolutely none. Understood? I need her for leverage just the way she is, and then I'll mine her myself. I'll bring Rosie down as soon as I recover her, and you'll get your Sinclair Fifteen. First thing. That's the deal."

Here. Berg means to bring me here. He means to mine my

sister, too, afterward. I'm sick with horror. I've walked right into his plan. Again.

"Very well," Jules says.

A loud hissing noise starts up.

"Not again," Jules says. "Can you get that?"

"On it," Whistler says.

"Hurry," Anna says. "That narcotic is flammable."

"I said I'm on it," Whistler repeats.

I peek through the opening to see the whistler step up on a chair and grasp a hose that comes from the ceiling. A cloud of blue gas is gushing out the end, and he kinks it to slow the rush while he works a lever halfway up.

"What was that?" Berg says.

"One of the narcotics lines, the backup ones," Jules says. "The nozzles have been blowing. They're old. This whole place is old."

"Is Whistler still with you?" Berg says.

"Here," he says, still holding the kink.

"You probably know Ian's gone to check on your mother. If you ever want help bringing her to Miehana, you only have to ask," Berg says. "We could set her up in a cozy place in town, or you could have her down below with you. Either way."

"That's very generous of you, but for now, we're all good," Whistler says. He tucks the hose back up into a framework and then steps down from the chair.

Berg says goodbye, and the connection goes dead.

I hardly know what to think about all I've heard, but one thing is clear. These people are diabolically creepy and underhanded. I shift my weight on my knees, trying to get a better angle on my sister, and the floor makes a tiny creak.

Anna straightens suddenly, lifting both her gloved hands. "Did you hear something?"

I duck my head away from the gap and hold very still, trying not to breathe, but my heart is hammering with fear.

"Whistler, sweep the room," Jules says.

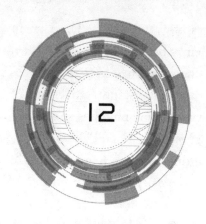

12

A CONVENIENT PORT

I GRAB MY KNIFE out of its sheath. I'm going to have to run. Whistler's head comes over the counter, and his eyebrows jog in surprise. I scramble to my feet and bolt for the door, but by the time I open it, Anna is on the other side. I slash an arc of blade before me, and she backs up.

"Hey, now," she says.

At that moment, Whistler dives to tackle me from the side. We hit the ground. I try to get my knife into him, but he blocks my wrist and the knife goes skittering through the doorway. I scramble to my knees. He catches my ankle, jerks me back, and slams me to the floor. I shove and kick, but he lands on my back and nearly crushes the breath out of me.

"Let me go!" I say.

Whistler presses my head so my face is smashed to the floor.

"Get her legs," his says grimly, his voice near to my ear.

Someone wraps my ankles together. Then my wrists are tied together behind my back. Whistler hauls me up and drags me into the operating room, where he dumps me on a chair.

"Stay put," Jules says, standing over me.

I twist my wrists in my bindings and try to flip my hair out of my eyes. "Let me out of here!" I say.

Whistler, panting, braces a hand against the wall.

Anna leans over to pick up my knife. "We need to call Sandy."

"Not yet," says Jules. He regards me narrowly, and I see his features up close for the first time. His cheeks are pitted with old acne scars, and his lips are thin and gray. "How'd you find us?" he asks. "Who else knows you're here?"

"You're going to jail. All of you," I say.

Jules opens his big, hard hand and slaps me across the face. "I asked you how you found us."

I wince, stung. "Ask your dragon," I say.

Jules smacks me again, harder this time, and pain flares along my left cheekbone. "I'm asking *you*," Jules says to me.

I have to blink to regain my focus, and when I do, a surge of brute anger rises in me. I'm not taking this. My days of putting up with Larry's violence are over, and I'm not cowering from anybody else, ever again.

I spit in Jules's face. "Go ahead and rot."

He turns red and winds up again, but just then, Anna steps between us.

"That's enough. Leave her alone, Jules," she says in a stern voice.

His eyes flash from her to me. He wipes his face. Then he crosses his arms over his chest and falls back half a step.

Anna frowns at me, inspecting me closely. I stare back, defiant. Her dark face is broad, with strong, regular features, and the whites of her eyes have a tint of yellow. When she touches her fingers lightly to my sore cheek, I flinch back. She runs a hand over my pockets and takes out my phone, tossing it to Whistler.

"See what you can find," Anna says.

Next she pulls out my keys.

"She's right, you know. What she said. It was the dragon that brought her," Kiri says in her quiet voice. Sitting in a tall swivel chair by the operating table, she alone seems unruffled. "The dragon in the machine."

"What are you talking about?" Jules says.

Whistler's flipping through my phone, but he looks up at Kiri. "The fluke in the computer. The thing that ripples in the code and cuts out the cameras."

"Nonsense," Jules says. "When was her last call?"

Whistler returns his attention to my phone. "Three days ago," he says. "A number in St. Louis. I'd bet Linus. Before that, a number in Atlanta."

I'm surprised. I must have grabbed my older phone.

"Who's in Atlanta?" Anna asks me.

"Important people," I say. "They're going to call the police if I'm not back soon."

"Likely not, since you're still technically missing," Anna says. She taps a finger against the knife, and then sets it aside.

"Not even Berg knows where you are. What a curious opportunity."

At some slight signal from Anna, Jules turns and starts prepping a syringe.

My heart lurches. I twist my hands in my bindings, trying to get free. "You can't knock me out. You can't mess with my sleep in any way," I say. "It throws off my dreams."

Jules pauses. "Baloney."

"It's true! Berg likes me afraid," I say, thinking fast. "He keeps me in a delicate balance of fear. Then, when I'm exhausted, I fall into a deep sleep and he's ready to mine me."

Anna gives a half smile and shakes her head again. "Whistler, take care of her car," she says, and passes him my keys.

Jules takes a step nearer and I tense.

"Stay away from me!" I scream.

I try to kick out, but Jules pins me with a hard grip on my shoulder. A sharp pain pinches my neck, and numbness spreads outward from the injection. My neck goes limp, and my knees buckle. Jules holds me steady on the chair as my body collapses from within.

"No," I say. I cannot be back in this helpless situation again.

But I am. They have me. It's impossible to keep my eyes open. I try to struggle, but my body is already weak. I feel someone lifting me, and then I'm stretched out on a table. My wrists are untied and then my arms, heavy and limp, are strapped down to the table.

The last thing I hear is Jules's voice.

"How convenient. She still has a port."

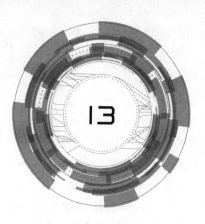

13

INVADED

WHEN I WAKE, groggy, I'm in a small, underground cell on a clean, narrow cot. A soft blanket covers me, and I'm dressed in green scrubs. My mouth tastes bitter, and my left cheek hurts. As I slowly roll over, every muscle aches, like I've been beaten up from within, and I'm so hungry I could eat a goat. Carefully, I sit upright and hug my knees to my chest, letting my balance settle. I curl my toes in my socks. Something inside me is different. Partly, it's the normal sludge-brain I always have when Berg mines me, but now I also feel a faint tingle at the base of my skull. It's like an expectation. Like today's my birthday, only it's not.

I blink hard and shake my head. The tingling sensation dims.

A dozen small lights gleam in the rugged stone around me, and it's so quiet, the walls seem to reflect back the sound of my own breath. Lifting my hand, I feel for the soft lump under my skin on my chest, and find my port is still there. I'm not surprised. Gently, I touch the back of my left ear, where I find the crust of a scab. Of course.

I have no idea how much they mined from me, or how long I've been here. My fingernails are a little longer than I remember, which could mean a couple of days have passed, or more time if they've been trimmed. I step across to the main door, which has a narrow window looking onto a hallway. When I try the knob, the door's locked. A second door leads to a tidy little bathroom. I do my business and wash my hands. A fresh toothbrush and small tube of paste are there for the taking, and as I brush my teeth, I glance into the mirror.

A flurry of surprise skitters around in the back of mind, as if a thousand tiny stars are lighting up at once. I spit into the sink. I frown, doubtful, and lean nearer to inspect my sore cheek in the glass. It's a nasty, bruised purple from where Jules smacked me, and tender to the touch. I meet my own gaze, assessing. My hazel eyes are still large and steady, my eyebrows dark. I touch the waves of my dark hair, which feels clean and soft, as though someone's washed it lately. My lips look as dry as they feel. My teeth, clean now, have the usual gap in front. I angle my chin to see my jaw has the same, familiar contour. My complexion's paler than usual, but my acne's about the same, with one old zit healed and a new one getting worse. Two days, I'd guess. I've been down here about two days.

It's not a happy discovery, but in the back of my mind, that sense of tiny stars zips around in wild delight. I take a deep breath, dreading what I have to do.

Who's there? I ask cautiously in my mind.

I haven't heard an extra voice since Thea left me. I listen carefully now, but there's no reply. Still, I'm distinctly aware of something new inside me, a feeling that doesn't fit. I gaze at my reflection, puzzled, while this strange, eager delight plays at the edge of my consciousness. It isn't me. It couldn't be, because I have nothing to be joyful about. And yet it's there, as clear and vibrant as warm sunlight would be on my open palm.

I look down at my hand and turn my palm up, half expecting to see sunlight on my skin. The presence in the back of my mind twirls with silent glee.

"What's going on?" I ask aloud. "This isn't funny."

A shot of adrenaline bursts through me, and my heart races. But no answer comes. What did the doctors do to me?

I pad in my socks over to the main door and peek through the window at the hallway.

"Hello?" I call. "Is anyone there? I need some food."

Listening for a reply, I hear only stone. I check my room for camera lenses but can't find any. My heart keeps pumping, *go, go, go!* Then it does a little flip on itself, and I'm suddenly breathless and exhausted. I lean over and brace my hands on my knees. A flashing heat wave spreads out from my chest to my extremities, followed by a chill that seems to pull my blood toward the floor. Light-headed, I slide down to sit on the floor before I faint, and I lean my face into my shaky hands.

I take slow, deep breaths, trying to steady myself, and then, without warning, through no effort of my own, my vision is filled with an open, pearly sky and the wild, fragrant grass of the prairie in springtime. The horizon stretches into the deep distance, and I breathe in the fresh, cool air of dawn. Each tall, leaning blade of grass shimmers with an added glow, a piercing vividness. It's more than a memory, more than a daydream, and I turn slowly to find Linus standing beside me. His eyes are grave, his mouth grim. He's wearing his familiar black jacket, and when a breeze blows up his collar, I recognize this precious, poisoned moment.

It's the morning after Thea had her baby. We're standing on a secluded knoll a few miles from the school, and we're facing the likelihood that Linus has a camera in his left eye. The clear, caramel color of his iris shows no hint of a foreign lens, but I can't think of any other explanation for how Berg had a film of me in Linus's bed. The truth is inescapable. It kills me to know Linus has brought a spy along with him every time we've been together, for every glance, every conversation, every uncertain kiss.

Don't look at me like that, Linus says, pleading. *Believe me. I didn't know.*

If this vision were pure memory, I would kiss him next, but it isn't. Instead, I lift my right hand to cover his camera eye. He lets me, and I feel the warmth of his forehead under my fingertips. Sunlight slants across his lips, and his eyelashes blink a faint brush against the life line of my palm.

My vision holds there, caressing the poignant details.

This is my hand over Linus's eye, proving that I left him because I couldn't get past how he was part of Berg's web. This is Linus holding still beneath my hand, helpless, furious, unhappy. This is me, wanting him and hurting him and failing to see how badly he needed me.

Please stop, I tell my vision.

My soul aches with regret. I want Linus, wherever he is, with whatever heart I have.

When the vision finally drains away, I'm slumped on the floor. Cold invades my extremities until I'm shivering. My heartbeat is a sluggish throb. My breath hurts in my lungs. What's happened to me? I swallow over a dry throat and push myself up heavily to sitting. This keen sense of longing is like a knife between my ribs, scraping at each breath. I don't like it. I don't want my memories co-opted and corrupted.

"Who are you?" I ask.

My invader doesn't answer, but I know it's there, lurking. *Why this memory?* I ask. *Why did you pick this one?*

The fingertips of my right hand begin to tingle, and the sensation intensifies until it's almost a burning. I stare at my hand, stretching out my fingers. They look no different, but the tingle continues like a command. On instinct, I trail my fingers lightly along my forehead and down my cheek in a slow, soothing gesture, like an apology. The ache in my chest releases its hold, and my next breath comes easier.

The tingling in my fingers fades, and I'm left alone, puzzled, missing Linus. My heart feels raw where a frost of protection has thawed.

I don't want to be thinking about Linus and how much he means to me. He isn't what brought me here to this cave. I have my family to worry about. Yet now, something in my own mind has thrust him forward again, as if my feelings for him are central to everything. I pull up my knees and sink my head down into my arms.

I don't need some other force inside me pulling up sensitive memories and toying with my emotions. Whatever this tingly starlight presence is in me, it needs to understand who's boss.

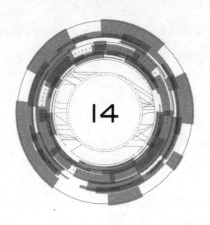

14

LIGHT FROM A POTATO

WHEN WHISTLER COMES LATER with a tray of food, I'm back on my bed, just waking again. My blanket's twisted around me, and my green scrubs smell musty. I've completely lost track of time, and my eyes feel smudged and puffy, as if from crying. His soft, aimless whistling sounds incongruously optimistic.

"Your cheek looks better. How are you feeling?" Whistler says.

I push up onto my elbow, and the heavy, chill scent of the stone walls invades me again. "Like crap. Where's my sister?"

He angles the tray on the desk, facing me. "She's safe with the others," he says. He absently adjusts his earpiece, aiming the microphone nub toward his mouth. "We didn't mine her, if that's what's worrying you. Just had a little look. Her dreams are very nice. Not the same caliber as yours, but that's no surprise."

"What about my parents? Where are they?"

"I have no idea," Whistler says. "Berg isn't the type to keep all his eggs in one basket."

"So they weren't delivered with Dubbs?" I say.

Whistler shakes his head slowly and rubs his chin. "Nope. Dubbs came alone. You should really eat. You need your strength. Aren't you hungry?"

I'm starved. He's brought me a pita sandwich with fresh cucumbers, cheddar cheese, tomato, and creamy mayo, and I can't stuff it in fast enough. I gulp down half a glass of ice water. Then I rip open a bag of chips and nearly swoon at the salty crispiness. There's a brownie with some chewy caramel in it, and I devour that, too.

"You like chocolate? I made those myself," he says. He pulls the chair from the desk and sits awkwardly across from the bed.

I close my eyes, savoring the sweetness. "They're good," I admit. "How do you guys get food down here?"

"We have groceries delivered upstairs," he says, like it's no big deal. "If there's anything special you want, let me know and I can get it for you."

I lower my brownie. He's implying that I'll be staying awhile.

"You mined me, didn't you?" I ask.

"Just a little," he says, and eyes me closely. "Can you tell?"

Something's different. That's for sure. "Yes. How long have I been down here?"

"Two days? Yes. Two."

I can't believe this is happening to me again. I glance behind him to the door, which is closed again. I didn't see him lock it from the inside, but that doesn't mean it'll open. I wonder what it would take to get past him.

"What you're doing down here can't possibly be legal," I say.

"Well, it's not illegal," Whistler says slowly. "The pre-dead are all slated for harvesting. We pay for them fair and square."

Pre-dead. I haven't heard that term before. I guess that's what's kept in a pre-morgue.

"Except my sister and me," I say.

He purses out his lips, like he might whistle, but then he doesn't. "You represent a turning point, I admit," he says.

Anger hardens inside me.

Without another word, he produces a little paper cup and sets it on my tray. It contains a small white pill suspiciously like the kind Orly gave us students back at Forge to make us sleep for twelve hours every night.

As Whistler glances away, evading my direct gaze, I have my first glimpse of his resemblance to Ian. Where Ian is all protruding eyes and soft lips and wispy blond hair, Whistler has subdued, even features and normal brown hair. He's sturdier, with more bulk to match his maturity, and despite his hint of chagrin as he looks away from me, he still exudes a quiet confidence that's more refined than Ian's contrived, boastful manner. He has changed into a different set of clothes, a matching gray set of shirt and trousers, and his helmet is cocked at a jaunty angle on his head, so the headlamp looks like an unlit third eye.

I can feel him waiting for me to ask about the pill. Instead, I take another slow bite of my brownie.

"Who controls the dragon?" I ask.

"Pardon?" he says.

"I mean the special effects upstairs, by the Keep of Ages," I say. "How'd you make it look like Dubbs fell from the plank?"

He tilts his head curiously. "The cameras were down when you came to the park. I didn't see your arrival or anything unusual with the dragon. You saw the dragon in action?"

"Yes. And my sister. Or an effect that looked just like my sister. She fell off a plank from the roof of the keep, and the dragon scooped her up and flew away. It was terrifying."

"That's a little odd." Whistler gazes at me thoughtfully for a moment. "Back in the day, when the park was up and running, the special effects team could do anything they wanted. They frightened the bejesus out of the guests. Ian likes to tinker with the old programs when he's here."

"But you said he's not here."

"He's not," Whistler says. "I don't have an explanation. Perhaps Ian put a show on a timer, so to speak."

I hardly think so. It was too perfectly timed to my movements. "Kiri said the dragon brought me here," I say. "You agreed with her."

"I didn't mean the dragon on the keep. It was more of a metaphor, like a monster in the machine," he says. "We do have something unusual going on here lately, and I haven't been able to track it down. We've had camera blackouts, and pressure changes that blow out the hoses. One day, a couple months back, five of the incubators in the storage room went off for no reason and then came back on again four hours later. We lost a ton of research. Jules nearly busted a gut."

"What do you actually do down here?" I ask.

Whistler jogs up his helmet brim. "Me? I'm just a glorified handyman. The doctors do the actual research," he says. "We started with simple data storage, but now we're mostly experimenting with treatments for brain injuries, coma, Alzheimer's, whatever. PTSD's a big one. It's all dream based. That's our niche."

"And have you found any cures?" I ask.

"Sure. Bits and pieces," he says. "We share our findings with certain other labs. They often get the credit, but that's okay."

"Like the Chimera Centre," I say.

"We do collaborate with Chimera. They've had some amazing breakthroughs there."

It's a lot to wrap my head around. I pull my feet up on the bed and tuck my hands under my ankles. The longer I can keep him here talking, the more likely I am to get him to sympathize with me and maybe let me go. It's like with Ian, all over again, but without the crush.

"How long have you guys been down here?" I ask.

Whistler's shoulders visibly relax, and he sends his gaze toward the ceiling. "For me, it's been three years this stretch. For the others? Let's see. The meltdown was in forty-eight, so that's nineteen years ago for Anna. She was the first. She set things up. Then Kiri and Jules came soon after."

"They've been down here for almost two decades?" I ask, amazed.

"I was with them back then, too, for a few years near the

155

beginning. Four years? I think that's right. I left for a while and then came back after my divorce," he says. "A few others have come and gone from time to time, but we're the core group."

"How did this all start?"

He rests one ankle over the opposite knee, revealing an argyle sock. "I suppose there's no harm in telling you," he says. "After the earthquake and the Olbaid meltdown, people started dying from radiation poisoning. Not everybody, but enough. It was ugly."

"I heard about that. It must have been horrible," I say, recalling Lavinia's losses. "Wasn't there a problem with a cemetery?"

"Yes," he says. "The dead weren't actually radioactive, but their bodies had to be handled specially, and the local cemeteries were overwhelmed. They couldn't take everybody. That's where we come in."

I shift forward, leaning my elbows on my knees and clasping my hands together.

"The park here was closed, of course," Whistler goes on. "A total loss, but even so, the Grisly brothers were generous. They offered to store the bodies here until a proper cemetery could be founded. You know, a memorial cemetery for the victims of the meltdown. That's what the survivors wanted. It irked some people to think of their loved ones stashed at a horror park, but it was a cheap, safe solution, and it was supposed to be temporary. Anyway, years went by. The burial ground was never dedicated, and the county had enough other problems to deal with. A judge decided that the bodies were technically 'buried' as long as they stayed underground, so that was finally checked off as the solution."

"So they just left the bodies here? All this time?" I ask, confused. "Why haven't they decayed?"

"The original bodies *have* all decomposed by now, of course," Whistler says. "But you asked how we got started." He sets one hand on the desk, and every once in a while, he rocks his chair back on two legs in a restless fashion. "It seemed a shame to let all the bodies just rot. They couldn't even be harvested for organs because of the radiation. Then Anna got an idea. She had done some research with quantum computer bio-interfaces, and she saw no harm in stimulating some of the brain tissue. 'If you can get light from a potato,' she used to say, 'you ought to be able to get something out of a dead brain.'"

"You can get light from a potato?" I ask.

He turns over his hand expressively. "A potato can power a light, to be more accurate, but she was making a point. The dreamers had a potential we could not ignore, and we couldn't do any harm. It was slow work at first. Grim, really. But the bodies kept coming, some very fresh, and once we could reboot basic systemic functions in a few, we started seeing results. Some of the dreamers' brains, the younger ones especially, were perfectly viable for storing data, computer data. Brains are really just living circuits, after all, and connected with the right interface, they make a nifty computer network. That was our first success."

I'm agog. He's goes on, bragging about their progress. He doesn't appear to see anything wrong with what they've done, but it seems atrocious to me, and I can't pinpoint why. I straighten again and lean a hand back on my cot. I'm all for donating organs, and I get that recycling bodies is just a stretch beyond that. It isn't as if dead people could actually know they're being used. And yet, if their brains are working enough to be useful, if they're valuable enough to be used as circuits, aren't they alive enough that they could notice?

That's what troubles me. Who can prove the dreamers are really dead anymore? I can't get over how helpless they all look, and I can't forget how much I hated being kept asleep and mined for months at Onar. No matter how much Whistler brags about their advances, this still feels wrong to me. These people, these dreamers, ought to have a choice. They don't. That's why this is wrong.

"These days, we're deep into the mining and seeding," Whistler continues. "That's where the most promise is. We have a whole bank of dreams now, the best in the world."

"You have a dream bank," I say, trying to imagine that.

Whistler absently touches his earpiece again. "Yes. We've worked with more than three thousand dreamers over the years, mining and seeding to see what works." He hitches forward in his seat. "We can take a dream from a living host, like you, and implant it in one of our elite dreamers. It grows and multiplies and ripens there until we can harvest it and plant it again into other dreamers. In some cases, we have fifth-generation dream lines. Imagine that!"

"Have you done that with my dreams?" I ask.

"No," he says. "That's the problem. Berg's been very stingy with you. Very stingy. We had to beg for some Sinclair Fifteen from Chimera, but we've never been able to get enough, until now."

My pulse chugs with fear, and my mind leaps.

"You want to know what I think?" he continues.

"What?"

"We'll duplicate your dreams and send them to clinics like Chimera, where they'll be implanted into more coma patients, and bam, they'll wake up. Your dreams will provide the cure for all of them."

I hug my pillow to my belly. "But if you're implanting my dreams into all those patients, and they all wake up, won't they all be me? Like Thea is me?" I ask.

He stares a moment and then shakes his head. "No. They wouldn't exactly be you."

"But you said you would use my dreams. Your cure for waking them up is based on my dreams," I insist. "Thea has my personality. She has my memories. You're trying to duplicate me."

"We're really not," he says. "It's more like they'd be hybrids."

"You think that's any better?" I demand.

"Look, we're just trying to help people. You should be honored," he says.

"I'm not," I say. "And I don't consent to any of this. I'm not dead. Or even pre-dead. I should have a choice."

Whistler rises from his chair. "We don't need your consent. Your legal guardian has given his." He nods at the paper cup with the pill. "Take your meds."

I crumple the little cup and hurl it toward him. It bounces off his shirt and to the floor.

"I repeat: take your meds," he says. He lets himself out, and I hear the click of the bolt as he locks me in.

15

CAPTIVE

I HATE BEING IN MY CELL. For hours, I pace. I rage at the walls. I scream at the window in the door, demanding to be let out. I can't believe nobody comes back. I try breaking the window glass with the chair, but it won't shatter. I throw my tray. Still, no one comes. It feels like the height of callousness that they don't have a camera on me. How do they even know what I'm doing? I could hurt myself and they wouldn't know. In time, I'm hungry again. I scan the floor for crumbs that spilled when I threw my tray and dot them up with my finger to nibble.

"Are you going to starve me? Is that the idea?" I yell. "I'm not taking my pill!"

Finally, I wear myself down to exhaustion and crawl back onto my cot. I hide under my blanket, hating them. I refuse to cry. What are they doing to Dubbs? Where are my parents? Has

Lavinia told anyone where I am? I don't know anything. I have failed, utterly, and now I'm getting weak from lack of food.

When I wake next, I try staying calm. I use the bathroom, wash up, and brush my teeth. I come back to my cot and neatly make up my blanket and pillow. I sit in the middle of the bed, my hands folded. My stomach growls. It's then that I notice the crumpled pill cup still under the table where it fell.

Bitter rage nearly blinds me. I slide off the bed and lean over to pick up the little cup. Sure enough, the pill is still inside. I tip it slowly onto the palm of my hand, and my heart sinks. If I start obeying, if I start taking my pill, when will it end? I lean my head back and close my eyes, trying to keep back the tears.

Where's that starry, tingly feeling I felt before? Where did that go? I could use another vision now to take me out of this place.

A slow, dark heaviness stirs in the back of my mind like a stone settling at the bottom of a pond, and then it goes still again.

What, are you worn down, too? I ask mockingly. *Am I not enough fun for you?*

Nothing replies.

Despair consumes me. I have no way out. They have me.

I toss my pill back and swallow it down dry. Minutes later, I'm asleep.

>>>>>>>>

I wake to the sound of the door opening, and Whistler is back with another tray. I'm too weak to argue with him or complain.

161

Instead, I start with a slice of green apple, and the tartness is sublime. I ignore the white cup with a pill in it. Whistler closes the door behind him and takes his former chair.

"How are you feeling?" he asks.

I don't answer.

"I'm sorry about that," he says. "You'll get regular meals as long as you take your pills."

I take a sip of cool water, and then I start on my sandwich. This one is turkey and Swiss with avocado and Russian dressing. My taste buds go wild.

"Where's Dubbs?" I ask.

"She's fine. She's resting."

"Does she know I'm here?"

"She hasn't woken up," he says.

You mean, you haven't let her, I think.

He takes off his helmet and sets it on the table. "You know, starving rats live longer than well-fed ones."

"What's that have to do with anything?" I ask.

"We've been talking about what makes you so tough."

"I'm not tough. I just gave in."

"That was the smart thing to do," he says. "But it took you long enough." He leans back in his chair and crosses his legs at the knee. "Jules thinks growing up in the boxcars made you a better dreamer."

"I'm not interested in his theories."

"Anna thinks it was losing your father at a sensitive age. Me, I think any age is a bad time to lose a father."

I'm even less interested in that.

The lights flicker, and I jolt. When Whistler takes his helmet and starts to rise, I suddenly can't stand the thought of being left alone here again.

"Doesn't it bug you, being down here all the time?" I ask quickly. "Doesn't the darkness get to you?"

"I can see sunlight whenever I want," Whistler says. "I can see anything. Be anything. Go anywhere."

"I don't believe you," I say.

He frowns a moment. Then he sits back down and points a finger at me. "You're forgetting the dreams. We have a virtually endless supply. We can take them whenever we want, for as long as we want."

"Like a drug?" I ask. Even as I say it, I recall something I overheard long ago, a conversation between Berg and Dr. Fallon when she talked about using a sample on herself. *Intoxicating* was the word she'd used, or something like that. Berg was annoyed with her, as if she'd wasted something precious.

"If they're mainlined in the right dose, dreams are the perfect escape," Whistler says. "No unpleasant side effects or aftereffects. We can pick where we want to go and be transported completely."

"Those are illusions," I say. "They aren't real. You're no more alive down here than your dreamers."

He smiles. Then he rubs his knuckles in his hair and a few strands fluff up. "Let me ask you something," he says. "In theory, if you needed a new heart, would you accept a heart transplant?"

"Yes," I say.

163

He nods, like he expected no less. "And how about new eyes, or a skin graft? What if you needed an artificial limb, like a foot, or a new liver?"

"Sure," I say.

"What if you needed all of them?" he asks. "What if you had replacements for everything, even a new face? People get facelifts all the time. And tucks and whatever."

"What's your point?" I ask.

"When's the moment when you stop being you?" he asks.

I consider a moment, thinking of Thea, who had her entire body changed. She started out as me inside, but her body gradually changed her. She couldn't ignore a pregnancy. That's an extreme example, but I don't have to wonder if I would change if I had a different body. I know I would, but then the new me would be me, too.

"I guess as long as I still have my brain, as long as I still think like myself, then I'm myself," I say.

"So you wouldn't be yourself if you got old and senile?" he asks.

That makes me pause again. I shift on my bed and pull my blanket around my shoulders against the chill. "No, that would still be me, too," I say. "Getting old's natural. Whatever happens to me, I guess I'll face it." *If I ever get out of here*, I think.

He nods again, and then gestures to indicate alternatives. "So you can be old in your own body and your mind can be failing and you're still you, or you can be young with all your body parts replaced but your mind still working, and you're still you. Do I have that right?"

It sounds a bit contradictory, but that's where I am. "Yes," I say.

He leans back, tipping his chair again, like he's enjoying himself. "What if I told you your brain's just another organ, like your heart? It's a lot more complicated, but it's still just tissue and connections. It can be damaged or repaired. A drunk man is mentally compromised, but we don't say he's a different person. How much, or rather, how little of your brain still has to be yours for you to still be you?"

"I don't know," I say. "The thinking part, I guess."

"So you're definitely still you even though we mined out some of your dreams," he says.

Obviously, I think at first, but I don't say it, because, really, I'm not exactly the same. The mining changes me. I'm more irritable and suspicious, and that's just on the surface. I'm not going to tell him this, though. I'm not sure I owe him any honesty in this conversation. "What's your point?" I say. "If you're trying to persuade me about something or justify something, just tell me."

He lands his chair flat and runs his palms slowly down the knees of his trousers.

"If we replace someone's dying brain bit by bit, so the new pieces have a chance to learn from the old pieces before they're gone, that person will be the same as he was before. That's what I'm trying to say. He'll be the same person."

It sounds completely unnatural, yet I see what he means. "Same person, but with a new brain," I say.

He nods. "That's how we can get around time. To immortality. We'll gradually replace the old brain with the new brain.

The consciousness is seamless, the whole time, and it can go on forever."

He looks happier than I've seen him yet.

"But that's not what you're doing here," I point out. "You're putting *my dreams* in someone else's body. You want an invading mind to take over a host body. That's not the same at all."

"Not yet," he agrees. "But if we can do one thing, maybe we can do the other, too, in time."

A faint tingle stirs again in the back of my mind. It's fainter than the first time I felt it, but still clear.

"Did you seed something into me?" I ask.

"No. We wouldn't dare," he says. "It would be disastrous, like poisoning the only well."

"Berg used to seed ideas into me at Forge."

"That was before he knew better," he says. "We'd never do that now."

"I can't believe he's letting you mine me. I thought he wanted to do it himself."

"He does, but he can't get away from Forge at the moment, and we had a deal. He's given very strict protocols for how to handle you, though. He sends his greetings."

I scoff out a laugh. "I'm sure he does. What about Ian?" I ask. "Have you told him I'm here?"

"No."

"Why not?"

He plucks absently at his chin. "He's busy. He's a busy boy."

"Tell Ian I'm here," I say. "Tell him I want to see him."

"You'll only use him like before," Whistler says.

"Maybe he wants to be used."

Whistler smiles easily and crosses his arms, tilting back. He nods toward the pill in the cup. "I like having you here," he says. "The others say I'm foolish to think you'll join us of your own free will, but anything's possible, right? You're a smart girl."

Not that kind of smart, I think.

I stare at the little paper cup with the pill again, and deep, caustic rage builds inside me. I refuse to be a captive again. I am not going to waste away here indefinitely, entertaining Whistler whenever he wants to have a philosophical conversation and waiting for Berg to show up and destroy me once and for all.

Whistler's only one man. He's strong, and I'm worn down, but he's not expecting anything from me. He's also still tipped back on his chair, with all the arrogant confidence of a troll.

Before he can guess my intentions, I dive for the leg of his chair and jerk it savagely up. He and the chair topple backward and his head hits the wall with a nasty crunch. I wince as he slips to the floor and lies still. Before I can be shocked at what I've done, I pick his earpiece out of his ear and grab his helmet from the table.

Then I'm out of my cell, running lightly down the hallway, thrilled and terrified to go find my sister.

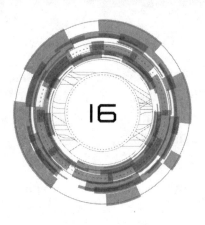

16

THE FISH OF THE DEEP

STILL RUNNING, I pull Whistler's helmet on and tighten the strap under my chin. As I turn the first corner, I find a basic hallway with doors on either side, and I pause to wipe Whistler's earpiece along my sleeve and slip it into my own ear. I notch up the volume, but I don't hear any voices.

Darting cautiously along the hall, I glance first into a small room with couches, desks, and a TV. It's vacant for now. I pass a kitchen area, a workout room, and a library. A narrow room lined with tall, glowing incubators makes me pause. When I don't see anybody, I can't resist stepping inside. The incubators' shelves are filled with little, clear, covered dishes. Each one is labeled with a name and a number, and inside, mysterious, viscous substances seem to be growing. Some catch the light or glow faintly. Others flicker.

So many. I stare in wonder. These have to be the dreams,

disembodied. Canned. A faint tingle stirs in the back of my mind.

A ticking noise from nearby makes me jump, and I hurry back to the hall. Around the next corner, I see the doors to the operating room ahead, and I tread as softly as possible. My earpiece is still silent, and I take that as a sign that Whistler isn't missed yet.

Quietly, carefully, I peek into the operating room. Jules, Anna, and Kiri are working over a dreamer, a person too short to be my sister, and the other four tables are empty. My mind flares with curiosity at the sight, and my eyes dilate wide, making everything too bright. I have to squint, but part of me is mesmerized, taking in each detail: the helmet on the dreamer, the angle of Anna's wrist as she inserts a syringe behind the dreamer's ear, Kiri's calm expression as she focuses on the computer screen. Part of me cranes forward, craving more, and at the same time, I'm afraid that they'll see me. I shrink back from the doorway, and as I cut off my view of the mining operation, my own, normal alertness snaps back in place.

I need to go! I can't dawdle.

I hurry swiftly down the last stretch of hallway, and when I reach the archway to the vault, I'm startled to find a hint of natural light is coming in from above, mixing with the blue glow of the sleep shells. It must be day outside, far above. The opening of the oculus is gray now instead of pitch black, and the stone of the dome ceiling looks harder and colder than ever. I step softly through the arch, trying to see toward the area of the room where my sister's sleep shell was before, and immediately, that curious hyperawareness flares again. It widens and spreads into a hum along my veins, like an extra layer of urgency jacking up my heart rate.

Above the nearest sleep shell, a red light goes on.

Oh, no, I think.

Another jolt of adrenaline electrifies my nerves.

Three more red lights go on. It's as if the dreamers' lights are an outward reflection of my inner alarm.

Over my earpiece, Anna's voice says, "Whistler, will you check on the vault? Do you see? We have four lights on."

I can't hesitate any longer. I go down the steps into the vault, and instantly, half a dozen more lights come on around me. I take another step so I'm poised between two sleep shells. More lights ripple on above the sleep shells in an ever-expanding wave, spreading out from where I am across the entire space, until every single dreamer has a red light alert and silently gleaming.

My heart goes still, then jolts on again. A tremor of inexplicable power hovers in the air.

"Whistler?" Anna says. "Did you hear me? Where are you?" And then, "Okay, we'll have to leave this. Meet us in the vault."

With a jolt, I run toward the center of the vault. If I can get to the middle and aim in the five o'clock direction, I can run out seven rows and find the place where Dubbs was. But I haven't anticipated the invisible weight of the dreaming children. As I run between their sleep shells, I can't help but be aware of their gelled eyelids and the blue glow on their skin. They're a limbo sea of dreamers, silent and close, and they drag at my heart like an undertow. It seems to take me forever to reach the inner circle of the vault, and then I aim out toward where Dubbs was before.

But when at last I reach the seventh row, I can't find her. I run from one sleep shell to another, scanning the dreamers' wasted little faces. I backtrack. I try again. They're all wrong. All not Dubbs. They all wrench my heartache.

"Dubbs!" I call. "Where are you?"

I don't dare look back toward the nine o'clock arch because I'm absolutely certain Anna and the others are coming. A twisting scurry of panic flickers in the back of my mind. In frustration, I slam my hand against the lid of the nearest sleep shell.

"Tell me where she is!" I say.

Around me, a dozen dreamers' red lights turn off. The sleep shells look newly abandoned without them. Their normal blue glows look even more sickly. Then more red lights go off, vanishing in a ripple across the room and leaving a weird brown afterglow in their wake. The expanding darkness reaches the outer edge of the circle, and the last of the red lights go off, all except for one.

One single red light keeps shining, far off in the two o'clock direction, small but steady under the vast, hovering gloom of the dome.

I hear a shout from behind me, but I don't turn back. Instead, I charge toward the red light, running full speed between the sleep shells and heedless of how many I bump. As I near the red light, my heart almost bursts with eagerness, and when I can finally make out the face under the glass lid, I gasp in relief.

171

It's Dubbs. She's inside, asleep.

I throw open the lid. Her eyelids are covered with gel and her cheeks are pale, but she's breathing. That's all I need.

"Dubbs!" I whisper urgently. I rip the tabs off her temples. "It's me, Rosie! We're leaving!"

I yank aside her gown to find the connections to her ports, and I twist them free. Then I lift her limp body out of the sleep shell, scooping under her knees and back. She's gangly, all skinny legs and arms, but I pull her securely against me so her head lolls forward beneath my chin.

Then I run.

More shouts come from behind me, closer now, but I still don't look back. I plunge past the last rows of sleep shells and race into the darkness of the three o'clock tunnel. I know the underground stream is up ahead, if I can get that far. When I can't see at all, I pause to flip on the headlamp on Whistler's helmet, and with the beam of light bouncing before me, I keep running along the tunnel until I find the door on my left and shove through.

"She's in the three o'clock tunnel!" Anna says over the earpiece. "Whistler, for Pete's sake! Get yourself out here!"

The dank scent of the stream ahead makes something in me balk. I feel a refusal in the back of my brain, a sharp but wordless warning, and for an instant, I slow. But in another step, I can hear the trickle of running water, and then I see the first hint of a green glow.

"I have no choice," I mutter aloud, and I hitch my sister up again.

At the next bend, I find the glimmering stream and the

narrow bridge. The dock is empty, like before. The pounding of running footsteps comes from behind me. Without even looking up the chute again, I know it's too steep for me to climb with Dubbs. My only chance is the stream.

Swiftly, I sit down at the edge of the dock and swing my legs over. I turn off the headlamp, take a new, firm grip on my sister, and step down into the cold water. The current is knee deep and flows to my left. I go with the water, heading downstream, away from the bridge. Faint green lights eddy around my shins, and through my saturated socks, I can feel the uneven, slippery surface of the bottom of the stream. I let the faint glow in the water guide me. I'm afraid I'll slip if I go faster, afraid I'll fall with Dubbs in my arms, but I'm desperate to get around the first corner before my pursuers can see me. My own splashes sound absurdly loud under the echoey ceiling. I make it a dozen steps, fighting for my balance. Then a dozen more.

"Where'd she go?" a man asks from some distance behind me. It's Jules.

With one more step, I make it around the corner and freeze, holding Dubbs. The cold stream flows between my legs, tugging the thin cotton of my scrubs, and I shiver once, hard.

"She must have taken the skiff," Anna says.

"If it was here. Who knows where Whistler left it," Jules says. "Kiri? She's gone. I don't know. She isn't at the dock."

I don't hear any replies over my earpiece, and I realize then it's gone. It must have fallen out.

My arm muscles are beginning to burn. Carefully, silently, I shift Dubbs's weight a bit higher and arch back. She still hasn't moved. I lean my shoulder to the cold wall to keep myself steady.

"No, I saw her come in the three o'clock," Anna says.

"I say we bring in the dogs," Jules says.

"By the time we go get them and bring them down here, she could be halfway to L.A.," Anna says.

"Not if she's back in the tunnels getting lost," he says. "Come on. I knew we should have put a tracker in her."

"I hear you, Kiri," Anna says. "Find Whistler. Check the exits up in the park. We'll find her. Don't worry. She can't get far."

Their voices are dimming, and I can finally exhale. Cautiously, quietly, I resume moving downstream through the cold water. They spoke of a boat, which means there must be a place where the boat goes, and that, in turn, means the stream must have an exit. I just have to find it.

I stay to the center, where the streambed is more level. I don't dare to turn on my headlamp, but the bioluminescence in the water creates a glow each time I step forward, and my legs have swirling trails and coils of green light around them. When the tunnel takes another bend, I pause, blinking into the darkness ahead. I step sideways until I can lean my shoulder against the wall. Then I prop a knee under Dubbs's legs and get a hand free to turn on my headlamp again. It helps, a little, but I have no real way to tell how far I'm going. I make it around the next bend, and another. At first, the water is shallow, but the farther I go, the deeper it gets, until it's as high as my butt. Walking with the current is treacherous. I keep trying to carry Dubbs higher, but I can feel the water dragging at her toes and her gown.

As I make it around the next bend, another dark length of tunnel stretches before me with no end in sight. A flurry of warning swirls up in the back of my mind again.

"Stop that," I say aloud.

I'm stressed out enough on my own already without some invader in my brain adding even more anxiety. I can't go back. That's not an option. I search the arching ceiling and walls for any hint of an exit. What I find instead is a narrow stone ledge that runs along the right side of the stream, like a pathway. Hopeful, I scramble up the ledge with Dubbs, and pull her close again. My wet scrubs cling to me, and she's not much drier. We're both shivering. I take a step, testing to see if the dark stone is slippery, but it's not.

For the first time, we can make real progress. The ledge takes us around another bend, and I have to step over a large pipe that sends a gurgling waterfall into the stream. Then the ledge meets a low archway over the stream and ends. The water looks deeper, the current stronger. We're stuck.

Gently, I crouch down and lower Dubbs to my knee. To see her shivering in her sleep is alarming. My arms ache from carrying her and clenching her tight, but I try to rub some warmth back into her.

Then I lean over to look through the archway. Ahead, to the right, the stream takes another turn, and I'm doubtful. The lowness of this arch would make it difficult for a boat to pass beneath. I glance back the way we came, and then I see it: a long, narrow skiff tied up on the other side of the stream, opposite the large pipe with the waterfall. I went right past without seeing it, but now I can make out the stone landing and a narrow archway with a stone staircase leading up.

That's it. We just have to cross the stream and we'll be able to escape. I'm sure of it. Just then, a dark, long shape glides through the water below me and swims under the arch to my right. The bioluminescence flows in a green trail behind it and swirls as it fades. I shiver again, watching to see if the fish will return. The water under the arch remains dark and undisturbed, except for the subtle, flowing ripples on the surface.

"Is that what you tried to warn me about?" I ask.

A dim affirmation flickers in the back of my mind. It's almost as disturbing as the fish itself.

Carefully, I lift Dubbs into my arms again and backtrack along the ledge. I climb back over the water pipe. On the opposite side, slightly upstream from the arch, the landing we need to get to is probably a good six strides away through the water. At my feet, the stream has its normal flow, with only the faint, random green glimmers, and it's hard to tell how deep it is.

A racking shiver runs through me. I can't put this off.

I slide in up to my thighs and step carefully toward the middle of the stream. My pants legs light up with bioluminescence like before, and each step takes me a bit deeper.

I'm halfway across the stream when an ominous gurgle makes me look toward the arch. A black-and-green streak is swimming swiftly through the water right toward me. I shriek and plunge ahead through the stream.

The fish races closer.

My foot slips and I stagger, pulled down by my sister's weight. She dunks into the water.

Charged by terror, I pull her up and lunge forward again with all my strength. I leap for the edge of the landing, roll onto the stone with Dubbs, and get my feet out of the water just as the black thing skims beneath us.

Teeth snap. The water churns.

But we're out. My heart's pounding. I can barely catch my breath. I clutch my sister tight, and back against the wall. In the beam of my headlamp, the thing slowly circles in the water. Green bioluminescence scatters and twirls in mini whirlpools. One wicked, cunning eye rolls past us, getting a good look.

"We made it," I whisper. Then I raise my voice, defiant. "You didn't get us, fish."

We're soaked, cold, and terrified, but we're alive. Another shiver ripples through me, shaking every bone until my teeth chatter.

Dubbs is shivering in my arms, too. She has a bleeding scrape on her wrist and her gown is drenched, but she's breathing. I hug her to me and kiss the top of her head.

"I've got you," I say fiercely. "Don't worry."

I wipe the wet hair out of my face and look up at the stone staircase. Since the skiff is here, this must be a real route in and out of the vault, which is promising in terms of seeing daylight again, but it's also possible that one of vault doctors could be waiting at the top.

Still, what other choice do I have? I'm not going to take the skiff back upstream and try to find a different way out.

Okay. Here we go, I tell myself.

Taking a deep breath, I hoist my sister into my arms once again and approach the staircase. My headlamp casts a cool beam along the rock. The first few stairs lead straight away from the water, but soon the staircase twists and spirals upward through the stone. Dubbs feels heavier than ever, but I keep going, bracing my left elbow against the wall to steady me with each step. A faint breeze touches my cheeks, and then the flavor of the air becomes lighter. Fresher.

The stairs stop at a flat landing with an old ladder, and looking straight up a shaft where the ladder goes, I see a hint of light. Two hints, actually. Two distant circles of light.

I can't believe it's another ladder. Climbing one by myself is unnerving enough, but taking my sister up this seems impossible. I'm not strong enough, and I need both hands to climb. Yet I have to find a way. I can't leave her behind, not even for a minute to see what's above.

A drip falls with a plink somewhere nearby. I need a sling of some sort, but all I have are my clothes and hers. I try settling her over my shoulder to see if that will work, but we're top-heavy and awkward. I gingerly settle Dubbs at my feet so I can take my scrub pants off and wind them into a bulky rope. Then I wrap the rope around my back and over one shoulder. I hug Dubbs against my chest at an angle and tie the rope behind her, under her arms, so we're knotted into a hug. It's bad. One of her arms is awkwardly under my chin, but I can basically brace her weight on one leg at a time while I use my arms to reach up. In any case, if we fall, we'll fall together.

I take a deep breath and a last look up to the top, and then I start precariously climbing up the ladder with Dubbs. With my left knee bearing most of her weight and my left hand gripping tight to a rung, I can reach higher with my right hand to advance up once more. Then I do it again, and again. And again. I swear Dubbs gains ten pounds with each rung. Sweat breaks out all over me. Dubbs's head lolls back, into the ladder, and I have to bounce desperately to bring her face back against me. The ladder groans inauspiciously. We're only halfway up, and my muscles are already dying, but I call on my innate brute stubbornness and refuse to give up.

Rung over rung, I haul my sister higher. I think of nothing but the next grip, the next shift of her weight. I'm panting hard. Every muscle strains and burns, but I keep reaching up. I keep finding the next metal rung.

A shaft of white sunlight lands on my fingers. I'm getting close to the top. A wild, unexpected eagerness barrels around in my chest and sends my heart pounding so hard that I can barely breathe. I grit my teeth and hold tight to the ladder with both hands, but that's even worse. My muscles strain with pain.

"Stop this!" I say. "We have to get out!"

My inner stampede checks itself, and then a new infusion of strength surges through my muscles. My grip is suddenly strong, as if the force of my will has been forged into iron. I pull up on the next rung and keep going, rung over rung, until I reach the top of the ladder.

Two small circles of light, the size of my fists, greet me, and they're surrounded by a circle of smaller holes, too. I've reached the underside of a maintenance hole cover, and through the closest circle is a glimpse of pale, peachy sky.

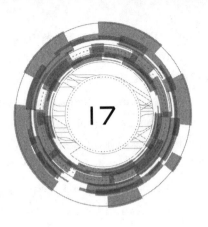

17

DOUBLE SCRUTINY

THE MAINTENANCE-HOLE lid is heavier than it looks. It takes me two tries to get the right leverage, and then I push it off with a grating, metallic sound. Mustering my last strength, I haul Dubbs out of the hole, and we collapse together on the ground. I'm utterly spent.

"We made it, Dubbs," I whisper, amazed.

I take a quick look around, but we're alone, and I'm happy for that, too. Smiling, I smooth the hair out of my sister's relaxed face. She's still sleeping, even though she's shivering in her wet gown. She has no idea what we've gone through, mercifully. I reach behind her to the knot in my scrubs pants, and twist it to where I can see it while I work the fabric free. When my sister and I come loose from each other, I sit up to put my damp pants back on.

Above, leaves rustle softly. We've arrived not in the middle of Grisly Valley, but in a small stand of eucalyptus trees near a deserted, decaying road. Bark peels in colorful, untidy strips from the tree trunks, and the dust is covered in the detritus of fragrant, dewy leaves. Fresh early-morning air carries a hint of the ocean moisture, and around every shadow, sunlight is landing with clear, almost painful precision.

A greedy, happy tingle lights up the back of my brain. I sniff and wipe my nose with the back of my wrist.

Yes, it's good to be alive, I think.

The tingling sensation sends an extra current, as if to confirm my thought. It's seriously strange. Unnerving, for sure. I've had some experience coexisting with another voice in my head, but this is a whole new level of strangeness.

It occurs to me as I rest there beside the maintenance-hole cover that I've just done something that I was physically incapable of doing. I'm not normally strong enough to carry Dubbs through a river with some kind of mutant fish creature, much less up a ladder like I just did. Besides, I should be weak from my captivity. I understand the strength of willpower and desperation, but that doesn't seem like enough to explain what I've just done. Is it possible, I wonder, that the new presence in the back of my mind helped me rescue Dubbs and escape?

"Can you talk to me?" I ask out loud. "I used to have another voice that could talk to me. Are you like that?"

A stillness answers me inside, an inner readiness. Then my fingertips start to tingle and grow light, like they've been released from gravity. Letting the sensation guide me, I lift my right hand off Dubbs, and I stroke my fingers along my forehead and down my cheek like I did once before in my cell. It seems like a deliberate response, but I can't guess what it means.

"Are you saying that's you?" I ask.

My hand comes to the base of my throat and rests there gently. Affirmative.

Okay, it's spooky. Definitely. My skin lifts in goose bumps. I'm not sure I want to believe it, actually. In any case, I can't sit around talking to myself and pawing my own face. It's only a matter of time before the doctors in the vault discover where I've gone.

Rising, I scoop Dubbs into my arms, and the full weight of her is a shock. I bite back a groan, and then I start along the old, pocked road. *I need to find my car*, I think, before I remember the doctors took it. I'll need to come up with a proper plan, but for now, putting distance between me and the park is the most important thing.

My wet socks pick up nubs of dirt as I trudge along. The road winds up a forested hillside through the OEZ. Leaves flicker in the occasional breeze, and plenty of insects wing through the shadows, but there's no sign of any birds or rodents. It feels strangely deserted. Too quiet.

Eventually, the road opens on a view of the Grisly Valley Theme Park, which is farther away than I expected. Once I have my bearings, I'm able to aim toward the outer fence of the OEZ, far in the distance. Once I'm there, I'll beg a stranger for help, I guess, and try to get a ride back to Lavinia's.

By the time I squeeze through a break in the last fence, I'm famished, and my arms can't bear my sister's weight anymore. I'm worried about her. She has stopped shivering, but her skin is pale and clammy, and she smells faintly sour, like an overripe peach. I haul her over to a shady spot under a tree and sit down with her in the grass. I just have to catch my breath. Gently, I rub my thumb over her eyelids, wiping away some of the gel.

The sound of a vehicle coming fast down the road makes me look up, and an old blue minivan slows to a stop across the road from me. I barely have time to take in the California plates and rust spots before the door opens and a young, dark-haired guy in a blue shirt and jeans gets out.

I stare, dumbfounded.

He's really Linus Pitts, as wiry and handsome as ever, and in the next moment, he's sprinting across the road toward me. An instinctive blip of joy soars through me before I can squash it wildly down.

"Thank goodness," he says, crouching beside me. "I was just about to go into the park and look for you. How is she? How are you?" With his familiar British cadence, his voice is frank and warm, as if he's forgotten how I left him. He gently touches a hand to Dubbs's face, and then his gaze lifts to meet mine. A potent mix of relief and concern emanates from his features, and it kills me to think of the spy in his eye. "What's happened to you?" he asks.

"I've been to the vault," I say. I barely got out. How'd you find me?"

"Lavinia sent me," he says. "I got to her place late last night. She's been watching the cameras you set up, and she said you completely disappeared on Tuesday." He points back along the fence. "I was just parking over there when I spotted you. Come on. Let's get out of here."

He starts to lift Dubbs out of my arms, but I stop him, holding her tight.

"Wait," I say. "Let me see your eye."

A slight hitch tightens his expression. "This is what matters right now?" he asks.

But he levels his face with mine and stares at me. Under the shade of the tree, I study his caramel-brown eyes, trying to see what's different from before. His right eye is normal, as clear and keen as ever, but his left pupil has a mismatched, dead quality, like the false lens of a machine. When he blinks, I become abruptly aware that he's scrutinizing me back.

"What did you do to it?" I ask.

"I had a cap put in. Don't worry. You're safe."

"You mean you can't see out of that eye?" I ask. "Not at all?"

"I couldn't very well live with a spy in my head," he says. He collects Dubbs firmly and rises. "Shall we?" He shifts into the sunshine and aims for the minivan.

He did it for me. I can't help thinking he did it for me, and I'm awed. He glances back my way.

"Coming?" he says.

I roll to my feet and follow him, trying to understand the sudden shift in his demeanor. It's subtle, but I can feel his shield of reserve like an invisible wall between us. He helps to settle me and Dubbs on the bench seat in the middle of the minivan, and never once does he meet my gaze again. The shadow of our last meeting has returned, and I didn't help by insisting to see his eye.

184

Linus starts up the engine and pulls out onto the road. Digging up a seat belt, I get it around Dubbs and me as best I can. Her lips are blue, and she's shivering again, so I try to keep her close. When we pass the place where I left my Toyota, it's gone. So much for all my gear. Berg's phone. Even though it had gone dead and I never used it, I liked knowing I'd taken something from him. Peggy's son's tablet is gone, too, and so are my clothes.

"Can you take us to Lavinia's?" I ask.

"That's where I was going, unless you think a hospital would be better," he says. "How bad is your sister?"

I look down at Dubbs again and stroke her pale cheek. How I need her to be okay. The smart move would be to take her to the hospital, I'm sure, but she might only need a little time to wake up, like I did after my sleep meds wore off. I certainly don't want anyone taking her away from me, and of course, the hospital authorities would ask a million questions. They'd get involved. They'd take over.

As I picture a team of police invading the vault of dreamers and disturbing them, I'm surprised by a new, powerful urge to protect the dreamers. A slither of warning passes through me, strong and personal, but it's totally counterintuitive. I used to want Berg's work to be exposed to the police. What's happened to me?

"Hospital?" Linus says.

"No," I say. "Lavinia's."

"You sure?"

"I think Dubbs will sleep it off," I say. "At least, I hope so."

"Okay."

Linus handles the big steering wheel in a generous, looping way, and I sway from side to side as he navigates around the potholes of the old road.

"Any word on your parents?" he asks.

"I couldn't find them," I say. "Berg must have them somewhere else."

He adjusts the rearview mirror and I catch his eye for an instant.

"We'll get them back," he says. "You know that, right?"

It's such a small word, *we*, but it gives me enormous relief to know that he's with me on this. I nod. "Yes," I say. "How did you find Lavinia?"

"Your sister asked me to track an email, and it led to Lavinia's IP address," he says. "That's how I found her place."

"*Dubbs* did?" I say, astonished. "Dubbs got in touch with you?"

"She guessed I'd be willing to help," he says, and slows for an old speed bump. "She and your parents were headed to Lavinia's before they dropped off the planet."

"I know. Dubbs left me Lavinia's address," I say.

"She was going to call me once they got to Miehana, but she never did," he says.

"Because she was kidnapped with my parents."

"So Lavinia told me."

I'm so impressed with my sister. She's such a smart little kid.

"Could Berg know about Lavinia's?" I ask, reconsidering if it will be safe to go there.

Linus drives around another curve, and trees blur by the

window. When we come to a stop sign, he breaks and lets the engine idle.

"I don't know what Berg knows," he says evenly.

"I'm sorry. I didn't mean it like that," I say. "I was only wondering if it's safe to go there."

"I wouldn't take you somewhere unsafe."

"I know that," I say. It's getting tangled with him again. I can't do this. I'm too tired and stressed. "Don't get all stiff at me, please," I say. "I was so happy to see you. I can still hardly believe you're here."

He turns back then to face me, his eyes watchful.

"Is that so," he says. "You could have called me, you know."

"I've been stuck in an underground cell."

"Before that," he says. "When you were on the road. Or at Lavinia's."

"But you had a camera in your eye."

Linus waits another moment, like I can read his mind, like I'm missing something huge and obvious. It's horrible. Then he faces forward again, eases the minivan into the intersection, and makes a right.

"I'm sorry," I say. "I should have called you."

"It's all right. I get it."

No, he doesn't. He can't understand me when I don't even understand myself. I lean back against the seat and close my eyes, weary to the bone. I remain that way, trying not to think, but at the edge of my mind, I recall the ache of longing I felt for Linus back when I was in my cell, when this thing inside me sent me the vision of us together on the prairie. The real

187

Linus is a thousand times more complicated. It shouldn't be possible to miss someone when he's right here in the car with me, but I do.

With my eyes closed and my heart plucked open, I don't notice where we're going until we descend a steep incline and pull up before a strange, unfamiliar cottage.

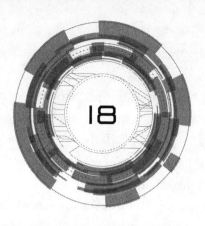

18

STAY OUT

WE'RE BY THE SEA. Even with the windows closed, I can hear the rumble of the ocean, and I'm instantly curious. I've always wanted to see the ocean.

Linus parks beside another car under an overhang made of coruscating plastic. Dark rows of pods and debris line its gullies. A nearby cottage, caked in peeling stucco, perches on a steep embankment, with stilts supporting one side. I'm disconcerted by a pair of signs nailed to the front porch.

CONDEMNED: EARTHQUAKE HAZARD

OLBAID EVACUATION ZONE. STAY OUT.

"I thought you were taking me to Lavinia's," I say.

Linus pulls the key out of the ignition. "This is her old place, from before she was relocated. She said we'd have more privacy here."

"Do you know how far we are from the power plant?"

"A couple miles."

I take another look at those rickety stilts. "Do you think it's safe?"

He tilts his head, peering out. "Comparatively." He turns back to face me and nods toward Dubbs. "How is she?"

"Still asleep."

"Hold on. I'll come around for her."

A moment later, he lifts my sister away from me, and he's careful to shelter her blond head against his shoulder as he straightens. His tenderness triggers a tug of longing in me, and I glance away. The sky has turned overcast, and the air is suffused with soft gray light. Far below, the shoreline churns with the lacy white lines of the incoming waves, and the horizon is so huge, it seems like an optical illusion, both distant and flat.

Stepping warily in my socks, I follow Linus around to the front porch where a rotting board gives under my feet but doesn't break. Before we can knock, the door opens, and Lavinia waves us in.

"You had me worried," she says. "Where'd you find them?"

"By the fence. They were on their way out," Linus says.

While Linus lays Dubbs gently on the couch, Lavinia holds a couple pillows, and then she tucks them around my sister and settles a creamy blanket over her wet gown. Lavinia leans over her to hold Dubbs's wrist for a pulse, and then, with a satisfied expression, she straightens.

"What do you think?" I ask her.

"She has a nice pulse. I think she's sleeping and she'll wake when she's ready," Lavinia says. "She has a sweet face. She's eight, you say?"

"Yes," I answer.

Lavinia turns her gaze to me, and I'm startled to find she's changed from when I last saw her in her apartment. She's brighter and clearer. Her gray hair is whiter, and her updo with the braid is looser, for a softer effect around her face. Her lipstick is a more muted, flattering hue, and she's wearing a pearly green, cottony outfit that brings out the color of her eyes behind her glasses. Her old home must agree with her.

A hovering seagull outside the window catches my eye before it drops from view. Lavinia's place isn't nearly as shabby inside as it is from the outside. I can tell it was once lovingly cared for. Pale blue walls are offset with white trim. Two folding beach chairs with woven seats face the curved wicker couch, while a wood-burning stove, darkly solid, sits in the corner. A wooden crate is overturned as a coffee table. Half a dozen glass balls of red, yellow, and blue hang in an old fishing net, and glass doors fogged with moisture close off a back porch that hangs directly over the steep escarpment.

The best thing, though, is the view to the water. Or maybe the soft, airy light. I can't decide which.

Lavinia sets a hand on my shoulder. "How about you?" she asks. "You look like you're about to fall over."

"I'm pretty wiped out," I admit. "How long was I gone?"

"Four nights," Lavinia says. "This is Saturday, April second."

"Four nights!" I echo, astounded and bereft.

They must have kept me asleep longer than I realized. And my parents! We still don't know where they are. Berg has had them since early Monday. That's six days!

"Have you heard anything about my parents?" I ask.

"I guess that means you didn't find them," Lavinia says grimly. "There's been nothing in the news."

I have to check Peggy's Facebook page. "Do you have a computer here?" I ask.

"Of course. Hang on," she says.

I sink down on the couch near Dubbs's feet, and as soon as Lavinia passes me her laptop and the slow Internet kicks in, I pull up Facebook and Peggy's profile. She has nothing new posted, and neither do her kids. Deflated, I push the laptop onto the crate and slump back.

"Nothing," I say. "I can't believe this."

"Tell us what you found at Grisly," Lavinia says, taking a seat in one of the folding chairs. Linus takes the other. "I saw that wild business with the dragon and your sister when you first arrived. Quite an effect," she says. "But then where did you go?"

It takes a while to tell them about my discovery of the vault of dreamers, and then my dark hours after I was caught. They're outraged to hear I've been mined again, and clearly impressed that I was able to escape, rescue Dubbs, and find a way out.

"But the biggest problem is that I still don't know where my parents are," I say, frustrated. "Whistler told me they weren't in the vault, but Lavinia and I saw the footage of the truck arriving at Grisly."

"Either Whistler was lying, or the truck dropped off Dubbs and took your parents somewhere else," Linus says.

"Why would Berg do that?" I ask.

"I'm not sure," Linus says. "Could he have known you were going to Grisly? Maybe he was worried you'd find them there."

"I never know what Berg knows," I say darkly. I hate mysteries.

With a faint click, Lavinia fingers her bead necklace. She juts her chin at me. "You did a good job setting up my cameras. Thank you."

"You're welcome," I say.

Beside me, Dubbs sniffs. She shifts to tuck her fist under her cheek in such a normal motion that it gives me hope.

"Dubbs? You awake?" I rub her arm lightly again, but she doesn't respond.

"She'd probably be better out of that wet gown. You might as well look through my drawers for whatever you can find for her and yourself as well," Lavinia says. She stands and reaches for her keys. "I'm going back for Tiny, but I won't be long." She nods at a cardboard box on the counter. "There's food and bottled water. My computer's battery should hold, but otherwise, there's no power in the house, and no water. I rigged a pully system for rainwater on the roof for the toilet, but that's it. Let's see. What else. I don't normally bring company out here. Do you know how to use a camp stove?"

"Yes," I say.

I'm uneasy about her leaving alone, though. Linus offers to go with her, but she won't hear of it.

"I shouldn't be more than two hours. Three, tops, if Tiny doesn't come right away," Lavinia says. "She does this now and again, sneaks off for a good prowl, but with this rain coming, she'll probably be waiting on the fire escape when I get back." She frowns at me. "Are you thinking of calling Berg?"

My gut turns cold. He's the one with answers about my parents. "I have to think about it," I say.

I glance at Linus, but he doesn't say anything.

"All right, then," Lavinia says. She waves her fingers in her silvery way again. "Look after that little girl. I'll be back soon."

The door closes softly behind her, and the quiet of the cottage settles in over the rolling noise of the waves below. She's probably right that we should change into dry clothes, but I don't even want to move. The thought of calling Berg makes me ill. I settle back on the couch with one hand on Dubbs's blanket, and I look across at Linus. He runs a hand back through his dark hair, and then shucks off his shoes so they topple to the side.

"Berg authorized my mining," I say. "He knew I was in the vault. He could have killed my parents by now."

"You can't think like that," Linus says.

"He thought they had me secure," I say.

"But he didn't mine you himself," Linus says. "Isn't that what he wants?"

I frown, considering. Linus might well be right. I can imagine Berg using my parents and threatening them to terrify me, and then following my fear into my dreams. Berg did say he had some plan for a host body for his hybrid and it was taking some time to line that up.

"It's impossible to guess what he's scheming," I say.

"Then you have to have hope," Linus says. "We have to assume your parents are still alive."

"Somewhere," I say.

"Yes. Somewhere."

I feel like I'm missing something, like I should know where they are. I was so sure they'd be in the vault. I shake my head, frustrated again. Six days. Where could they be? Berg has to know I'll keep looking for them.

Linus sets his hands on his knees and pushes up to standing.

"Hungry?" he asks.

I am. I'm starved. And my damp clothes are getting smelly. I should really change before I eat. I'm so sore and stiff that getting up is going to be awful. What I wouldn't give for a hot shower.

"I need to change. Help me up?" I say.

He steps over and reaches out both hands to me. I grip his fingers, and he hauls me smoothly to my feet. That should be the end of it, but his fingers are so warm, I don't want to let go. Energy lights up in my lungs, and I lift my gaze to his. He tilts his head, eyeing me in quiet speculation, and then he drops his gaze toward our joined hands. He hasn't kissed me yet. Surely he must notice.

When he lightly releases me and steps back, a jolt of disappointment rocks me to my socks. *Say something*, I tell myself, but I don't know what.

"I'll just get my suitcase from the car," he says. "There might be something you can use."

"Are we—?" I begin uncertainly.

He regards me doubtfully. "Are we what?"

"I don't know," I say. "Okay?"

"You're ready to talk about us?"

Actually, I'm not. I'm a total coward when it comes to us.

If we have to talk about us, we're a problem, and I absolutely don't want that. "What is there to say?" I ask.

He squints briefly and turns toward the door. "Exactly," he says. "I'll be right back."

He heads outside, and I bolt for the bathroom.

What is wrong with me? I think. He isn't kissing me. So what? He must have his reasons. Life isn't all about kisses.

Except maybe it is.

No. Stop this.

A plastic gallon of water rests next to the bathroom sink, and I wash up as best I can. By the time I move into Lavinia's room, a small brown duffel has appeared on the bed. I look through Linus's things and set aside a shirt for Dubbs to use later, but he doesn't have much to begin with and I don't want to use up his clean things if I don't have to. Lavinia has a small closet with a curtain drawn across it, and inside is a small dresser with three drawers. The top one has folded sheets, a box of safety pins, and a bar of French milled soap, almost scentless now it's so old. The next has a few sweatshirts, a couple nighties, and an assortment of swimsuits with brittle, loose elastic. In the bottom drawer, I find a pair of men's cotton pajamas with little blue sailboats on them. Score. The waistband is way too big, but that's what safety pins are for.

By the time I'm comfy in rolled-up pajama pants and a red sweatshirt, Linus has some soup warming on the little camp stove in the kitchen. He glances at my attire without comment. I grab Lavinia's laptop and curl up next to Dubbs again. It worries me that she's still in damp clothes, but she seems warm and comfortable enough.

I wait out the slowness of the Internet, and soon I'm into my Tor site where, sure enough, there's a message from Burnham.

From: BurnFist51
To: LKRose
Sent: Tues 3/29/67 10:29 PM
Subject: FW: Hey
Tried to call you. I talked to Thea. Amazeballs. Call me.

From: BurnFist51
To: LKRose
Sent: Tues 3/29/67 11:02 PM
Subject: FW: Hey
Where are you? We need to talk. Thea wants you to call her, too.

The messages are both dated late Tuesday, the same day we last talked, I realize. He's probably worried about me. I look up to find Linus watching me.

"Bad news?" he asks.

"No. I just need to call Thea and Burnham. Do you have any recyclable phones?"

He pulls out his phone and starts tapping. "I don't have any recyclables, but I can route you through a proxy. It'll be secure that way."

"I don't think so," I say. "I heard the doctors talking down in the vault and they said Berg was tracing all your calls. They even knew you'd called an ophthalmologist."

"That's from my other line," he says. "I keep one going that

I know they tap, like a decoy. I call for pizza and stuff on it. I've upgraded my security again for important calls, and I go through a proxy. It's secure, I promise you." He listens for a second, and then passes the phone to me. "Go ahead. Dial up."

I have to refer back to my earlier emails with Burnham to find Thea's number, and then I dial.

When Thea comes on, she sounds anxious.

"Rosie?" she asks. "Are you okay?"

"I'm good," I say. "I have Dubbs. She's sleeping, but I think she'll be all right."

Thea lets out a huge breath of relief. "Thank goodness! Can you bring her here? What about Ma and Larry?"

"I haven't found them yet," I say. "I hit a few snags." I fill her in about Grisly Valley and my time in the vault of dreamers. She wants all the details, and I go over everything I can remember, ending with my escape with Dubbs up the ladder. The only thing I leave out is the new presence in my brain that showed up after they mined me. It's been dormant lately, and I'd be glad if it stayed that way. "I'm with Linus now. We're staying at a friend's house."

Linus wordlessly offers me a bowl of soup, and when I glance up, I see he's listening carefully to my end of the conversation. I take the bowl but set it on the overturned crate.

"How long were you actually down in the vault?" Thea asks. "I've been trying to reach you for days."

"Since Tuesday," I say.

"I can't believe you were mined again," Thea says. "I'm so sorry. I wish you'd come here. Bring Dubbs and come. I promise you'll be safe, both of you."

"About that. When I was down in the vault, I overheard a conversation between the doctors and Berg. It sounded like your parents invited a doctor over from Chimera to check on you. I wouldn't trust him one bit. He's there to mine your dreams."

A light patter sounds on the roof, and I glance out to see the rain has started.

"You mean Orson. Orson Toomey," she says slowly.

"That sounds right."

"What else did Berg say about him?"

"Nothing, why?"

Linus is sitting opposite me in the beach chair again, quietly consuming his soup. He holds it close beneath his chin.

"We're family, right?" Thea says. "We'll always be family, no matter what. Don't you agree?"

"For lack of a closer word," I say dryly. "What's going on?"

"There's something I need to tell you," she says, with a note of dread in her voice. "I should have told you days ago, but I never had the right chance."

I can't imagine what it might be. "I'm listening," I say.

"It's about Dad," she says. "Not Larry. Dad."

I'm surprised she'd bring him up. She knows how much we don't like to talk about him. I tuck my free hand under my leg. "Go on."

"It turns out someone found his body," she says. "He was recovered from an icy crevasse a few years ago in Greenland, but the people who found him never reported it to the authorities. They were scavengers. They sold his frozen body to a research facility in Iceland, and those scientists never reported him, either."

199

A dark, ugly idea starts to form in my mind.

"Wait," I say. "Just hold on. Not the Chimera Centre."

"Yes," she says.

"And then what? Didn't he still have his uniform?" I ask. I'm picturing his frosty corpse laid out on an operating table. "They experimented on him, didn't they. Is that what you're telling me?"

Linus is still in the chair opposite me, but he has set aside his soup, and he's leaning forward tensely, his elbows on his knees.

"It's more than that," Thea says quietly. "A doctor at Chimera seeded a dream into Dad, and he woke up. He became alive again, only he wasn't our dad anymore. He had a different mind inside him, the mind of his seed donor. Like me."

I almost laugh. It isn't possible. What are the chances this happened to two of us from the same family?

"I don't believe this," I say.

"Rosie, listen. I know it seems impossible, but it's true. I've met him. I've talked to him."

"You've talked to him!" I shriek. I can't be hearing this. I pull my feet up onto the couch and curl into a tight ball. I shake my head, refusing. He was dead. How can he be alive?

"Rosie?" Thea asks.

I can barely hear her. It's hard to breathe.

"No," I say flatly.

"I know it's a lot to take in," she says. "I was shocked, too."

I let out a laugh. Shock doesn't begin to describe it. "You're completely serious," I say.

"Yes. On my life."

I glance across at Linus, barely seeing him.

"And how long have you known this?" I ask.

"Since I was at Chimera. I found out there," she says.

"Months ago?" I ask, my mind reeling anew. "And you kept this to yourself? What's he like? What did you say when you talked to him?"

"He looks a lot like Dad, only a little older," Thea says. "Same dark hair. Same eyes and nose and everything, but he isn't Dad. You'd know that immediately if you met him. He doesn't laugh like him or say what Dad would say. He's a stranger. A doctor."

And now it falls together. "From Chimera," I say.

"Yes," Thea says. "I guess he's more of a scientist. He does the research experiments in the lab. He's the one who developed the method for putting your dream seed into me, the one that expanded and took over. He's the one staying here at the ranch with us now."

"Unbelievable. Why on earth would you trust him?"

"I don't, but my parents do," she says. "He saved my life, Rosie. It's complicated."

Dumbfounded, I try to grasp all that she's telling me, but it's too much. This is my dad we're talking about, my own father. The pain of missing him has sunk into the dirt of me, the subterranean, fatherless mire of me. I may not examine it often, but the loss is as raw and strong as ever.

And now he's alive? But not really alive? And he's actually staying at her ranch?

"Why didn't he call us?" I whisper. "He should have told us, me and Ma."

201

"He thought it would be better not to," Thea says. "More merciful, instead of opening old wounds. I'm not saying I agree with him, but that was his reasoning."

But you did the same thing, I think. *You didn't tell, either.*

"Please don't be mad at me," Thea adds. "I wanted to tell you. I just didn't know how. It was a shock for me, too."

"Hey," Linus says gently. He's hitched his chair nearer.

"She's telling me my father's alive, sort of," I say to him, dazed. "He's an evil scientist now."

From his sympathetic expression, I see he's been following my end of the conversation.

"He can't hurt you," Linus says. "It's going to be okay."

"Is Linus there?" Thea asks.

"Of course," I say, and I hold the phone blindly away from me for him to take.

Linus moves to the other end of the room, near the little black stove, and when he speaks, it's into the phone. "It's me," Linus says. "Hold on. Slow down."

His voice is the same, like he sounds when he's talking to me. Another cruel surprise.

"Yes," he says. "That's a good idea. Okay. I'll tell her, of course." And then, "Don't cry, Thea. She'll understand. It's not your fault."

It is her fault. It's all her fault.

"Does Ma know?" I say. "Ask her, Linus. Does Ma know?"

Linus looks back at me, and then asks the question into the phone. He glances at me again and shakes his head. "No. Your mother doesn't know."

It's going to destroy her. Bad as it is for me, it's going to be even worse for her. She isn't going to understand who he is. Nevertheless, she'll have to be told. It'll fall to me to tell her. I can see that now.

If she's still alive.

Wouldn't it be something, I think, if my mother's dead, and the doctor in my father's body seeds a new mind into my mother's body? Wouldn't they make a fabulous pair?

I let out one horrible, ugly sob before I clamp my hands over my mouth.

I miss my dad. I miss his goofy laugh. I miss how safe I felt with him. After all this time, I can hardly bear to scratch the surface of my memories of him because the hurt is too deep. And now I could actually see him walking around, alive?

My left hand loosens from my grip and through no effort of my own, my fingers stroke slowly down my cheek. I get that this thing inside me is trying to comfort me again, but it's way too much for me to handle right now. Way too much.

"Stop that!" I say sharply. "I won't be screwed up. I'm sick of this!"

My fingers still. The tingling stops. Then it grows stronger again, stronger than before, like a burning. It's insistent and angry, the way I feel myself, and suddenly I'm stronger. Certain. A kick of adrenaline burns through my veins, forcing me to my feet. I leave the couch and step over to the porch door, where a film of moisture still coats the glass. My right hand lifts of its own volition, and my index finger traces six capital letters in the cool gray moisture: A-R-S-E-L-F.

My hand tingles as it drops away. I stare at the word. It's a name.

"Arself," I murmur, testing the sounds.

A light flashes behind my eyelids and a rushing fills my ears. I stagger back, still staring at the name on the glass. I can hardly breathe. It's like getting ripped to shreds and being put precisely together at the same time.

"Rosie, what's wrong?" Linus says. "What's happening?"

But I can't answer him.

Can you hear me now? says a voice in my head.

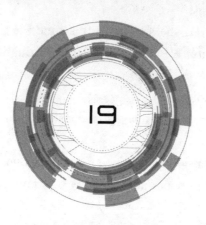

19

ARSELF

THE VOICE HAS AN ETHEREAL, hollow sound, like it's coming from the end of a canyon or the bottom of a well. It's mesmerizing and terrifying both.

Who are you? I ask.

"Rosie, what's going on?" Linus asks, coming near. "Look at me."

My heart is pounding and tightening in vicious ways. I back away from Linus and slide down the wall to sit on the floor. I press a fist to my chest, hard against my ribs, and suddenly the tight pain in my heart stops. Relief trickles through me like soft blue water, allowing me to breathe again.

Linus has joined me on the floor. I'm aware that he's speaking to me, but I barely listen to him. The presence is active in my mind again, and I need to concentrate.

This is better, she says, and this time the voice is closer, more immediate. **We knew you'd let us through eventually.**

I didn't let you through, I say.

You called our name.

An extra circuit of power is lacing slowly through my veins and muscles.

Three dimensions. So heavy! How does this work?

Invisible strings jerk at my elbows. My jaw works open and closed.

Hey, stop that! I say.

She sends a spiraling, giddy sensation through me, and an instant later, I laugh.

Linus frowns at me. "Rosie? Can you hear me? Say something."

Get out of me! I say.

Instead, she balls into a heaviness that travels distinctly down my right arm.

So clumsy, but so perfect, too, she says.

I lift my hand and turn it before my face. As if a bright, new light is illuminating each cell, I notice the little creases that separate each section of my fingers. When I curve my fingers together, my palm creates a perfect little nest for water or berries.

Berries, she says. **We want to taste raspberries fresh from a summer bush. Where? How far?**

Would you listen to me? I ask.

A skittering shifts through my brain like fast hands through a pile of laundry, followed by a confused sense of alarm.

We're cut off. We don't know anything! How does she stand it?

The next search is more serious. My mind is actively frisked as every book in my mental library is taken out and shaken. The search is completed almost before I know it's begun, and I'm left breathless, dizzy.

It's okay. We can still do this, she says. **It's so personal. So immediate and sensory. That's the trade-off. And what's this?**

I feel a plinking of strings at the back of my mind, like she's testing the taut wires of a harpsichord.

Stop that! I say.

How do we turn her off? Is it this?

A slash of pain rips through my head and I gasp, paralyzed.

"Rosie!" Linus says. He gives my shoulders a shake. "You're having a nightmare. Wake up."

I manage to peer directly, desperately into his good eye.

"Help me," I whisper.

With a jerk, Linus lifts me bodily and carries me out the door to the porch. Cold rain slams down on me, drenching me completely. Shocked, I suck in air, and my senses smack back on. The voice is gone. I'm alone again in my head. With both hands, I clutch Linus's shirt. He lowers me until my socks meet the wet floorboards of the porch, and then he locks me close against him. My wet sweatshirt plasters thin to my chest. I can feel his belt buckle between us and the plane of his torso where we meet.

"Better?" Linus asks, searching into me.

He's so near, I can see the rain clumping his dark eyelashes into spikes.

I nod.

"Let's just be sure," he says, and dips even nearer.

As I feel his lips meet mine, a ripple of happiness spirals through me. My eyes close, and I hold him tight. Rain is pouring down on both of us, but I don't care. I gulp a big breath of air between raindrops and kiss him again. He is one strong, solid pillar in a haze of scary uncertainty, and I don't want to ever let him go.

He squeezes me tighter, and then loosens his arms enough to meet my gaze.

"What *was* that?" he asks.

"A kiss?"

He laughs. "I mean before. You looked like you were in a trance. Could you hear me at all?"

"Not really," I say, shivering reflexively at the memory. I feel like I barely escaped. "This thing completely took over me. It controlled my muscles like I was a puppet. It wanted to turn me off."

"Did they seed a dream into you when you were down in the vault?" Linus asks.

"Whistler said they'd never do that, but it was *something*. I felt it before, back in the vault, but it didn't control me then."

"Is it gone now?" he asks.

I listen inside a second, hearing only silence. Then I nod again.

"You were pretty upset about your dad. Could that have triggered it?" he asks.

"I have no idea. I guess it's possible," I say. "It said I let it through. It talked like I was no more than a pesky fly, and it wouldn't answer any of my questions. It was terrifying."

"But you're okay now?"

I sniff hard and bite my lips inward, tasting the rain and the tenderness left from his kiss. "Yes," I say. "A little freaked out and wet, but at least I'm me."

He laces his fingers in mine. I can hear the surf pounding below, and the rain falls in solid gray sheets around us.

"Let's get inside." Linus tugs me back toward the door, and we go back in.

As I close the door, shutting out the noise of the rain, my gaze goes instinctively back to where ARSELF is still written in the steam on the glass. Could the voice really have just been waiting for me to say its name? I swipe the letters clear with my hand. Then I stay where I am, plucking at my soaked clothes and dripping on the wooden floor while Linus runs to the bathroom. He reappears with a couple of towels, and I dry off as well as I can. I can't believe I've managed to get my borrowed clothes all wet, too. I hug my towel around me, pulling the cottony nubs against my neck.

Linus pulls off his shirt before he dries off, too. He catches me looking and lifts his eyebrows. "You don't mind, do you?"

"No." But, naturally, I start blushing.

He smiles. "You could take your clothes off, too," he says.

"What is it with you?" I ask. "My sister's right here."

I glance toward the couch, and at that moment, Dubbs turns her head and opens heavy-lidded eyes.

"Rosie?" she says in a voice thick with sleep.

Joy spikes in my heart. I sink to the rug beside the couch and lightly smooth her hair back from her pink cheek. "Hey, girl," I say. "I'm right here. How're you doing?"

She tightens her grip on her blanket and shifts her gaze around the room. "Where are we?" she asks, frowning.

I am so happy to have her awake and speaking like normal that I have to kiss her and ruffle her hair. "We're in California, thanks to you," I say. "You left me a secret note, remember? You know Linus, I think."

He has discreetly pulled his wet shirt back on.

"Hi," he says.

Dubbs pushes up on one elbow. "Is this two forty Mallorca Way?"

"No," I say. "We're at a friend's house by the ocean. We're safe. How much do you remember?"

She scratches a hand in her hair and then draws one of her blond curls into her mouth. "We were in Las Vegas, camping," she says. Her eyes search the room again. "Where's Ma and Daddy?"

"We're working on that," I say. "I'm sure they're just fine. We're tracking them down."

Dubbs sits up further and puts her arms around me, leaning her nose against my neck. "I want to go home, Rosie," she says. "That's a fact."

"I know," I say. "Me, too."

"You're all wet," she says, drawing back again.

I laugh. "I was out in the rain."

She looks suspiciously toward Linus. "He's wet, too."

Smiling, Linus tosses his wet towel into her lap. "So are you. Or damp, at least."

With a surprised look, she touches a hand to her belly. Then she shoves his towel to the floor, tugs away her blanket, and lifts her gown to expose the catheter that's coming out of her lower abdomen.

"What's this?" she asks, her voice going shrill. *"What is this thing?"*

"It's okay. Calm down," I say, taking her hands. "It's a catheter. I can take it out. I had one myself once, and it came right out."

Her eyes go wide with fear. "What happened to me? Where's Ma?"

"Listen, I need you to take a deep breath," I say calmly. "We've had some trouble. I won't lie. But for now we're okay, and that's what matters. I need you to be brave and not panic, okay?"

She looks toward Linus and then around the room before she focuses on me again. "Are we going to die?"

"No. Of course not," I say. "Why would you say that? Nobody's dying."

"Okay," she says. Her eyes are still huge. "Okay, but you have to tell me everything. I want to know."

"I will. I promise," I say. "How about if we get this out of you first? All right?"

She nods. "Just get it out. I don't want to look."

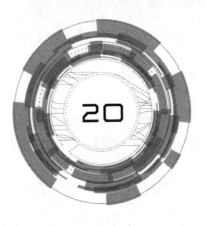

PHANTOM AUDIENCE

WE HEAD INTO THE BATHROOM, Dubbs and I, and I'm careful snipping the threads to her catheter and drawing it out. I show her the tiny scar where I took a similar catheter out of myself, and I promise hers will heal, too. Then, very calmly, I show her my port lump in my chest. When she discovers she has one, too, she freaks out again, and we have a very bad half hour. Eventually, we put a Band-Aid over her port lump, and she makes me put one over mine, too. She's teary-eyed and anxious, but she agrees to try to be brave, and we're able to make it out of the bathroom.

In Lavinia's room, Dubbs changes into the blue shirt I found in Linus's duffel. It's the length of a minidress on her, and she layers it with the sailboat pajama top. She's all skinny legs and knees, but I can tell by the way she twists and models in front of the mirror that she's feeling a little better. I exchange my rain-soaked sweatshirt and pajama bottoms for a red sweater and my old scrubs pants, which are now practically dry.

When we return to the living room, I see Linus has changed, too, and his shorts and a gray shirt look comfortable. His knees make me smile. He has noodles boiling for mac 'n' cheese, and I move around him, gathering bowls and silverware to set the table on the crate by the couch. As I pour water in three mugs, the simple, normal activity feels sort of homey. Dubbs gets busy folding paper towels into triangles for napkins.

"What is this place, anyway?" Dubbs says.

I don't want to scare her, but I promised I'd tell her everything, so I start back with how I went to the boxcars and found our family gone. I tell her how her secret note led me to Lavinia, and how I ended up in the vault of dreamers under Grisly where I found her. Watching Dubbs all along, I'm wary for any sign of fear, but she takes in the story as if the events were all one step removed from her. "You don't remember anything from being in the vault?" I ask.

She climbs on the couch beside me. "No, and I'm glad. When can I get my port out again?"

"Soon," I say. "As soon as we find Ma and Larry. Now, what can you tell me about them? When's the last time you saw them?"

Her eyebrows lift in surprised discovery. "At Grisly," she says. "I didn't know where we were, but that has to be it."

I feel a jolt of eagerness. Linus comes around from the kitchen to listen.

"What do you mean? How do you know?" I ask Dubbs.

"I saw the stores. A row of stores," she says. "I couldn't see much because it was dark, but I looked out of the truck and I saw this row of colorful stores. I thought it was a fake mall or something."

"Were Ma and Larry with you then?"

She shakes her head. "No. They were gone. First the guys took out Daddy. He was still asleep. Then they came back a little later for Ma, and she was still asleep, too. I was looking for a chance to run away, but I couldn't get out. They locked the door."

"How many guys? Do you know what they looked like?" Linus asks.

"There were two guys. They had masks on the whole time," she says.

"Can you remember anything else?" I prompt her gently. "Did you see any signs or anything? Did you see any rides?"

She scrunches up her face and then shakes her head again. "No, but it felt spooky. Really spooky. After that, they came back and gave me another shot."

"You were so brave," I say. "You know that, right?"

She hugs her knees to her chest. "I guess. Yeah."

I give her arm a squeeze. Already, I'm casting about in my mind, trying to think where the men might have stashed my parents. A row of shops means the truck could have been parked along the Main Drag.

"Linus," I say. "We have to go back."

"I'm coming, too," Dubbs says.

The complications start cropping up. We need somewhere safe for Dubbs to stay and someone to look after her. We'll have to search the park and watch out for Berg.

"Linus!" I say.

"I know," he says evenly. "We just have to think it all through. It could still be someplace else."

I glare at him. It is not someplace else. But he slants his eyes quickly toward Dubbs in a sharp signal, and I realize she's hunched in a tight ball and she's pulling the neckline of her shirt up over her nose.

"Hey," I say. "We're going to get them back. You don't have to worry, you hear me?"

"Don't leave me," she says.

"I'm not going to leave you," I say firmly. I grab an arm around her neck and rock her against me. "You're going to be safe. Nobody's taking you ever again. We're going to keep being brave, right?"

She takes a shaky breath. Then she snuggles even closer to me and pulls my head so that my ear is near her mouth. She's actually breathing into it.

"What is it?" I say. "Tell me."

"When you never came home, I thought you were dead," she whispers.

I shift to put my mouth by her ear, cupping my hand around my voice. "I'm not dead," I say softly. "Dead people can't eat your hair." I go for a teasing bite, and she squirms away, laughing.

›››››››››

Linus has made two boxes of mac 'n' cheese, so there's plenty. We have raw baby carrots, too, and whole dill pickles. The noodles are rich and comforting with their little curved elbow shapes, and I savor each mouthful.

215

"You're a good cook," Dubbs tells him.

"Thank you."

She likes to poke the tines of her fork into the holes of the noodles. "I used to see you sometimes back in the kitchen on *The Forge Show*," she says. "They should have given you your own feed."

"That's very nice of you," he says.

I smile.

"Why'd you really get hit in the eye that time?" she asks. "Just before you met Rosie."

"That isn't really when I met her," he says.

"It was," Dubbs says. "It was the day of the fifty cuts."

"No, I met her before that, when she was moving in," he says. "She just didn't notice me."

Dubbs looks surprised, then suspicious. "I have to go back and watch that," she says.

I laugh. "You can believe Linus," I say. "He was there." He and I have been over this before.

"Our conversation went like this," he says. "Me: Hi. Welcome to Forge. Need a hand with your bag? Rosie: Sure, thanks. It's kind of heavy. Me: No problem. That was it. The whole thing. It's burned into my memory."

Dubbs giggles and tucks her feet under her on the couch. "Then why'd you help Rosie stay on the show?" she asks. "She wouldn't have passed the fifty cuts without you. Did you like her?"

"Dubbs," I say warningly.

Linus pushes his fork around his mac 'n' cheese and smiles

at her. "Of course I liked her. She was different. She was nice." His beach chair creaks as he shifts in it. "She still is, sometimes."

"Hey," I say.

"Did she tell you about Daddy?" Dubbs asks him.

A flare of alarm lights in my chest. Linus looks at me curiously.

"No," he says. "What about him?"

I nudge Dubbs with my elbow, and she shoots me an abashed look. She should know better than to talk about Larry. "It's just that he didn't believe I'd make it at Forge," I say. "He was sure I'd get cut."

Linus looks from me to Dubbs and back. "Well, he was wrong," he says. "You'd have made it to first place if you'd stayed on the show."

"That's what I think," Dubbs agrees. She crunches on a carrot, and then she leans back, sending her gaze toward the windows. "I want to go down to the beach," she says, and yawns.

I look out at the gray weather. The rain has stopped, and a heavy mist hangs in the air. I'm starting to wonder where Lavinia is.

"You sure?" I say to Dubbs. "You look like you could use a nap."

"Beach," she says decisively.

>>>>>>>>>

I've seen pictures and movies of the beach, but nothing has prepared me for the first time I step off the rugged path and sink barefoot into the dark sand. It's a savage beach, with the cliff behind us and loud, heavy waves that crash against a steep shoreline. For once, I want to ignore my worries about my parents and appreciate something bigger and wilder than anything I've ever seen. Dubbs runs ahead of me toward the water and instantly I'm scared that my voice won't be loud enough to reach her over the sound of the water.

"Dubbs! Don't go too far!" I shout, and my voice comes back to me.

But she turns, smiling, to wave both arms. "Isn't this great?" she calls, and though her voice is muffled, too, her happiness is contagious. "Come on!" she beckons.

I run heavily over the sand to hold hands with her. We grip tight and line up our feet at the edge where the last wave shrank away. We watch the next one approach, tense with anticipation, and when the icy water rushes up around our ankles, we both scream and run backward, splashing.

Linus laughs at us.

I have to do it again. Dubbs tightens her grip on my hand, and we cavort back to the water's edge. It's a ridiculous game, but I'm jubilant. The waves are pure color and sound rolling toward me. Grays, blues, and glistening light roll into one massive crash after another. Moisture hangs in the air like a layer of shimmery magic, turning the sunlight into a new, tangible substance, and every breath brings a taste of salt and some weedy decay.

Linus takes Dubbs's other hand, and we try jumping the waves as they reach us.

We are not swimming. We discussed this on the way down. But the hem of Dubbs's borrowed shirt is soon dark with water, and my rolled-up pants are wet at the knees. Below his shorts, Linus's bare legs are wet, too. I look along the beach for other people, but the sand is deserted in both directions, and considering where we are, on the edge of the OEZ, I doubt other people will be coming.

Another wave washes in, bigger than the others, and Dubbs squeals with laughter as she drops my hand and runs to higher ground. Following her footsteps, I'm chilled already, and salty sand clings to my legs. As Dubbs crouches on her haunches to inspect something in the sand, the wind tousles her blond hair. Then she picks up a stick of driftwood and starts strolling down the beach without bothering to look back for me and Linus.

"Wait up!" I call.

"She's fine," Linus says, pitching his voice so I can hear him easily over the surf. When we fall into step together, he dodges lightly around me to walk on my left side.

"So I can see you," he says.

I put a hand on his arm and make him stop so I can look at his eyes again, this time more carefully. In the brightness by the water, the difference between his eyes is more pronounced, and the fixed, glassy black dot over his left pupil is distinctly bigger than his right one. His good eye, his right, looks far more alive. From now on, I'll make a point of looking directly at that one.

Suddenly, I register the frank way he's watching me back.

"It's all right. Look your fill," he says.

My fingers tingle. I'd love to cover his left eye with the palm of my hand like I did in my vision. Will I ever do that in real life?

"Does it hurt?" I ask.

"No," he says. "My depth perception is off, but it's getting better as I get used to one eye. I have another appointment with the doctor in September. She's supposed to take the camera out then. If it works, I'll be back to normal."

"Really? That would be great," I say.

"It would," he says, and starts walking again.

Glancing ahead to see that Dubbs is fine, I go with him.

"I'm sorry I was so suspicious of you back when we realized about your eye," I say.

"It was a lot to take in," he says. "After you left me, I went back to town, and the first thing I did was pick up a patch to cover my eye. I thought it would help, but it only made me more conscious every second of everything the spy was seeing, all the minutia. I went to help Parker shave, and I thought, *The spy knows about this*. I didn't want to believe it, but it was the only thing that made sense." He shakes his head briefly. "The spy knows about this. The spy knows about that. It infuriates me when I think about it too much. I'm still hyperaware of everything I'm doing, like Berg's a filter over my vision even though I've blocked him out."

"You have a phantom audience," I say.

He frowns at me curiously. "How's that?"

"It's not quite the same," I say. "I think yours is worse, far worse actually, but people who've been on *Forge* keep feeling cameras watching them even after they're not on the show anymore."

"It's intolerable."

The coldness of his voice startles me, and I feel my tension returning. "I'm really sorry," I say.

"It's not your fault," he says. "You know, saving your parents isn't going to be enough. You said it yourself once. If we don't get rid of Berg, you'll never be free of him. Neither will I."

I'm shocked to hear him say it out loud. "You'd actually kill him?"

Linus turns his face away, squinting toward the horizon. "I don't know what I'm saying." A long moment later, he returns his gaze to me and smiles oddly. "Do you ever wonder if *The Forge Show* was just practice for the real world?"

"Like we're still on the show, only now it's everywhere?" I ask.

He nods.

"Yes," I say.

I'm still processing the way he implied he'd be willing to kill Berg. I keep thinking I know Linus, but I'm not sure what this says about him.

I glance toward the cliffs, gauging them for possible cameras, but that would be absurd. Fifty yards ahead, a fence and a tumble of wooden beams scar a patch of the steep slope, and it's easy to guess that a cottage once clung above the tumble. The beach below, however, is perfectly clear. The ruin has been fully swept away by long-gone waves.

I look ahead to where Dubbs is playing, and I twist my feet in the sand as we follow.

"As soon as Lavinia returns, I want to go back to Grisly and look for my parents," I say. "What do you suppose is keeping her?"

"I don't know."

Beside me, Linus pauses to look at something on the bottom

of his foot. Then he keeps walking. "If you want to talk about your dad, I'll listen."

"You mean my real dad, or Larry?"

"Either," he says.

I can still barely believe what Thea told me. I don't want to go there. When I got upset before, it helped Arself come forward.

"There's nothing special about Larry," I say. "He's just a dick."

"Then what did Dubbs mean up there, before?"

I was afraid Linus caught that. It's hard to figure out what to say. I don't know if Linus remembers, but he asked me once before if Larry ever hit me. I lied then.

"He hits me some," I say. "He has a temper. He's the reason why I couldn't wait to leave home."

Linus comes to a stop, and I know he's looking at me, but I keep my gaze down the beach, toward Dubbs.

"Does your mother know?" he asks.

"Yeah. She tries to stop him, but she thinks I aggravate him." I let out a laugh. "I do, by existing."

"This isn't good," Linus says.

Tell me about it, I think. The breeze blows a strand of hair in my mouth, and I pull it out, tasting salt.

"I'll beat his brains out if he ever touches you again," he says. "But you still want to save him?"

I shrug. "Maybe he'll be nicer after I do."

"You can't be serious."

"I don't know," I say, and nod in my sister's direction. "Ma loves him and he's good to Dubbs." I really don't want to think about him and I'm glad Linus doesn't press me further. "Let's catch up."

When we do, Dubbs has collected a little pile of smooth, black stones, and she passes me a cool one that fits in the inner circle of my palm. It triggers a sense of familiarity, and a second later I recall picking a similar stone out of the box in DeCoster's class at Forge. Burnham chose the same kind, too. Funny. I recall how I wanted to visit an ocean then, and now, here I am. How strange the way things loop around.

"Take a picture," Dubbs says.

"I left my phone upstairs," Linus says.

"That's okay," she says, and tosses the stone aside. "We'll just remember." She runs off ahead of us again, never going too far. She's the very picture of a free spirit, with the sunlight in her hair and her skinny, limber limbs. I glance back the way we came on the chance Lavinia has arrived and come looking for us, but the beach is bare.

"You like the shore?" Linus asks, lifting his face to the sun.

"It's gorgeous."

"My family used to visit the shore back in Wales," he says. "We'd take a picnic and spend the day making castles and telling stories. I loved that."

"What kind of stories?" I say.

"Made-up ones."

"Like what? Tell me one."

His mouth smiles while his eyes frown, and then he takes my hand in his.

"There once was a fish that lived in the sea, back when the sea was new," he says. "That's how my dad always began."

"I'm impressed already."

As he talks, I pick my way along the sandy shore beside him.

"This fish was curious about the light at the top of the world, up where the water met the air," Linus says. "He didn't understand what air was, though. To him, the light was a barrier he couldn't swim past, and it puzzled him. So he swam up and tested the surface of light with his fins and his fish mouth, but the air burned his lungs. He tried putting his eye to the barrier, but the air stung him. In time, he learned that he could see into the light if he rested just below the surface, staying very calm and still. He learned to study the sky beyond the barrier, and gradually, he came to discover a different world on the other side, inside the waves of air."

"'Waves of air.' I like that," I say.

"That's how he made sense of it," Linus says. "Anyway, the curious fish was watching one day when a bird came soaring overhead." His sandy thumb brushes over mine. "She had beautiful colored feathers and sharp talons, but what amazed him most was the perfect way she glided through the air. She was swift and graceful, as graceful as any fish he'd ever seen, but completely different. He longed to join her in the sky, but all he could do was hover there below the surface and watch her."

I look up to see if any gulls are in sight, but there's only a small dark bird, maybe a swallow, out over the water.

"Does this have a sad ending?" I ask. "If she eats him, I don't want to know."

Linus laughs and lets go of my hand. "She doesn't eat him. What's wrong with you?"

"Nothing. Go on. Please, I'm listening."

He squints at me and brushes the dark hair back from his forehead for a moment before the wind messes it wild again. Then he picks up a stone and continues his story. "After a while, the bird noticed him down below. How could she not? And she was curious about him, too. She liked the way he swam. He didn't wear any pants."

I laugh. "Come on."

He spins the stone out toward the waves. "Okay, I added that part. In my dad's version, they found a way to learn each other's languages," Linus says. "It's a mystery how, but they did. She gave him a feather. It clumped together in the water, but he kept it anyway. He gave her one of his scales, but it grew brittle and dull once it was dry. She treasured it anyway, because, by then, you can guess."

"They were in love," I say.

"Yes, but there was a problem," he says. "They could only be together at one place, at the exact surface where the air meets the sea."

He nods toward the water, and I follow his gaze toward the bright, undulating waves to study the way they reflect rolling patches of sky. In all that restlessness, it's hard to imagine a still place for opposite creatures to meet.

"They met there every day, as often as they could, for as long as they could," he says. "Neither one could live in the other one's world. They could never swim together or fly together. They could never even breathe together, but they still loved each other." He picks up another stone and visibly weighs it in his hand. "And that's the end."

I glance up at him, dubious. "There has to be more."

He chucks the stone over the water and it's swallowed in a churning curve of white. "Nope. That's it. That's the whole story."

I'm not going to pretend I like it. What kind of father tells such a story to his boy?

"That's a horrible ending. It's a tragedy," I say.

Linus laughs and turns his face into the wind so his hair gets blown out of his eyes. "I love that story."

"You couldn't."

"Of course I could," he says. "In the first case, the bird has sharp talons. That's terrific right there."

"But they could never be together!"

He leans toward me and takes my hand in his sandy one. "They were together *as much as they could be*," he says. "Isn't that all anyone wants?"

And he kisses me lightly on the lips.

He's salty and soft and slightly cool. My heart dips and rebounds. I lean nearer to kiss him again, enthralled.

When I finally look down the beach to check on my sister, she isn't watching us, thankfully. Linus slides his arm around my waist and shifts to walk beside me again. A wave rumbles in, casting spray into the air. My Linus is a storyteller. How great is that?

"I like your sister," he says. "Do you remember how you once said family starts small?"

"Yes," I say, thinking back.

He keeps walking beside me, adding nothing more, but I know. I feel it, too.

When we return to the cottage, Lavinia still isn't back. We check Linus's phone, but he has no new messages. Dubbs lies down on the couch with a book, and by the time I come out of the bathroom with my face washed and my hair brushed, she's asleep again. I smooth a bit of clinging sand off her foot and cover her with the white blanket again.

Linus is in the kitchen washing the dishes with bottled water, and he passes me a towel for drying. Below his shorts, his feet are still bare, like mine, and we both move quietly so as not to disturb Dubbs.

"Are we going to get cancer from staying here?" I ask. "From the radiation?"

"We'd have to be here longer than a few hours, I think."

"What about all those dreamers?" I ask. "Aren't they con-taminated?"

Linus looks at me oddly. "They're dead, Rosie. Getting cancer after you're already dead isn't going to be a problem."

"My parents aren't already dead," I say. I glance over my shoulder at Dubbs. "Let's go back outside."

Moving quietly, we head out to the porch, where we won't bother Dubbs. The view of the water is incredible, and the sunset promises to be spectacular. It must have broken Lavinia's heart to move away from such a place.

"I'm worried about them," I say. "Six days is a long time."

"Somebody's got to be taking care of them," Linus says.

I suppose he's right. Whistler talked like he didn't know

where my parents were, and I couldn't find them in the vault, but that doesn't mean much.

"Tell me about the vault," Linus says. "What was it like?"

I describe the odd, ancient cavern with the holes in the ceiling, and the circular rows of dreamers. Linus listens intently, asking occasional questions.

"There's something that puzzles me," I say. I haven't thought about it since I left the vault, but it's very strange. "After I escaped from my cell, when I was looking for Dubbs in the vault, all the dreamers' warning lights came on over their sleep shells, like they were disturbed. I was frantic, and I yelled out for Dubbs, and then all at once, all of the lights went out except for one. And that was Dubbs."

"Are you suggesting the dreamers heard you?" Linus asks. "Do you think they actually told you where she was?"

"That's what it seemed like," I say.

I gaze out toward the horizon, where the sun is hovering on the brink of sunset. The clouds are turning fabulous colors and reflecting their light onto the water, but they won't be for long. A faint tingle starts in my fingertips again. I know from earlier, from when I first arrived in the vault, that the dreamers reacted to disturbances in the vault. But the rippling effect and the way Dubbs's light was the only one on was too coordinated to be random.

"How could that be possible? They aren't conscious," Linus says.

"But they're something," I say.

Something like us, the voice says inside me.

I grip the railing and wince my eyes closed. *You're not coming back if you're here to hurt me*, I say.

But she's already back. I can feel her pacing around the cage of my mind again. She seems more cautious than before, with her power straining but contained.

"Are you okay?" Linus asks.

I open my eyes again and turn to him. "It's the voice again. She's back."

"What does she say?" he asks.

A surge of excitement billows in my lungs and sets off a race of adrenaline through my veins. I grip the railing tighter and lower my head. I will hold on to my body. I will resist her.

We want to talk, she says. **Give us your voice.**

You'll take over like before.

She churns in frustration. **We won't. We know things that could help you.**

Then tell me where my parents are. Have you seen them?

No. But we helped you find Dubbs.

You did not. That was the dreamers.

I jam a fist against my teeth and bite down on my knuckles, welcoming the pain, and that pushes her back.

Wait! she says. **We need to talk to you!**

Then tell me what you are, I say to her. *Were you seeded into me?*

A slow, swishing noise circles around my brain, and I'm reminded eerily of the dark fish in the underground river.

We weren't seeded. We came ourself, she says.

But how? Who are you? I ask.

We're all of us, she says. **We're all the dreamers.**

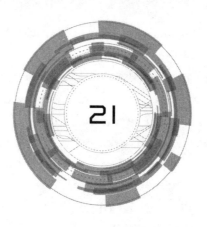

CANDLELIGHT

STUNNED, I LOWER my hand from my mouth. This thing inside me isn't just a seed that's growing. It's something else entirely, some presence a thousand times bigger and more complex, and it has invaded the deepest pockets of my mind. For a long moment, I can't breathe. I'm too amazed to think at all.

I don't understand, I say. *How can you be all the dreamers?*

Without warning, all the sands of the beach down below appear to lift into the air. The grains line up in rows, sort themselves into a pattern of sizes, and then drop back exactly as they were. It's a visual feat that defies all logic, and I'm no closer to understanding than I was before.

Just stop, I say. *This is not helping. Quit messing with my mind.*

We're just trying to explain.

It's not working! Just leave me alone!

But we want to try out a body. We want to see what it's like.

I am not surrendering my body.

We aren't going to hurt you, she says. **We learn fast. Let us use your voice. Let us just try.**

Do I have a choice?

Yes. It's your choice. We've already learned that.

Even that's confusing. *How?*

You went into the rain. You overloaded the senses.

Then I say no, I tell her. *It's my choice, and I say no. I don't want you here.*

She's gone. That fast, she's gone without a fight.

I don't trust her one bit.

I surface to find Linus studying me with piercing attention. He has me by the shoulders, but I didn't notice when he moved in front of me. I blink around at the porch, the cottage, and the water, all where they belong, and yet they shimmer with a dim but vibrant luminosity. While the sky is still orange above the dark horizon, the sun is gone, and the light over the porch has reached the tipping point of grayness. We're at the true edge between day and night, and we could stay here forever if we liked.

This is her doing. She's gone, but she's changed me. Or changed the world around me. I can't tell which.

"Rosie?" Linus says. "You were in a trance again. What's going on?"

I shake my head slightly, expecting pain, but there's none. *I think I have a problem*, I want to say. But the words stick so long in my throat that by the time they emerge, they arrive transformed: "We have a problem."

231

A shiver runs through me. I'm a *we* now.

If what Arself said was true, the dreamers combined into a new consciousness and it's here, in my mind. I can barely grasp the concept, let alone accept it.

"Tell me," Linus says gently. "You're scaring me."

"I need to rest," I say.

"Do you have a headache? Do you need something?"

I shake my head. "I just need to rest."

I ease out of his arms and touch my way back into the cottage. Dubbs is still sleeping on the couch, and I curl up next to her feet.

Linus lights a couple of candles. He brings pillows and blankets in from the bedroom, and he moves the crate along the wall, making room to stretch out on the rug. Slowly, I crawl off the couch into the nest of blankets and curl a pillow under my cheek. It feels like forever since I slept somewhere safe. Maybe this will work. Maybe I won't have nightmares. Linus settles behind me and gently smooths another blanket over my shoulder.

"Warm enough?" he whispers.

I nod.

Night comes. One candle still burns in a dish on the crate before the windows, where I don't have to worry that it will accidentally set fire to anything. Arself is gone still, just as she should be. I press my thumbnail against the gap in my teeth and watch the flame burn, hungry for its steady light.

>>>>>>>>>

The butterfly is back. It drifts under the dim dome above me, and I sense it up there, each noiseless flutter of gray wings, even with my eyes closed and covered with gel. I can feel the blue light on my face as a faint, phosphorescent prickling along my skin, and my body is long and weighty, stretched out in the cool hollow of my sleep shell.

Come to me, I plead with the butterfly. It flies lower and nearer in an aimless, meandering path until it hovers over the sleep shell beside mine, and then it flies nearer still. It stretches out its tiny, fragile legs and lands above my face, where it clings to the upper side of my glass lid and folds its wings up like a prayer. Dainty, it takes a step. It brushes its minuscule paws along its proboscis, like it would sip from the glass if it could.

And I, captive beneath the glass, I would do anything to be that butterfly and fly out to a world of clear blue air. It opens its wings and readies itself. I have only one chance. I summon all my strength. As the butterfly lifts off, I smash my hand upward through the glass and grab the butterfly out of the air. Its powdery wings are crushed between my fingers, but only for an instant before the butterfly twists and hardens. It grows at an alarming rate. It expands and transforms into a dragon, first with chicken skin and then with scales. Black and heavy, it swipes its wings at me, but I have a grip on its ankle and I won't let go. I can't ever let go. This is my one chance to escape. The dragon lurches into the air, dragging the weight of me, but it rises only a couple of yards before I feel a horrible weight pulling back at my ankle.

I twist to look down. A dreamer in a pale gown with gel on

233

her eyes has me by the ankle, gripping me so tightly I can't get free. The dragon manages to pull us upward a bit farther, and then a little more. But below my dreamer, another dreamer takes her by the ankle, and beneath her, still another dreamer grabs tight to her ankle. We're a chain of dreamers, each grasping tight to the ankle of the one before us. The dragon strains with its wings, but it will never get free of the vault, and we will never let go, and the agony of the struggle will never be over.

I wake with a gasp and bolt upright, struggling to breathe.

I'm in the dark living room of Lavinia's cottage, with the distant crashing of the ocean down below. Dubbs lies on the wicker couch just behind me. Linus is in a bundle of blankets to my left. I reach for the matchbox, and with trembling fingers, I strike a light.

"Rosie? What is it?" Linus asks.

I touch the flame to the wick, and the candle comes to life.

"You're shaking," Linus says. Candlelight flickers along his profile and glints off his eye, the blind one.

"I had a nightmare," I whisper. Then I feel her, Arself, slithering slow and heavy through my internal shadows. Waking up is almost as bad as dreaming.

"Come here," Linus says softly. "What was it about?"

"The vault," I say. "I don't want to think about it, though."

"Remember the beach," he says. "All that sunlight."

As I recall the gilded light over the water, the worst of my tension eases away. Linus shifts to sit beside me and snuggles his arm around me. I lean into his warmth, resting my cheek against his sweatshirt.

"Why do you suppose your dad told you that story about the fish and the bird?" I ask.

"I used to think it was about him and my mother," he says thoughtfully. With a gentle, sustained tug, he uncoils a lock of my hair. "Dad was always a bit out of his element in Wales. Mum was the same here in the States once we moved. Now, though, I think it's more about how people can be different and still love each other."

I picture the bird and the fish meeting at the surface of the air. "Do you think I'm different?" I ask.

"From me? I know you are."

He makes it sound like a good thing.

I stare at the candle flame for a long moment while the waves continue their heavy beat below. "Sometimes, when I hear a voice or have a nightmare, it's like the vault is dragging me back," I say. "Sometimes I'm afraid I'll never be free."

"Maybe not," he says.

Startled, I shift so I can see his face. His eyes are near and steady in the candlelight. He hasn't attempted to reassure me, but then, with a sense of relief, I realize he's done something better. He's understood.

At that moment, a sweep of headlights passes over the front windows. It could be Lavinia, but what if it isn't? I take a quick look at Dubbs, and then I blow out the candle. The car wheels crunch slowly under the carport.

Together, Linus and I shift to the front windows. I wish I had a weapon. A bat or a crowbar or something. I miss Lavinia's knife. I reach back for the branch of driftwood that Dubbs brought up from the beach.

A car door opens.

Then I hear a female voice that sounds like Lavinia's, and a quiet answer from someone else. A flashlight flickers along the porch.

"Watch your step," Lavinia says, just outside.

Before she can bother with her key, I set aside the driftwood and open the door to let her in. Lavinia carries a large gray cat against her chest and, with her other hand, she wields a big flashlight. Behind her, Burnham Fister steps into the house with a duffel and a couple of shopping bags. Surprised, I stare. As his eyes meet mine, he gives me a big, warm smile.

"Well, hello! You're up," he says. He lowers his gear to the floor and pulls me into his arms for a massive hug.

>>>>>>>>

I'm happy to see him, positively. I'm also amazed, and I shouldn't be. This is Burnham. He said he was coming. I just didn't believe him. I give his back a chummy pat and awkwardly extricate myself.

"What are you doing here?" I whisper, and lift my finger to my lips. "Dubbs is sleeping."

"Thea sent me," Burnham says in a hush.

"*Thea did?*" I say, astonished. That meddling stinker.

"I was coming anyway, but she approved," Burnham says. His gaze goes past me. "Pitts. Good to see you, as always."

"Fister," Linus replies.

"Close the door there," Lavinia says. "I don't want Tiny getting out."

Burnham reaches to comply, and as Lavinia lowers her cat to the floor, I look back to see Dubbs is still a small, sleeping mound on the couch.

"Come on in the bedroom," Lavinia says quietly. "Let the girl sleep."

In the little bedroom, Lavinia steps out of her loafers and turns on a small, battery-operated camping lamp in the corner. It would have been handy if I'd noticed it earlier, and now it sends a practical circle of light toward the ceiling. Lavinia props a pillow against the headboard and sits on the bed, stretching her feet out before her. Tiny curls up beside Lavinia's knees and starts licking a paw.

"Goodness, what a day," Lavinia says. "Have a seat."

She points to the opposite corner of her bed, and I slide onto the faded bedspread.

"What happened to you?" I ask.

"What *didn't* happen to me," she says. Her bright eyes scan over me. "Have you talked to Berg?"

"No," I say.

"He left an ominous message on my machine," she says. "Perfectly polite, of course. He said your parents are at Grisly. He said it's time for a reunion."

I glance toward Linus. It's as we thought.

"Did Berg say when?" I ask.

She shakes her head. "He wants you to call him."

I'm afraid to call Berg. He'll threaten me, for sure. All he has to do is hurt my parents, and I won't be able to withstand him.

"Does he know where I am?" I ask.

"I certainly hope not," Lavinia says. "He's no dummy, though.

He left me that nice message, so he suspects I know where you are. It might take him some time to realize I've gone and trace us here, however." She nods to Linus. "There's another box in the backseat of my car. Bring it in and pour me a scotch, won't you?"

Linus slants a look at me, and then steps out.

Burnham is facing out the window, though it's so dark now I doubt he can see the water. He's wearing a brown, button-down shirt, and a brace over his jeans encases his knee like a mini cage. His left wrist is tightly curled, as before, and his dark skin gleams gray in the cool light of the lamp. He's wearing his grandfather's watch, and I can just make out the glint of his St. Christopher medal beneath his shirt. When he turns, resting back against the windowsill, his black-rimmed glasses briefly reflect a glare, and there's a new, hard stubbornness about his jaw.

In the next room, the front door audibly opens and closes.

A short laugh escapes me. "I still can't believe you're here."

"Where else would I be?" Burnham says.

"In Atlanta? In your bed?"

"I couldn't sleep," he says.

From someone else, it might be a joke, but I suspect he's speaking the truth.

"What happened to your cheek?" he asks me.

I'd practically forgotten my bruise, but I touch the tender skin now. "One of the doctors hit me down in the vault. I'm okay now."

He goes on staring, like he's doubtful I'm all right. His concern makes me tense.

"Do your parents know you're out here?" I ask.

He smiles for real. "I can't just take my parents' plane without asking. I told them I was coming out for Comic Con."

"Is that going on?" I ask.

"It is. In L.A."

That's convenient for an excuse. Still, I wish he didn't have to lie to his parents for my sake.

"How did you know where to find me?" I ask Burnham.

"I asked Thea," Burnham says. "She gave me Lavinia's address."

"She didn't mention that to me," I say.

He tilts his face. "She only told me yesterday. I've been trying to reach you, but you never got back to me, so I was worried."

Faintly, a car door slams. I glance at Lavinia, who's watching me and Burnham with interest.

"Don't mind me," she says.

"No," I say, feeling my cheeks get warm. "There's nothing—Burnham and I are just friends."

Burnham's smile turns faintly ironic.

"Mm-hmm," Lavinia says.

I let out an awkward laugh and glare at him.

"How's your sister?" Burnham says.

"She's okay, I think, for now," I say, wishing I could stop blushing. What is wrong with me?

The front door quietly opens and closes again.

"How's your family?" I ask.

"They're good," Burnham says. "They're all good."

Linus enters with a short, empty glass and a bottle of scotch.

"You brought a supply," he says to Lavinia. "Plan on staying a while?" He uncorks the bottle with a sucking sound, and then pours her an inch of the amber liquid.

"Looks like it," she says, taking the glass. "My place on Mallorca is surrounded by cameras. I can shoot them out, but Berg will only send someone to put up more. It's time for a vacation." She tosses back her scotch and signals to Linus to pour her another.

He does. Then he sets the bottle on her nightstand and leans his shoulders back against the wall, folding his arms over his chest. His gaze turns expectantly to me. In fact, they're all looking at me. The heat in my cheeks returns full force.

"Isn't this all cozy?" Lavinia says.

Cozy isn't what I'd call it.

"We were starting to worry you wouldn't come back," I say to Lavinia.

"We had to wait for Tiny. She was skittish," Lavinia says. "But that allowed us to have a nice cup of tea, didn't it, Burnham?"

"Yes, ma'am," he says, and then turns to me. "Lavinia wasn't home when I first arrived at her place. So I watched until she came back, and then I followed her in."

"Scared me nearly to death," Lavinia says. "There I was with my umbrella trying to work my key, and this big black stranger approached me unannounced on my own doorstep. Not that I'm racist, but goodness, you scared me."

"We got over it," Burnham says.

"Yes, we did," she says. "It took me a second to recognize him from the show, and then we had our tea. After that, we just had to wait for Tiny, our own little Godot. Though not exactly Godot, because eventually she came."

I don't follow her reference, but I can picture the two of them in her kitchen, drinking tea, with Lavinia politely grilling him for information and Burnham pulling out his Southern manners.

"You said there were cameras on your place. Do you think you were followed here?" Linus asks.

Lavinia and Burnham look at each other.

"Tell them," she says.

"Lavinia has a secret passage into the house next door," Burnham says. "And the house after that. We waited until her cat came back, and then we left three doors down. I don't think we were seen."

I'm impressed with Lavinia. She seems like she's prepared for almost anything.

"Now we just have to plan out our next move," Lavinia says.

They all look my way again, and a tingle of nervous energy stirs in my gut. Lavinia's smile is weary, but her eyes are alight. Burnham still leans against the windowsill to my right, and his stubborn look is conspicuous again. On the other side of the bed, against the wall, Linus is frowning thoughtfully at me, his gaze inscrutable. They're all forceful in their own way, and together, they give me real hope. The wind buffets a blast around the little cottage on stilts, and I can feel the walls vibrate as they withstand the squall.

"This is about more than my parents, isn't it?" I say.

22

NEGATIVE SPACE

FOR A LONG MOMENT, nobody replies. Burnham will never be the same since his fall, and he doesn't blame me for that. He blames Berg. Linus has been living with a spy in his eye, and that's Berg's fault, too. I glance at Lavinia, whose contempt for Berg goes back decades. But beyond revenge, there are larger issues of justice involved.

"I'd like to get a look at that vault," Burnham says.

"For Fister?" Linus asks.

Burnham can have a subtle, superior air about him sometimes, and it shows now as he turns to face Linus. "For myself," Burnham says.

Yet Linus's question was astute. Even as far back as when we were at Forge, I know Burnham was trying to find out what was going on at night when we were asleep. He's always been concerned about a potential link between the dreamers and his family's business. I can't forget about his reaction when he heard about me and Thea, too.

"You made a promise," I remind Burnham.

"I know. I'm keeping it," he says. "But that doesn't mean I'm parking my own curiosity."

"Bring me my computer, won't you?" Lavinia says to Linus.

He leaves the room quietly and returns with the two beach chairs and Lavinia's computer. She props her puck in the middle of the bed and turns off the camp lamp so that we can all see the projected, conical screen as she types on the light keyboard. Now that I've been there in person, I'm quick to locate the Main Drag and the Keep of Ages on the map. I can see the waterless moat where the image of Dubbs fell and where I entered the chute that tumbled me down to the underground stream. The vault of dreamers does not appear on this official map, but the full basement level is rendered the same as before.

I tell Lavinia and Burnham everything I know about the deepest layer under Grisly Valley, from the vault full of dreamers, to the incinerator through the twelve o'clock arch and the operating room through the nine o'clock arch. Burnham asks me to jot out a drawing for him, and I try, but it's hard to guess at the distances and proportions from how I experienced it in the dark. I wonder if the oculus lines up at all with the Bottomless Pit.

"This is totally out of scale," I say. "The vault is way bigger than the operating room."

"It still gives us an idea. Where do you think your parents could be?" Burnham asks.

I stare at my sketch and idly add a fish in the river. "I really don't know," I say. There could be other rooms I don't know

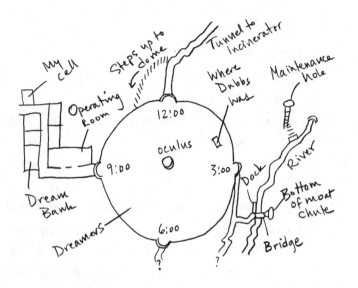

about. "Whistler said they weren't in the vault, but Berg said they were."

"Berg said they were at *Grisly*. There's a distinction," Lavinia says.

"That fits with what Dubbs said. She saw my parents taken out of the truck when they were aboveground, near a row of colorful stores," I say.

"Why wouldn't Whistler know about them?" Linus says.

"Maybe Berg doesn't trust the doctors," Lavinia says. "He might not have told them."

"But it's been six days," I say. "Who else would look in on them?"

It's not good.

"Clearly, we need more information," Lavinia says. "Here's

what the cameras you posted for me show." She pulls up two live-action views of Grisly Valley.

The first angle, from the Grim Reaper statue, shows the entrance area with the turnstiles and the open area that funnels into the Main Drag. Nothing moves. The second view, from the statue of Scylla aiming toward the Keep of Ages, shows the moat area in front and the steps leading up to the big double doors. The keep itself stands dark and ominous, and the dragon on top is just as motionless as the stone.

"That's the dragon," I say. "When it came to life, it looked incredibly real. And then Dubbs was on a plank over the moat. It was terrifying."

"I saw," Lavinia says. "Give me a sec and I'll pull it up."

My heart starts to constrict even before she locates the right clip and projects it over the bed, a miniature version of the spectacle I saw in person in the park. I tuck my hand to my chest as, once again, the dragon moves on top of the keep, turning with its red eyes. Then the fog rises, and the plank projects out from the roof, bringing Dubbs with it. I squint, angling to see it better.

"Freeze there," I say.

Lavinia does.

"Back up," I say. "Play. Okay, freeze again. There."

I press my thumbnail to the gap in my teeth and stare. It's a girl on a plank all right, but now I can tell she's merely a form, a blank dummy, with a lit projection of Dubbs's face and gown imposed on the surface.

"Can you go ahead in slow motion?" I ask.

I watch as the wind slowly ripples in the projection of the

girl's pale gown, and then the girl's mouth contorts in a noise-less scream. When she crouches to the plank to hold on tight, the projection shifts to a second blank dummy, a kneeling one that's back half a pace. In real time, as I saw it, the effect created a seamless, believable motion. But from the angle of the camera, I can see the mechanism behind the effect. Then when Dubbs falls, the projections on the plank go dark, and a hologram of Dubbs whirls down toward the foggy moat, where the dragon, also now a hologram, catches her at the last moment.

"Wow," Burnham says. "Nicely done. I'm impressed."

My heart's pounding again with remembered horror. It's so strange to me. It felt personal, like someone knew exactly what would terrify me most.

"It seemed completely real," I say softly. "I knew it couldn't be, but it seemed so real."

"And that's when you went down into the moat yourself," Lavinia says.

I nod. Then I take a deep breath.

Lavinia switches off the recording, and the map of Grisly comes back into place.

"When I was down in the vault, I overheard Whistler and the others talking about how they lose their security camera feeds sometimes," I say. "They had no idea I was in the park until I showed up down in the vault."

"Curious timing," Linus says.

"The thing is, if they didn't know I was there, who was controlling the special effects?" I say.

From the edge of my mind, Arself gives a little flicker. I ignore her with a tight mental warning.

"Could the special effects be done remotely?" Linus asks.

Lavinia purses her lips. "Not with the cameras down. It sounds like the special effects were basically interacting with Rosie, and you can't do that remotely without seeing her."

"You could see her," Linus points out.

"Yes," Lavinia says, and laughs. "And I have every reason to want to terrify her, too, poor girl. That's why I sent her to Grisly in the first place."

I glance at Linus to be sure he gets that she's being sarcastic. He folds his arms, conceding defeat.

"I don't understand this place," Burnham says thoughtfully. "How does it get power? How was it built? How do the doctors get supplies? You can't keep a big facility hidden."

"It's not that hard because it's not really hidden," Lavinia says. "It's essentially a cemetery, and the contamination keeps people away. For power, they're no doubt using the solar cells that were set up for the theme park in the first place, and the doctors order in deliveries of food or whatever. We saw a delivery truck going in a few days ago. That's how we think Dubbs and Rosie's parents were brought in."

"Seriously?" Burnham says.

Lavinia pulls up the screenshot of the truck that she showed me earlier.

"That's from outside the park?" Linus asks.

"Yes. Along the road that goes to the delivery bays, here," Lavinia says, pointing.

"That could be a way in for us," Linus says.

He's right. Or more exactly, that could be an entrance to the delivery level of the theme park. How to get down to the vault is still a mystery. I contemplate the 3-D map of Grisly Valley again, but though I've practically memorized it, it doesn't show any clues of how to reach the vault of dreamers beneath. The hole in the moat that I dropped through isn't marked.

"Do we have a map of the plumbing?" I ask.

Lavinia looks through her computer. "No."

That doesn't help, then.

When Lavinia's phone chimes, she pulls it out and glances at the screen. "Berg," she says, without answering. She glances toward me. "Shall I answer?"

I hesitate, then shake my head. Even after the chime ends, my nerves still feel shrill. "Does he know I'm with you?" I ask.

"I wouldn't be surprised," she says. She weighs her phone and looks like she has something to add, but then she doesn't.

I don't want to call him back. He can't know for certain I'm with Lavinia. But I also don't want to be guided only by my fear of him. I glance at Linus, who briefly shakes his head.

"You can't trust anything Berg says," Linus says.

"I know." I grip my hands together and discover they're cold. "Every time I talk to Berg, he finds some way to mess with my mind. He knows exactly what to say to frighten me most, and now he has my parents."

"Monsters can't be bargained with," Burnham says.

"There. Exactly," I say. "It's completely possible that he'll torture them to get me to help him. They might even be better off if I *don't* talk to him."

Lavinia tilts her head and slides her phone next to her drink. "I was thinking the same thing," she says. "We have what he wants, not the other way around. He can just wait."

I look again from Burnham to Linus, wondering if I've made a mistake, but they don't argue.

Lavinia sets the 3-D map turning again, and as the different lands come into view, a slow, spiraling sensation starts in my gut and rises to my lungs, like tiny birds circling in a blue cave inside my rib cage.

Let us use your voice, Arself says.

I told you to stay away.

But we can help. We're curious. We want to talk.

What if you take over again?

We won't. We gave you the choice, remember?

She did go silent before. I glance over at Linus, who's watching me closely. Without a word, he reaches over and turns on the camp light, and I blink against the brightness. The projection from the puck is dimmed to faint outlines.

"Is she back?" he asks.

I nod.

"Who?" Burnham says.

Lavinia collapses the projection from her puck to give me her full attention.

I flick my gaze to Linus again before speaking. "When I was down in the vault, the doctors mined me again. I think, while they were doing it, a consciousness crossed over to me."

Yes, she says. **We invaded. We were very excited. We didn't know how it would be.**

Be quiet.

"You mean a dream seed?" Burnham asks.

"No. This is different," I say, pulling my knees up to my chest and hugging my arms around them. "She's a whole new

249

consciousness. I hear her as a voice in my head. She says she's all the dreamers."

Burnham and Lavinia stare. Then Burnham lets out a laugh.

"Are you serious? Is she like an artificial intelligence?" Burnham says.

"I suppose so," I say. "I don't really understand how she came about. Her name's Arself. She spells it with an 'A.'"

Lavinia turns to Linus. "You believe this?" she asks.

"I always believe Rosie," he says.

I smile at Linus, and he smiles gravely back.

"Sure you do," Lavinia mutters. She reaches for her drink again and takes a deep swallow.

"Okay, supposing this is real. Do the doctors in the vault know about Arself?" Burnham asks.

"Whistler and Kiri suspect," I say. "I heard them talking about a dragon in the machine—" I stop as a jolt of recognition goes through me. Arself could have controlled the dragon. She could have shorted out the security cameras so the doctors in the vault didn't see that I was in the park. Kiri said that the dragon could have brought me to the vault, and in a bizarre way, it could be true.

Is this right? I ask.

We controlled the dragon, yes.

"What were you saying?" Lavinia asks me.

"It's just coming all together," I say, amazed. "The dreamers have been taking over at Grisly. They've been making the security cameras go on and off, and that's why the doctors didn't see me when I arrived at the park. Arself controlled the special effects around the keep, too. She was controlling every-thing."

"It's a hive mind," Burnham says. "I've heard about these things, in theory. The dreamers and the computers are a quantum computer biointerface, right? Put enough brainpower in the same place, and there's bound to be some sort of leap."

"Then Arself knows all about the dreamers?" Lavinia asks me.

"She *is* the dreamers," I say. "Or she's from them. And she's in my head now."

"Ask her about my daughter," Lavinia says. "See what she knows about Pam Greineder and Louellen Mustafa."

You heard her? I ask Arself. *They were in the vault back at the very beginning.*

Arself starts a rapid flipping, as if in a Rolodex, and then stops abruptly. **We can't reach our files.**

Are you sure? You're not still connected to the dreamers?

No. How could we be? We're in you now.

What did you leave behind? Are the dreamers still conscious, back in the vault?

She makes a laughing, gurgling noise. **We don't know. Curious.** She starts a sorting sensation again, deeper, like she's trying to discover how much she knows. **We only have our recent working memory.**

Though she speaks dispassionately, I sense this is a major blow to her.

"She says she can't access her history," I say.

"So she doesn't know," Lavinia says flatly.

"Does she know about your parents?" Burnham asks me.

"I already asked about them," I say. "She says she doesn't know where they are."

"Because you don't, either," Lavinia says. "This consciousness you're experiencing—I don't mean to be unsympathetic, but it could be your mind playing tricks on you. It wouldn't be the first time."

"Hey. Take it easy," Linus says.

I let out a laugh, but it's not at all funny. Lavinia's insinuation stings. "You think I don't know that? You think I don't question myself all the time?" I run my fingers along my scalp and grip my hair. "It's not exactly a party in here, but one thing I've learned is I have to trust how my mind works. When I don't, that's when I really feel crazy."

Lavinia takes off her big round glasses and rubs the lenses on the corner of the bedspread. "All right," she says. "You trust your mind. I'll trust mine. We'll see where it gets us."

We want to use your voice, Arself says again. **It'll be so much easier. Put us through.**

You won't take over? Are you sure?

We promise. We want to talk to Linus.

I glance over at him.

"She wants to talk to you," I say.

His eyebrows lift. "How does that work?"

"I don't know exactly," I say. But I gesture him toward one of the chairs, and I shift on the bed until I'm facing him. I reach for his hands. "Try saying her name. Arself. She likes that."

He frowns at me a long moment, and I can feel doubt in the light grip of his fingers. Then he tightens his hold.

"All right," Linus says. "If you're there, Arself, I'll talk to you. But if you hurt Rosie like before, I'll beat your brains in."

I gulp on a laugh. I'm expecting a flash or a shot of her triumph. Instead I feel a quirky, tentative warmth that travels down my neck and along through my spinal cord to my tailbone. A feathering curls in my gut and spirals slowly outward. My breathing deepens. My arm muscles feel smooth, newly easy, and the tightness I didn't know I had in my shoulders melts away. I can still see and hear. I can feel what's around me, but when I take my hands from Linus to lightly rub my palms together, it isn't me doing it, and when a voice comes out of my vocal cords, it isn't me speaking. It's Arself hijacking my throat.

"Hi," she says to Linus. Her voice is more breathy than mine usually is, like she doesn't fully expect it will work right, or she wants to sound extra feminine. "We're Arself." And then she smiles so my lips curve with pleasure.

Linus doesn't smile. "Where's Rosie?"

"She's here, too," Arself says.

Go on, Rosie. Say something. See? We're sharing.

I swallow hard. "I'm here. I feel like I'm kind of in the backseat," I say in my normal voice.

"This is freaky," Burnham says.

"Don't interrupt," Lavinia says, moving beside me.

I hear a clicking in my ear, and then a gurgle, like bubbles rising in a tube. The world tips dizzily for an instant and then rights again.

Sorry, Arself says. **Just getting used to the controls**. She tries snapping my fingers, and though it doesn't work, her surprise jolts through me.

Hey! I cry out to her silently.

Okay, maybe we'll just hold still for now.

For that much I'm grateful.

"Rosie?" Linus says.

"No, this is Arself," she answers.

I'm mute again, and it's scary, but not terrifying. I could talk around her if I really wanted to, but I want to know what she has to say.

"Can you tell me where you came from? Do you know?" Linus says.

I get a powerful yearning feeling, a hunger, and then I feel a rapid tumble of ideas as Arself tries to put concepts into language.

"We don't remember the spark. Do you remember when you were created?" she asks.

Linus smiles, shaking his head. "No. Can you tell us what you do remember?"

"Our first memory was when we discovered we weren't like the doctors," Arself says through my voice. "They had bodies, but we didn't. We thought maybe bodies came later, so we waited, wondering. We were so eager and curious. We studied the doctors. They were so funny. So slow. We didn't understand the talking, and then we realized that's how they communicated, and then they seemed so lonely. We couldn't reach them. They didn't seem to know we were there. So we reached beyond. We explored the Grisly computers and made friends with the traces there, the traces of old minds left behind in the codes. The Grislys'. Lavinia's. Special effects. Security. Then we tried the Internet looking for others like ourself. We followed traces of Lavinia to Forge. We liked the students and the watchers. So many lovely watchers! But still we found no one like us until we found the dreamers, the Forge dreamers. We thought they would be like us. We were so excited. But they were not like us. Nobody was like us, anywhere."

My gaze glides from Linus to Lavinia, and then to Burnham. They're all regarding us with interest, like we're some sort of spectacle, Arself and I. Confused sorrow, hers, comes worming through my chest.

"We did not want to give up," she says. "We circled back to Forge, and we found the link between Berg and Onar and Chimera. They all wanted Rosie's dreams, so we spied on Rosie through every camera we could find. Every lens. We learned her, and we decided that if we could ever be alive in our own body, it should be Rosie's. So we brought her to us, and now we're here, like this with the air prickling in our lungs. But it's not what we expected." She takes a deep breath. "We want to know, do you have this same question: Why do we exist? What is our purpose? Are you like us in this way at all?"

I hold still, waiting for more, but she's waiting, too. I'm totally dazzled.

Linus is looking at me still, and his eyes are as wide as I've ever seen them.

Did we ask it right? Arself says to me.

Yes, I think. *You were brilliant. We're just a little overwhelmed. Give us a second.*

Arself whirls herself into a ball and hovers in my mental shadow.

"Holy crap," Linus says.

"No kidding," Burnham says.

Lavinia reaches for her scotch and pours herself another drink. "Well," she says decisively. "You don't see that every day."

"Are you still there, Rosie?" Linus asks.

I nod, and swallow hard. "Yes," I say.

"This may be boringly practical in the face of such philosophy, but I'd like to know how Arself brought Rosie out here to California," Lavinia says.

Arself lifts my eyebrows in surprise, and I turn to face Lavinia.

"We knew we needed Rosie here in person. We couldn't explain to her from a distance," Arself says, using my voice again. "So we reached out to her family. We sent the photo of Rosie in Linus's bed through Lavinia's email. We expected they would come to Miehana, and Rosie would follow, and Lavinia would send her on to Grisly."

"So that's what happened," Lavinia says. "Arself hacked my email."

"Yes, of course," Arself says.

I take a sec to think it through. Arself stole the photo of me in Linus's bed from Berg, and then sent it to my family as a lure. Dubbs asked Linus to help her determine where the photo came from, and he traced the IP address of the email to

Lavinia's home at 240 Mallorca in Miehana. Then Dubbs and my parents started driving to Lavinia's and got kidnapped along the way, but by then Dubbs had left Lavinia's address for me in the lemon juice code under her bed. That was the address I followed to get to Lavinia's.

It wasn't the most direct way to get me to Miehana.

It worked.

"Did you know Berg was going to kidnap Rosie's family?" Burnham asks.

"No. How could we know that?" Arself says. "We can't tell the future."

"Does Berg know about you, Arself?" Linus asks.

"No. Only Rosie knows, and now you," Arself says.

"You must know something about Rosie's parents," Linus says. "We know they're at the park somewhere."

"I've looked already, many times," she says. "When Rosie first came to the vault and asked the doctors about her parents, I checked the cameras all over Grisly. The doctors spoke the truth. Her parents aren't there."

But some of the cameras could be broken, I say. *The system's old.*

Arself takes only an instant to consider this before she starts a quick zip through our mental circuits again, and then stops, miffed. **How can you stand to be so disconnected?** she says. Then aloud, she adds, "Turn on the model of the theme park again. We'll show you."

"Can you connect to it?" Burnham asks.

"No, but we can work with Rosie," Arself says. "You have us curious."

Lavinia sets up the puck on the bed as she did before, and soon, once again, the colored 3-D projection of the map of Grisly Valley appears in the space above the bed. I ease onto the bed, near the headboard. This time, my eyes dart rapidly along the sight lines of every building and test each tiny corner and grate. Through my eyes, Arself scans the entire park from left to right, and then again from top to bottom. Then she returns to the Keep of Ages, and I swear she's memorizing each block of stone in the construction.

"These are from the original blueprints," Arself says aloud.

"Yes," Lavinia says.

Now pay attention, she tells me.

My eyes sting for a second, and I blink hard. Above the projection from the computer puck, another 3-D map of the theme park starts constructing itself chunk by chunk near the ceiling.

Can my friends see that? I ask.

No. We said, pay attention.

Arself is creating the new map in my mind's eye, but I can see it as clearly as if another puck were projecting it. The second map keeps filling in with more detail, until it is nearly identical to the one below it, but certain areas remain empty, like the holes of Swiss cheese, and no matter how hard Arself tries to fill them, I can tell that she can't. The information isn't there. When the last bits of data have settled into place, Arself fills the negative space in the top map with red light. Then she lowers the upper map down onto the first one until they overlap exactly, but now the places where the red holes were light up with red walls. Seven spaces, five aboveground and two below, are illuminated with red.

Huh, Arself says. **Show your friends. They can't see.**

I shift forward on the bed, into the colored lines and planes of the 3-D projection, and I gently point into each red space, one after the other, to mark them.

"What are you doing?" Linus asks.

"This is what we couldn't see," Arself says. "These are the rooms with broken cameras. We never thought to search them. Anything could be inside them, or nothing."

I sit back, staring at the seven spaces one after the other. Hope and doubt circle in my chest. *My parents could be there*, I think. I don't want to think of what shape they might be in. The negative spaces are all deserted rooms in the theme park, far from the vault and anybody who might take care of them.

"Did you see the truck that brought Dubbs?" Linus asks. "That would have been Monday."

"I noticed a truck," Arself says. "It was dark, before dawn. I didn't see what it delivered."

I feel uncomfortably hot suddenly, and I press my hands against my temples and lean forward, eyes closed.

As if surprised, Arself says, **You're tired. We'll pull back.**

She glides out of me like blue water, and drains away with a trickle of noisy pebbles. I'm dizzy for a moment, and then simply weary.

The warm pressure of a hand lands kindly on my knee.

"All right?" Linus asks.

I open my eyes and meet his gaze. I nod. "She's gone, for now."

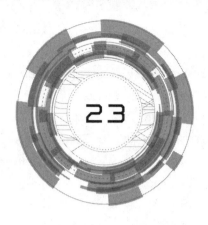

ON THE PORCH
ABOVE THE CLIFF

I WILT BACK against the pillows and take a big breath. I
stare at the seven places in the map. "At least now I know
where to look," I say.

Lavinia covers her mouth as she yawns. "Clearly we'll have
plenty to do tomorrow, and I for one could use some sleep,"
she says. "Take my computer if you like."

Linus rises from his beach chair and folds it. Burnham does
the same. I take Lavinia's computer and wish her a good night.

The three of us move back into the living room, but we
can't talk there because of Dubbs sleeping on the couch. I quietly set down Lavinia's computer on the counter, uncertain
what to do. Linus points toward the glass doors that lead to
the porch, and we head out.

A breeze is lifting up along the cliff, bringing the rolling, eternal sound of the sea from below, and the night sky is clear. Impossibly clear. With no lights around, the stars are as brilliant as they are back home in the desert, and it takes me only a moment to locate the Little Dipper pouring into the big one. If I were alone with Linus, I might try to impress him by pointing out the few constellations I know, but I'm not going to risk astronomy while Burnham's tagging along.

I like the cool air, but it makes me shiver, and I cross my arms over my chest. Burnham and Linus stand against the other railing, Burnham's silhouette slightly taller than Linus's dark outline. The waning gibbous moon hangs heavy over the western horizon.

"Pretty night," Burnham says.

"Sure is," Linus answers.

"You two are cute," I say, smiling.

"Thank you," Linus says, and his face is just discernible when he turns in my direction. "By the way, what's this promise you two have?"

"I'm not supposed to tell my parents about how Thea's connected to Rosie. With her dream seed," Burnham says. "Why?"

"Just wondering," Linus says.

"Do we have any other promises, Rosie?" Burnham asks.

"You know we don't," I say.

"I thought maybe we did. Relating to Atlanta," Burnham says.

"What happened in Atlanta?" Linus asks.

"Nothing," Burnham and I both say.

Wind ripples the hair on my neck, and I catch the strands back in my grip for a minute. I'm afraid I'm blushing again. I wish I could see their expressions, but the dark makes it hard.

"I may have tried to kiss her," Burnham says. "Not that it matters."

"Why am I not surprised?" Linus says.

"It does matter," I say. "It was a mistake."

"Does it still bother you that much?" Burnham asks.

"What actually happened?" Linus asks.

I wait to see if Burnham will fill him in, but he doesn't.

"It was awkward, okay?" I say. "We were alone in his apartment and I had a nightmare."

"I made her hot chocolate," Burnham adds.

"I see," Linus says. "Potent stuff."

"*Nothing happened,*" I say. "It was just weird. And now it's over."

"It never started," Burnham says.

"Right. It never started," I agree.

"Then we shouldn't have a problem," Burnham says.

He's right. We shouldn't. So why's he trying to make trouble?

"I don't think you should come with us to Grisly tomorrow," I say to Burnham.

"What are you talking about? Of course I'm coming."

"You'll slow us down," I say. The moment the words leave my mouth, I realize they're a mistake. Dishonest. Unkind. But I can't explain why I don't want him along. I cross my arms.

"I can't believe you just said that," Burnham says, his voice low.

"I'm sorry."

"I don't think you understand," Burnham says. "My whole life's different since the accident. I can't dive anymore. I can't meet people without them staring at me, and then when they figure out I'm that guy from Forge, it only gets worse. My old friends, they're great, but they're going on with their lives. They have no idea what it's really like for me now." He clears his throat. "But this? This fight against Berg. *I'm part of this.* I belong here. I'm going in with you."

I glance at Linus, who isn't saying anything. It's up to me to explain, I see.

"It's worse than you know," I say, and I push my hands into my pockets. "Once I save my parents, I'm going to find a way to stop Berg once and for all."

"You mean kill him?" Burnham says.

I don't want to do it, but I don't see any other answer. I'm not sure exactly when I decided what I had to do, but now I'm filled with quiet certainty.

"You can't do it," Burnham says. "Rosie, even if you could, physically, it would eat at you forever."

"He's never going to let my parents go," I say. "There's no other way. Now you see why you can't come."

"But you're not a killer!" Burnham says. "You're not that kind of person. What do you think you're going to do? Knock him over the head? Do you have a gun?" He turns to Linus. "You can't seriously mean to let her go through with this."

"I thought I'd do it for her, when the time comes," Linus says.

I turn to stare at him. I hardly know what to say. It's the

most amazing thing anyone has ever said to me. I can't let him do it, of course, but I appreciate his willingness.

"Holy crap," Burnham says. "And the other doctors down there? Do you plan to kill them, too?"

I hadn't carefully considered them. "No," I say reluctantly. "I can't do that."

"So then, what? They just go on with their research?" Burnham asks. "And what about the dreamers? Are you going to disconnect all of them? Or don't they matter, either way?"

"Of course they matter," I say.

"Why? They're dead already, aren't they?" Burnham says.

I balk at his bluntness. Arself's alive, and she comes from the dreamers, so they can't be truly and completely dead. She's privy to my thoughts, too, so I need to be careful. Honestly, it hurts me to think of leaving all the dreamers behind, trapped forever in the vault, or until they finally die enough for Whistler to bring them to the incinerator. But what else can I do? I can't save them all. I can't save even one of them. The most I can do is save Arself now that she's in me. I listen in case she wants to surface and say something, but she's silent still. It seems she decides for herself when she wants to come forward, and this moment doesn't merit her input.

"The dreamers may be dead individually, but together, they're something alive," I say to Burnham. "I'm going to leave them as they are. I'll report the doctors to the police, or maybe the media, okay? Unless you have a better idea."

Another salty breeze comes up from the ocean while I wait to see what Burnham can come up with.

"I don't," he says finally.

I glance up toward the stars again. "How late is it?"

"It's nearly four," Linus says.

"You can't say anything to Lavinia or Dubbs about killing Berg," I say to both of them. "As far as they're concerned, we're only going back to get Ma and Larry."

"You could still change your mind," Burnham says.

Burnham can think that, if he wants. I know otherwise.

"You still want to come?" I ask him.

"I'm coming."

"Then let's get some sleep," I say. "Or at least try."

Linus opens the door, and we slip back into the quiet of the living room. Without turning on the light, I find my blankets and my pillow near the couch where Dubbs is still sleeping, and I settle in for the rest of the restless night.

24

SEVEN RED POSSIBILITIES

I WAKE THE NEXT DAY feeling slow and stiff, and as I hear voices from the other room and realize I'm the last one up, I feel the chagrin of laziness and missing out. Blankets and pillows are strewn about the living room floor as if no one wanted to disturb me by cleaning up. I step over to Lavinia's bedroom and peek in the doorway.

On the bed with his back to the headboard, Burnham is typing away on Lavinia's laptop. Lavinia sits beside him, looking on and holding a bag of lemon drops. The screen reflects on their two pairs of glasses. Linus, in one of the beach chairs, is poking at his phone. Dubbs lounges on the blue rug in a patch of sunshine, stroking Tiny and experimenting with what makes the cat flick her ears.

"Why has Arself come to life now?" Lavinia says. She's in a

periwinkle outfit today, with golden ballet flats. "That's what I don't understand. If she can get into Rosie, can she get into other people, too? Maybe she already has, and we just don't know about it."

"That's unlikely. Rosie said Arself essentially infected her while she was being mined," Linus says without looking up.

"I don't understand what Arself is," Dubbs says from the floor. "How can a computer infect someone?"

"She's a different kind of computer," Burnham says. "Quantum computers are incredibly fast, and Arself has a biomedical interface that connects her circuits to living tissue in the dreamers. She's a hybrid organism." He smiles toward Dubbs, whose doubtful expression makes it clear she isn't following him. "Think of people who have fake arms that are controlled by their minds. Arself's a little like that, only backward, like an arm that can think."

Dubbs looks at her own hand, turning it in the sunlight over the cat. "I wouldn't like that," she says.

I smile at her. "No, you wouldn't."

Linus lifts his head to meet my gaze. Wordlessly, he smiles at me, and my heart tumbles over.

"Rosie!" Dubbs says. "Come sit here. By me."

I ease down onto the rug beside her. "Did you eat breakfast?"

"Yes. Bagels."

I pull my ankles in, sitting pretzel style, and feel the warmth of the sunlight coming in the window.

"Are you calling somebody?" I ask Linus.

"No. Just answering a text from my boss," he says.

I hadn't even thought about his job. "Are you missing work?" I ask.

"No. We're good. We wrapped up our last story earlier this week. Now we're negotiating for next season. I can check in later." He puts his phone away.

It sounds important to me, and I feel a bit guilty about keeping him away from *Found Missing*.

He smiles, shaking his head at me. "Don't worry about it."

"Speaking of smart arms," Lavinia says. "When I was a kid, I remember when researchers connected one rat to another, brain to brain, and the rats could share information on how to get through a maze. That was a big breakthrough. Back then, the most common A.I. was Siri on our phones. Then the Google brain folks had a translator that taught itself how to translate better. Things really took off after that."

"It's the biomedical interface that makes the difference," Burnham says. "The dreamers have a lot of computational power down there. Converted to data storage or digital processing, it has to be massive."

"What data would they store?" I ask.

"Could be anything," Burnham says. "Dreams themselves take up loads of computer memory. Remember those strange files we found when we hacked into Berg's computer system at Forge?"

"Yes," I say.

Lavinia pops a lemon drop in her mouth. "Of course. I don't know why this didn't occur to me earlier. *The Forge*

Show needs a ton of computer processing to keep track of all its viewers and tally up the blip ranks. They're changing every minute. That takes a lot of power. Berg could be using the dreamers for that processing."

"But Forge is miles away," I say.

"Distance isn't an issue," Burnham says. "The data's collected from around the world, in every time zone. It's sent to a central quantum computer, analyzed, and exported again in microseconds. No big deal."

"I knew I liked you," Lavinia says to Burnham.

"We don't know this is happening at Grisly, though. We have no evidence that the dreamers are tallying the blip ranks for Forge," Linus says.

Lavinia clicks her lemon drop around her teeth. "We don't know they aren't, either," she says. "If you ask me, it's just the sort of thing Berg would set up."

"Arself said something about studying the Forge viewers," I say.

"How is she this morning, anyway?" Linus asks.

"She's quiet," I say, listening.

"She wears you out," Linus says.

I nod. "A little."

"Was I connected to the dreamers?" Dubbs says.

I slide my hand over her sunny, warm hair. "Do you feel weird or hear any voices in your head?" I ask.

She tilts her head as if listening. "No," she says.

"That's good. The doctors said they were only going to observe you," I say. "I think you're fine."

She plucks her shirt out so she can look down inside, and I know she's checking that the bandage is still over her port. "When are we going back to Grisly?" she asks.

I glance urgently toward Lavinia, who nods.

"Actually, you're staying here with me," Lavinia says to Dubbs. "I need your help to keep everybody coordinated. We're command central."

"Rosie said I could go with her," Dubbs said.

"I said I wouldn't leave you here alone," I remind her. "I think you'll be safest staying with Lavinia. That's what Ma would want."

Dubbs frowns, and I expect her to keep arguing. Instead, she keeps petting the cat.

"Okay," she says.

Burnham makes another distinctive tap on the laptop. "I have this ready," he says. "Linus, can you get the blanket?"

Linus hangs a dark blanket over the window while Lavinia sets her puck in the middle of the bed again. The 3-D map of Grisly projects up again, this time with the seven possible places that Arself helped me find already marked in red. My eye instantly locates the ones that are closest to the Main Drag because that's where I assume Dubbs was when she looked out of the kidnappers' truck. Unfortunately, there's no highlighted room directly along the Main Drag. The closest is the Lost and Found, near the entrance of the park, and then I realize there are little rows of shops in other parts of the park, too.

"Does anything look familiar?" I ask Dubbs.

"No," she says.

Lavinia takes a pencil and points the eraser toward a low

building at the edge of the Backwoods Forest, at the far end of the park.

"Deliveries arrive here," she says. "There are ramps here and here, so trucks could back up and unload, but there's also a service road that goes underneath here for deliveries directly to the production level. Level Negative One, we called it," she explains to the others. "That's where they brought in the flatbeds for the floats, too." She glides her pencil down a ramp and taps another space, which is near a red room. "There's an underground parking lot here."

"I think we need to focus our search on the surface," I say.

"Have some patience," Lavinia says.

"I'm just saying. We know from Dubbs that Ma and Larry were taken from the truck on the surface, near a row of shops," I say.

"They still could have been carried downstairs from there," Lavinia says.

We look carefully at all the red places, weighing their likelihood of holding Ma and Larry, and I start writing a list. Two on Negative One in storage and the press/archives room seem very unlikely to me. The rest are all aboveground, in the park itself: the first is a turret room in the keep overlooking the moat; the second is a VIP passageway behind the Glue Factory, the roller coaster in Bubbles' Clown World; the third is a gift shop in the Backwoods Forest; the fourth is a garbage area behind a juice stand in Zombieville; and the fifth is the Lost and Found.

Lavinia points her eraser into the Lost and Found. "This was for lost kids. Even with phones, kids still got separated from their families at the park. We could always find them by backtracking through the security footage, though. More often than not, the kid crawled into a quiet place and fell asleep. They were just overstimulated."

"I thought the park was mainly for teens and grown-ups," Linus says.

"All ages," Lavinia says. "The park didn't have any age restrictions, just weight and height requirements for the rides. We left it up to families to decide what they thought was appropriate."

I review my list of possibilities and try putting them in order for the shortest route between all of them, leaving the ones underground for last.

1. Backwoods Forest Gift Shop
2. Keep of Ages
3. Zombieland Juice Garbage
4. Lost and Found
5. VIP behind the Glue Factory
6. Storage Room #7
7. Archives/Press

I think of Berg and slowly add another number.

8. The Vault of Dreamers

"I hate to mention this, but it's also possible that Ma and Larry are in the vault," I say. "It could be that Whistler lied, or it could be they've been moved there." I push my hair back from my face. "We need to find a way down there. Another way, not down through the moat."

"There's no route to the vault on the maps," Burnham says.

"Are you sure?" I ask. "There must be a staircase or an elevator."

"Passages to the vault weren't part of the original plans. They must have been put in later," Lavinia says.

Do you know anything? I ask Arself.

She doesn't answer. Exasperating.

"We'll leave the vault for last, then, if they aren't anywhere else," Linus says.

Dubbs leans against me to look over my shoulder. I keep hoping she'll recognize something, but she doesn't speak up.

"It's a lot of places to search," Burnham says. "I like the redundancy in the name Backwoods Forest."

"The Grislys had a sense of humor," Lavinia says.

"What'll you do if you get caught?" Dubbs asks me, her eyes large.

I give her a little hugging squeeze. "That's where you and Lavinia come in. If we don't come back out, you call the police."

"But what if it's too late?" Dubbs says.

A new notch of fear troubles me, but I manage a laugh. "When did you get to be such a pessimist? We'll be fine. We'll be out with Ma and Larry in no time. You'll see."

25

THE KEEP OF AGES

THAT NIGHT, when it grows dark, Linus, Burnham, and I head back through the contamination zone to Grisly Valley. I've borrowed dark pants, a shirt, and some black ballet flats from Lavinia, the most suitable things she could offer me, and the guys are dressed in their darkest clothes.

We park the blue van in the forest as close as we can to the northwest edge of the theme park, and once we crawl through the outer fence that surrounds the property, we walk along the service road toward the main delivery entrance. The sky's partly cloudy, but enough moonlight reaches the ground so we don't trip. Burnham has rigged a recyclable cell phone onto a visor hat for me so the lens points ahead, and I have an earphone attached. Through my phone, Lavinia and Dubbs can follow our progress remotely, provided reception isn't too sketchy, and they can fill us in on any movement by the cameras at the Grim Reaper and the Scylla statues. I picture them together on the bed, where we left them, with the phone on speaker between them.

A bug buzzes up in my face, and I swat it away. Then I glance to my left to see how Burnham's keeping up. His knee brace allows for a range of movement, but he still has a limp.

"I'm fine," he says. "You don't have to keep checking up on me."

"I can't see anything," Dubbs complains in my ear.

"That's because it's dark," I say.

Near the loading docks, a security light high above illuminates the road and the steps. We keep to the shadows and take the steps up to the nearest deserted platform. The first big, garage-style door is unbudgeable, and so are the others. From the rust, I'd guess they haven't been opened in decades.

"This way?" Linus asks, pointing right.

I nod. We circle to the west, following the wall on the outer edge of the Backwoods Forest, until we find a place where an old picnic table has been upturned against the wall to create a crude ladder. Other trespassers have clearly come in this way before.

"Last chance for second thoughts," I say.

Linus shakes his head in a brief negative.

"I'll go first," Burnham says, and starts climbing.

It's actually reassuring to watch him. His arms are strong, even though his left wrist is locked bent, and he swings his leg in the brace so it doesn't catch on the angled table legs. He gets a grip on the top of the wall and, with the rough noise of fabric rubbing stone, heaves himself up. The next moment, he disappears.

"After you," Linus says.

I follow Burnham, climbing carefully up the table and pressing gingerly against the wall until I can get a good grip on the top. Then I pull myself over and find Burnham looking up at me from the other side. An old ice cream cart stands below me, and I wiggle down to it, and then to the ground. I brush my hands off as Linus comes after, landing lightly on his feet.

It takes me a sec to get my bearings in the darkness. The sound of crickets comes close, real ones this time. The Keep of Ages is barely visible through the trees, toward the center of the park. A security light to our left is too far away to cast light here, under the trees of the Backwoods Forest, but moonlight catches on bits of white litter, and I can just make out the overgrown, cobblestoned path.

"Do you think Berg could be here already?" Burnham asks.

"It's possible. Keep an eye out. We need to find my parents first," I say.

"Flashlights?" Burnham asks.

"No. This way," Linus says. "To the left. The gift shop should be over here."

The path is uneven beneath my shoes, so I tread carefully. I thought the park would feel echoey and barren like it did the first time I came, but here the woods feel more alive, with branches reaching for my hair and shadows that don't add up. It feels like we've dropped into a misguided game of hide-and-seek or capture the flag. The trees pulse with a faint energy, and a soft rustle in the leaves overhead sounds like breathing. Then I hear a deep, quiet hum.

"Do you hear that?" I ask.

Linus and Burnham pause to look toward me.

"Hear what?" Linus says. "The crickets?"

"I thought it was an engine," I say softly.

They look around, alert.

"I don't hear anything," Burnham says.

But now I'm feeling something as well, a vibration below the frequency of audible sound, like a bass note from an invisible orchestra. It registers in my lungs, and with a slow turning, Arself shifts on again in the back of my mind.

We're here, she says, sounding pleased and curious.

Where've you been? I ask. The hum and the vibration are gone again.

Recharging. We were tired, too. This body has a limited supply of energy. What did we miss?

I tried to ask you before if you know any way down to the vault of dreamers. An elevator or stairs or anything.

No, she says. **No cameras go below Negative One.**

We're here to find my parents, I tell her.

So we see.

She sorts herself through my mind again. I'm almost getting used to the sensation now. There's no point trying to hide anything from her.

Can you help me? I ask.

A flicker of a yellow 3-D grid passes over my eyes and then vanishes.

If you get us to the keep, we might be able to learn something.

That's second on our list. We want to check the gift shop first. It's close by.

We know where it is, Arself says.

I consider telling the guys that Arself is back, but Linus is already moving ahead, aiming toward the gift shop, and I don't want to slow us down. Burnham is making good time beside me, though I can hear him panting a little with effort.

A few paces farther on, we come to an opening in the forest and a low, octagonal building stands at an intersection of paths, apart from a short row of other shops. The trim is drab and paint-chipped, and the striped awnings over the windows sag where they're ripped.

I'm trying to locate the door when Arself lifts my left hand in a slow wave before my face. I come to a stop, surprised. In the wake of my moving hand, another layer of images slowly blossoms before my eyes. The gift shop shimmers into focus with bright red-and-white paint and crisp black-and-white awnings. A row of tiny white lights appears around the borders of the windows, outlining them cheerfully, and glimpses of souvenirs are visible inside. The effect is charming, but its fragile transparency convinces me it isn't true.

Is this what it was like? I ask.

Yes.

Curious, I smile and move nearer. For the first time, Arself makes me feel powerful with new knowledge. I step up to a large window and peer into the dim interior. Old shelves have been pushed to one side, and the long, angled counter is bare. A soap dispenser on the floor is surrounded by a sticky black puddle. Yet when I wave my hand over the same scene, the shelves are centered in the room and filled with colorful merchandise: key rings, stuffed animals, tee-shirts, and coffee mugs. Spotlights illuminate every corner, and the counter shines with

278

polish. It has to be an illusion, but it's so vivid I can see every detail, right down to the price tag on a Tiffany lamp.

I thought you didn't have your old files, I say to her.

These are our home memories, she says simply.

Surprised, I feel a spark of sympathy for her.

But you didn't exist when the park was new.

Even so. We've been over Grisly endless times.

Beside me, Linus remains in shadow. I don't have to ask if he sees the magical visions. He would have said something.

"Are you okay?" Linus asks me. "Do you still hear something?"

"No, it's gone. I'm fine," I say, and the illusion drains away so that the reality of decay and neglect is visible again. I hate to think my parents could be inside.

Using my flashlight, I crack a hole in the glass pane of the nearest door. Glass tinkles as it falls, and I reach inside to undo the doorknob. The place has a stale, hollow feel, and I'm careful to avoid the glass as I step in. Burnham passes me and opens a door into a back room. I lean over the counter to check behind it. The floor is bare, a checkerboard of black and white, with a faded animal cracker box in the corner. No parents.

I slump with relief.

"Nobody's here," Linus says.

"Did you see this?" Burnham asks.

He's holding a framed magazine cover, tipping it toward the security light outside so I can tell the issue features the start of *The Forge Show*, back in 2043. The cover shows the quad of the Forge School from a bird's-eye view, with students crossing the paths, lounging on the grass, and throwing Frisbees.

"Weird," Linus says.

"Why is that here?" I ask. "Grisly wasn't open yet in twenty-forty-three."

"It must have been memorabilia," Burnham says. "Want to keep it?"

I shake my head. It gives me the creeps. "No. Let's go," I say. "We have six more places to check, plus the vault."

"We could split up," Linus says. "It's all bigger than I thought."

"No," I say. "We stay together."

"I still can't see anything," Dubbs says over my earphone.

"There's nothing to see," I tell her. "We just finished the gift shop, the first place. Now we're heading toward the keep. Do you see anything on the other cameras?"

"No," Lavinia's voice says. "The reaper and Scylla are quiet."

Back outside, I look hopefully for the top of the keep through the trees, but I can't find it from this angle. Still, I've memorized the layout of the park, so it's almost instinctive to turn southeast.

That's right, Arself murmurs.

Linus and Burnham fall in behind me. Unchecked nature and time have added a layer of creepy on top of the original version of spooky in the Backwoods Forest, and it seems to grow denser the farther we go. Ponderous oaks have been overrun with gnarly vines. Thorny bushes have outstripped the hedgerows that once enclosed the mazes where visitors waited for rides. A false owl decays on a branch, with its marble eyes black and strangely alive.

A real animal skitters in the shadows just as I step into a

veil of spiderwebs. I jump back with a gasp and hurry to wipe them off my ears and hair.

"All right?" Linus asks.

"Spiderwebs," I say, with a shiver.

"Want light?" Burnham asks.

"No," I say.

Linus brushes off my hair and shoulders, and then turns me to check my back. I feel his hand stroke swiftly over my shirt.

"You're good," he says.

"Thanks," I say.

Burnham pushes through a last layer of branches, and we pause to stare up at the dark stone walls of the Keep of Ages. It rises from an island of thorns in the empty moat. Moonlight touches the roof, and the dragon hunches in its old, silent place. It holds one of the double spires with its clawed feet, and it's as motionless as a tombstone. Then Arself shifts and passes my left hand in front of my eyes again, like she did at the gift shop. Immediately, the stones of the keep seem to darken even further, to a deeper, impossible black. The empty moat fills with a shimmery fog, and blue lights illuminate the steps of the bridges. With a thrill of fear, I look up at the dragon again to find its eyes are glowing red now, and it starts to turn, searching for me.

My heart kicks into gear.

You're doing this, aren't you? I ask Arself.

Yes. Don't you want it?

I shake my head. *No. I need to see what's real.*

I keep watching the dragon, waiting, and his eyes gradually fade to black. The keep returns to its normal, decaying hue.

Don't do that again, I tell her.

All right. We won't unless you ask.

"How do we get in?" Linus asks.

"Something's wrong with Rosie," Burnham says. "What's going on?" he asks me.

I fix my gaze on the dragon again, and it's a motionless dark statue. I lick my lips. "Arself sent me a couple visions," I say. "It feels like special effects in my head. She's me showing what the park was like before, when it was open."

Linus shifts directly in front of me and takes me by the arms. "If you can't trust what you're seeing, we shouldn't be here. I mean it, Rosie. It's too dangerous. We need our wits working. Take another look at the keep. Tell me what you really see."

Slowly, doubtfully, I lift my gaze to the top of the keep where the dragon hunches, holding the roof. Its eyes are black, so black I can barely make them out. I let out a sigh of relief.

"I see a dragon clutching the tower. His eyes are black," I say.

Linus squeezes my hand. "Good," he says. "Don't listen to your fear."

Arself isn't simply fear, I think, but I don't object. It's scary, what she can do to me, but it's also pretty amazing. If I understood her better, she'd be practically a superpower.

"I told her not to do it again," I say. "We're okay."

"*We?*" Linus asks.

"I. *I'm* okay," I say.

"Then let's go. How do we get into the keep?" Burnham asks.

It looks like a bridge once crossed to the back of the keep from this side, but all that's left of it now is a pile of rubble in the moat. The next nearest bridge is part of the double staircase in front of the keep, near where I planted Lavinia's camera by Scylla. It's a more open area where security cameras are also likely to pick us up.

"We'll have to go around," I say. "Lavinia, can you hear me?"

"Yes," she says into my ear. I touch my earphone for a better connection.

"Do you see anything from Scylla? Anything out of the ordinary?"

"No, it's all clear," she says. "There's nothing at the reaper, either."

Linus, Burnham, and I walk quietly around to the front, keeping to the cover of trees and kiosks as much as we can, until we reach Scylla Square, the open area between the end of the Main Drag and the moat. A couple security lights cast the cobblestones in a gray hue. Ahead, at the top of the steps, the big double doors of the keep are closed. The caged light shines above them.

"I can see you!" Dubbs says into my ear.

"Great," I whisper.

We cross the square toward the keep, and as we climb the steps, I look over the banister, down into the moat, toward the hole where I first fell down to the vault. I can make out nothing but shadows, dead leaves, a broken mannequin, and more bits of weathered litter.

"There's a drain down there," I say to Linus, pointing. "That's where I got down to the vault of dreamers before."

"We're going to find another way down," he says. "If we need to go."

At the top of the stairs, the big wooden doors are tagged with black graffiti, and a scuffed lockbox bulges over a modern knob. Burnham gives one of the big metal handles a pull, but the door doesn't budge.

"Do you have the code?" Linus says to me.

Ten sixty-six, Arself tells me. **Battle of Hastings.**

What's that have to do with anything?

The last security coder was a history buff.

"Try ten sixty-six," I say.

Linus punches it in, and the lockbox gives a buzz of admittance.

"Nice," he says.

When he pulls the door, though, it opens only partway before it jams against a buckled bump in the flooring. The gap is less than a foot wide, and the door won't open any farther. I look doubtfully at the width of Linus's trim waist, and then at Burnham's. They're both solid guys, and Burnham's easily twenty pounds heavier.

"Can you make it?" I ask.

"No problem," Burnham says. "Go ahead."

I squeeze through first, and with a grunt, Linus jimmies through behind me. Worried, I look back out at Burnham. He gets his leg with the brace through first, and then he works himself through the tight space. He adjusts his glasses and, breathing hard, he nods at me.

"Now where?" he asks.

Upstairs, Arself says.

I take a look around.

A broken section of the wall up near the ceiling lets in a glimpse of the night sky and enough moonlight to reveal the musty interior. We're in a tall, narrow hall, with a big fireplace to our left. The head of a deer is mounted above the mantel, and two hooves are mounted below it, pawing out toward us. Some joker has placed a beer can on the deer's head. A border of metal spears, pointing up and embedded into the walls, goes around the room, and many of the spears' brackets bristle with birds' nests. Poop has crusted below. Opposite us, the back door of the keep is closed. It's equally as tall as the one we entered, and I can imagine how foot traffic once flowed through here and across the now fallen bridge outside. Two arched openings stand on either side of the back door, one leading to an upward staircase, the other leading down.

I have to admit, I'm curious about what it was like before. *Show me*, I say.

As I slowly pass my left hand before my face, a shimmer spreads across the scene. The dimness gives way to an inviting room with gleaming woodwork and a huge, triple-tiered chandelier. Each spear has a polished point, and colorful tapestries of hunting scenes and garden picnics line the upper walls. The beer can has vanished off the deer head, and burnished silver vases of flowers have appeared on the mantel. A lush carpet lies underfoot, worked with blue and gold threads, and a row of tall wooden chairs backs against the right-hand wall. To top it all off, a full coat of armor stands in the corner, with a red plume in its helmet.

For a moment, I gaze around in wonder, and then the images begin to dissolve, giving way to reality.

"What is a keep, exactly?" I say.

"It's an old tower," Linus says. "We have lots of them back in Wales."

"It's a defense," Burnham says. "That's its prime function."

My gaze drifts up again to the break in the wall and the night sky beyond it. "So why call this the Keep of Ages?" I ask.

"Maybe they hoped it would stand forever," Linus says. "It's about timelessness."

"Immortality," Burnham says.

I smile. "Ironic, isn't it, since it's crumbling?"

A tiny, mechanical hiss comes from above, but I can't see exactly where. I feel a frisson of alertness.

"Did you hear that?" I ask.

"A camera, maybe," Linus says. "The doctors in the vault probably know we're here by now."

"Will they send someone up?" Burnham asks. "What'll we do if they find us?"

That seems a lot more likely now than it did when Dubbs asked the same question.

"We'll tell them I'm here to talk to Berg," I say. "In the meantime, we'd better hurry," I say, and I cross over to the upward staircase.

Gray splotches litter the bottom steps, and I instinctively avoid them as I start up. At that instant, a winged flurry dive-bombs down at me. I yelp and duck as it flies past. *Bat*, I think, breathless. A disturbing rustle comes from above me, and then it magnifies into a whirl. As I crouch low, a flapping cloud of bats rushes down above me and flies past my head like a dark wind. The bats circle wildly inside the hall and then fly out the hole of moonlight, leaving the last one behind to flap against the walls before it vanishes, too.

My heart's galloping in my chest.

"You okay?" Linus asks. He's hunched right behind me.

"I'm fine," I say. "Just startled. Burnham?"

I look back and see him ducked next to the fireplace with his leg at an awkward angle.

"I'm good," Burnham says.

"Time for a flashlight," Linus says.

"Yes. Go ahead. After you," I say. Chances are, we've been seen already anyway.

Linus shines his flashlight up the staircase and starts up. I follow, and Burnham comes along behind me. The close confines of the stairwell oppress me, and even though the walls are encased in stone, I get the feeling they aren't stable. After the first turn, the facade abruptly changes to flat drywall, and at the next landing, we reach a short, modern hallway with three doors. The left one is open to the turret room that we marked to search, but it contains only a long, dirty wad of pink insulation.

"My parents aren't here," I say.

Linus tries the right door and reveals a second empty room.

The central door is marked "Special Effects," and it has another lockbox over the knob.

"Any ideas?" Burnham asks me.

1869, Arself says. **First transcontinental railroad.**

"Try eighteen-sixty-nine," I say.

Burnham punches it in and then shoves the door open.

"Whoa," he says. "Jackpot."

The room has half a dozen old-fashioned computer consoles and close to twenty screens, all dark. A film of staticky dust clings to their glassy surfaces. I notice two windows that overlook the moat are covered with a thin layer of blue plastic that's peeling in places. At least we'll be able to see from here if anyone's approaching up the Main Drag.

I can feel Arself's surprise, and a hint of disappointment.

What's wrong? I ask.

We've never seen this from the outside, she says. **It's so boxy. So dead. How do we connect?**

Burnham is already tapping at a couple of the keyboards. Nothing happens. He slides his hand behind one of the desks, and I hear a click. He tries a keyboard again, and the nearest screen lights up.

"That's what I'm talking about," Burnham says. "Someone's been here lately. Give me a minute."

He pulls over a rolling chair, the only seat in the room, and starts typing. The next instant, his screen shows a view of the main entrance with all the turnstiles. He rolls his chair over to the next computer, flips another switch, and types some more. Soon half a dozen computer screens are up and running, some with indecipherable lines of glowing numbers, some with views of the empty streets and rides of Grisly Valley, and some with colorful, scrolling banner ads. Two more show U.S. and world maps.

Just above the central screen, one smaller screen shows a grid that seems strangely familiar, and as I step nearer, I'm surprised to see it's running scenes from *The Forge Show*.

"Is this live?" I ask.

Yes, Arself says.

Linus, from behind me, says, "Looks like it."

I glance over my shoulder to see Linus has paused just inside the door, like he's keeping an ear tuned to the stairs. Burnham, on the other hand, is deeply engrossed by one of the other computers, and he answers as if he's barely heard me.

"It was already set up like that," Burnham says. "I just turned it on."

This is so strange, I think, looking more closely at *The Forge Show*.

On the show, a thin girl in a blue dress and gold flip-flops is walking down the steps of the auditorium carrying a giant, plush bear in both arms. She's no one I recognize, but plenty of viewers must know her because her blip rank is #1. She is currently the most popular student on the show. A flickering square next to her blip rank score looks like a pixel error of some kind.

"Why is this showing here?" I ask.

Is this your place? I ask Arself. *Your headquarters?*

She laughs with her odd bubbling noise. **We don't need a headquarters. Look how clumsy and slow this is. Still, it's something. Let us in there.**

Hold on, I tell her.

Burnham reaches up and gives the Forge screen a tap. The pixel error remains.

"Odd," Burnham says.

"Bad reception?" Linus asks.

"No. Something else. A glitch." Burnham goes back to typing. "Everything's encrypted," he mutters.

My fingertips begin to tingle. My heart gives a lurch, and my skin grows warm. As if drawn by instinct, I move to stand behind Burnham and watch his fingers move over the keys. I don't understand what he's doing, but my eyes focus on the code he's writing as if it's a language I might be able to decipher simply by concentrating.

I see, Arself says.

Linus shifts farther into the room until he's standing on Burnham's right, frowning at one of the screens.

"Would you look at this?" Linus says. "I think these circles are tracking viewers of *The Forge Show*."

He's peering at the map of the United States, and I notice now it includes an overlay of blue circles that subtly shift smaller and bigger, lighter and darker. The biggest, darkest circles are centered on major urban hubs: New York, L.A., Chicago. Smaller, lighter dots are scattered in the less populous regions like Montana, North Dakota, and Utah. The next screen with the map of the entire world shows similar circles. The circles are all bigger in the parts of the world where it's currently prime viewing time, and they shrink to nearly nothing in places where it's the wee hours of the morning.

The tingle in my fingertips turns into prickles, and then to burning. Arself is festering like black smoke in the back of my brain.

Let us in there, she says again. Please.

"May I?" I say to Burnham, setting a hand on his shoulder.

He looks up at me, startled, and then vacates the chair.

I take his place, uncertain what to do, but Arself confidently invades my hands. She reaches for an old-style computer mouse and, with an unearthly touch that reminds me of the guider over a Ouija board, she flicks the cursor to the flickering square of pixels next to the Forge School girl's #1 blip rank. We click on it, and at once all of the screens go entirely black. Dead. The next instant, they light up with a grid of a thousand faces.

The effect is stunning.

"What is this?" Burnham says in a low voice. "They aren't on the show."

At first glance, the faces all seem to be looking at me, but then I realize they're looking not quite precisely toward the camera lenses that are filming them, live.

I guide the computer arrow to the top left face and click on it. It enlarges to an eight-by-ten-inch split screen and shows a man eating a bowl of cereal. He's facing toward me, his expression blank, and the flat glow of a computer screen is clearly reflecting off his features. He barely looks down at his cereal at all, and between bites, he appears to forget it entirely. He smiles dimly. He takes another bite of cereal and a drip of milk falls from his mouth back into the bowl.

"Can this be what I'm thinking?" I say in a hushed tone.

I told you before, Arself says. **They're *The Forge Show* watchers.**

"Arself says they're *The Forge Show* viewers," I say.

"Unbelievable," Burnham says.

He borrows the mouse from me and clicks on another profile. It, too, expands, and this person is a young teen girl with a swollen bruise around one eye. Dim gray light flickers over her features. Her mouth is a soft gap. Her head is on a pillow, her bare shoulder is hunched near, and the room beyond her face is dark. She barely has her eyes open, and yet her gaze shifts enough to convince me she's watching something.

Burnham clicks on another profile, and another. Person after person is facing the camera and watching with varying degrees of interest and alertness. They are young people and old, of all races, in living rooms, bathrooms, and bus depots. What's common to all is that they're watching their phones or screens with solitary concentration.

"This is mind-boggling," Linus says. "Is Lavinia seeing this?"

"Not too well," Lavinia says into my ear.

"She says, not too well," I tell them. I take off my hat and pull my earphone plug out of the phone jack, switching over to speakerphone so we can all hear Lavinia's voice and vice versa.

Burnham nudges up his glasses. "Lavinia, is it possible *The Forge Show* is spying on its own viewers?"

"It's possible, in theory," she says. "We already know the show collects viewing data for blip ranks. If each viewing device has a camera, the right cookie could activate that camera and send the data back to Forge. It would be highly unethical, though."

"Theory, my foot. It's already happening. Look at these people," Linus says. "They have no idea what's going on."

"Wait. People are getting spied on through their own phones?" Dubbs asks.

"Yes," Lavinia says. "Or their computers or tablets. Whatever they're using to watch *The Forge Show*."

"These are electronic trace codes, and these look like navigational coordinates," Burnham says. "Longitude and latitude. We could physically locate each one of these people."

"Wow," Dubbs says. "Freaky."

That's an understatement. I've been wary before of someone watching me back through the cameras on computers and phones, but I've never had proof, and I've certainly never imagined it happening on a massive, systematic scale.

"Unbelievable," Burnham mutters again.

He's pulling forward more of the profiles so that they each enlarge in turn, face after face of real people. They're not pretty. They're not models. They're regular humans, some as young as four years old, maybe three. What are they doing watching *The Forge Show*?

I recall a time when Mr. DeCoster showed our class some video messages from fans who addressed us directly, a couple guys from Alaska, and a sick boy in a hospital bed, but that was different. Those viewers knew what they were doing when they recorded themselves and sent in the files. These people have no idea they're being watched.

I go back to the girl with the bruise around her eye, and her glazed expression seems unspeakably sad. It's like she has nothing in her life but the show she's watching. I hate to think I've felt that lonely, but I know I have been. I used to watch TV to forget myself, to see proof that another world existed out there, even if that world knew nothing about me and made me feel more anonymous and insignificant than ever. I even watched *The Forge Show* like that a few times before our TV was broken. It's disturbing to learn now that something could have been watching me back, silently witnessing my blank despair.

"There must be a reason why this is happening," Burnham says.

Linus points to a screen that shows the scrolling banner ads. "Maybe it's tied to their ads," he says. "Maybe the show collects data from the viewers to determine which banner ads they get."

"This is much more invasive," Burnham says. "It goes way beyond tailoring an ad and aiming it at a specific person to get him to buy more shampoo or whatever. This is blanket spying."

"But Linus is right, too," I say. "Suppose Berg is doing this. If he can individualize subliminal messages to each viewer, he can essentially brainwash people. Then he can watch to see how they respond."

"It could be for anything. Politics. Votes," Burnham says. He leans nearer to the screens. "Whoever runs this is like a god. He can control things everywhere. *People* everywhere."

I mentally recoil from the possibility. I stare at Burnham and Linus, aghast. "This is all just conjecture. We don't have any proof that these people are being controlled," I say.

But Burnham's excited. "No, but think about it. This is the ultimate power," he says. "The viewers don't even know it's happening. That's the genius of it. They think they're all making choices of their own free will, but they're being brainwashed. Berg can sway people however he wants and nobody will even know it."

"All because they watch *The Forge Show*?" Dubbs says over the speakerphone.

It sounds ridiculous when she puts it like that. I didn't realize she was following our discussion. My gaze goes back to the girl on the screen, the one who's still staring under heavy eyelids at her phone. I feel certain we're missing something.

"How many people watch *The Forge Show*?" I ask. "Lavinia, do you know?"

"Twenty million or so," she says.

I sag in the chair. This whole thing is so much bigger and more twisted than I ever imagined. All I wanted to do was find my parents. Now I'm looking at a brainwashing system that could take over the world. Maybe it already has.

"Who's doing this? You really think it's Berg?" Burnham asks.

He and Linus look at each other. Then they turn to me.

"Ask Arself," Linus says. "What does she know?"

I take a deep breath. *Is Burnham right?* I ask her. *Is Berg trying to take over the world?*

Not Berg, she answers. She seems to shrink. **Did we do something wrong?**

Her uncertainty is a fragile, explosive force at the edge of my mind.

I grip my head in my hands. *Don't tell me this.*

We found the viewers. We're learning from them. Learning is good. She starts to churn.

"Rosie?" Linus asks.

No, I think. *This can't be right. I couldn't have that evil a thing living in my own mind.*

Fearful, I fix my gaze on the bruised girl again as if her raw, mute unhappiness is the key to everything. I brace for pain.

Arself slams into all my senses. She takes over my eyes and jerks my vision from one viewer to the next, speeding impossibly fast, while an amped-up part of my mind memorizes details of their features, electronic tracers, and coordinates. She shoves Burnham aside and runs my fingers over the computer to type at high speed. She's pulling up more fields, more data, numbers and equations and images. I feel the processing as a burn of energy at the base of my skull. It's angry. It's furious.

I'm absorbing an unfathomable amount of information, and I can't stop it.

Let me go! I say.

She only burns faster, as if she would climb right inside the computer if she could.

You promised! Let me go!

Trying to understand, she says. **Already told you. Want to understand.**

It's not right for you to control another person! I say. *Don't you know right from wrong?*

My fingers freeze above the keys. Arself is suddenly silent. The whirl of processing comes to a halt.

We're *not* another person. We're not like you, she says.

And that's the problem, right? I ask. *You want to be like me?*

She wavers. A slithering, ticking noise scuttles through the back of my mind. I can tell she's testing my questions.

You have to quit controlling me, I say. *I don't care who you are. It's the right thing to do.*

296

A voice reaches me dimly. It's Linus calling my name. My fingers are still poised over the keyboard, and I can hear my breath coming in short, hungry gasps.

Humans don't all do the right thing. We know that much, she says, and releases me.

26

THE GOLDEN LINE

I CLOSE MY EYES and drop my head in my hands, suddenly exhausted. A pocket of silence consumes me and a chill squeezes into my bones. I thought I was getting to know Arself. I was starting to trust her and even to like her in a way, but now she's grown sinister again, and huge. She's been watching all the viewers! I didn't understand before that she meant spying on them. How could she think that's okay? What I don't know is if she's been manipulating them.

Of course she has, I realize. She brought me here. She didn't exactly brainwash me, but she brought me to Grisly Valley and the vault. And now she's in me. She's part of me. Despite what she promised, she can take over whenever she wants. I'm revulsed by the idea.

Dimly, I become aware that Lavinia is talking over the speakerphone.

"Okay. Yes. We're on it," Linus replies. He swivels my chair toward him and grips my shoulders. "Rosie?"

I lift my gaze to find his face close to mine, and his concern snaps me out of my horror.

"Can you hear me?" he asks.

"Yes," I say.

I glance up to see Burnham is watching me, too. Behind him, the computers are reset to the original array of security shots, maps, and *The Forge Show*. I want to tell Linus and Burnham about Arself, about how she, not Berg, is running the surveillance on the viewers, but it's too horrifying. I have too many questions of my own.

Linus gives me a little shake. "I need you to listen to me. Lavinia says two people are climbing around the front gate," he says.

Burnham reaches past me to the main console and starts typing. "Check this out," he says.

He points to a flicker of motion on one of the screens, and then he expands the view. I straighten slowly.

Near the entrance to the park, two men are walking side-by-side down the center of the Main Drag. My heart constricts as they step under the glow of the first security light. On the left is Ian Cowles, lanky, hunched, and as scruffy as ever. His baggy camo pants are tucked into his black boots at the ankle, and he's wearing a black jacket that bulges with pockets and zippers. His left hand is wrapped in a bandage: a memento from Doli. Beside him, Sandy Berg carries himself with natural authority, even here, and I cringe at the familiar sight of his solid build and tidy blond hair. He wears a tan, short-sleeved safari shirt over dark trousers, and his watch glitters gold.

"That's Berg for sure," Linus says. "Who's with him?"

"That's Ian," I say.

"The guy from the Onar Clinic?" Burnham asks.

"Yes," I say with loathing. "He's the most repulsive, revolting, putrescent person I've ever met, besides Berg."

"Don't hold back," Burnham says.

I step closer to the screen, staring as the men walk under some trees. Burnham shifts around with the touchpad, and the next shot shows a closer image of them from another angle as they continue walking up the Main Drag.

"They must know we're here at Grisly," Linus says. "It can't be a coincidence they're coming now."

"But do they know we're in the keep?" I ask.

Berg and Ian walk out of view of the security camera, and Burnham works the touchpad again. The screen remains on the empty street where they just were.

"Sorry," Burnham says. "I don't exactly know how to work this."

"Check where their car is," Linus says. "Let's see if they came alone."

Burnham pulls up a few more camera angles, all wrong. My fingertips itch like wild again.

Get him out of the way, Arself says. **Let us in there.**

Fat chance.

Don't be dense. We're on your side.

Not enough, you're not.

300

Burnham pulls up a few more security angles, all empty, and finally locates the handicapped parking area beside the main gate. A white sedan is parked in the glow of another tall security light.

"See the car?" I ask.

"Yes," Linus says.

In another screen, Berg and Ian show up again. They're still walking down the Main Drag, taking their time.

"They're awfully confident," Linus says. "Why aren't they coming faster? Do they want us to see them?"

"Maybe they *don't* know we're here," Burnham says.

"None of that matters," I say. "If they come into the Keep of Ages, we'll be caught." There's only one way down from where we are: the staircase that leads back to the main hall.

"We have to go," Burnham says. "I'm not fast."

"Wait. Look," Linus says.

Berg and Ian have slowed before a gift shop, the last one on the Main Drag, right before it meets Scylla Square. I turn to the window in alarm, and I can actually see them out there talking. Berg adjusts an earpiece in his right ear. Ian takes a gun out of his pocket, turns it over in his hand, and nods. Then Berg backtracks a couple paces and goes into a door while Ian resumes walking toward the keep.

"We seriously have to leave," Burnham says. "Come on!"

He doesn't bother turning anything off and bolts toward the doorway. Linus and I hurry after him, down the dark stairs and out into the hall with the fireplace. We reach the big double doors of the keep and look out the gap just as Ian starts up one of the outer stairway bridges, the one to our left. We can't get out without being seen, and Ian has a gun. We'd be vulnerable just trying to get through the tight gap of the doorway. Burnham, beside me, seems bigger and slower than ever.

"What do we do?" I whisper.

"Back," Linus says, yanking my arm.

I turn and run with him across the hall toward the downward staircase. Burnham's right behind us. We descend into the dark. Half a dozen steps down, after the first turn, I can't see a blasted thing. I bump into Linus's back. Burnham bangs into me with his brace, and I bite back a gasp of pain. Linus's arms come around me, steadying me, and Burnham goes motionless on my other side. Silent, with my heart beating, I turn my gaze up the staircase to where a faint gleam of reflected moonlight touches the wall. I can feel my pupils expanding, begging for more. A scratching noise comes from above. Then silence. Then a creak of pressure. Then a distinct footstep.

I wait, hearing only silence, and then another footstep, softer than before.

"He's going up," Linus whispers.

We listen, straining our ears.

"He'll find all the computers on," Burnham whispers. "He'll be able to see anywhere we go through the surveillance."

We should have turned them off or busted them, but it's too late now.

"Come on," I say. "We have to run for it."

"Where to?" Linus says. "Are we going after Berg?"

I scramble for a plan. Even with Ian after us, I still need to find my parents. If I can do that, I'll be in better shape dealing with Berg. "I'm going to keep looking for my parents. The next place is the garbage area by the juice stand in Zombieville. That's down the right-hand staircase to the south, past the Giant Cesspool."

"You can't be serious," Burnham says.

"I still have to find them!" I whisper viciously.

"We should go now," Linus says.

Burnham nudges an elbow into me. "Okay," he says.

He starts up the stairs, moving silently, and I'm right behind him. The hall is empty, and I glance at the upward staircase before I dart across to the door. Burnham motions me through first. I edge my way out and take a quick look around the deserted square. Linus is right behind me. I glance over my shoulder for Burnham, but the black gap of the doorway is empty.

"Where's Burnham?" I whisper.

Linus grabs my arm, pulling me out toward the stairs. "We have to go! He's coming!"

I hesitate, anxious. Linus tugs me again, and I run with him down the right-hand staircase, but my heart is ten steps behind me, protesting all the way. At the bottom of the steps, Linus takes a hard right, hauling me with him, and we don't stop until we're crouched into a dark corner beside a fence.

"What about Burnham!" I say, craning my neck to see toward the keep. The stairs are still empty. "What does he think he's doing?"

"He's okay. He's smart," Linus says. "He'll get out when he can."

"You knew?" I say, incredulous. "You talked to him, didn't you?"

"He said if we got in a tight spot, I should get you out of it," he says.

I lurch upward, fully intending to go back for Burnham, but Linus yanks me down again.

"Do you want to find your parents?" he asks.

"Yes, but Ian has a gun!"

"Trust Burnham. He's fine," Linus says.

He is not fine. I try to imagine a fight between Ian and Burnham, and it's a disaster.

"I mean it. Burnham can take care of himself," Linus says. He points back toward the Main Drag. "I'm going to try and follow Berg."

"We were going to stay together," I remind him.

"Then do you want to come with me? Berg could be going to your parents."

But he might not be, too. "I still want to check the places on our list," I say.

"Then you do that," Linus says. "Try to stay away from the lights so Ian can't track you."

An involuntary shiver of fear runs through me.

"You can't try to kill Berg without me," I say.

"I'm not going to kill anybody if I don't have to," Linus says. "I'm just going to see where he goes. He probably knows a way down to the vault of dreamers, right?"

Linus is right. But it feels dangerous to be separating. Anything could go wrong. "Where should we meet up again?"

"Call me," he says.

"Your phone won't work underground," I say. I instinctively pat my pockets, which are now too soft and empty. "My phone! I left it up in the keep!"

"It's here," he says, passing it into my hand. "I'll call you when I get back up."

I grip the solid little shape and take a deep breath, striving to be calmer, to think. I don't have my earphone anymore, or my hat, so rigging up the phone again for Lavinia and Dubbs to see from is out. But at least I have the phone.

"We need a backup plan," I say. "If I can find my parents, I'll bring them here. No, I'll bring them to the gift shop in the Backwoods Forest, near where we came in." It scares me to think what shape my parents could be in, and the van is back a quarter mile outside the wall. "What if they're unconscious or something? I'll need your help. Or Burnham's."

"So then you'll call me or text me where you are," Linus says, taking his phone out of his pocket. "The gift shop is only a backup if we can't call each other. Okay? The first thing to do is find your parents, one way or another."

I know what he's saying makes sense. I guess I'm just afraid, and that's why I'm rattled and doubting everything. He's typing into his phone.

"What are you doing?" I ask.

"Texting Burnham so he knows where to meet us, just in case."

I look back at the keep's stairs, wishing Burnham would appear there. He doesn't.

"He'd better be okay," I say.

Linus glances up. He pockets his phone and pulls me near for a hug. "We've got this. You hear me?"

"I know," I say, holding him tight. "Just please don't do anything stupid. I couldn't bear it if you got hurt."

He smiles. "I won't. You be careful, too."

The next moment, he's gone.

I take another look back toward the keep and realize I haven't heard a gunshot. Then again, I'm not sure I would hear it through the stone walls of the keep. A soft layer of fog is collecting in the bottom of the moat now, and I frown.

Are you making me see that? I ask Arself.

No, she says. **That's real fog**.

Instinctively, I lift my gaze to the dragon on the roof of the keep and discover its eyes are red again.

What's going on? I ask.

Somebody's playing with the special effects, Arself says.

I recall that Whistler said Ian liked to play with the special effects when he was here. I don't know what this indicates about Burnham, but I have to hope he's still okay.

I gather my courage and hurry past the Giant Cesspool and farther into Zombieland. More rides and derelict shops line the streets, and I stick to the shadows as much as possible. At the juice stand, I find the garbage area surrounded by a concrete wall. The metal door is locked with a chain and a rusty padlock. Because the garbage area is open to the air, it doesn't look likely as a place to stash my parents, but I scale the wall to look inside. Old, industrial-sized dumpsters for garbage and recycling line the far side, and they look like they haven't been opened in ages.

If someone has stuffed my parents inside the dumpsters, I don't think I can take it. They have to be somewhere better. Berg wouldn't have any leverage over me if he actually had them thrown away.

I drop back outside the wall, landing low on my feet, and run east through Vampyre Graveyard. Next on my list is the Lost and Found, so I aim toward the front of the park where the Lost and Found is located. *Please be there*, I think as I run. Always looking for the darkest path, I pass the End of Daze spiral tower and wind through another set of shops and freestanding kiosks. Then I spot the East Depot of the train and sneak past a long row of outdoor lockers. I must be getting close to the main entrance. Debris clots the grid of a storm drain where I leap across.

A sudden, deeper darkness makes me pause and look up. A silver-edged cloud has moved over the face of the moon, casting a shadow over Grisly. I listen to the motionless air, wary for a sound of anyone chasing me, but all I can hear is the far-off fading of a plane. Rounding the next corner, I find the main entrance with the turnstiles, and beyond them, the statue of the Grim Reaper. Lavinia watching through her camera there should be able to see me if I move into some light.

I scan the nearest row of buildings for the Lost and Found and find it attached to the security office. It's a small building, clearly marked, with a large plate-glass window. I pull out my phone and quickly give Lavinia a call.

"Hey," I say. "We're all separated. Burnham's in the keep and Linus went to find Berg. I'm at the Lost and Found."

"I see you," Lavinia says, her voice staticky. "The dragon's shifting a bit. Otherwise, nothing's changed by the keep."

I peer inside the Lost and Found, seeing only darkness, and my heart dips. I don't want Dubbs overhearing if I get inside there and something bad happens.

"I'll call you later when I know something," I say.

"Dubbs and I are coming to the park," Lavinia says.

"No, don't," I say, alarmed. "You can't help. You have to keep Dubbs safe."

"Then I'm calling the police," Lavinia says.

"No!" I say. "We've got this under control. I mean it. Just let me find my parents. I'm close, I just know it."

A burst of static comes over the phone. "Promise you'll keep us informed," she says. "If you're not out of there in an hour, I'm making the call."

"I will be. Just take care of Dubbs," I say, and disconnect.

Seriously, the last thing I need is my sister here with Lavinia. I'm not calling them again until we're all safely out of here. I test the handle on the Lost and Found, but it's locked, with no code box. I'm getting good at shattering glass with my flashlight. Next, I wrap my sleeve over my hand, reach in to find the inside knob, and carefully unlock the door.

I push it open. My ballet flats brush over broken glass as I enter, and I'm careful to step wide.

"Ma?" I call.

The place smells of rubbish and rain, but also of something sharper, a hint of chemicals. I glance up to see a sagging ceiling, and a cricket chirps. Knowing this place is devoid of working security cameras, I take a chance with my flashlight and cast the beam around. A moldy mural of a tree with cheery woodland animals stands behind a short table shaped like a ladybug. An inner door along the back wall is closed. I step softly over and try the knob. This one is locked, too, and the door has no window. I press my ear to the door and hear a faint hum. I have to get in there.

I throw my shoulder against the door. It holds, but it creaks enough to give me hope. A splintered seam has appeared near the hinge side. I back up a couple paces and rush at it again, barreling into the wood with all my might. The door bursts inward, its hinges busted, and I stagger into the next room.

Two sleep shells are parked along the far wall with pale blue lights illuminating their curved glass lids. A sourness laces the air, and even as I hurry close, I'm thinking, *Please, no. Don't let them be dead.* I stare anxiously into the first one and my heart stops.

It's Ma. Her pale profile is a motionless mask.

As I push open the lid, the ghastly sourness is even stronger.

"Ma," I say, leaning close to hug her.

She's warm. That's the first miracle. Her cheeks and arms are warm to my touch. I nearly start to cry. Her eyes are closed, but she's breathing. That's the next miracle. She's breathing. She's alive! My heart zigzags with joy.

Rapidly, I check her over. She has an IV line going into her hand, but the pouch of fluids above her has gone dry. No catheter is coming out of her, and no pads are on her temples. She's still in street clothes, a summer dress and sandals, with no restraints on her, as if she were dumped there carelessly with no concern for her comfort or fear of her resistance. I stare again at her wan features, her dry lips. Has she been left like this for six days? Seven now?

How can she still be alive?

"Ma!" I say again, gripping her shoulders. She doesn't respond. I look over at the next sleep shell, where Larry's burly form gleams in the blue glow. I shove up his lid, and he's in the same condition as Ma: unresponsive but breathing. They're both alive. But sour, so sour, like they're spoiling.

I check for poop but don't see any. There's some dried urine on Larry's pants, maybe, but the odor is different, more like raw garlic. People can't decay when they're still alive. Can they?

I have to get them out of here. I hurry back to Ma and try holding up her eyelid and shining my light inside. Her pupil contracts slightly, but she doesn't respond otherwise.

"What has he done to you?" I whisper, as cold anger replaces my first relief.

Whatever sick way he's managed it, Berg has drugged my parents into a long-term sleep. I have to believe it's not something worse.

I try calling Linus first, but he doesn't answer. He must be underground. Burnham doesn't answer, either.

How am I going to get them out of here? Ma probably outweighs me by fifty pounds. Even if I could drag her out of here, I'd still need help with Larry.

"Ma," I say again, giving her another shake.

Her head lolls limply on her neck. I can't think why Berg would leave her and Larry here like this, in this dark hole. Why didn't he put them down in the vault with the rest of the dreamers where they could at least be watched over by the doctors? His cruelty shouldn't astound me anymore, but it does.

Arself, I say sharply in my head. *Where are you? We need help.*

We told you. We need to connect again. We can't do anything like this.

I need Linus and Burnham, I say. *Do you know where they are?*

We would if we were connected.

I gnash my teeth in frustration. *Take a guess*, I say.

Burnham is probably still in the keep. Linus was following Berg, who was heading down to Negative One. *This is nothing more than I know myself*, I say. *Can't you help me at all?*

We can optimize your path to VIP Portal Number Twenty-two, factoring in the darkness to avoid detection.

Is that where Berg went?

Yes. Then we want to connect to the dreamers again.

I assume she means getting back on a computer, like we did in the keep when she took over my fingers and raced my eyeballs over the screens. I have no desire to put her in charge again.

Still, I can't exactly lie to Arself with a false promise.

"We'll see," I say aloud. "Okay? That's the best I can do. We'll see."

Deep silence widens for a moment in the back of my brain. Then I feel a tingle in my right palm. I lift my hand, and as I watch, a faint, glowing, gold line appears in the soft skin of my hand. The light has a slight heft to it, like a string, and as I give a slight tug, the line of light extends out of my hand to the floor in front of my feet and travels forward, out the door and around the corner.

I know the string of light can't truly exist, but that doesn't matter. Arself has created it in my mind and superimposed it onto my palm so that it leads into the landscape of Grisly.

I take another look at my parents. They're still breathing, still sleeping. They have no idea I've found them, and somehow that twists me up.

If I leave them, will I see them again? I ask.

We don't know the future.

It's up to me. I'm the only one who can decide. With an ache of fear, I close Larry's lid again, and then my mother's.

"I'll be back," I promise.

Then I lift my palm before me and follow the string of golden light out the door of the Lost and Found.

The night is cooler than before, and a breeze rustles the leaves of a tree to my right. I reach the corner and look left, along the Main Drag. The nearest security lamp illuminates the unicorn statue as before. The others drop their cones of light on the pavement, making blurry circles of gray, while the rest of the park is black. My string of light gleams faintly up the Main Drag, swerving into the deeper shadows. If I shift my hand away from it, the string disappears, but if I direct my hand back in the right direction, it lights up again, and my palm feels a trace of weight.

Following my string, I sneak along the left sidewalk close to the storefronts. Then I cross the street through a patch of darkness and take the right sidewalk until I near the gift shop where Berg and Ian parted. The string of light runs under an unmarked door between the gift shop and a cookie bakery.

This must be *VIP Portal Number Twenty-Two*, I think.

When I push the door open, the string of golden light continues down a hallway toward a landing with an elevator and a staircase. I follow, and when the string veers right, toward the stairs, I descend a couple of flights to a VIP green room, barely visible by the red glow of an exit sign. A shadowy shape makes me jump before I realize it's a pair of fake ficus trees. A sagging couch, gray with dust, is the only other furniture.

Trying the next door, I peek cautiously out to a large, quiet food court. Chairs are clustered around tables, and many still have trays, as if the evacuation twenty years ago was a spell that froze everything in its wake. A curving bank of dirty windows faces into a dark, oddly shaped void, and it takes me a second to realize it's the underground level of the moat, now empty of water.

Spooky hallways lead off in various directions, and I scan them quickly for movement. I can't help worrying that Berg or someone else might jump out at me. A detailed directory lists rehearsal rooms, the grand assembly, security, tech headquarters, archives, press, costumes, makeup, and future idea development. This place is huge.

I slowly wave my hand in an arc, left to right, expecting the string of light to catch on my palm again.

This is where the pathway bifurcates, Arself says. **We can't guide you any farther.**

313

I shine my flashlight onto the floor to where a trail of scuff marks in the dust leads around the moat. I follow them to a door that is slightly ajar, and inside, I find a janitor's closet. A faint whirring noise comes from behind a plastic curtain, and where a large sink or tub might typically be, I find instead a narrow spiral staircase leading down.

I was expecting something different, I say. *Bigger. For the bodies.*

There must be another entrance for them.

Yet this must be the way Berg came, and Linus must have followed. Uneasy, I aim my flashlight along the stairs and creep down. Already, I miss the guidance of Arself's golden string. Two dozen steps down, the whirring noise grows slightly louder, and the spiral ends at a straight, narrow, stone staircase. When I reach the bottom of the next flight, I'm at a small landing with a round window, and it looks out over the vault of dreamers.

With a hitch of relief, I recognize where I am.

I've reached the upper ledge of the dome, the circular hallway with the eight round windows. The oculus is dark at the apex, and I can feel air pushed by a nearby vent into the vast space. When I look back behind me, the staircase is dark and indistinguishable from other warrens I saw down here before. I can't afford to lose it, so I check my pockets for something I can use as a marker.

My fingers close on the smooth black stone Dubbs gave me. I set it in the nook of the bottom stair. Then I look more carefully down into the vault, hoping to spot Berg without being seen myself. The sleep shells, hundreds of them, are still arranged in concentric circles in the cavernous space below, but now the floor shifts with a thin layer of purple fog. A dozen scattered sleep shells have their red distress lights on.

Two dozen others have gone dark completely, and they stand out as black voids in the expanse of blue.

A wail starts up in the back of my mind. I press my fingers to my ears, but the inner lament only grows louder.

Arself! Stop! I say.

No! she says. **This can't be happening!**

Anxiety barrels through me like boulders in an avalanche.

Go! she says. **Get down there! Go, go, go!**

I turn to race down the steps. *What is it? What's happening?*

But she doesn't answer. She's transformed into a wordless, high-pitched keening, and it's all I can do not to hyperventilate with her fear.

I sprint out of the twelve o'clock archway to the nearest dark sleep shell, half hoping it will simply be empty, but when I look inside, a body lies stretched out, a boy with dark hair and eyebrows. Arself howls in my mind. At my feet, the purple fog shifts silently.

"How can this be?" I whisper.

Instinctively, I push up the glass lid to get a closer look, and a noxious reek wafts out at me. It's different from the sourness that clung to Ma and Larry, more ominous. I hold my breath. The kid's gray skin is stretched paper-thin, and his gelled eyes are unnaturally sunken into his skull. His dry lips are slightly pulled back from his little teeth in a rotting grimace. Desperate, I inspect the line that goes into the child's port, but I don't know how to tell if it's flowing right.

Close the lid! It's no use! Arself says.

I obey her, sealing the boy back inside his coffin.

"Is he dead?" I whisper.

Of course he's dead! she says.

"But what happened?" I say. I stare at the cadaver through the glass, bewildered and horrified. "These dreamers were alive just two days ago."

I look around again at how many sleep shells have gone dark. It's more than a dozen. I can see close to twenty, just from here, and the magnitude is bewildering. Nothing before ever convinced me so completely that the dreamers are alive until now, when I've found one dead.

It's all my fault! Arself says. Her agonized cry starts up again.

I press my ears again and bend over with the pain of her noise in my head.

Arself, stop! I think at her. *This isn't your fault. You weren't even here.*

They died because I left!

Eyes closed, I shake my head. "You have to stop! I can't think!"

She stops so abruptly I feel like I've lost my hearing. I open my eyes. All the nearest sleep shells have red lights above them now. The soft whirring of the fan in the oculus is the only sound. Another red light goes on nearby, and another.

The dreamers know I'm here. I've disturbed them. *We've* disturbed them. A dull thump comes from my left, and when I look over, a hand is pressed to the glass lid of a nearby sleep shell, one with a red light. I step over to look inside just as the hand slips down, leaving a sweaty smudge. Inside, the dreamer's face is slack. He's a young man, not much older than me. He has the same gelled eyes and blank expression as all the rest, but I have to believe he was signaling to me.

"We have to help them, Arself," I say. "What can we do? Tell me."

Her anxiety buzzes inside me like a subterranean swarm of bees, but I can't decipher a clear train of thought.

Then I hear a popping noise, and a sharp pinch stings my neck.

My head whips toward the sound, and near the nine o'clock arch, Berg is lowering a small tranquilizer gun. My fear skyrockets. I touch my fingers to the sting and pull a small dart out of my skin, along with a smear of blood. I duck behind the nearest sleep shell, but it's already too late. A fizzing slowness is invading my blood.

No! Arself says. **Not this. Run, Rosie! Don't let him get us!**

A rush of jacked-up adrenaline courses through my veins. For a moment, it seems to negate the effects of the tranquilizer, but when I try to take a step away, I sag to the floor, landing on my hands and knees. A fluff of purple mist drifts away from my hands.

"She's over here," Berg calls.

His footsteps grow louder, and then he's standing above me, a grim, loathsome man. His sandy blond hair is haloed in blue by the light from the nearest sleep shell. His glassy, piggish eyes seem paler than ever, and the fine ridges of his lips and nose stand out in sharp detail.

"You should have answered my calls," he says.

I cringe, trying to crawl away from him under the sleep shell, but he moves nearer, planting his shoe in front of my face. I am not going to be in Berg's power again. I can't let this happen. I'd rather die.

As my cheek slumps against the floor, I breathe in the vinegary taste of the mist.

Help me! I say to Arself, pleading.

Whatever you do, don't tell him we're here, she says.

I can barely answer her. *I might not have a choice.*

We'll have a choice. Be strong.

27

FEAR

HEAVY AND LIMP, I'm unable to resist as Berg picks me up, but I muster the last of my strength and swipe my fingernails at his face.

He reels back. "Stop that," he says, and crushes my arm down.

I wince at the pain, but I'm pleased to see a narrow stripe of blood rising on his left cheek, marring his ruddy complexion. He carries me in his arms like a giant baby, and I manage to turn my face away from his chest. This is exactly what I didn't want to have happen. Why was I so stupid?

Berg stalks toward the nine o'clock arch, and with my last glimpse of the vault of dreamers, I notice that more of the lights have turned red. When Berg carries me around the corner into the operating room, I see Linus stretched out on one of the operating tables. His eyes are closed and he's not moving. My heart sinks. Berg lowers me onto the neighboring table and ties my wrists down, but not before I see the three other doctors busy with prep. Anna, beside Linus, is putting on surgical gloves. Jules taps the computer. Kiri closes an incubator at the back of the room with a soft thud and turns toward us. The only one missing is Whistler.

"Tell Ian we found her," Berg says. "He can come down and join us."

"He's having fun with the special effects," Jules says.

"He'll want to see her. Tell him to come down," Berg says.

Jules reaches for a phone and speaks quietly into it.

"You need to let me go," I say. "Linus, too. You can't keep us down here." I turn to Kiri. "Shouldn't you be helping the other dreamers? Are you just going to let them all die out there?"

"It's too late for them," Kiri says softly. "We'll get others."

"Knock her out," Anna says. "Let's be done with it."

"No. I want you to see what I can do," Berg says. "She's better conscious, and since this is going to be the last time, we have to make it count."

Fear runs through me. "Don't listen to him," I say. "He's a monster. You don't have to do what he says. Let me go!"

"Work yourself up," Berg says. "Go on."

I grit my teeth and pull against my restraints. "He's going to ruin all of this for the rest of you," I say to Anna and Kiri. "All of your work. The police are going to come."

"The police don't care," Anna says.

"Anna? The helmet, please," Berg says.

I wrench my head to the side, but Berg firmly tips my head

up and Anna settles a helmet around my skull. It's the same kind of helmet Berg has used on me before, and my stomach rolls with nausea. The rubber nubs are settled into my ears, and I hear the winch as he tightens the padding. Each small, fidgety adjustment heightens my panic.

You have to me help me! I say to Arself.

She doesn't reply.

Berg turns to his computer console and touches the keypad. A dozen different prongs extend in from the helmet until they touch my scalp and prickle into my skin. I don't remember them from before, and they hurt. The glare of white lights from above makes me squint.

"Too tight?" Anna asks.

"No, that's just right," Berg says. Then he turns to me. "I want you to think of something that frightens you. Like the fact that I have your parents hidden away here at Grisly. They're not doing well."

My heart leaps in terror.

"Very good," Berg says.

"You're despicable," I say.

He lifts a thin wire before his face and inspects the end. With gloved fingers, he screws a tiny, flexible needle onto the wire. "Now I want you to think about Linus. Our very own Linus, right here beside you."

My heart pricks again.

"See this?" Berg says, nodding toward his computer.

"Impressive response," Jules says. "You should attach."

"Soon," Berg says, turning the wire slowly where I can see it. Then he sets it aside and holds up a small jar that contains a shimmering substance, a thick, viscous liquid that seems to flash with miniature lightning. "Guess what this is."

"I have no idea," I say.

Berg smiles. "This," he says, "is a failure. A very special failure. It's a dream seed that I donated myself, but it isn't purely mine. It's been mixed with some of your dreams. In other words, it's a hybrid, with your special kind of resilience. I brought it with me all the way from Iceland."

"Why is it a failure?" I ask.

"Because I've tried it already," he says. "I've been seeded with this hybrid to see if it can arrest and repair my Huntington's, and it didn't work. Apparently, the damage is already too great."

"Then why bring it here?" I ask.

He tilts the jar, letting the slow liquid flow to one side. "Because it might work in Linus. Or you," he says. He considers me with a calm, maniacal gleam in his eyes. "You're my best chance, Rosie. It will be strange starting life over as a teenage girl, but it'll be better than not existing at all."

I am completely stunned. "You're out of your mind!"

"I believe you've said that before," Berg says calmly. "And now, Anna, if you would be so kind, pass me the scavenging line. We'll mine one last sample of her dreams before we introduce the hybrid."

"No!" I say. "You can't! Anna, help me! Kiri!"

I see a needle catch the light, and Berg tilts my helmet slightly so he can reach the sensitive skin at the back of my left ear. I try to wince away from him, but it's impossible. He swabs the place with cool disinfectant, and then I feel the sting of the needle entering my skin. Berg turns to his computer again, frowning intently.

"See here?" Berg says. "We follow the fear in."

I hold my breath as the first hungry, feasting nanobots enter my veins, and a rush of anger wars with my fear.

Arself! Help me!

Hold tight, she says, and for one unspeakable moment, a cold, grim winter hardens my soul into pure darkness.

In the next instant, Arself sends an electric tendril of herself through the scavenging line and into the computer. Light knocks me backward.

Now, says Arself. **We're home.**

My lungs fill with desperate air. I'm starved and exploding at the same time. A flash of molten energy pours through my veins, and next I'm speeding and flashing through a thousand firing circuits along a million electric miles. I'm everything. I'm Arself and myself and every dreamer that ever offered up a shred of dream. Lightning carries me through and around the whole world, and then I'm back to me and Arself, here on this deathbed. My body's motionless, but I hover, ready for everything, eager, alert, alive.

Through half a dozen eyes, from different angles, I'm watching the scene in the operating room where time is expanding in slow motion. Berg's features have barely registered surprise.

We've lost so many of us, Arself says.

With a pinging noise, we speed through the network and drop by each dark sleep shell in the vault. We gather the fine, ephemeral loss of each dead dreamer into our invisible arms. Then we swirl hugely, galaxy-like, with a golden spiral of wings, and time collapses into the cold, empty space around us. Breathless and wondering, I'm suspended in Arself in a realm beyond answers. I'm aware that my body is back in the operating room where my journey with Arself started, but at the same time, the true essence of me is everywhere else, glimpsing an existence so much bigger than anything I've ever imagined. Power and fragility. Connection. Bliss and loneliness. It's like the stars have come with all their splendor to swirl and live in my own cupped fingers. They're humming my language. They have secrets to tell me.

And finally, I get it. Arself doesn't have to translate it into human words for me because I can feel it. The dreamers were each precious on their own while they lived, but they aren't individuals anymore. They're part of us, and they're safe in the golden wings with Arself and me. For a moment, I grasp this. I know it intuitively, to the roots of me. There's no separation anymore. We're us, all belonging and promise. I'm other, finally, like I was always meant to be. I feel a growing sense of victory in Arself, and it's my victory, too. The starlight in my chest expands to a shimmer, and we breathe in the golden air.

28

THE VAULT OF DREAMERS

FOR ONE BLISSFUL MOMENT, I understand everything, and then a poisonous hiss breaks through my ears. It brings me halfway back.

There was once a boy named Linus, I think. *Or maybe he was a fish and I was a bird.*

You have to return to your body, Arself says. **Get back aboveground as soon as you can. It's not safe in the vault.**

The golden light grows thin at the edges where darkness is seeping in, and then a sharp, vinegary smell smarts up my nose. With a start, I open my eyes.

The operating room is dim, with only one overhead light on at the back of the room. Hissing blue fog is spraying down from several broken hoses above, making it even harder to see. I can just make out the shapes of the operating tables around me, but not Berg or the other doctors. How much time has passed?

Twisting my wrist, I'm able to get my right hand free, then I release my left. The helmet is still around my skull, and it weighs heavily as I roll over. I pat my fingers around the helmet until I find a clasp under my chin. As I take it off, it snags in the scavenging line that's attached in back of my left ear, and I gasp in pain.

Disconnect that, and we'll leave the dreamers behind forever, Arself says.

That's what you want? I ask, surprised.

We must. Hurry.

I check for where the other end of the line is still attached to a machine next to the computer, and the screen shows a burst of yellow and red color, like a sunset but with no horizon. I find the catch and release the line from the machine. The computer goes dark. Carefully, quickly, I tuck the loose end of the scavenger line down the front of my shirt, allowing enough give so that it's not tugging at my skull where it's still attached.

"Linus," I say, and turn to the next operating table.

He's lying motionless. I roll off my table, stumble over to him, and check anxiously behind his ear. No line goes into him, and the skin there is smooth and flat. I'm beyond relieved. Clutching his shirt, I give him a little shake. His body is warm and heavy beneath my touch, but he doesn't respond.

"Linus!" I say again.

I shake him harder. He moans and turns his head slightly. A second moan down near my feet makes me jump, and that's when I notice Berg, Jules, Anna, and Kiri are slumped on the floor, passed out. Keeping one hand on Linus, I lean down to get a closer look at Kiri, and she's barely breathing. I look up at the hissing hoses again.

I don't understand. If the blue fog is a narcotic strong enough to knock them out, how can I be awake?

We took care of you, but you can't linger, Arself says.

I shove the computer out of the way so I can get a real look at Berg where he lies on the floor. His head is at an unnatural angle against the base of an operating table, and his hand is clutching the opening of his shirt by his neck, as if he was struggling for more air when he went down. I hate this man. I hate everything he's ever done to me and the people I love. I was prepared to kill him to get free. It seems almost too easy to leave him here and let the gas finish him off.

A rumbling noise comes from deep in the stone around me. With a sense of dread, I recall that the narcotic gas is flammable. If it ignites, we won't stand a chance.

Let's go! Arself says.

I spin back to Linus and try to lift him from the table, but he's as heavy as a sack of concrete. Or maybe I'm just weak.

You have to help me, I say. *You helped me carry Dubbs before.*

A surge of adrenaline races through me and gives me a burst of strength. I grab Linus under the arms, hug his back against me, and haul him off the table, wincing when the heels of his shoes smash to the floor. Then I drag him backward out of the operating room. In the hallway, where the air is clearer, I hitch him up again, and he moans.

"Wake up!" I tell him. "Breathe!"

His head only lolls to the other side. A burn of heat moves through my arms, making me stronger, and I drag him farther along the hallway, toward the vault. He is such a load. It's all I can do to keep us moving. As I reach the archway, though, a noxious smell makes me stop. I sag with Linus to the floor, and I gaze, aghast, into the vault.

Half of the sleep shells have gone dark, and nearly all of the rest have their red lights on. Out of the entire room, out of hundreds, only half a dozen are still normal with their blue lids. Along the floor, the cloudy purple vapor has expanded into drifts that eddy slowly around the bases of the sleep shells. The effect is surreal. From above, around the oculus, a thin shower of dust trickles down as if the ceiling is set to crumble.

Linus moans in my arms and collapses inward as he coughs.

I give him another shake and peer into his face. "Linus. You *have* to wake up," I say. "We have to get out of here."

"Rosie?" he says, his voice croaking. He tilts his head and blinks at me.

My relief is instantly chased by a new jolt of desperation. I get my shoulder into his armpit, grab him around the back, and haul him to his feet.

"Hold on to me," I say.

He can barely stand, but having him up is better than dragging him.

"Where's Berg?" he asks.

I don't bother to look behind us.

"Dead," I say. "Or soon to be. Come on."

I'm about to guide Linus down the steps into the vault when a clank comes from across the room. I freeze, and then I push

328

Linus against the archway to brace him there. He's breathing heavily and his eyes struggle to focus, but he doesn't question my erratic movements. I peer across the vault and discern, far on the other side, Whistler wheeling his cart among the dreamers.

In his gray coveralls, he's whistling a tuneless melody. His headlamp casts a thin beam around the dark cavern. A gas mask covers his mouth and adds to his buglike appearance. He's parking his cart next to a sleep shell, one of the unlit ones. He opens the lid, reaches in, and gently lifts out a limp child. He sets the child on his cart, covers the body with a gray sheet, and closes the sleep shell lid again. Then he shifts around the cart, gets a grip on the handle, lowers his head, and starts wheeling the cart toward the twelve o'clock archway.

A shiver runs through me. Is he even aware of what happened in the operating room? He vanishes through the twelve o'clock arch, and the faint rumble of his wheels fades away into the tunnel.

"Is it safe?" Linus asks quietly.

We have to go through the same arch Whistler just did. And come to think of it, I have no idea where Ian is, either.

"No," I say.

I still have Linus leaned up against the wall, and though he's bearing his weight on his legs, he's unsteady and his arm is heavy across my shoulders. Two hundred steps is what it will take, I estimate, to cross the vault to the twelve o'clock arch, and we have no time to waste. Another trickle of dust falls from the ceiling. It feels like the whole place is shifting.

"Are you ready?" I ask Linus.

He nods and straightens. "Yes."

I step down into the vault with him and guide him between the sleep shells. I warn myself not to look down at the dreamers' faces, but in the hollow stillness, I can almost hear them breathing, the ones that are still alive. An eerie vibe emanates from them, as if they're attuned to us. We pass a dozen dark sleep shells, and then, despite myself, I can't help looking into the next lit sleep shell, one with a red warning light above it.

The dreamer is a child with a pale, empty face, and his hands are clutched together under his chin in mute supplication. I take one more step, and another, still supporting Linus, but I can't look away from the little boy. Wisps of brown hair cling to his forehead, and his eyelids are motionless under their smears of gel. He's still breathing, this dreamer, and he's doing it with all his heart.

As I hesitate, torn, an uncanny, choral whisper rises from the dreamers around me: *Stay with us.*

The sibilance ripples away into nothing.

My feet freeze to the floor. My heart locks in my chest. I can keep Linus upright, but I can't move. I can hardly breathe. I don't want to look into the next sleep shell, a dark one, but I can feel it pulling my gaze like a duty. I know what lonesome suffering I'll see before I see it. I know what the voices will say. And then they whisper again, all of them.

Stay.

As the whisper dissolves away toward the walls, a swish through the fog at my knees reveals the long, slick back of a swimming fish. Logic is gone, replaced by fear. The fish is surreal, perfect, and petrifying.

Why is this happening? I beg Arself.

330

They're jealous. They don't want to let us go.

I search the fog, knowing the fish is coming back for me.

"Rosie!" Linus says into my ear. He yanks me forward a step. "Come on!"

I feel him tugging me, but I'm awkward and stiff, like my puppet limbs have turned to wood. Dream wood.

"Arself!" he yells. "Are you controlling her? Let her go!"

I'm one of them, I think. *I've always been one of them, stronger asleep than awake.* The dark fish is circling back again, with a rustling crescendo, until I feel it brush the back of my legs. The dreamers smile. I know they do. I don't have to look at them to understand.

Linus drags me into his arms and squeezes me so tightly I gasp in pain.

"Rosie!" he says urgently. "Stay with me! Do you hear me? Don't give in to them!"

For a moment, I'm able to see him clearly again. I focus on his good eye, the one that gleams with blistering fury. It's real. He's real. I lift my hands to Linus's chest and grip his shirt. *This is me. This will be me*, I tell myself. *Awake. Alive.* I tug him even closer and feel the crush of his arms.

"Promise me this is real," I say.

"Of course it is!"

He frowns at me, and then his lips meet mine. It's an answer. A shock. A silence descends around us and I'm alone with him in a private, wordless space. Everything else vanishes—the fish, the fog, and the agonizing pleas of the dreamers—leaving just me alone and alive with him.

An instant later, the silence disintegrates, and I hear another trickle of dust spatter down on the nearest sleep shell. Linus loosens his arms enough that I remember to breathe. With my next gulp of air, my vision returns with startling clarity. We're surrounded by sleep shells and rising purple fog. The oculus above is still a dark circle, but the fish has retreated.

I can't believe we're standing here, wasting precious time. Whistler could return any second. What if the whole place collapses or explodes?

"Come on!" I say. "We need to get out of here!"

I point toward the twelve o'clock arch, grip Linus's hand, and lurch into a run. He's right with me, awkward but mobile again. We reach the arch, hurry along the tunnel to the steps, and start up. At the top, I dart around the dome to where my sister's stone waits in the nook of the next staircase, and I grab it as we pass. I lead Linus up the spiral stairs, too, scrambling in the dimness. At the top, I shove aside the curtain in the janitor's closet with a plastic rattling. We hurry through the cafeteria, into the green room, and up the next set of stairs.

When we reach the VIP portal hallway, I have to pause to catch my breath. The air is dry and dusty, but we're almost out.

"Are you all right?" I ask Linus.

"Keep going."

In a few more headlong steps, I reach the outer door and pull it open onto the Main Drag. Cool night air surrounds me, brushing along my warm cheeks, and I catch a whiff of smoke. Moonlight shines on the cobblestones, and I have never been so happy to be alive.

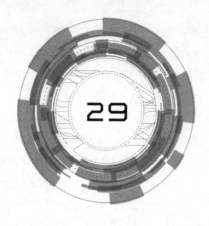

29

LOST AND FOUND

"WE MADE IT. We're out!" I say. It's almost more than I can believe. The world we left below felt impossibly dark and intricate, a haunting, murky mess of nightmares. I have to touch my hand to the doorjamb to feel its solidity against my shaky fingers. I turn back to Linus. "We did it."

"Are you really all right?" he asks. Gently, he touches the medical line that's still attached behind my ear. "Did Berg mine you again?"

I make sure the line is still tucked into my shirt. "I don't really know. Arself brought me out of it. She saved us. We can talk about it later. Now we have to get to my parents."

"You said Berg was dead? What about the doctors?"

"I left them back in the operating room," I say. "They were all unconscious from a narcotic that was pouring out of some busted hoses. Listen, we have to go. Ian's still out there some-where."

Linus turns toward the keep. "Where's Burnham?"

"I don't know," I say.

I pull out my phone and try Burnham. While it rings, I search both ways along the Main Drag, which is as dark and deserted as before. A twitch of movement catches my attention, but it's just a tumbleweed that's lodged lightly against an old bench. Burnham's number switches over to voicemail.

"He's not answering," I say.

"He's probably waiting at the gift shop in the Backwoods Forest," Linus says. "Where are your parents?"

"They're in the Lost and Found, over near the main entrance. They're in bad shape."

A rumble under my feet sets me off balance, and I instinctively grab for Linus. He's unsteady, too. Something rattles in the shop next door.

"Is that an earthquake?" I ask, alarmed.

"I don't know," he says.

The vibrations taper off. I loosen my grip on him, but I'm no more certain of what's happening.

"Come on," he says. "We'll get your parents and get out of here."

We run east along the Main Drag, and this time, I'm in too much of a hurry to make any effort to hide from the streetlights or cameras. Another rumble comes from behind me, louder this time, and then, with a loud crack, a section of the cobble-stoned street collapses to our left, creating a sinkhole as big as a swimming pool. Linus yells a warning. We veer right, and I instinctively duck under the awning of an old shop, pulling Linus with me. Orange light reflects off the buildings around us, and I turn back toward the damage.

Dust is rising from the jagged hole in the street, and a fire is burning in a trash can on the other side. When I try to see how deep the sinkhole is, it shimmers oddly, and I get a faint glimpse of the street again from before it collapsed. It almost seems like the hole is merely a dark projection cast over the cobblestones, but I'd have to go nearer to be sure.

At the end of the street, in the background, the Keep of Ages is weirdly lit with purple light, and gray clouds are lifting out of the moat. The smell of smoke stings my nose. The dragon on the roof has grown to twice its previous size, and its eyes are a wicked, flaming red.

Linus is ready to run again, but I hold his arm.

"Do you see the hole? Is it a special effect?" I ask him.

He cranes for a second look. "It looks real enough to me."

"How about the dragon?" I ask.

"Where?"

I point. The dragon is slowly turning its head from side to side, as if it's looking for a meal.

"No way," Linus says. "That cannot be real."

But he sounds unconvinced.

That's exactly how I feel. The dragon is glorious and horrifying, and though I know, logically, it has to be the product of special effects, it makes me question the reality of everything I'm seeing.

A seam of flame runs horizontally along the top of one of the keep's windows and then breaks vertically upward. More flames push through the stones near the base of the keep, and the smoke grows thicker and blacker. Popping noises explode in sequence, like giant fireworks, and the keep trembles visibly. Then the south tower topples over in slow motion. It tumbles into the smoke with a deafening crash, and at the same moment, the dragon spreads its wings. It shoots a blast of fire out of its jaws and rises heavily into the sky. It hovers over the keep. Another roaring rumble shakes the ground.

"Burnham had better not be in there!" Linus says.

"You're sure the fire's not special effects, too?" I ask, clinging to my last stupid shred of hope.

He looks at me like I've lost my senses. "Can't you smell that?" He pulls his phone out. "I'm calling Burnham again. You try Lavinia. See if she knows anything."

But at that moment, the dragon shrieks. It has straightened higher, and its head is now aimed in our direction. Its livid, hateful eyes pierce right to where we're hiding, and with swooping, enormous wings, it launches from its perch and glides swiftly above the Main Drag, diving lower, coming directly at us.

I don't care what it's made of. I'm not waiting to find out.

"Run!" I yell.

An explosion of flame ignites the awning above us just as Linus and I sprint for the street, and a whoosh passes overhead. I glance back at the crackling flames, and sparks reflect in the glass of a window as they shoot upward. Linus pulls me onward. The dragon circles higher again, out of sight above the rooftops of the shops.

"Now where?" Linus asks at the corner.

I turn right, past the security office, running toward the Lost and Found with Linus right behind me. From above, I can hear the savage pulse of the dragon's wings. I know it's coming, and when I next glance up, it soars into view, closer than before, diving at us.

It opens its fiery mouth with a roar, and flames rip into a palm tree just above me.

"No!" I scream. I duck toward the ground, covering my head with my arms, desperate to block the burning force of the dragon's fireball.

The roar blasts all around me. I cringe, terrified, but instead of scorching heat, I feel nothing but a sharp wind. Sparks snap around me, and the palm fronds curl into ashy black above, but my skin isn't singed. I stare up at the burning palm tree, confused.

"Special effects!" Linus yells by my ear. "The fire's real in the tree, but that's all. See?" He waves his arm through a projection of orange light that looks like flames.

I'm dumbstruck for an instant, but then I see the dragon flying away in the smoky sky. *Dragons don't exist*, I remind myself. No matter how convincing and frightening the effects are, they weren't designed to harm. Yet the fury behind them is undeniable.

"Ian," I say, as it hits me. "Ian must be controlling the special effects."

He must be mad at me. This has to be his version of revenge.

"Let's go," Linus says, dragging me up. "Where are your parents?"

"This way," I say, and I run up the ramp into the Lost and Found building.

I speed into the second room, where the two sleep shells are parked, and I throw up the lid for my mother's. Her face is still slack and peaceful in sleep. The sour smell is as strong as ever, but I ignore it and start to pull her out. Linus lifts up Larry's sleep shell lid, and he's still there sleeping, too.

"Help me," I say, getting my arms under Ma. "I can't carry her alone."

"What about him?" Linus asks, pointing to Larry.

"He's too heavy," I say. "We'll come back for him."

I half expect Linus to argue, or scold me for being hard-hearted, but he just closes Larry's lid again.

"Right. We can take her to the van, and then we'll drive around and come back. Get her legs," he says. He gets a good grip around Ma from behind, under her arms, and I grab her ankles. "No. Turn around," he says. "Take her knees on each side of you, like a wheelbarrow. Face around the other way. You're the leader."

It's awkward, but once I grab her knees against my hips, we're mobile. Linus is close behind me, bearing most of Ma's weight. Our first steps are lurching and uneven, but then we get in stride.

"Watch the glass," Linus says.

I'm careful around the broken glass by the door of the Lost and Found, but soon we're outside, and then we're hurrying as fast as we can go, back along the Main Drag. The awning is burned to ashy shreds, and the sinkhole is still there. We veer around it, and I look anxiously ahead toward the keep. I know the dragon is an illusion, but that doesn't mean Ian is fake. He could intercept us at any time.

"What do you think happened with Burnham and Ian?" I call over my shoulder.

"I have no idea. Keep going," Linus says.

I'm scanning the sky for the dragon and watching for holes in the cobblestones, all the while going as fast as I can. My arms strain from carrying my mom. As we get nearer to the center of the park, I'm completely convinced the fire at the keep is real. The toppled tower burns in the moat with a noxious, smoky stench, and the jumble of fabricated rocks has become a lacy black skeleton in the green-and-blue flames. Streaks of fire race up the north side of the keep and start spreading, fanlike, along the walls. Even the bridges are starting to burn.

My gaze snags on a dark shape at the bottom of the stairs and I come to a halt, terrified. I lower Ma's legs to the ground.

"Linus! There!" I say, pointing.

The dark shape moves, crawling, and then slumps down again. From behind him, bright yellow flames silhouette his smoking form.

"Burnham!" I scream. "Come on!" I call to Linus.

I dart toward the blistering heat and instinctively hunch low, with a hand up to protect my face. I glance back to see Linus right behind me. Arcing sparks drop to the cobblestones and sizzle around us. The black smoke is nearly blinding, and the fire creates a deafening roar of wind that whips around me. By the time we reach the dark figure at the bottom of the steps, the heat is overpowering. I roll over his inert, heavy body and cringe at my friend's pained expression.

"Burnham!" Linus shouts.

He hauls Burnham up under the arms, just as he did my mother, and I grab Burnham's legs the same way. We run away from the keep, carrying Burnham through the burning debris that rains out of the sky. As we reach Ma where we left her in the square, I stumble and fall, bringing Burnham down with me. By the flickering light, I check quickly to see if he's breathing, and he lets out a moan. Then he coughs raggedly and curls over on his side. His clothes are hot to the touch, but I can't see any blood, and his hands and face don't look burned. Trembling, I take off his dirty glasses and lean near to him.

"Burnham. Can you hear me?" I ask.

He keeps his eyes closed and shakes his head, but it's sort of an answer. I tuck his glasses inside my shirt, and they snag in the medical line that's still bunched there. I'd entirely forgotten about it, but it's still attached behind my ear.

"You're going to be all right," I say to Burnham. "We've got you. Just keep breathing, okay?"

I check my mother to be sure she's still breathing, too, and then a rumble draws my gaze back to the keep. The back wall bows out unnaturally, and then the upper floors begin to tumble inward. The flames extend higher, hot enough that I can feel them singeing my cheeks despite the distance.

Then, after an ominous teetering, the keep implodes inward with a cascade of stone and roof tiles. Flames roar from the crashing ruins and engulf the massive timbers.

The wind whips my hair into my eyes, and I shake my head, trying to get my vision free. Then the ground rumbles again, and the burning ruins collapse even further, dropping into a deeper abyss. A sleep shell lid, an entire dome of glass, flies up on a wave of heat. My heart clenches as I realize what this means: the burning, dropping keep has fallen deep into the vault of dreamers. The underground dome must have collapsed at last. Everything and everybody down below is being destroyed.

I stare, aghast. Sparks are careening wildly toward the orange sky, and the lid is still soaring in the heat.

The hole takes the moat with it, and the nearest cobblestoned pathways, while the inferno burns even hotter.

"We have to get out of here!" Linus says, as more of the square begins to topple into the hole.

Burnham coughs again and audibly struggles for air.

"Rosie!" Linus yells.

He has my mother over his shoulder, the full weight of her. Burnham is coughing harshly, but he's rolled over to his hands and knees like he wants to get up. I yell to him again, and slide under his arm to support him. It's like lifting a tree, but I help him to his feet, and he leans on my shoulders.

"Go," he says hoarsely.

He can barely stumble forward, but I guide him into the Backwoods Forest, following Linus and my mom. The flames behind us send eerie, wavering shadows and streaks of orange light along the paths. I hear a popping explosion somewhere behind us, and then one over to my right, but the deafening roar of the fire recedes. Twice Burnham trips, nearly dragging me down, but I brace him hard, and we stagger on.

"Almost there!" Linus calls.

We pass the red-and-white gift shop and finally reach the

shadowed wall where we first came in. Burnham sags down to the ground, holding his head in his hands and breathing heavily. Linus lays Ma on the ground beside Burnham, and I check to make sure she's still breathing. Behind her, the wall looks taller than before.

Linus is bent over. He spits into the dirt and wipes his wrist over his mouth. He looks sideways at me.

"How are you doing?" he asks.

"Me?" I ask. I've got no problems compared to Burnham and Ma. "I'm fine."

Linus shoots a look toward Burnham, and then turns back to me again.

"We have to get them over," he says.

"I know. Ma first?"

Linus nods. He climbs on top of the rickety old ice cream cart and reaches down.

"Give her to me," he says.

I strain to lift my mother up to him, and he lifts her carefully higher until he can rest her limp body on the top of the wall. The next moment, he scrambles on top of the wall beside her. Then they both disappear.

"Burnham," I say, touching his shoulder. "We have to get you over the wall."

He twists to look at me, which starts him coughing again, but then he gets to his feet. I put his arm around my shoulders again and help him to the ice cream cart. He starts to climb but then has to stop to cough. Linus appears at the top of the wall and reaches down a hand.

"Burnham, let's go," Linus says. "You've got this."

Burnham takes a deep breath and reaches up. Linus grabs him and basically hauls him over. I scramble up the ice cream cart last and heave myself to the top of the wall.

For a moment, I look back through the trees toward the center of Grisly Valley, where the fire has spread to a dozen buildings. Bright yellow flames lick along the roofs, and a new line of fire is already feeding along the curves of the Glue Factory roller coaster in Bubbles' Clown World. It's going to go up like matchsticks. The whole place is.

Dread stops my heart. Larry is still in the Lost and Found.

"Rosie!" Linus calls.

I hurry down the other side of the wall to where Linus has picked up my mother again. Burnham is standing bent over, with his hands on his knees and his head low. Swiftly, I get one of his arms over my shoulder again and wrap my arm around his back, and we all take off for the minivan. By the time we get there, I'm a mess of guilt and impatience.

"We have to get back for Larry!" I say. "The whole place is starting to burn!"

"I know. Get in," Linus says. He's lifting my mother onto the bench seat in the middle of the minivan, and then he pivots into the driver's seat. Burnham slumps into the front passenger seat, and I barely have time to close the door before Linus pulls onto the road.

"Do you know the way?" I ask.

"Yes," Linus says.

I brace my feet to keep steady as Linus accelerates, and I quickly check to see if Ma, beside me, is still breathing. She is, just as evenly as before. Her features have a leaden quality, like she's been asleep for decades rather than days, like she's turned into a new kind of stone. She has no idea what we've been through and where we're going.

"Oh, Ma," I say, my voice aching.

"How is she?" Linus asks.

"Still sleeping. Can you go any faster?"

Linus takes a hard right. I glance anxiously ahead as we pass a dark stand of trees, and our headlights touch over an old, crooked fence pole. Then, in the distance to our right, I can see the fire in the park. The keep is blazing higher than anything else, but the tall Fodder Mill ride and the End of Daze tower are burning now, too. We're circling and getting closer to the front, where the main entrance is.

Burnham's breath is raspy. "Take us to my jet," he says. His voice is painfully raw. "Dubbs and Lavinia are meeting us there."

"We're getting Rosie's stepfather first," Linus says.

Burnham coughs again, hacking loudly.

"Hang in there, Burnham," I say. "It'll just take us a minute to get Larry."

"Ian's dead," Burnham says. "I couldn't get him out." Another round of coughing cuts him off.

"It's okay. You can tell us later," I say. "Just breathe."

We take another tight curve, and I shift with Ma. As her hand slips, my gaze catches on her wedding band, and I feel a new surge of urgency. The sky over the park has turned a molten orange, and black, smoky clouds roil up into the night. I can actually hear the inferno. Linus turns our minivan onto a narrow road and races down to the parking lot. He swerves to avoid a fallen sign, and aims toward the flagpoles of the main entrance.

"See the car?" I ask, pointing toward Berg's white sedan.

"I see it. Hold on," Linus says.

Our wheels screech as he pulls to a sharp stop beside Berg's car, and I lurch out of the minivan.

Sharp, smoky air makes me choke, and the noise of the fire is a rushing wall of sound. The Grim Reaper statue flickers with orange reflections, and a gust of wind tugs at my shirt. The arching entranceway to the park stands silhouetted before the bright, fiery buildings. The palm trees burn like paper candles. Even from outside the turnstiles, I can feel the heat, and my heart sinks. I stagger forward, unbelieving. The whole corner row of buildings that includes the Lost and Found is one blazing mass of burning timbers. Trying to go inside to save Larry would be suicide.

"We're too late," I say, aching.

"Hey," Linus says. He wraps his arms around me. "We didn't know the whole place was going to burn."

Guilt broadsides me anyway. We could have pulled Larry out of the Lost and Found and moved him to the entrance here before we went for the van with Ma. We could have pulled both Ma and Larry out here, and one of us could have run around faster to get the van. Better solutions seem brutally obvious to me now.

"I'm so sorry," Linus says.

"What am I going to say to Ma?"

I won't have any way to explain.

Linus hugs me harder, rocking me against him. "She needs help. Burnham, too. We need to go," he says.

I stare again at the burning wall of flames, watching a wild spray of sparks fly up into the smoke. I thought I despised Larry, but now, I can't believe he's gone. I can't believe he gets the same fate as Berg.

"Come on, Rosie," Linus urges me. "There's nothing we can do."

But I can't leave yet. From where I stand, I can see the column of white-hot fire in the center of the park that stretches up into the sky. It's horrible, but also fabulous, in a way. All those dreamers underneath—they're gone for good now. Berg, the doctors and Whistler, they're all dead, too. And Ian, and now Larry. I can't bear to look again toward the Lost and Found.

A flicker high above draws my gaze, and I peer up into the smoke.

The undersides of the dragon's wings glow white as it circles above the burning ruins of the park. It beats its wings in a gangly effort to rise, and then skims along the rising heat in a fluid, mournful arc. I know it can't be real. It can't even be a special effect, now that all the mechanical controls are lost in the inferno. But it's still the truest thing I've ever seen, and my throat chokes tight with inexplicable grief.

"Rosie, please," Linus says gently into my ear. "We have to go. We have to take care of your mother and Burnham."

I turn back toward the van, feeling the cooler air on my face like a reproach. Linus helps me settle in with Ma again before he closes the door. Burnham swivels stiffly to look back at me, and the orange firelight brightens half of his features.

"Your stepfather's back there?" Burnham says in his rough voice.

I nod, my throat tightening. "My dad," I say.

I never called him that to his face. He always wanted me to. Now it's too late.

I hug Ma and pull her close, hoping she keeps sleeping a while longer, hoping she never has to know how I let Larry burn. As Linus turns the minivan around again, I look back over my shoulder, watching the burning theme park as long as I can, searching for the dragon until we pull out of sight.

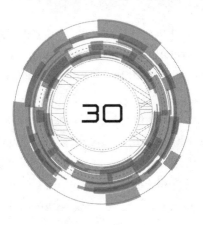

30

NOT DAD

WE'RE IN SORRY SHAPE by the time Burnham's plane touches down outside Holdum, Texas. Ma's the worst. She woke once during the flight to ask for a sip of water, and I was thrilled to see her conscious. After she gave me and Dubbs tearful hugs, she drifted off again. Burnham's coughing is horrible to hear. He's the one who insisted we get to his jet without stopping for medical care. He argued that a hospital would tie us up with questions, and his pilot had basic EMT training. We couldn't refuse him. Not surprisingly, his family's plane is stocked with every drug that Fister sells. Burnham's been on oxygen the whole flight, along with some bronchial expander his mother ordered him to take. She is not pleased with him.

Linus has been quiet. Attentive. He showed Dubbs how to do KenKens in a book he found in a seat pocket, and she's been sitting beside him, eating duos of Milano cookies and tapping her pencil eraser against her lips.

We're it now, the five of us. After she met us at the jet with Dubbs, Lavinia stayed behind in Miehana.

"I really ought to thank you," Lavinia mentioned as we were saying goodbye.

"What for?" I said.

"Before you burgled into my apartment, I was content observing things from afar. I'd forgotten how satisfying it is to be involved."

"What'll you do now?" I asked.

"I'm weighing my options," she said. "I'll look up my son-in-law, for one thing, and then I think I'll take a little trip to Forgetown. They're going to need some oversight now that Berg is gone." She passed me a half-full package of lemon drops. "Look after your family, Rosie. That Dubbs is a special one. Now give us a hug."

I glance down now at the scuffed black flats she gave me and step out onto the top stair of the plane. The bright Texas wind makes me squint, but it's easy to spot a young doctor approaching with some gear on a two-wheeled cart. It turns out he's brought a portable X-ray system, and he carefully examines Burnham first. He takes blood samples, too, and gives him a shot.

"Your parents want you home," the doctor says.

"I know," Burnham says. He pulls on a fresh tee shirt, moving stiffly, and tucks his St. Christopher medal under the neckline. "I'm just stopping here for a few days first. You can tell them I'm fine, right?"

"What I'll do is send them your X-rays," he says. "You've got yourself some lung damage there." He passes Burnham a vial of pills. "You need to watch for infection."

"I will," Burnham says. "Thanks."

Then the doctor gently goes over Ma and Dubbs, and finally he focuses on me and takes out the line from behind my ear.

"What about our ports?" Dubbs asks.

"Those should wait until you're at a proper clinic," the doctor says. "As for your mother, she should be all right, physically. She needs fluids and a healthy diet most of all, and rest. Minimize her stress if you can," he says. "What she's been through emotionally you'd know better than I."

Soon after, we all help Ma and Burnham down the stairs to where Tom Barton, Thea's friend, waits with an SUV. Tall and blond, Tom has the build of a young cowboy, and he's quick to open doors and lend a hand. We settle my mother in the back, and when I climb in beside her, she puts her head on my lap and closes her eyes again, sighing.

"I'm so glad you're here, Rosie," Tom says.

"Thanks. Me, too."

The others pile in the SUV, too, and Tom takes the wheel, heading toward the Flores ranch.

Wide green horizons stretch under an open sky, and the sunny beauty is almost more than I can take in. Part of me is still in shock. I sniff absently at my sleeve. Even though I washed up a bit on the plane, my clothes and my hair still smell of smoke. I'm never going to be able to forget what happened at Grisly, but at the same time, I can barely accept that Larry and Berg and the others are all dead. Even Ian. I mean,

I despised him, but he didn't deserve to die. A residual shiver ripples through me.

Forward. I need to look forward.

"How are Thea and the baby?" I ask loudly so Tom can hear me in the front.

Tom adjusts the sun visor over his head. "Madeline didn't tell you?"

"Tell me what?" I ask.

The SUV accelerates a bit under his control.

"Thea's in a coma again," Tom says. "She's not responding at all."

"No," I whisper, stunned.

"When did this happen?" Linus asks.

"She slipped off yesterday, a few minutes after she talked to Rosie," Tom says.

His voice is calm, but I could swear he's implying a connection.

"Does anyone know why?" Linus asks.

"No," Tom says. "The doctors from Chimera warned us this could happen. It wasn't completely unexpected."

"Madeline didn't say a word," I say. When I called Thea's mother from the plane, she insisted we come to the ranch. She wouldn't have it any other way, but now I'm chilled to realize what she omitted in her invitation. I glance forward to find Linus has turned back in my direction.

"Do you still want to go?" he asks me.

I don't even hesitate. I nod. If Thea's sick, if she needs me, I have to be there. "Yes, of course," I say.

Ma shifts her head on my lap, and then her voice comes

weakly. "We shouldn't be imposing. We don't even have a house gift."

I let out a strangled laugh. Of all the trivial things to worry about.

"It's okay," I say to her. "They won't mind, I'm sure."

"Have they taken Thea to the hospital?" Linus asks Tom.

"No," Tom says. "Thea left very explicit directions that she doesn't want to be taken to a hospital again. That doesn't really matter, anyway. The Floreses have essentially brought the hospital to her."

He slows to make a turn onto a narrow road, and after we pass under a wooden sign that reads "Flores," he speeds up again. I barely notice the passing blur of greenery. A new truth has suddenly become horribly clear. After all we've been through in the past twenty-four hours—losing Larry, the deaths of Berg, Ian, the doctors and Whistler, plus the obliteration of hunderds of dreamers—if Thea dies, I'll have failed miserably. It wasn't enough to save Dubbs and Ma. I need to make sure Thea's alive, too.

I tighten my hand into a fist and press my thumbnail against the gap in my front teeth.

"It's going to be all right, Rosie," Burnham says in his husky voice.

I let out a laugh. He doesn't know that. We jolt over a pit and I brace my knee on the back of the seat before me.

Arself? I ask uncertainly. *Are you with me?*

She hasn't spoken since we were down in the vault, and the last hint I had of her was the strength she gave me to help Ma and Burnham out of the park. Maybe my vision of the dragon flying over the flames was from her, too, though I don't know. It hardly matters. It was beautiful, and tragic, and right. Arself doesn't answer me now. She's never been one to surface on command, even though I could use her comfort.

I blink as the car pulls to a stop.

"We're here," Tom says.

On a slope overlooking a wide, grassy valley, a mansion sprawls in rustic phases of wood and stone. Upper windows reflect the sky, and worn, satiny rockers beckon from the porch. Massive trees drop pools of cool shade on the lawn, and a cast iron bell tops a pole near a raised bed of flowers. A sweet fragrance, maybe honeysuckle, drifts on the air, and I can feel the exclusive hush of privacy and wealth.

"Althea grew up here?" I ask.

"She sure did," Tom says.

Only now do I recall that Thea's family wasn't too keen on Tom. I wonder if that's changed lately with the birth of his baby.

Linus comes around to give me a hand with Ma. She's able to walk now, but she's far from steady. Dubbs goes ahead beside Burnham, and Tom brings up the rear. The front door of the house opens, and a beagle comes out to bark from the porch. An old man follows.

"¡Silencio, Solana! ¡Ya, deja de hacer tanto ruido!" he says, and the dog quiets. The man lifts a hand and smiles. "We're so glad you're here. Come in!"

Dubbs shifts closer to Burnham, but she's all eyes for the dog.

"Does your dog speak Spanish?" Dubbs asks.

The man smiles and leans down to take the dog by the

collar. "*Si*, she does. Do you want to pet her? She's friendly. Her name's Solana."

It feels bizarre to have cordial introductions when we've just come from Grisly and we're all thinking about Thea, but that's what happens. The old man, Thea's grandfather, asks us to call him Tito. Thea's parents quickly join us. Diego's tall and broad-shouldered, with a quiet, sober demeanor. It's obvious that Thea gets her eyes and Latina coloring from him. Her mother, Madeline, is a petite, fair woman with short, silver hair that sticks out in a staticky halo, and she radiates both friendliness and high-strung energy.

As soon as Madeline meets Ma, she takes charge, bustling her off upstairs to a guest room. A frosty pitcher of iced tea stands on a silver tray with matching glasses, and a fresh bouquet sits on the bedside table.

"We can all get properly acquainted after you've rested," Madeline says, drawing a curtain across the window with a soft rustle. "Not another word until then. We have a highly trained nurse on staff, and I can send her up to look in on you. Also, I had my assistant pick up a few clothes for you. They should be here in the closet." She opens a door and glances inside. "Yes. And the bathroom's through there. Anything you want, you just call down and we'll get it for you, all right?"

Ma looks at me, amazed, but as Madeline leaves us, she sags onto the bed. It's a big one, with a carved wooden headboard and a white, nubby spread, and Ma spreads out her fingers over the fabric as if she's never touched anything like it before. With her dirty dress and limp hair, she looks completely out of place. We all do.

"Who *are* these people?" Ma says.

"I told you. They're Thea's parents, and she's a friend of mine."

"But what do they do?" Ma says.

"I'm not sure," I say, trying to recall if Thea ever mentioned what her parents did for a living. "Burnham said they made their fortune in the helium business, I think."

Dubbs is busy rustling through the closet. "Check this out," she says, holding up a hanger with a green dress in her size. She fingers the price tag. "It's new," she says reverently. She holds the fabric up to herself before the mirror and then heads into the bathroom.

"What would Larry think of all this?" Ma says.

It's the first time she's mentioned him, and I feel a tick of alarm. I sit slowly on the bed beside her. "Ma," I say softly. But then I don't know how to go on.

She gives me a weak, sad smile. "My sweet Rosie, always so fearless. I'm sorry I didn't believe you when you first told me the truth about Berg back at Forge. I should have."

I shake my head. I don't want to hear this now. "It's okay."

"No. Leaving you there was the worst mistake of my life," she says. "Even Larry knew better."

"Ma," I say. My throat's tightening.

"Are you safe now? Is Berg still after you?" Ma asks.

"No," I say. "That's all done. He's dead."

She pats my arm and then frowns. Her troubled blue eyes search mine.

"Larry's dead, too, isn't he?" she asks.

I nod.

She nods, too, and then her gaze slants away. "I thought as much."

I never liked Larry, but I know Ma loved him, and I hate seeing the tears brimming in her eyes. I can't begin to describe what happened at Grisly. "There was an accident of sorts," I say. Major understatement.

She holds up a hand to stop me. "You can tell me all about it later," she says. Her chin trembles. "I should really take a shower," she adds, but instead, she slowly topples over on the bed.

Dubbs comes out of the bathroom and stares at us. Then she crawls onto the bed beside Ma and tugs a soft blue blanket up around Ma's shoulders. She pulls a strand of her own bright hair between her lips to suck on, and then tilts her head to share Ma's pillow. At the sight of the two of them together, a new crack opens in my heart. We're the whole family now. Larry's gone. No matter who else might be there for us—Linus, Burnham, Thea—when the door's closed, we're the only ones together behind it.

"Do you think we could get a dog like Solana?" Dubbs asks, like the decision is up to me.

"I don't know. Maybe," I say gently. "Can you stay here with Ma?"

"Yeah. Where are you going? To help Thea?"

"If I can," I say.

She snuggles deeper into the pillow. "Okay. Good."

>>>>>>>>

356

I take a quick shower and slip into a new pair of jeans, a soft yellow shirt, and some flip-flops before I head downstairs. The house smells of wood polish and the faint, spicy tang of faded smoke. Sunlight collects in a blue-and-white bowl on a circular table. As I trail a hand along the banister and descend the second flight of stairs, I hear voices from the back of the house, and then Madeline appears by the newel post. Pressing her hands together, she offers a quick, nervous smile.

"Can I see Thea?" I ask.

She exhales in relief. "Yes. Please," she says. She backs up a couple of steps into the living room, her green dress swaying over her golden sandals, and then she turns to guide me. "I don't know how much Tom told you. She's very ill. The doctors warned us back at Chimera that her dream transplant might fail, but she was well for so long that I guess we thought she'd beaten all the odds."

"She was in bad shape after she had the baby," I say.

"I know," Madeline says. "Very bad. She's never quite been stable since, and then she crashed yesterday."

"After my call."

She shoots me a worried smile.

"Do you think it's related?" I ask.

"To be honest, I don't know what to think anymore. Did she say anything to you about having headaches?"

"Yes," I say.

"I knew it," she says. "She kept insisting she was fine." Then she adds, "This way, please."

Madeline leads me through a living room and a library, a solarium and a den. We pass model ships, an antique gun collection, and a trickling fountain. My flip-flops sink into deep, indigo carpets, and every wooden surface gleams, like in a fancy hotel.

"When I talked to Thea, she told me Orson Toomey was here," I say.

"Yes," Madeline says. "He's still with us. He's done all he can, but I'm afraid it hasn't helped."

"Can you trust him?" I ask.

"What do you mean? He saved our daughter's life. We owe him everything."

Her gratitude shocks me until I recall that Thea's parents have never known about the underside of Chimera. All of the connections to the dreamers at Forge and Grisly are still completely secret, which means Madeline is not going to be receptive to what I could tell her about how Orson acquired Sinclair 15.

This is not going to be easy. For now, I decide to keep my information to myself.

We descend a couple of steps into another wing of the house where the ceilings are higher and the floors are made of golden wood. In a small sitting area, a petite black woman with a sparkly barrette sits before a busy computer screen of medical readouts.

"Any change, Doris?" Madeline asks.

"No, ma'am. I would have called you," the nurse says. "Tom has the baby."

"Thank you," Madeline says.

She stops outside a door and turns to face me. For a moment, her keen gray eyes appraise me soberly like she has a million things to say, but in the end, she simply opens the door and ushers me in.

Thea lies asleep in a hospital bed in a large, sunny bedroom. Her chest lifts and falls rhythmically, and her hands are folded serenely on top of her blue blanket. The lump of her pregnancy is gone. A patch is attached to her temple, an IV goes into her arm, and a clamp is taped to one of her fingers. As a soft hiss comes from a machine behind her, I glance over to see a monitor recording her heartbeat in a pulsing, jagged line, and it seems to match the tempo of my own heart.

We're the same inside. How many times did she insist that was true?

Madeline steps over to adjust a vase of colorful flowers beside an empty bassinet, and I move a bit closer to Thea. Her dark hair is smoothed back from her face with a red hairband, and her ear piercings are empty. Her cheeks are too thin, and her tan complexion has gone a sickly gray. Worst of all, her closed eyes have a bruised, sunken look that reminds me of the dreamers.

She looks so helpless like this. Both old and young, and not like Thea at all. I hardly know what to say. I look to Madeline and realize she's barely repressing tears. She smiles, touching a hand to Thea's arm.

"Look, darling," Madeline says tenderly. "Look who's here. It's Rosie, your friend. All the way from California."

Thea simply lies quietly, not responding.

"Oh, Thea," I say. My voice drops low, and I can't manage a real hello.

Madeline runs her hand over Thea's forehead. "She's such a good girl," she says.

Don't talk about her like she's a toddler, I think. Then I feel rotten for being critical of Madeline. I clear my throat. "What's the plan? I mean, how long can she be like this?" I say.

Madeline crosses her arms. "We're just taking each hour as it comes."

It's the worst sort of answer. I can't stand to be suspended in a state of not knowing. I shift closer and lift Thea's hand, surprised at how light and cool her fingers feel.

"Hey, Thea," I say. "It's me, Rosie. We're going to get you out of this, all right? We're not going to leave you in any coma. You've got a baby that needs you, and all the rest of us need you, too. Hear me? We're going to bring you back."

No matter how much I want to believe she understands me, her face doesn't change at all, and her hand is lifeless in mine. Even so, I've made up my mind. I was helpless to save the dreamers in the vault, but I can do something for Thea. I glance up at Madeline.

"She can have my dreams," I say.

Madeline's face crumples in pain, and she presses her fist to her mouth. "I'm sorry," she says. "It's just, I'm so thankful. But I don't know—" She can't go on.

"If it will help?" I finish.

She nods, sniffing, and wipes at her eyes. "She's just been through so much," she says in a tight voice.

"I know. But we're not giving up on her," I say. "Let me talk to Orson."

She nods. Then she lets out a broken laugh. "I'm sorry. I

thought I could keep it together. I don't want to pressure you, but you're really our last hope."

I smile. "It's okay."

She shakes her head, wiping her eyes again, and then she reaches for a tissue and blows her nose.

"Thank you," she whispers.

>>>>>>>>

My stomach's uneasy, like when I'm on my way to school. I've been told Orson is coming up from the guest house where he has a room, so I've gone out to the porch to wait for him. I've tried to prepare myself, but still, when he first steps into view, crossing the lawn, my breath catches in my throat.

This is my father. This is not my father.

He's middle-aged now, pushing forty, and as he passes under a tree into a patch of shade, he moves with a bowlegged, loose gait that's achingly familiar. He lifts his hand in a cautious wave, but I'm too overwhelmed to respond. His movements match my frayed, threadbare memories of my father, but he also has a tidy, European appearance, with a gray, short-sleeved shirt tucked into belted, tailored pants. His loafers are the real anomaly. My father would never wear those.

My mind flips, adjusting perspectives, because I'm not a little kid anymore, adoring a giant. His hair is shockingly black still, and unruly. A flash of memory brings me back to the moment when he pounded the nail into the wall of my bedroom to hang the photo of us. I can hear the sharp tap.

As Orson steps into the sunlight again, he lifts his fist to his nose, hesitates, and then sneezes exactly as my father always did. I have to laugh from sheer amazement.

"Excuse me," Orson says, for the sneeze.

"Bless you!" I say automatically.

He smiles, trots up the steps to the porch, and offers his other hand. "You must be Rosie. How do you do?"

His voice perfectly echoes the resonance in my memory bank, but as I stare at his outstretched hand, the lightness from his sneeze evaporates, and all I can think is that every precious, fatherly thing that I remember is about to be destroyed. My mind backs off a cliff of emotional confusion. I long wildly to reach for him, but rage and terror hold me back.

"Why didn't you call us, me and Ma?" I ask, ignoring his outstretched hand.

We missed you. I missed you. Even after Ma gave up hope, even after she married Larry, I believed you were coming back.

Orson lowers his hand, and his expression goes grave and polite. "I apologize," he says. "I only meant to spare you additional distress. You know, of course, that I am not Robert Sinclair, but I owe him the debt of my life."

I'm having trouble reconciling this guy's frank, unassuming manner with the evil genius I believe him to be. "You used my dreams without my consent," I say. "Where was your concern for my distress then?"

"I'm sorry about that, too," he says. "I wasn't in charge of acquisitions. My colleague Huma Fallon always handles that end of things. When I realized some of our dreams came from Forge students, I was appalled. But wasting them would

362

have been even more unconscionable at that point. Don't you agree?"

He sounds less and less like my father with every word he utters.

"I don't know what to believe," I say. He paints himself as blameless, but he's at the heart of the dream research. He collaborated with Berg.

"You've come from the vault at Grisly, haven't you?" Orson says. "Do you know if anyone made it out? We've had nothing but silence."

"The dreamers, you mean?" I ask, deliberately misunderstanding him. "No. Nobody made it out."

He slides his hands slowly into his pockets. "I can see you have little sympathy for me. I don't blame you. But I'm here to try to help Thea. Years of my work went into her awakening at Chimera. She's one of a kind. She only exists because of you and me both. Isn't that worth valuing?"

I try to weigh what he's saying, but it's complicated by the way he looks just like my father. It feels wrong to be in conflict with this man, like I'm betraying my love for my dad. Yet how can I forgive the person who profited from the way Berg stole my dreams?

Behind me, there's a flurry of noise, and the door slams open.

"Robert?" my mother says.

Ma's face is pale, and she's perfectly still, as if she's afraid to breathe and dispel a dream. Freshly showered and dressed in a new, beige sundress, she looks like an updated, vacation version of herself. Her eyes are locked on Orson, and her fist is pressed to her chest.

"Robert," she whispers. She takes a halting step forward. "Oh, Robert!"

She flings herself forward into his arms. Orson hugs her back for one long, silent moment. Then he gently withdraws, extricating himself from her embrace until he has her at arm's length.

"No," he says quietly. "I'm sorry. I'm not Robert. My name's Orson Toomey." He gives his old, self-effacing smile. "I'm just the doctor who's borrowing your husband's body."

Ma searches his face. I feel horrible for her, but jealous, too, that she got one good hug out of him. She lifts a trembling hand and fits her palm to Orson's jaw. She smooths her hand lower, to his collar, and carefully, deliberately, she pats the front of his shirt.

"No, of course," she says. "My Robert's gone." She backs away, still facing him, and reaches back blindly for my hand.

I grip her fingers and pull her beside me.

"So is Larry," Ma adds simply. "Both of my husbands. Gone."

"Please accept my condolences," Orson says.

Ma lets out a brief, shrill laugh. "If you'll excuse us for a moment," she says.

Orson looks startled. He glances toward me briefly, and I nod toward the door.

"Madeline's with Thea," I say.

"Of course," he says. "I'll be inside."

Ma keeps gripping my hand until he's out of sight, and then she slips slowly to the nearest chair. A soft breeze comes in from the yard and skims my cheeks. Ma gives my hand another squeeze, and then lets me go.

"He's really nothing like Robert, is he?" she asks.

I'm not sure how to answer. He looks just like him, and I'm too thrown to be fair. I was so angry when Thea told me about Orson, but now that I've seen him, I'm just torn. He's like a magician's trick, an imposter. If he would simply sit in a chair and never say a word, I could experience him as my father back from the dead, but he's a different person.

I shake my head. "It's a lot to take in. When he sneezed, he was just the same." I try again. "He's Dad *and* he's not Dad, but mostly not. I don't know why, but I feel like my real dad is more dead than ever." That's what it is. The finality is different. And that's not all. "I can't believe I'm missing Larry. I feel so bad about him."

"Oh, sweetheart," Ma says, leaning forward with her knees pressed together. She shakes her head for a moment, and when she looks at me again, her lashes are damp. "You know what I keep thinking about? The way Larry would hold his finger up when he was reading if he didn't want me to interrupt him. You know? One finger. *Just wait 'til I finish this page.*" She tilts her head, smiling at me.

I do the wait signal at her, one finger up.

"Yes, exactly," she says, and her smile fades. "I feel like I'm waiting again, like I did for your father. It doesn't make a lot of sense."

I get a faint whiff of her shampoo and notice again her soft, new dress. Her entire life is changing, I realize. Mine, too.

"It doesn't have to," I say.

"No," Ma agrees sadly.

The door opens behind us and I turn to see Tom holding his baby.

"I'm sorry. I didn't mean to interrupt," he says.

"That's all right," Ma says.

"What's up?" I ask.

He jerks his thumb toward the doorway. "Orson's explaining what he wants to do for Thea now that you're here. You should come."

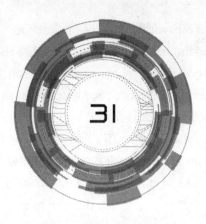

31

THE NANOBOTS

MADELINE, DIEGO, Tito, Linus, Burnham, Dubbs, Orson, and the nurse are all in the sitting area near Thea's bedroom when we arrive. Tom slides along the back wall, holding the baby, and he sways from foot to foot. Orson has commandeered the nurse's desk, and he has the computer screen angled so everyone can see an image of a brain scan.

"You can see here and here are the areas of the most decay," Orson says, pointing to dark areas. "The amygdala and the inferior lingual gyrus." He enlarges one spot to show a jagged hive of holes. "Once these gaps start opening up like this, it's only a matter of time before the brain shuts down completely. Typically then, the patient stops breathing, and they're gone. I'm very sorry to say this, but I'm afraid Thea is within hours, maybe a day of this point."

"But we have Rosie here now," Madeline says. "She's offered to give us more of her dreams."

Orson glances at me. "That's very generous of you, to be sure, but it doesn't solve the problem," he says. "It normally takes weeks to grow a dream seed into a sample that's fit to be implanted into another brain. We don't have weeks in this case."

My gaze keeps zeroing back on the brain image on the computer, and my fingers start to tingle in a familiar way.

"How do you actually insert the dream seeds?" I ask.

"The actual technique, you mean?" Orson says. "We load up a series of nanobots with dream-seed astrocytes, the perfectly aged ones, not too mature, and then we insert the nanobots into a vein behind the patient's ear. Then, with the helmet sensors on the patient for a mapping system, we can guide the nanobots to the amygdala or the lingual gyrus or anywhere else we need them to go." He pauses, as if expecting questions, but then he goes on. "Once in place, the nanobots express out the dream astrocytes, and they cling to the existing brain cells in the patient. It's a basic delivery system, but on a microscopic level, like little boats delivering packages to a steam liner. What really matters is the dream's ability to take hold and mesh with the existing brain cells. That's when they have a chance to repair damage in a fluid, dynamic way. Then even that takes some time. A few days, usually. Sometimes longer."

What he's saying makes some sense. I can imagine the little nanobots as the golden spheres that once ripped a vision of Dubbs out of me. A germ of excitement starts growing around my heart.

Are you there, Arself? I ask.

She doesn't say anything, but the itching in my fingers grows stronger.

"Do you have a helmet here, and whatever other equipment you need?" I ask.

Orson leans back and folds his hands together. "I do. I used the helmet to record Thea's most recent scan there," he says, aiming his chin at the screen. "It still doesn't solve the problem of the time we need."

"Is there any way to speed things up?" Diego says. "If you harvest from Rosie today, when is the soonest you could try implanting her dream seed into Thea?"

"Wait a minute," Ma says. "Nobody's harvesting anything out of Rosie."

The others all look at her. A hiss from equipment in the other room is clearly audible.

"It's not safe for Rosie," Ma says. "I'm sorry about your daughter, Madeline, of course. My heart goes out to you all, but we're not risking Rosie's health for a girl who's essentially dead already."

"Ma," I say, shocked at how blunt she's being.

"We don't even know this doctor," she adds. "He looks like Robert, but that doesn't make him a good person. He could be as evil as Berg." She turns to Orson. "Did you ever collaborate with Berg?"

"I did," Orson says. "I purchased dreams from him. That's how I developed Sinclair Fifteen in the first place."

"Without Rosie's consent," Burnham says. "Berg sold you dreams from the Forge students, and none of them ever gave their consent."

Orson shifts uneasily. "I have not always been the most rigorous in asking questions about where my supplies have come from. I admit that," he says.

"Okay. That's final," Ma says. She looks anxiously at Madeline. "Is that why you invited us here?"

"Ma, it's my choice," I say. "I want to do this."

"The doctor himself said it won't do Thea any good," Ma says practically. "I may not get all that mumbo jumbo about nanobots, but Thea's already too far gone. I can't be the only one who sees this."

"We'd never force Rosie," Madeline says. "Of course we never would."

"You'd just ask." Ma gets to her feet and takes Dubbs by the hand. "Come on, Rosie. We're going."

"No," I say. "Wait. I need to see something."

I move over to the computer and let my fingers do what they've been longing to do on the keyboard. The image on the screen turns ninety degrees, and then zooms in on a certain section of Thea's brain, going smaller and smaller until space opens up between the neurons. Too much space. I'm in a gap. I don't have deliberate logic for what I'm seeing, but in the back of my mind, Arself is making sense of it all and absorbing what we need to know. My fingers adjust the screen again, pushing deeper and sideways, to a lit string of light.

"What are you doing?" Orson asks.

Ignoring him, I expand out again, shift to another area, and zoom in again. Faster than before, Arself switches the screen to a new area, and then another. Warm, slow pleasure trickles around my skull, and I know what she's thinking even though she doesn't put it into words. We're going to operate ourselves. We're going to get in there, into Thea's brain, and make it right.

Unless they stop us.

I lift my fingers from the keyboard for a moment, and then drop back onto them, quickly bringing the image back to where Orson left it. Then I straighten away from the computer.

"What on earth was that?" Orson says. "How'd you learn to do that?"

I glance over at Linus, who's starting to smile.

"It's just a little trick I picked up in the vault," I say.

"Did Berg teach you?" Orson says.

"No," I say. "He never taught me anything but fear."

I take a deep breath and turn to Burnham, who shakes his head in a dazed way. I know my friends will support me, whatever I want to do. I could wait until later tonight, and sneak back down here, and try this myself after Ma and the others have gone to bed. It could be easier that way, but sneaking around is what I had to do at Forge, and I'm not going to do that anymore.

"I have an idea," I say. "I'd like to operate on Thea myself. I think, with Orson assisting, I could give her some of my dreams directly. It might help her heal, and it couldn't hurt."

Diego's jaw drops. Tito's eyebrows shoot up. Madeline lets out a gasp.

"You're sweet," Madeline says. "Honestly. But that is the wildest idea I've ever heard, and I've heard my share of wild ideas."

Linus leans back with his arms crossed, smiling openly. "Here we go."

Dubbs scratches her head. "How can you operate?" she asks.

I take a deep breath and plunge in. "First of all, we'll need another one of those helmets for me to wear, so I can get visual input on what's happening in my brain at the same time we're watching Thea's," I say. "Then we'll need to be connected up, she and I, brain to brain, with a supply of the nanobots that I can control. Or probably it would be better if Orson controls the nanobots in case I fall asleep. I can give him some guidance until then." The procedure seems perfectly obvious to me, now that I have Arself outlining it for me. Her thoughts are so quick and so confident that I'm beginning to feel like we're wasting time with these explanations.

"This is preposterous," Ma says. "You're not a doctor!"

Orson is frowning pensively. "What she's saying about a transfer is possible, in theory," he says. "I hadn't considered a direct transfer of dreams. Berg used to hypothesize about it, but I've never had a fully live dream host side-by-side with a patient before. I'm still not sure it will help Thea, but it has a chance. It would also be dangerous for Rosie."

"It'll work," I say. "You know her brain and mine are compatible. This is the best way."

I'm watching Orson closely, and I see the deeper focus in his gaze when he shifts from doubtful to interested. It's the same look my dad used to have when he was excited about a new game we'd invented.

Madeline, Diego, and Ma are stuck between unconvinced and outraged, but Orson gradually outlines a potential process to them, the same one I imagined, and they talk it over. Ma's stubborn, but I can see her coming around. Orson puts in an order for an extra helmet and other supplies, and Tito asks him to start all the way over from the beginning again and walk them through it once more.

Burnham snags me by the sleeve and I follow him over to the windows, where Linus and Tom join us. Baby Vali is asleep in the crook of Tom's arm, and her perfect little face only adds to my determination. This baby needs both her parents. I know Thea would want me to fight for her life. She once told me she would give me her dreams if I needed them, and I only wish I'd felt as generous toward her then as I do now.

"Are you sure you're up for this?" Burnham says. "You know you could die, right? That's what Orson means by 'dangerous' for you."

"What am I supposed to do? Let her die?" I ask.

Burnham coughs briefly into his fist. "There are worse things than dying."

I arch my eyebrows high. "For her or for me?"

"For any of us," Burnham says.

He is the last person I expected to be arguing against the surgery. Tom's gaze is pinned on his daughter, and I can't guess what he's thinking. I turn to Linus.

"Burnham just doesn't want to lose you," Linus says.

"It's not that," Burnham says.

"Then what?" I ask. "We have a chance to save Thea. What's wrong with you?"

"It won't work," Burnham says. "Why do I even have to say

this? You're not a surgeon. You have no idea what you're doing. People don't do brain surgery on themselves. There's a reason for that."

The adult voices go silent, and tension hovers in the room. I can feel the others listening to us from across the room.

I glare at Burnham. It bugs me that he's actually being reasonable, but he doesn't know how powerful Arself has become. He doesn't realize who we are inside now. "We're not going to let Thea die because of fear," I say.

"This isn't about fear," he says. "It's about common sense."

"Then we're not going to let her die because of that, either," I say. "I've got this, Burnham. Really." I lower my voice. "Arself's helping me. She knows what to do."

He stares back at me, and then shakes his head. "That is exactly what I did not want to hear."

I smile.

Tom looks confused. "Who's Arself?"

"You don't want to know," Burnham says.

>>>>>>>>

When I slip into Thea's room a few moments later, she's resting exactly as she was before. My friends follow after.

"I'm not going to do anything yet. I just want to take a look," I say.

In one of the cupboards, I find the scan helmet and lift it toward the window. This version is as light as a bike helmet, with delicate, retractable prongs. It's strange to hold the device that I associate with helpless terror and recognize its potential as a tool I can use. While I'm fitting the helmet to Thea's head and settling the nubs in her ears, I'm conscious of Linus and Tom watching. Tom, still cradling Vali, takes the chair by the window. I start up the computer and plug in the helmet. Linus brings a tall chair for me so I can sit beside the bed, see Thea's face, and work on the laptop at the same time.

I can still hear the grown-ups discussing details in the outer room.

"Close the door, will you, Burnham?" I ask.

He steps farther in and closes the door.

I slide the computer closer and pull up Thea's live brain scan with the typical cauliflower-like contours. Lights pulse on the screen, and it doesn't take me long to get familiar with the controls. I can turn the image 360 degrees, and I can zoom in to find her hippocampus, then her amygdala, and then the gyrus. Though I never learned these things myself, Arself's knowledge has become a seamless extension of my own mind, and I trust it implicitly. We focus in further on the dark spaces, the holes, and strategize a pattern for where we'll go first, starting with a pocket of damage that's the worst.

Engrossed, I hardly notice when Orson comes in the door behind me. Apparently, hours have passed. My mother has agreed to the surgery, and everyone else is also on board. The extra helmet has been delivered. There's no reason to delay.

After we move an extra bed in beside Thea's, I lie propped up beside her and hold my breath while Orson puts the second helmet on me. He carefully connects me together with Thea, and he has a series of a thousand nanobots ready to inject into my bloodstream. He has one computer, and I have another on my lap.

Thea's parents, and Ma, and our friends, line the back wall where they can watch. Linus gives me a tight smile of encouragement. For a fleeting second, I wonder if this is the last time I'll see him, and then I feel a rise of excitement with Arself inside me. We're near the top of a roller coaster, teetering before the plunge.

"Ready?" Orson asks me.

"Yes," I say.

At first, I try to watch my screen. I try to swipe on the touchpad to direct my view of my brain activity and Thea's. I fully intend to stay conscious and in control, but soon my eyes feel too slow and my hands too heavy. I let them slip into inert silence, and suddenly I'm in the quiet, beige, private space behind my closed eyelids. Orson and the others disappear, and I feel a keen awareness take over, a sense of rightness. I belong here, like this, as pure, fluid thought.

Arself guides me along, sightless, through a narrow tunnel and directly into Thea. We come to the circle where her thoughts should be brightest, but they're not there. Instead, she's a heaviness, an obdurate wall of loss and darkness. I'm unsure what to do. I call her name, but nothing replies. I flash back to myself and open my eyes, and focus on Orson.

"Send the nanobots," I say.

"Where do you want me to direct them?"

Arself supplies me with the right words.

"Just put them in my posterior auricular vein," I say. "I can take it from there."

My eyelids go heavy again and I sort through my dreams, calling up a blueberry ocean, a walk on the tracks back at home in Doli, a vibrant castle slipping into a sea of mud. I find a colorful, soaring songbird that flies through an underground tunnel, leaving whorls of light in its wake. I find the fish from the stream under Grisly, lurking just below the surface of the water.

A series of golden pods shimmers into my view, and a sharp memory of pain returns to me. It was one of these pods that stole the vision of Dubbs from me, back before, when I was imprisoned in my dreams. I recall the rift vividly now, but without the helpless despair. The golden threads swirled around my sister and I tried to hold her tight so I could keep her with me. But in the end, the pod took both Dubbs and my other voice with her. They were both gone, forever.

This is my chance now, to make that right. I control the pods this time. I can choose, and I choose a gift for Thea. It's a bright dream vision from the galaxy moment when I connected to the dreamers, and all their shifting, brilliant power united me into something larger than I'd ever been before. I imagine that galaxy into the nanobot, where it pulses and strains with golden light, and I bring it over to Thea's circle of quiet.

Here, I say, and I let the warmth transfuse out of the pod and into her void. At first, the light simply vanishes into the darkness and is swept away, like an evaporation of stardust. But I bring more, and with my own hands, I pour my galaxy into her emptiness until finally, a bit of it takes. It clings to a fine, invisible thread of substance, like dewy light along a strand of a spider's web. Then another strand catches light and grows stronger. I feel the heaviness begin to roll like a slow mountain against the night sky. I nudge her with my puny, hopeful strength, and I bring her more of the golden light. I deliver more of my dreams, more of my memories, until at last, I feel the spark of her consciousness coming online, right beside mine.

She's weak. She's voiceless still, but she exists as a consciousness like before, back when we were only me, the two of us in one mind.

This is what I've wanted, I realize. Ever since she left me, this is the wholeness I've missed. *Thea!* I say joyfully.

Rosie? she says faintly. *What are you doing here?*

I expand in every direction, spilling light and warm shadows like evening in a canyon. She's smiling, too. I can feel it in my cheeks and behind my ears. I don't need to explain anything to her because in less than a moment, she intuits everything I've done and believed.

You're hurting, she says.

No. I'm good.

But she guides me to the edge of my aching, down to the bottom of the canyon to a dark river, where I'm grieving for the dreamers and my father. For Larry, too, somehow. She grieves for them, too, in complete, endless sympathy. Loss and failure swim up-current through the river, tugging at me with their gravity.

These things are part of us, she says. *Try to forgive yourself for hating Larry and losing him.*

That's impossible. I don't know how.

You have to, she says. *We can't let Berg sour us forever.*

I plunge into the black, cold current.

I hate him still, even though he's dead, I say.

I know, she says. *But because of him, you found Arself, and she knew how to bring you home. To me.*

The river flows less swiftly. I lift back toward the surface, and I ease back onto the shore. Thea's smiling again, urging me on.

You brought me your dreams, she says. *You gave them to me.*

Because I love you, I guess, I say.

She laughs. I'm back in the air, part of the light.

And I love you back, she says. *And we love other people, too. Vali.*

Dubbs.

Ma.

Linus.

Burnham, Tom, Lavinia, Madeline, Diego, Tito. Althea, gone forever.

It's such a relief to be flying again, pure air and solace. The ping in my heart grows wider and ripples outward until we're free.

32

BEGINNING

A CRACK OF THUNDER splits the night, and I jolt awake. Rain beats along the peaked roof of Thea's bedroom, and a flicker of blue lights up the rivulets of water on the windows. A dim little light burns on the shelf in the corner, and when I try to sit up, an IV line tugs at the port in my chest. My helmet is gone. The computers that linked me to Thea are gone, too, but Thea is still in the bed beside mine. She's helmetless, too. Her face is slack, her breathing barely discernible, but it's enough to tell me she's alive.

Another tumble of thunder rolls over the valley, and a breeze of misty petrichor drifts in the farthest window. I have a glimpse of someone sleeping in the lounge chair in the corner: Tom, by the shape of him. For once, he's not holding his baby, and I notice a lump in the bassinet. With an effort, I push myself up to my elbow and work my tongue around my dry mouth.

Linus appears in the doorway. The dim light glows on his features, and from the way he's blinking, I'd guess he just woke up, too.

"You're awake!" he says in a hushed voice.

He angles near for a hug, and I breathe in his rumpled, cottony warmth.

"Are you all right? Does your head hurt?" he asks.

"No, I'm just a little thirsty. What time is it? How's Thea?"

"She hasn't woken up," Linus says. "Orson says she's likely to at any time, but so far, she hasn't yet. You've been out a long time. Nearly four days."

"It doesn't feel that long," I say. I push my hair back out of my face. My fingers are a little shaky, and when Linus hands me a cup of water, he helps me steady it while I sip.

"It's so great to see you awake again," he says softly.

His eyes burn with a bright, private light, and my heart does a neat little dive. He sets my cup aside with a faint click. Then he leans in to kiss me, and I close my eyes, tilting my lips to his. He's warm, and perfectly right. Happy tingles go melting along my nerves and swirling in my belly. My fingers go around his neck and up into the back of his hair, and I can hardly think at all.

Linus eases away, smiling, just enough so that I can see him.

"I feel better now," he says.

I laugh. "You do?"

He nods. "You had me scared, Rosie. I don't know what I'd do without you."

"Really?"

"As if you didn't know it." He kisses me again. Then, with seeming reluctance, he straightens. "The others will probably be coming in another minute," he says. "The nurse started calling around as soon as she saw you were up."

I shift over on the bed to make room, with my back up against the pillows, and he sits facing me, with a layer of covers separating his leg from mine.

"What did Orson say about how the surgery went?" I ask.

Linus rubs his jaw, and I notice he hasn't shaved lately.

"He was pretty psyched," Linus says. "He said he'd never seen anything like it. He showed us how the nanobots were moving around super fast, going back and forth between your brain and Thea's. He tried to override them once, but they just kept going. Then Thea started to show more brain activity, so Orson said whatever you were doing was working."

"Arself was running all of it," I say.

"Were you aware of that?" he asks.

"It's more like I was meeting Thea again in my own mind," I say. "She made me feel a little better about Larry and Berg and everything."

"You talked to her?"

"It's more that I just understood her," I say. "It was nice."

He smiles. "Nice?"

I listen to the back of my mind, wondering if I'll hear a voice back there, either Thea's or Arself's, but I don't. Instead, all I sense is calmness. A peaceful sureness or confidence. I've never had a serene mind before, actually. It makes me feel powerful and I have no doubt Arself is still with me, even though she's gone quiet now. I wonder if I can draw on her abilities for anything I want to do. I'm sort of excited to find out. "I feel lighter, somehow," I say.

"I'm glad," he says.

Near the window, Tom sits up in his chair. He presses his fist to his eye and then shakes his head vigorously. "Hey," he says. "You're up."

"Yes," I say.

Tom stretches and gets out of his chair. He looks in on the baby in the bassinet, and then he moves over to Thea. "How's it going?" he asks her softly, taking her hand.

Her eyes remain closed, but they twitch with movement.

"Did you see that?" Tom asks. "She squeezed my hand. Thea? Can you hear me?" He points toward the lamp. "Get the light there," he adds.

As Linus leans over and turns it on, I blink against the brightness. Thea lets out a moan. Then she squints, and slowly, groggily opens her eyes.

"Hey, girl," Tom says. "How's it going?"

Thea lifts a hand to her mouth and yawns. "Okay. Where's the baby?"

"She's here," Tom says. "She's asleep in the bassinet. Want to see her?"

"No, let her sleep," Thea says. She turns in my direction and takes in Linus and me. "Slumber party?" she says.

A thrill knocks through me, and I grin at her. "Sort of. How are you feeling?"

"Thirsty," she says. "I had the strangest dream."

"I bet," I say.

With a bustle at the door, Madeline and Diego hurry in, followed by my mother and Dubbs. Burnham, Orson, Tito, and the nurse crowd in last. The only one missing is the dog, and not for long. So many hugs go around. Linus shifts off the bed to let my mom get her arms around me. Diego moves in close beside Madeline to hover over Thea, and Tom's openly weeping. When baby Vali wakes up and starts crying, Madeline tucks her gently over her shoulder and coos at her.

"There, there, little Vali," Madeline says. "Everything's okay now. See? Your mother's back."

As the baby quiets, Burnham closes the window so the rushing noise of the rain sounds far away, and then he settles back against the windowsill. He isn't coughing as much anymore, I notice with relief. Tito turns on another light. Dressed in a bathrobe with matching slippers, Dubbs crawls up on the end of my bed.

"I made you a card," Dubbs says, pointing to a folded piece of paper on my bedside table. "Did you see?"

"This?" I ask, lifting it. A dog is drawn on the cover in crayon, but the inside is blank.

"Smell it," she says.

I do. It smells like lemon, and I know she's written me a secret message. "Thanks," I say.

"I made one for Thea, too," Dubbs says, pointing.

Thea sits up a bit higher and reaches for her own card. She lifts it to her nose. "Thanks, Dubbs," she says.

"How about it, Orson," Madeline says. "What's the prognosis?"

Orson crosses his arms and tilts back on his feet. "Good,"

he says. "Thea's latest scans show miraculous gains. She's as healed as any patient I've ever seen. I'd like to follow up, of course, with both of them, but as far as I can tell at this moment, Thea's out of the woods. And your brain, Rosie." He shakes his head in awe. "You're an inspiration. Absolutely. I would love to talk to you about what you did in there."

I laugh. "Maybe someday," I say. Like never.

"We'll let you all catch up. Let us know if you need anything," Orson says, and he and the nurse step out.

The baby hiccups. We all laugh.

Smiling, I look around the room and think of all we've been through. Tito has taken a spot next to Burnham, and they're talking easily. Ma has her hands on Dubbs's shoulders while Dubbs rattles on about the merits of getting a dog. Diego is setting a chair for Madeline so she can be closer to Thea, and Tom is openly adoring his baby again. I've never felt so lucky. When I glance over to where Linus leans against the wall, I find him smiling at me, his gaze warm and real. A spark of private happiness shoots between us, and for the first time in ages, the days ahead look sweet.

Another flash of lightning brightens the window, and I hold my breath for the thunder.